YOUNG-HEE
and the
PULLOCHO

To my son James, who is just starting
a long journey of his own

——————————— ✳ ✳ ✳ ✳ ✳ ✳ ✳ ✳ ✳ ———————————

YOUNG-HEE
and the
PULLOCHO

MARK JAMES RUSSELL

TUTTLE Publishing

Tokyo | Rutland, Vermont | Singapore

Published by Tuttle Publishing, an imprint of Periplus Editions (HK) Ltd.

www.tuttlepublishing.com

Library of Congress Cataloging in Publication Data for this title is in progress.
ISBN 978-0-8048-4497-0

Distributed by

North America, Latin America & Europe
Tuttle Publishing
364 Innovation Drive,
North Clarendon VT 05759-9436, USA
Tel: 1 (802) 773 8930
Fax: 1 (802) 773 6993
info@tuttlepublishing.com
www.tuttlepublishing.com

Japan
Tuttle Publishing, Yaekari Building 3F
5-4-12 Osaki, Shinagawa-ku
Tokyo 141-0032, Japan
Tel: (81) 3 5437 0171
Fax: (81) 3 5437 0755
sales@tuttle.co.jp
www.tuttle.co.jp

Asia Pacific
Berkeley Books Pte. Ltd.
61 Tai Seng Avenue #02-12
Singapore 534167
Tel: (65) 6280-1330
Fax: (65) 6280-6290
inquiries@periplus.com.sg
www.periplus.com

Printed in China   1501CM
18 17 16 15   5 4 3 2 1

TUTTLE PUBLISHING® is a
registered trademark of Tuttle
Publishing, a division of Periplus
Editions (HK) Ltd.

The Tuttle Story "Books to Span the East and West"

Many people are surprised to learn that the world's leading publisher of books on Asia had humble beginnings in the tiny American state of Vermont. The company's founder, Charles E. Tuttle, belonged to a New England family steeped in publishing.

Tuttle's father was a noted antiquarian book dealer in Rutland, Vermont. Young Charles honed his knowledge of the trade working in the family bookstore, and later in the rare books section of Columbia University Library. His passion for beautiful books—old and new—never wavered throughout his long career as a bookseller and publisher.

After graduating from Harvard, Tuttle enlisted in the military and in 1945 was sent to Tokyo to work on General Douglas MacArthur's staff. He was tasked with helping to revive the Japanese publishing industry, which had been utterly devastated by the war. When his tour of duty was completed, he left the military, married a talented and beautiful singer, Reiko Chiba, and in 1948 began several successful business ventures.

To his astonishment, Tuttle discovered that postwar Tokyo was actually a book-lover's paradise. He befriended dealers in the Kanda district and began supplying rare Japanese editions to American libraries. He also imported American books to sell to the thousands of GIs stationed in Japan. By 1949, Tuttle's business was thriving, and he opened Tokyo's very first English-language bookstore in the Takashimaya Department Store in Nihonbashi, to great success. Two years later, he began publishing books to fulfill the growing interest of foreigners in all things Asian.

Though a westerner, Tuttle was hugely instrumental in bringing a knowledge of Japan and Asia to a world hungry for information about the East. By the time of his death in 1993, he had published over 6,000 books on Asian culture, history and art—a legacy honored by Emperor Hirohito in 1983 with the "Order of the Sacred Treasure," the highest honor Japan can bestow upon a non-Japanese.

The Tuttle company today maintains an active backlist of some 1,500 titles, many of which have been continuously in print since the 1950s and 1960s—a great testament to Charles Tuttle's skill as a publisher. More than 60 years after its founding, Tuttle Publishing is more active today than at any time in its history, still inspired by Charles Tuttle's core mission—to publish fine books to span the East and West and provide a greater understanding of each.

1

"Give him *back*!" Young-hee shouted, trying to sound commanding.

She stared in desperate terror at the creature grinning malevolently in front of her. Short and grotesque, with the stump of a horn in the middle of his forehead, he smelled of ash and deceit. He was a *dokkaebi*, a goblin. And he had her little brother.

"No, he's my servant now," the dokkaebi answered, "fair and square."

Young-hee's thoughts raced. Around them, crowds of bizarre creatures—elegant fairies, entrepreneurial witches, clay golem servants, and people-that-weren't-really-people surged through the market, ignoring the overstuffed stall where Young-hee faced off against the dokkaebi. She was on her own. *Think!* she urged herself, but she barely understood the rules of this strange place, and this goblin was clearly happy with his prize.

Oblivious, Young-beom turned his dirt-smudged face to his big sister and chewed happily on his *yakgwa* honey biscuit. *Stupid! I never should have brought Bum to a place like this.* "Bum" being her nickname for her annoying little brother. She had been to the goblin market before, but not without a guide, and never with Bum. She had been told it was treacherous, but thought she could handle it. Now, because of her recklessness, her brother had been taken.

"He's not your servant," she said. "He's my brother."

"Oh, I must differ. I offered an exchange of services: I'd fill his hunger with a delicious cake, if he'd enter my service for a year. He accepted."

"No!" cried Bum, growing upset. "I did *not*!"

The goblin scowled. "And yet, there's one of Woo's half-eaten *yakgwa* in your hand, and its crumbs around your mouth. Or is the boy a thief?"

"Woo?"

"Woo," he grunted, pointing a lumpy goblin thumb at himself.

Scared by the goblin's snarl, Bum tried to run, but the moment he reached the shop limits he stopped short—as if held by a chain. Young-hee rushed to Bum and put a comforting hand on his head.

"He couldn't have agreed to anything," said Young-hee, watching her brother begin to understand that something was very wrong. "He's too young. He's just a little kid."

"*Pfft*," said the dokkaebi dismissively. "He accepted the offered. Now he must pay the price. That's the way of things."

"But he didn't know," she said weakly. She ran a hand down Bum's side to his ankle, feeling the invisible thread that held him fast. She had narrowly avoided similar capture on her first market visit.

"Few people know the true cost of the things they buy," the goblin snapped. "That is not my concern. Woo never made the rules. That's just the way things are."

Young-hee tried to imagine what her mom would do. "Look, Mr. Woo ... I'll get my friends—the *jangseung* guardians and, uh, and the giant toads, and the fairies. I'll bring them all here, and they'll make you give me my brother back."

Woo shrugged. "Tell whomever you like. Everything's fair and square. This is a goblin market, and goblin rules apply."

"*Jigyeowo*," screamed Young-hee, her emotions exploding, and her face turning red. Bum cringed. "Give me my brother back! *Right now!* Or I *swear* I'll make you sorry!"

Woo spread his fingers and pressed his open hand against Young-hee's chest, pushing her hard against the wall behind her, just beyond Bum's reach.

"You will do *no* such thing," said the dokkaebi with low menace. "You think you can threaten me, girl, in my own shop?" He stuck a fat, earthen finger from his other hand in her face. "Do you know anything about dokkaebi power? Your little brother is *mine* now, for at least the next year, and there is so much I can do to him. I could sell him to something big and nasty, some creature that likes to eat little boys. He's not very big, but many creatures would find him juicy and delicious. Or maybe I could just vanish him, send him somewhere far away—another realm, another time even. I have many, many cruel options if you rub Woo the wrong way."

Woo took a slight step back, removing his hand from Young-hee, his voice softening. "The fact of the matter is, rules are rules. Without laws and contracts, all would be chaos. No one would ever close a deal, would ever make any money."

Young-hee breathed in, the scratchy pressure of the goblin's touch fresh on her skin. She felt broken. But just then, one of the dokkaebi's words reverberated. "Money?" she said. "I could give you something for him, to get him back. That would be fair, right?"

"Like what?" asked the dokkaebi, rubbing its chin skeptically.

She rooted through her jacket pockets, one stuffed with her brother's doll, but the other full of hair bands. "Uh… I have all the hair bands you want."

"Hair bands?" said the nearly hairless creature, "Why would I want hair bands?"

"Money, then?" she implored. "I have some money."

"Gold!?"

"No, it's regular money," said Young-hee, digging through her pants pockets. "But it's worth a bit. It's my birthday money."

The dokkaebi looked disdainfully at the crumbled won notes. "Paper money? I never heard of anything so silly. This isn't even mulberry paper. No!"

"But I have to get Bum back. I'll do *anything* to get him."

"Anything?" he said, his voice betraying his attempt to look uninterested.

"Yes!"

"Well, I like the sound of 'anything.' "

"Please, just tell me."

The dokkaebi looked thoughtful. "Would you go anywhere?"

"Yes!"

"Would you brave great danger?"

"Y-Yes."

"Would you … get a *pullocho* for me?"

"Yes, anything!" she exclaimed, grasping at hope. "Er, what's a pullocho?"

"It is a very special plant," explained the dokkaebi, "A root, like ginseng." The dokkaebi turned and went digging into a pile of papers.

But suddenly, Bum shouted "*Hiya!*" and he put all the fury of a frightened four-year-old into a kick to the dokkaebi's ankle.

The goblin looked momentarily surprised, then merely annoyed. "Don't do that," he commanded, and immediately Bum went quiet. "Stand over there," he said, and Bum obeyed. "Part of being a servant is doing what you're told," he explained, returning his attention to the piles of papers and extracting an old drawing—simple, but quite vivid, of a green, wrinkled root. "They used to be rare, but you could find one with a bit of work. Now, though, I cannot remember the last time I saw even a piece of a pullocho. Some think they no longer exist."

"So how can I find one?"

"That's your problem. That is, if you really want your brother back."

"I do!"

"Good. It so happens I heard a rumor that a noble-hearted *simmani* might be able to find a pullocho in the ruins of the great Sacred City, in the shadow of the first sandalwood tree."

"And where is the Sacred City?" Young-hee could barely understand anything the dokkaebi was saying.

"I only know that it is far away, across the lake of Mey, over the Cheongyong Mountains, past the Great Woods. You will need to ask the animal-spirit women to find out where exactly."

"The animal-spirit women?"

"Yes, three sisters: Bear, Fox, and Snake. They live on their own near the Hungry River. They are very old and know many things."

"Oh. That sounds far…."

"Doubtlessly. Or I would have gone myself."

Young-hee racked her brain, trying to think of what else she could do. She doubted whether the great frogs or the Grannie Dol would help her. The jangseung couldn't walk, of course. Besides, Woo didn't seem worried about anyone she might be able to enlist. She could go back to the real world and get help from her mom or someone, but how could she begin to explain all of this? Who would believe her? And how could she find this world again without her brother? There were no good options. The dokkaebi had won.

"Okay, I'll do it," she said. Woo seemed pleased, but Young-hee wasn't finished. "But you have to promise me something, too."

Woo immediately stopped smiling. "Promise what? You're in no position to demand anything of Woo."

"If I am going to go on your stupid quest, you need to promise you'll take care of my brother."

"Agreed."

"You cannot sell him or do anything to him or let anything bad happen to him."

"Agreed."

"And you have to promise to be here, in this market, in the same place, and return him to me safely once I bring you your pullocho. No tricks."

He sighed, looking impatient. "Agreed."

"That's a promise?"

The dokkaebi's face grew very serious. "It is a true vow. But, little human, understand you must keep your part of our bargain too. Do not try to trick me or take back your brother by force. He is mine now, and if you break our deal, I can do with him whatever I will— sell him or maybe just eat him myself. I bet he is tender and juicy."

"I want a contract," said Young-hee impulsively.

"A true vow is binding," said Woo, turning into his shop to root through his piles. He emerged with a small, fiery-red jewel. "Put this under your tongue," he said, handing the jewel to Young-hee. She held it between her thumb and finger. "It's a *yeouiju*," explained the dokkaebi, "a jewel from the jaw of a yellow dragon. If it is under your tongue when you make a promise, the promise cannot be undone."

Young-hee put the dragon jewel to her mouth, gave it a quick sniff, put it under her tongue, promised to get the pullocho, and then handed it back. Not bothering to wipe it off, Woo put it straight under his tongue. She could barely make out what he said, but it sounded like a promise to keep their bargain. He took out the jewel, wrapped it in a small bag, and put it away.

"I don't feel any different."

"Nor should you … as long as you don't break our agreement."

Young-hee looked down at her brother, standing at the far wall of the shop and watching. He seemed scared, even if he didn't grasp everything going on. *How can I leave him behind?* she wondered. *He won't understand. He'll be so scared and lonely.* But if she thought about Bum's feelings, she would never be able to go. A sadness— deeper and more painful than anything she had felt since her dad went away—cascaded through her. But she had to lock up those feelings and fears and frustrations. She gave Bum a big hug.

"I'm so sorry, Bum, but I have to go."

"No, *don't*," he pleaded. Young-hee was surprised at how much he seemed to have understood. "Don't leave."

"I don't want to. But I have to." She wished she could have hugged him for the whole year, until his contract with the dokkaebi was finished. She looked at the half-eaten biscuit in his hand. "Come on, you should at least eat your yakgwa."

"I'm not hungry anymore."

"Here, take your Gangjee," she said, pulling the ragged doll from her jacket pocket. "It's just his toy. No tricks," she told Woo. He glanced at it and nodded. "Gangjee is very strong and very brave. He'll keep you safe." Bum held the toy and looked up at his big sister.

"I suppose you want old Woo to give you food and supplies to help you on your way," said the goblin.

"I don't want anything from you," snapped Young-hee, more bitterly than she intended. "I just want to get my brother back."

"Then you better get going. The sooner you find the pullocho, the sooner you can have him back."

Young-hee hugged Bum once more. It took everything she had to walk away. Each step felt heavy as stone, as long as a mile. She kept looking back, but after just a couple of stalls, the trudging masses of indifferent shoppers and merchants swirled around her and hid Bum and Woo's stall. Young-hee dropped to the ground and sat against a wall, holding her knees and crying harder than she could remember. She cried until her tears were all gone and her eyes burned. Then she stood and started marching through the market. She knew what she had to do.

The Fox and the Farmer

Many years ago, high in the Taebak Mountains, there was a wealthy farmer who lived on a large property with his wife, many servants, and three strong, healthy sons whom he loved very much. But deep down, he was sad they had no daughters.

One day, while walking with his eldest two sons high in the mountains, he discovered a beautiful baby girl. The farmer and his sons searched high and low for the baby's mother, but to no avail. He returned to the farm and announced that he would raise and love the baby as his own daughter. For the next few years, the farm prospered, and everyone was happy.

But on the night after the daughter's fifth birthday, a wild animal killed one of the farmer's servants as he slept. The distraught farmer sent out many hunters, but they could not find the creature responsible.

The next night, another servant was killed by an animal, and the night after that, and the night after that. Soon, the whole farm was swamped by fear and swirling with rumors: Maybe it was a crazed bear. Maybe a pack of wolves. Maybe, some whispered, an evil ghost.

More nights passed and more servants died. Traps were set, but they caught nothing. They could not even find any footprints.

Finally, the farmer's eldest son vowed to hide and keep watch all night. At the darkest hour, he saw something move in the shadows. As it drew closer to his hiding place, he realized that it was his adopted sister. In horror, he watched as she snuck around a wall and transformed into a fox, but one with nine lush tails. The animal jumped through a high window, and what followed was the terrible noise of a fox killing a man.

The son ran to the window, crying out to wake the whole house.

The roused inhabitants found the servant dead, but no sign of any fox. When the son explained what he saw, his father grew enraged. "How dare you slander your sister?" yelled his father. "You are an ungrateful and jealous son, and I will not tolerate such evil scheming. Leave this farm."

The following night, the next-eldest son kept watch. Hidden in the tallest tree in the middle of the farm's central courtyard, he saw his sister emerge from the darkness, transform into a fox, steal into a servant's room, and kill him. When he, like his elder brother, sounded the alarm and tried to capture the fox, she was nowhere to be found. Asked what he had seen, he told his father the truth. Again the father was furious. "Another dishonest, scheming son!" he cried. "What did I do to deserve such an unfaithful family? Leave this house."

The next night, the youngest son hid in the darkness and witnessed his sister turn into a fox and kill yet again. But frightened of his father's wrath, he blamed a mountain tiger. "Ah, at last, the truth," said the anguished father. "Your older brothers really were wicked." But try as they might, no one could catch the tiger—because, of course, there was none. And each morning, another servant was dead.

Meanwhile, the two exiled brothers wandered the mountains together for many months, sad and alone. Until one day they met a venerable Taoist monk, begging for alms. The brothers gave the monk the little money they had, and shared the little food they carried. Seeing their sadness, the monk asked if he could help and listened as they told of their fox sister. The monk said, "Your family has been cursed by Gumiho, a truly evil and strong spirit. Do not underestimate her power or her need for blood. I fear it is too late for your family, but you must return and try to help." The monk wrote some holy verses for the brothers, and gave them three small vials: one white, one blue, and one red.

By the time they returned home, their youngest brother and mother had both been killed, and the servants had either been killed or ran off. Only their father remained, living in the run-down house, surviving on scraps. The father wept when he saw his exiled sons, and begged forgiveness.

As they cried together, the sun set, and the fox walked into the room, looking at the three of them, hungrily. "Sister! We know you are the Gumiho. Why are you doing this?" cried the eldest brother. "How could you hurt your father so, after he took you in and raised you as his own daughter?" asked the second brother. "Stop now, and leave our ruined family in peace."

The Gumiho, her eyes blood-red, her nine tails waving menacingly, grinned, and spoke with their sister's voice—but layered with ancient power. "Brothers, how good of you to return," she said. "But I have no interest in peace. I have already eaten the hearts of ninety-seven people from this farm, and with three more, I will be made a Queen of Heaven and rule all these wretched lands. Three more and I shall have the power over life and death, on earth and in the sky, from the furthest realms and across creation. How lucky for me that there are three of you."

As the fox crept forward the eldest son read the incantation the monk had provided. Just as the fox lunged, she heard the magic words and fell writhing to the floor. Howling, she covered her ears. Then the younger brother released a drop from white vial and, instantly, a vast thorny hedge sprang from the floor, and trapped her. The brothers took their father and started to run, but the fox pulled off the pricking thorns and ran after them. So the younger brother released a drop from the red vial. Instantly, a huge fire engulfed the fox, and she howled in agony. But she was strong with magic, and fought through the flames. So the elder son took out the last, blue vial, and let a drop fall. Instantly, a huge lake opened under the fox, swallowing her up in deep, cold water.

Free from the fox spirit, the sons and the father traveled far from their home and the sad memories it held. All three turned away from worldly things to study the scriptures and warn the world of the fox's evil.

As for Gumiho, she eventually swam to the shore of the lake to lick her wounds. She vowed to never forget how close she had come to getting what she wanted…

2

The metal crane zoomed high and clattery into the sky, jutting between the dingy concrete walls and dirty glass of the surrounding apartment buildings. On it, a platform stuffed with boxes and mismatched furniture rose noisily to an open window nine floors up.

It was moving day, about four months before the dokkaebi would take Bum. Before she discovered the existence of such fantastic and terrifying places as the goblin market, Young-hee's life had been mostly dull, unremarkable, and endlessly annoying.

The day she returned to Seoul with her mom and Bum after nearly five years abroad was one of the most annoying of all. They had lived in the *ático* of a beautiful old apartment in Buenos Aires for two years, then a nice home in Toronto for three years. She could even remember way back to their big, old house, high in the hills in Seoul.

Her new home was an apartment complex—sprawling, ugly, even by Seoul's standards. Twenty-story buildings, built quickly and badly before she was born, surrounded her like a concrete forest. Peeling paint, faded to rotten-egg yellow, was streaked with rust trails dripping from old window frames. *What a dump*, she thought.

On the ground, chaos reigned as scurrying movers carried boxes, furniture, and the bric-a-brac of their lives. Young-hee dodged one mover only to find herself in the path of another.

"Sorry," she said, and then, twisting away, arms flailing, knocked over a wooden coat rack. "Sorry," she repeated to no one in particular, and righted the rack.

"Young-hee!" said her mother, watching the slapstick awkwardness. The sharpness of her voice was tinged with exhaustion. "Try to stay out of the way. Please."

"Sorry," Young-hee said, dodged more movers and retreated to a tree-lined wall as her mother reappeared. She was walking at a fast clip, holding the hand of Young-hee's irritating, perpetually dirty younger brother, Bum.

"Young-hee, I need you to get Young-beom's Gangjee," she said—

"Gangjee" being Bum's childish mispronunciation of "*gangaji,*" or "puppy," what he called his favorite stuffed toy. As usual, Bum was completely clueless—distracted in this charming instance by some snot on his finger.

"I don't know where it is."

"It's in the car," mom said, barely containing her stress and digging into a pocket for the keys.

"I don't see the car," Young-hee said.

"It's down in the parking garage near the stairwell door."

Before Young-hee could think of an excuse, in one motion her mother had put the keys and Bum's dirty hand into Young-hee's, and returned to the chaos of the move.

As Bum giggled, a greenish snot bubble popped from his nose with a sickly splash. He may have been clueless but he was happy. "*Aish, jigyeowo,*" said Young-hee, grossed out. "So annoying."

Bum was bored and tired, and finding the Gangjee was their best bet if they didn't want him turning into a raging monster of sleep-deprivation. Maybe then he'd nap and she'd dig up a book to read. Or maybe a friend would send her an email. Letting Bum hold her little finger, she led him to the elevator, trying to remember the electronic lock's secret number. She found it horribly elusive, as if forgetting the number made the move less real—but, fortunately, someone had propped the door ajar with a cloth. Immediately inside, the smells of cooking and living drifted into the hallway.

A light indicated that someone, probably the movers, had locked the elevator on the ninth floor. Her floor. "Come on, Bum," she sighed. "Let's walk down to the garage."

Bum must have gone with her mom when she parked the car, because he rocketed down the stairs, spewing goofy four-year-old noises. Young-hee let out another annoyed sigh as she slowly followed down the poorly lit stairs, toward a spooky and foreboding darkness. *If Bum isn't scared, why should I be*? she told herself. The garage was deeper than she expected, and the stairs reversed four times before ending. At the bottom was a big, dark blue steel door, with her apartment building number written on it: 206.

W*ow!* she thought. Despite the gloom the garage seemed huge. Gray concrete and unremarkable cars stretched out impossibly far. One parking garage must connect all the apartment buildings in the complex. *How many levels did the thing have?* she wondered. *Three or four, at least.*

She located Bum by his *bloop* and *bleep* noises. He was playing with the car door handle, his face pressed against the glass. "Gangjee," he said, pointing inside. Young-hee opened the door and reached in for the puppy doll. With his dirty fur and a single, dangling button eye, Gangjee had definitely seen better days, but he made Bum happy and manageable. Snatching Gangjee, Bum whooshed the toy in Superman-like flying motions. Young-hee rolled her eyes, locked the car, and led her brother back. But as she walked through the dark blue door she found herself looking back into the garage, with a feeling she couldn't put into words.

Emerging into the lobby, Young-hee noticed the elevator was unstuck, quickly hit the button and heard a whir of response. She felt an irrational rush of joy at this tiny victory over the movers and the forces making her day so miserable.

She rode to the ninth floor, to door 901, her home—no, her *apartment*, she corrected herself. *This is definitely not home.* Inside, things were as chaotic as outside—and ugly, with that gray, poorly-fitted linoleum floor and mismatching, vaguely pastel molding and doorframes. Everything felt grimy, scratched and rundown, the depressing leftovers of years of other people's lives.

Young-hee helped Bum maneuver through moving mess to a bedroom piled high with boxes. Gangjee had been transformed from Superman to a pirate, slashing at invisible marauders; but Young-hee could tell he was mostly just fighting off sleep. Recognizing a box swollen with bedding, Young-hee found a big, soft comforter and laid it on the floor. Before Bum finished protesting her order to sleep, he had drifted off, mouth agape, holding Gangjee.

Deciding he was safe, Young-hee decided to explore, figuring her mom would prefer it if she weren't in the way. Outside in the sunlight, she passed some dubious-looking playground equipment, and near a side entrance to the apartment complex, found a waist-high gate bracketed by two totem poles adorned with strange, toothy faces and googly eyes. Their paint was flaked and faded, and the bearded figure on the right was missing half of its black hat. They were meant to evoke the traditional guardians that protected villages in old Korea, but Young-hee thought they just looked cheap.

Outside the gate was an unremarkable road lined with unremarkable buildings, four-storied and gray. It could have been anywhere in the city. Or nowhere. Restaurants and convenience stores filled the first floors, while basements were bloated with *PC Bang* Internet cafes and the occasional virtual golf driving range. The upper levels featured "health" clinics (for reshaping faces and sucking out fat) and *hagwon*, cram schools (for reshaping brains and sucking out joy), where desperate parents sent desperate kids to study math, science, and English. Aside from weekend Korean classes, Young-hee's life abroad had been wonderfully hagwon-less, but she dreaded that, soon, her days would be stuffed with extra classes.

Across the street was a small supermarket, and down the road a farmer's market, where old people gathered, buying and selling homegrown vegetables. Down the other way, the far side of a three-way intersection ended abruptly in recycling yards. There, all day long, poor people hauled in carts overflowing with cardboard and metal, and yard workers noisily loaded the scraps of other people's lives onto beaten-up trucks. But what drew Young-hee was the lonely, grassy hill behind the chaos. Overlooked by developers, it had turned half-feral.

Curious, Young-hee followed a steep path at the top of the hill and found a half-finished park with benches, a wooden gazebo, and some rusty exercise equipment.

It was a warm spring day, not deadly hot yet, and the air was surprisingly clear for the time of year, so Young-hee enjoyed the view. *Geez', Seoul is massive*, she thought, *and hideously drab.* Everywhere she looked was just more of the same. Concrete apartment complexes like hers and commercial buildings stretched in all directions, each more boastfully and strangely named than the last: Luxville, Besttown, Brownstone, Emerald. Her apartment complex was just as bad—Hanbit Mansion. She tried to remember what "hanbit" meant: *Light? Sun? Aish, my Korean's gotten terrible.* And with cracks and rust streaking the buildings, "mansion" was a joke.

It wasn't like this before, she thought. *I used to live in a house with a yard, trees, a beautiful view.* She remembered her grandfather proudly telling them that their house, with a mountain to the north and a river to the south, had great *pungsu*—a a kind of magical geography that was just right. She missed him, even though she barely remembered what he looked like. But she knew he wouldn't have approved of the pungsu here. "*Has everything changed while I was gone,*" she wondered, "*or just me?*"

She fished her cell phone from her pocket and checked for messages. Still none. Impulsively following a path that snaked down the hill, Young-hee lost sight of her apartment. The path passed a massive construction project, with high, corrugated steel walling off giant holes from which would likely grow another complex, just like hers. Leaving the construction trucks, dirt, and noise, she reached the main road, and momentarily panicked—until she spied the name of her apartment complex on the high walls of a building a block away.

At the old guard booth was, fittingly, an old guard—a *gyeongbi*—chatting with another guard inside the booth. All apartments in Korea hired old guys to act as security and keep an eye on things. The muffled sound of a television came from booth. He eyed her suspiciously. "Hey, girl. Are you looking for someone?" he asked in a thick rural accent.

She eyed the gyeongbi back, examining his blue, police-like uniform and deeply wrinkled face. Some gyeongbi could be nosy, others grouchy, and some, even scary. But all could be huge pains if you got off on the wrong foot. This one seemed gruff, rather than mean. "Um, I live here. Building 206," she said.

"Ah, you're the ones moving in today," he said, looking relieved.

"The manager talked about you this morning. The Jo's, right?"

"Yes. Nice to meet you. I got a little lost, walking around the neighborhood."

"It's a pretty big complex, easy to get lost, at first." he said. Then angling his head curiously, he asked, "You're not from around here?"

"We just moved back. We've been abroad for a few years." Young-hee squirmed, embarrassed by her own accent.

"Well, welcome back. I'm Gyeongbi Shin."

"Pleased to meet you, Mr. Shin," she said with a light bow.

Young-hee figured she should head home. As in most Korean apartment complexes, the towers were separated by parking lots and small playgrounds, full of busy, gossiping housewives and bored, gossiping men. Young-hee walked quickly with her head down. She passed a fountain quietly gushing and surrounded by puddles—evidence that local kids had ignored the "Keep out of fountain" sign.

She said "Hi," to three pretty girls about her age, wearing a peculiar mix of fancy and garish clothes. They kept walking, mimicking her "*Hi*," and giggled—evidently finding something about her greeting or appearance just hilarious.

"*Jigyeowo*," she said again, feeling her face flush with anger. "So annoying." A couple of buildings later, embarrassment replaced anger. Maybe she shouldn't have talked to strange girls. Or maybe it wasn't a big deal. Maybe the stress of moving made everything seem worse.

As Youngee approached her building, her mom came running up, frantic. "*Where's Young-beom?*" she asked, grabbing Young-hee's arm in panic.

"Wha?" said Young-hee, confused.

"Your brother, have you seen him?"

"No. I was walking around. I left him sleeping in your bedroom."

"He's not there now. He must have woken up and wandered off."

"He always wanders off."

Immediately Young-hee realized she had said the wrong thing. "*Young-hee!* I don't need your attitude, not now. He's your little brother. You should have been watching him." Young-hee frequently got lectured about her "attitude," although she often didn't know why. "The movers didn't notice him walk out," her mom went on. "He doesn't know this place at all. He's just a little boy. He's probably scared…"

Young-hee hated seeing her usually strong mother so fragile. "It's okay, mom. I'm sure he hasn't gone far. We'll find him."

They split up, with Young-hee's mom turning right and heading down the street. Young-hee zipped across to the supermarket, to see if he was lured by the treats, but nothing. Walking quickly, she saw no renegade four-year-old walking alone or checking out the cranes and machinery in the recycling yards. She frantically looped around the complex until she found herself by the gatehouse again.

The setting sun threw shadows up and down the apartment, giving everything a warmer glow. Remembering the fountain and her brother's unrelenting need to make messes, she took off, half-running.

Then Young-hee heard a familiar laugh from around the corner. And, sure enough, there was the fountain and there was Bum, giggling with a security guard. Bum's eyes were red from crying, but now he was laughing and happy. As she approached, she saw it was Mr. Shin. "They were all running away, but to Tiger, it looked like they were running from Rabbit," he said, making funny Tiger faces. "So Tiger says, 'I had no idea Rabbit was so strong,' and he ran away as fast as he could."

"Bum! There you are," said Young-hee.

Bum looked up and shouted "*Nuna*!"—"big sister." He jumped off the chair and ran to her.

"You know you shouldn't run off like that. Mom was so worried."

"Sorry," Bum said.

"I found him wandering by the side gate, crying," said the guard. "I could see he was lost, but he couldn't remember where he lived."

"Sorry, he likes to wonder off."

"Oh, he's a little adventurer," said the guard, tousling Bum's hair.

"No, he's just a dork." Young-hee crouched down to make sure Bum wasn't missing any limbs. "Thanks for the help. We're not usually such a strange family."

The gyeongbi laughed warmly. "We're here to help. Don't worry about it."

Young-hee spent most of the walk back trying to drill their address into Bum's scattered mind. "We live in building 206, apartment 901," she said. "Two-zero-six. Nine-zero-one. Remember that!"

"Uh-huh," said Bum.

As they neared the apartment building, their mom caught sight of them. "Young-beom!" she exclaimed, running over. "You can't just wander off like that. I was so worried." She held her boy tightly, so happy to have him back she forgot everything else. She took him by the hand and led him back to the apartment, barely looking at Young-hee.

Only then, watching them walk away together, did Young-hee realize that for at least five minutes, she hadn't felt stressed or frustrated by the move or the three rude girls or anything else. She had just been happy to find her brother—and just as suddenly, that good feeling was drifting away again. "So annoying," she muttered. *Yeah, what an adventurer.*

* * *

That evening, Young-hee sat at the kitchen table with her mom and brother, eating Chinese takeout. Black *jajang* sauce streaked the empty noodle bowls. Gooey, half-eaten *tangsuyuk* filled a cheap dish. Bum sat on his doting mother's lap.

"Who wants a big dumpling?" she asked, swirling a steamed *mandu* in front of Bum. "Does a big boy get a big dumpling?" Bum laughed as he tried to bite the dancing food. He had made his typical mess, and Young-hee felt herself scowl reflexively.

"He gets all the big dumplings?" asked Young-hee, looking at the small ones on her plate.

"It was a big day for Young-beom, wasn't it," said mom. "Oh, does somebody have a beggar in his belly? How does he eat so much?"

Young-hee scowled at the trite saying. *How did "beggar in the belly" even make sense?*, she wondered. Instead, she thought about their day—moving into this lousy apartment, Bum getting lost, the mean girls laughing at her. But then she recalled the old security guards. "Mom? What does *maok* mean?"

"Maok? That's not a word. Do you mean *maehok*?"

"Yeah, that was it."

"Oh, Young-hee, how did your Korean get so bad?"

That was not what Young-hee wanted to hear. Her parents had insisted on Korean school every Saturday when they lived abroad, and plenty of Korean homework every night. She had only forgotten one word. "But what does it mean?"

Her mom cleaned Bum's mouth with a napkin. "Fascinating. Or charming. Where did you hear it?"

"When I met a couple of the old gyeongbi guards this afternoon."

"Ah, they must have found you interesting, then."

Young-hee wondered if her mom was teasing. But no, she must have misheard the guard.

Then, at last, Young-hee's mom turned her attention to her daughter. "Young-hee," she said softly, "Could you do the dishes? There's still so much to get done tonight, and I need to be at work early tomorrow."

"If Bum's such a big boy, why doesn't he help?" she muttered, louder than she intended.

That earned her a sharp look that quickly softened. "Look, Young-hee," her mother said, "I know this isn't what you wanted. But we're trying to restart our lives, all of us, and I need your help."

For a moment Young-hee felt bad for her mom and all she had been through. She knew none of this was intentional, and that her mom needed her help. Young-hee could feel generous words on her tongue, but just couldn't say them. "I miss my friends," Young-hee complained, poking a cold dumpling.

Her mom cast a tired glance at Young-hee. "You can always chat online. That's why I got that camera for your computer." She stuck the chopsticks into another dumpling for Bum. "Besides, it's not like you had that many friends in Canada. You always used to complain about that."

That comment stung, and Young-hee felt her mood grow darker. "I miss dad," she said. Her mom stiffened briefly, as if absorbing a blow in a fight, then went back to playing with Bum.

Suddenly, Young-hee felt overwhelmed by emotions—from the move, the rude girls, her mom, her stupid brother, things she couldn't explain, and other things she couldn't admit. She left the table and stormed to her room, closing the door hard.

The Tiger and the Rabbit

One day Rabbit was strolling through the woods to the market to buy some vegetables when he heard the sad sound of someone crying. "Oh dear! Oh dear!" the voice cried. Rabbit looked and looked and finally found the voice. It belonged to Tiger, who had fallen into a tiger pit and was trapped.

"Hello?" said Rabbit, peering over the edge of the deep hole.

"Oh, Rabbit!" said Tiger, suddenly hopeful. "Please help me out of this hole."

But Rabbit was wary. "I know you, Tiger," he said. "If I got you out of that hole, you would only try to eat me."

"No!" he protested. "I would be ever so grateful. I could give you a reward."

"I fear my only reward would be being your dinner," said Rabbit skeptically.

"Definitely not. How could I do that to someone who helped me? Please, before the men find and kill me."

Rabbit took pity on Tiger, and decided to help. He found a strong length of rope, tied one end to a tree, and lowered the other to Tiger who climbed out. Once free, Tiger roared with joy. "That's so much better," he said. "I was trapped in that hole for days, cold and hungry. Ever so hungry." He looked at Rabbit, suddenly predatory.

"But Tiger, I just helped you," protested Rabbit.

"Yes, and I appreciate it, but I am hungry. And you are definitely a big, yummy-looking rabbit." Tiger moved forward ominously, intent on making a meal of the animal who saved him.

But Rabbit remained calm. "Oh, silly Tiger," he said casually, "You know you cannot eat me. I am far too strong and powerful. In fact, I might even eat you, if you anger me."

Tiger kept approaching. "Nonsense," he said, "I am far bigger than you. My claws are long, my teeth are sharp. There's no point resisting."

"Resisting?" said Rabbit, looking bored. "My teeth are pretty long and sharp, too. Why, I could swat you away with barely a thought."

Tiger slowed, his eyes narrowed, and he looked at Rabbit full of disbelief. "I have never heard such silliness. Everyone knows Rabbit is small and harmless."

"Oh, really? Everyone knows?" said Rabbit. "How about I show you just how strong I am? Follow me, Tiger, before you make me angry." He began to walk away.

So Tiger, skeptical but confused, followed Rabbit. "You better not try to run off," he warned.

"Who's running? I want you to see this." Rabbit led Tiger into town.

And as all the villagers saw them approach, they saw mighty Tiger and they fled in terror. Women and children, men and soldiers, all ran before Tiger—but because Rabbit was walking in front, to Tiger it looked like they were fleeing from Rabbit. "I had no idea Rabbit was so strong," said Tiger, and ran away before Rabbit could hurt him.

3

Bored, Young-hee bounced a tennis ball against the wall of her room. *Thump-bump*. It was the middle of the afternoon, but the sky was dark with purple clouds that poured down the hot, summer rains of *jangmacheol*.

The heavy humidity left everything soggy and disgusting; clothes hanging by the window felt nearly as wet as when taken from the washer the night before. *Gross*, thought Young-hee, looking at the wallpaper by the window that was turning green with mold.

Thump-bump.

It was the plainest, most unremarkable day ever.

With each *thump* of the tennis ball, Young-hee, surly and un-relenting, felt the glare of her mom struggling to work in the next room.

"Young-hee, could you use the Internet or something?" her mom called.

"Internet hasn't been working all day," Young-hee said sullenly. But, feeling her mother's glare, she stopped throwing the ball.

The weeks since the big move had not gone well. Knowing that thirteen-year-old girls anywhere could be cliquish and cruel, she had dreaded her new school, but it was worse than she feared. On the first day, she discovered that the three girls she met on moving day were in her class—and, of course, its unofficial leaders. They were eager for someone new to torture.

Young-hee tried putting her energies into schoolwork, but it was all either ridiculously easy or impossibly hard. Either way, it was nearly all endless memorization—no activities, no experiments, no creativity at all. Young-hee used to like science class, the way Ms. Thompson would lead them through experiments and let students try things out for themselves. But here there were just multiple choices and lists. "So annoying," she would say as she puzzled over some grammar problem or stupid history lesson. Sometimes she found herself looking out the window, daydreaming, only to be brought back, embarrassed, when a teacher slapped her desk with a ruler. Young-hee would sit fuming, her resentment piling higher than her homework.

Life at home was not much better. Sarah and Fei were already talking online with her less and less often, and Denda never emailed at all. She could still follow her friends from their homepages, but the new pics, updates, and inside jokes left her feeling increasingly distant. Her mother worked more than ever, even at home. Lousy takeout food containers stacked up, and Young-hee was sick of the same things all the time.

Bum seemed to get lost at least once a week, although now the kindly guard was pretty good at finding him and cheering him up. Half the time Bum would return soaking wet after a mess-making swim in one of the complex's fountains. Sometimes Mr. Shin would tell Bum stories until Young-hee could pick him up. The last time, she found them playing with a stray orange kitten while Bum made tiger noises. Young-hee apologized again for the inconvenience, but the guard said Bum couldn't help it because it was such a magical time, being young. Young-hee always hated it when adults said that kind of thing. *There is nothing magical about being young,* she thought. *Only someone who has never been young could think it was magical. Being young is boring.* That she knew for a certainty. *And frustrating and confusing. But mostly horribly, endlessly boring. Every minute takes an hour, every hour takes a day, and life just sprawls out ahead of you.* But she held her tongue and thanked him.

Soon after that, school took a turn for the worse after the girls heard gossip about her father, and used it to tease her. On the chalkboard one morning, there was the simple drawing of a stick-figure man, standing sadly behind bars in a simple prison. "Where is Mr. Jo?" asked the cartoon's caption. Furious but determined not to let anyone see her cry, Young-hee stormed out of the classroom, with cruel laughter trailing her down the hallway. At least her teacher didn't punish her. In fact, soon after that, school got a little less terrible, although Young-hee thought she was probably just getting used to it.

Today, though, she was at home, listening to incessant, pounding rain, determined to avoid her homework. "I'm going to watch TV," she announced.

"Please keep the sound down," said her mom.

Young-hee sighed dramatically, but when she turned it on, the TV hissed static so loud, she jumped. "Sorry," she said. She hit mute, but failed to find anything wrong. *Cable's out*, she concluded. She turned to the DVD collection, but had seen everything way too many times, even movies she didn't like. At last she decided that something with Gwenneth Paltrow would do—at least she was pretty.

When Young-hee pressed "eject," the DVD door jiggled and cracked slightly open, then made a sickly noise as gears ground against some unseen obstacle. Young-hee hit the eject button a couple more times until the DVD tray managed to open—revealing a sticky mix of peanut butter and Japanese robot toys.

"Mom! Bum ruined the DVD player!" She felt like she would explode. "He ruins everything!"

Suddenly Young-hee found herself facing an umbrella. Her mom jiggled it slightly. "Take it," she said, her voice clipped. "I need you to go for a walk. Or go shopping. Something."

"But … it's raining."

"I know. That's why I'm giving you the umbrella. Maybe you can visit your friend—what's her name?—Eunsu."

"Eunju. And she's not my friend."

"Whatever. I can't take it anymore. I have to get this work finished, and you've been impossible all day. All week. Longer."

Young-hee looked back at her mom as defiantly as she could for as long as she dared, then took the umbrella. "Fine."

She grabbed a light jacket and shoved a ball in her pocket, unsure if she was more furious or sad.

"Look, Young-hee," said her mom, her voice suddenly soft again, "I just need to get this work done. Give me a couple of hours, then we'll have something nice for dinner. Okay?"

Young-hee, not ready for a truce, stormed out. As the door closed behind her, she called out "So annoying!" one more time, so her mom could hear.

The elevator was out yet again, so she took the stairs, scared she might start crying, although she couldn't really say why. She knew she was being difficult and her mom needed to work, but it still wasn't fair. Bum ruined the DVD player, the rain was ruining her summer, her mom had ruined her life.

Outside, the rain was falling harder than ever, forming ankle-deep water pools. Even with the concrete entrance overhang and her umbrella, the wind-whipped downpour soaked her shoes and pants. *I can't believe this is my life*, she thought. A gust of wind blew the umbrella inside out, soaking her all over. *This is stupid*, she thought, *there's no way I can walk around in that.*

Giving up, she sat down, failed to wrangle the umbrella into shape, and angrily threw it to the ground. She checked her phone. No messages. She sulked, checked her phone again, then sulked some more. A rainy roar echoed through the stairwell. Far away, she could hear cars pushing through water-filled streets.

Just then, she heard the clank of a heavy door, followed by feet on stairs. She turned and saw Mrs. Park from apartment 201 coming up from the parking garage, carrying shopping bags. With her blotchy, white makeup and her pushiness, Mrs. Park had quickly become a staple of their lives, often offering to keep an eye on Bum or share some extra side dishes. Everyone agreed she was friendly and helpful, except for Young-hee, who secretly found her nosy and vaguely scary. "My goodness, child, what are you doing here?" she said on spotting Young-hee's broken umbrella. "You're not thinking of going out in that? You'll catch your death." She squeezed by Young-hee and kept going up the stairs, making complaining noises. "I can't believe the elevator is out in this terrible building again."

Young-hee looked down into the dark stairwell. The building's parking garage was not the most exciting place in the world, but it had to be drier than outside, assuming it hadn't flooded. Pushing her broken umbrella into a corner, she walked carefully down four flights of rain-slicked stairs to that familiar dark blue door marked with the big 206.

After the stairwell, the parking garage seemed almost bright. At midday, it was only half-full, mostly with smaller cars—husbands took the nicer, big cars to work, leaving their wives the "cute" cars for shopping and errands.

The parking garage stretched out endlessly, connecting all the apartment buildings above into one giant concrete cavern below. It was not a pretty place, but quiet and kind of interesting. She instantly felt a kind of ownership, and pleasure that no one here could tell her what to do.

She fished the ball from her pocket and walked deeper into the garage, hoping to find an emptier area for throwing things.

The next level was a lot less crowded, and she tried whipping the ball off of a wall, but an unlucky bounce left a dirty round mark on a white Hyundai Accent, so Young-hee thought it best to find somewhere even more deserted.

Her foot falls squeaked on the rubbery green floor and echoed throughout the huge underground space. She passed stairwells to other apartment buildings, their doors emblazoned with big white numbers: 205, 204; around a corner was 408 and 501. They didn't seem to be a clear order, and some doors had labels instead of numbers: storage, maintenance, or utilities. Curious, she tried them, but they were nearly always locked.

Turning another corner, she came to a promising place—darker than most of the garage, but with very few cars—so she tossed the ball off the wall and ceiling, in elaborate caroms. Soon a bad throw coupled with a bad bounce sent the ball ricocheting over a wall and into a lower level. Young-hee took a ramp down to chase the rogue ball. The car park ramp turned and turned again, and it seemed to be too long to be going just to the next level. Then, it opened up again into another parking level, and Young-hee stopped short.

Something was not right. Everything was just too … empty. No cars, no people, no anything, except a forlorn orange parking cone on its side in a corner. The garage's colors seemed off. Sounds had a weird flatness. Even the light felt wrong. *That doesn't make sense,* she thought. *It's just a parking garage.* Young-hee swallowed, trying to stop scaring herself. She wasn't looking for the ball anymore, just trying to figure out where she was. And that was when she realized: None of the doors had apartment numbers. No signs told what floor she was on. Or marked an exit. The floor no longer had the green rubbery finish or bright white and yellow lane markers. *Where on Earth am I?*

The feeling of dread grew overwhelming and, suddenly, Young-hee just wanted out. She tried a door that might be a stairwell, but it would not open. Nor would the next door, nor the one after that. Her heart raced. She took a couple of steps back and looked for a ramp up. There was one not far off, so Young-hee ran up it hard, but the next level looked the same as the one below—no signs, no numbers, no cars, no people. Young-hee ran up another level. And another. And another. *This is crazy,* she thought. *The garage wasn't this deep. And there definitely were cars around here.* She could feel a spiky ball of fear growing in her chest.

Her phone! She pulled it out and dialed mom, but nothing happened. Zero bars. No matter how many times she tried. *What's going on? What's happening?*

Think logically, she told herself. She must have wandered into some disused part of the garage. She tried to retrace her steps, but all the levels and ramps looked the same, no matter where she went. *That's it, I've gone insane.*

She refused to let herself cry. She just needed to figure things out. Every place with a way in must have a way out. There was definitely an explanation—it just seemed scary because she couldn't think of it yet.

And then she noticed the orange pylon, on its side. *Have I just looped around to where I started?* It hardly seemed possible, but that must be it. She went to another ramp and ran up and up. But when she walked into the next parking area, the pylon was still there, in the same place. Every level was exactly the same. She was nowhere. She was trapped.

Young-hee sat down. Out of ideas, she yelled, but no one answered.

And then, a doorway caught her eye, and she walked over to it. It was dark greenish-brown, not blue. It was wood, not metal. Taller and thinner than the other doors, it looked handmade, almost elegant, like the door to a traditional home. Instead of a regular knob, it had a heavy metal ring. Curious, she turned the ring and pushed.

Finally, a door that opened. It revealed a pitch black stairwell leading up, with no lights and no signs. She strained her eyes and, high above, she thought she could make out the distant, dull glow of daylight. And for a moment, she felt cool air against her face. Young-hee looked back at the eerie garage and, not knowing what else to do, she stepped into the darkness and began her ascent, using her mobile phone to light her way.

The stairwell turned a corner, turned again, and Young-hee found herself standing outside in the sun. For a brief second she wondered what had happened to the rain; but then her eyes adjusted to the light. This was not Seoul. This was nowhere Young-hee had ever been before.

The Hammer of Wealth

Long ago, when the Tiger used to smoke a pipe, there lived in a quiet village a hard-working young man named Hongjo. His family was very poor, so he traveled far and wide over the surrounding hills, chopping wood to sell so his parents and sister and brother would have a little more money.

One day, after a long day of chopping far from home, he came across a strange walnut tree. He picked a bag of walnuts for the family to enjoy. Hongjo realized it had grown too dark to go home. Fortunately, in a clearing by the walnut tree, he saw an empty, battered house in which to spend the night.

It was a cold evening, so he started a fire in the fireplace. As soon as the wood lit, strange sounds came from the fireplace. Scared and seeing nowhere else to hide, Hongjo climbed into the rafters.

From there, he saw half a dozen dokkaebi—goblins—tumble out of the fireplace. Like all dokkaebi, they were short and very ugly, with dark gray, leathery skin and a single, stubby horn on their foreheads. The gob-

lins danced around the house merrily, boasting of their mischief that day.

"I pulled the tail of a cow and made it kick his owner and run away," laughed one.

"Well, I snuck into a woman's kitchen and knocked the rice pot's lid into the hot pot, ha-ha."

"I danced under a rich man's home, making the floors creak and scaring the whole household."

After a time the goblins grew hungry. The head goblin took out a big, wooden hammer and slammed it against the floor. "Tukdak tukdak," he shouted. "Bring us food!" And—poof!—piles of hot meats and soups and rice appeared. Greedily the goblins ate, and working up a thirst, the goblin again swung his hammer. "Tukdak tukdak, bring us drink!" he shouted, And—poof!—bottles of soju and magkeolli appeared. Quickly, the goblins drank too much and became drunk and silly.

From high above, Hongjo watched their merrymaking and eating and drinking, and he grew very hungry. Suddenly, a huge kko-reu-reuk noise rumbled loudly from his hungry belly.

"What's that?" asked the drunken goblins, all confused. "It sounds like thunder. Rain will probably leak into this old house, and we hate rain."

Hongjo worried that any more stomach noises would reveal him to the dokkaebi, so he decided he had to eat something. But the only things in his pockets were the walnuts. Desperate to quiet his belly, he tried to open one quietly with his mouth, but it was no use. Ttak! The walnut made a huge noise as it cracked open.

"Oh no!" said the foolish dokkaebi again. "The roof is caving in. We're in danger! Run!" The goblins all ran away. But, in their haste, they forgot the wooden hammer.

Hongjo dropped down from the rafters and ate his full of the dok-kaebi's delicious food. But as he was eating, he saw the hammer and picked it up. "Tukdak tukdak," he said, "Bring me gold!" And—poof!— huge bags of gold appeared. From that day forward, Hongjo and his family were the richest people in the province, and they were very happy … at least until his younger brother found out where Hongjo got the magic hammer. But that is a story for another day.

4

Young-hee looked up, down and all around, confused and over-whelmed. She was surrounded by trees and a pine forest, but not like any she had seen before. The trees loomed huge, each the size of an apartment building, with thick gnarled branches like arthritic pretzels. The bark cracked with ridges as thick as her thigh and pine cones as big as watermelons. The trees were unreal, their greens and browns too vivid to take in.

Everything else was like those mammoth trees, bigger-than-life. And unreal. *No, super-real.* She was standing in a field of grass, but the blades ruffling against her legs felt soft as silk, and the wind blowing through them sounded like a gentle, faraway song.

Trying to take it all in, Young-hee stepped back and bumped into a door—wooden, like the one in the apartment basement. Set into a tree's giant root, it swung open easily, revealing ugly concrete stairs—the way back to the parking garage. Her first impulse was to run back down, to escape the scary strangeness. But, aside from the shock of wandering into a new world, she felt surprisingly little fear as she moved away from the door. It wasn't even like making a decision.

The sun was directly overhead, and yet the light was soft, bathing everything in a warm glow that felt more like evening. She was standing in a clearing. In the center, the branches of a big hedge twisted like playground equipment. To one side was a large and incredibly ornate fountain with multiple levels of water cascading from pool to pool. As she got closer, she realized that the water was flowing with gravity in some places, but against it in others. She carefully slid her fingers into a stream that poured upward, blithely disregarding physics. At least, any physics Young-hee had ever studied.

In the churning water she could see myriad fish in explosive colors and impossible shapes. She tried to try to touch one, but as soon as her hand broke the surface, the fish swam up the fountain, out of reach. She thought the laughing, gurgling of the fountain sounded a little like crying.

At first, this place almost hurt to look at, but increasingly Young-hee found it beautiful. Through a break in the woods, she made out a big, grassy hill and, further away, the purple points of mountains. It was hard to explain or understand—leaves looked like leaves, sky like sky, but everything familiar was also strange.

Reflexively she reached into her pocket for her cell phone to photograph the huge trees, but they were too big for the frame. She tried a selfie with a giant pine cone. But when she checked, the images were jumbles of unintelligible pixels. She checked for messages or emails. Nothing.

With soft, deep buzzing a dragonfly rose from behind a tree. Brightly colored as a peacock's tail, it was a bigger than real-world dragonflies and had more wings. Young-hee held out her hand, palm up, inviting it to land. After hesitating, it settled on her hand. Maybe she should try to pet it?

"What do you think you're doing?" came an angry voice behind her. Startled, she turned, but saw only forest. And two jangseung totem poles, like the ones at her apartment complex. "Don't pretend you didn't hear me," said the voice, coming from the jangseung.

"Er," said Young-hee, tongue-tied. "I was playing with the dragonfly."

"Do you want to lose a finger?" asked the second jangseung. "Or, *heavens forbid*, your whole hand?"

Young-hee was perplexed. It was just a cute little dragonfly. But as she turned to point at it, she saw its impossibly large mouth, open very wide and filled with long, sharp teeth.

Before it could chomp, a branch from a nearby tree swung down and gently bonked the toothy not-so-dragonfly in the head with a giant pine cone. Young-hee jerked her hand away. "*Tsk*! None of that," said the first jangseung. "You are free to eat what you will in the Jade Swamps and the Empty Forest, but not here. You know that." Young-hee could have sworn she saw the creature nod. "Now, be gone." The creature got back up on its six legs and took to the air.

"Thanks for your help," said Young-hee, feeling terribly dumb. "That was really..." Young-hee trailed off as she realized she was talking to two totem poles "... nice."

She checked out the defenders of her fingers. They were definitely jangseung—wooden carvings about two meters tall, stuck in the ground. Unlike the ones by her apartment building, these were real wood, wonderfully intricate, their paint fresh and bright, and most lively. The first jangseung had black hair and a big red mouth, with almost fleshy lips—Young-hee guessed it was female. The second had a black hat and a scruffy beard, clearly male. But they were alive.

"Tell us," said the female totem pole, "what manner of creature are you?"

"Creature?" repeated Young-hee, taken aback. "Excuse me?"

"No, you *may not* be excused," answered the male jangseung. "We are the guardians here and require an answer. What manner of creature are you?"

"You are not a fairy, obviously," said the female. "Or a witch or an imp. And I'm fairly certain you are not a fox."

Fairies?, Young-hee wondered. *Does Korea even have fairies? I thought they were a European thing.* "You're jangseung," she said, stating the obvious and feeling dumb for it.

"Of course we're jangseung," said the male. "What else would we be?"

"Maybe she's a golem," said the female. "They're not too bright."

"Are you a golem? The penalties for a golem crossing a jangseung's territory unbidden are most severe. How did you get here?"

"I'm not sure," said Young-hee, truthfully. "I just got lost, walked up some stairs and came out over there." She pointed across the clearing to the brown door in the tree root.

"Huh, I never noticed that door before," said the female.

"Me neither. Very *peculiar*. All the more reason to know what she is."

"I… I don't know what you mean," said Young-hee.

"She doesn't know very much."

"Definitely a golem."

"No, I mean, I'm nothing special. Just a girl."

"'Nothing special,'" echoed the female jangseung. "Just a … *waita-minute* … a *girl*?"

"From the mud world?" said the male totem pole. "A bear daughter?"

"A human girl?"

"Er, yeah," said Young-hee. "I mean, yes, to the human part. Not the bear part or the mud."

There was a brief pause, then both jangseung started talking rapidly at the same time.

"Could she be a true girl?"

"It's been an age since I saw a human. What could it mean?"

"Why now? We shouldn't be hasty."

"Do you think she's here to fight?"

"Could she tip the balance?"

"She doesn't look like much of a fighter."

Young-hee didn't understand. Fighting? Balance? This was way out of her league. "Uh, excuse me?" she ventured. "I never meant to make trouble or offend anyone."

"Oh, I'm sorry, dearie," said the female jangseung, her scowl softening. "We're being terribly rude. These are difficult times and sometimes Cheonha and I forget our manners."

"So … am I allowed to pass?"

"Oh, yes. A bear daughter? Of course."

It was a promising response, and Young-hee relaxed a bit. "You're the first real jangseung I've ever met, but you both look very beautiful and elegant. And you saved me from that nasty dragonfly thing, so I really owe you. Thank you so much." Young-hee bowed politely as she finished speaking.

"You are very gracious girl, and grace is always appreciated," said the male, bowing his wooden body politely. "I am General Cheonha, and my bride is General Jiha. We are the guardians of the *jureum* forest and surrounding lands, from the Crying Stream to the Swollen Pond, and from the Lonely Wastes, past the goblin market, to Haechi's Horn."

"Haechi's Horn?"

Jiha gave a flick of her head toward the steep grassy hill beyond the forest. "Haechi's Horn. Because the hill is so steep, like the horn of a haechi."

"Ah," said Young-hee, looking at the hill towering over them. "Well, it is wonderful to meet you both. I'm Young-hee. I'm nothing special like a general or a guardian, just a normal girl. I'm certainly not a bear."

"A bear *daughter*," corrected Jiha. "You are a human, descended from Ungnyeo the bear and the first son of heaven."

"Wait, are you talking about that Dangun story?" she asked, remembering the old Korean tale. Young-hee wasn't up on mythology, but had read the tale in a comic book. "Is that where I am? In the world of Dangun and stories like that, not the real world."

"Well, that depends," said Cheonha. "Our realm is as real as any other. But it hasn't been the first world in a long, long time. Not since your mud world took our place."

"Took your place …?"

"Yes, long ago, before the Second Great Giants' War," said Cheonha. "Before the nine-headed ogre Agwi Kwisin stole the daughter of the vice regent, when the river fairies still ran wild, and the evil yellow dragon came down from …"

"I'm sure the girl doesn't want to hear the convoluted history," interrupted Jiha. "Besides, as long as we are here, no one has to fear ogres or tigers or the like."

Cheonha seemed ready to argue with his wife, but a shadow passed across the sun, covering Young-hee and the forest in darkness. Young-hee looked up, expecting a cloud, but was surprised by the silhouette of a bird so immense that its shadow lingered for seconds. It had wings the length of a soccer field, and a body the size of a whale, but its glide was light and graceful as a helium balloon. One beat of its wings sped it out of sight behind Haechi's Horn, and a few seconds later, Young-hee was almost knocked off her feet by a gust of wind that whipped the trees and grass.

"Wow," she said again.

"Ah, a crane!" said Jiha. "One of the ten symbols of life. Very good luck."

"*That* was a crane?"

"A *great crane*. It's been a long time since I saw one."

Young-hee decided that, strange and overwhelming as it was, this world was *amazing*. Certainly more than school or her ugly apartment or the muggy Seoul summer. "Could I look around? You mentioned a goblin market?," she babbled with gleeful excitement. "Or maybe I should climb Haechi Horn."

"Hmm," said Jiha, thinking. "You are free to go where you will, of course. But care is always needed, especially for a bear-child."

"Oh, right," said Young-hee, remembering the toothy dragonfly. "But you said you were guardians of this forest and around here."

"True," said Cheonha, "but there are still dangers. What you need is a guide."

"I don't suppose jangseung can get up and walk around in this world, can they?"

"*Hehe*, no. But our friend Grandma Dol can," said Cheonha. "Isn't that right, grandmother?"

An old woman, large and lumpy, with chalky skin, shuffled out of the forest. She moved slowly but steadily, using a cane, with a large bag strapped to a wooden frame lashed to her back. She wore a bulky, gray traditional *hanbok*, like Korean peasants in old paintings. After a long pause, she asked, "Eh? What are our guardians rattling on about today? Never have I heard such a chatty couple of jangseungs." She talked as slowly as she walked, but with the same assuredness of purpose.

"Greetings, forest elder," said Cheonha, his beard swishing as he talked. "We do have a favor to ask of you. And your partners, of course."

"Oh, and what's that? To buy all of my wares, sparing me a tiring day in the market?"

"I'm afraid we don't have the *jungbo* for a single one of your famous lanterns. But we'd like you to show the market to our friend, Young-hee."

"Your … *friend*," said Grandma Dol.

"She is from far away and would like to learn more about our world and customs," said Jiha. "Could you show her around and keep her safe?"

Grandma Dol shifted her shoulders to adjust the heavy load. She flashed Young-hee a quick look, just a once-over, but it felt like the old woman had seen into her soul. Her face was heavily lined, stoic, and unreadable.

"Very well," she said, resuming her slow, steady pace. "Come along, child. The goblin market is fast-moving. You could get lost if you aren't careful. Stay close."

Young-hee leaned in close to Jiha. "You said I was the first person you'd seen in a long time," she whispered. "What about Grandma Dol?"

"Don't be fooled by appearances. Did you see her skin? She is really a stone."

"A *stone*?"

"Yes, a very old, wise stone. You may see many things that look like people, but you are the only bear-child around. Never make assumptions. Now, don't dawdle. Stay close, and she'll keep you out of trouble."

"Thank you so much, General Jiha," said Young-hee more loudly. "And General Cheonha. I won't be long." The jangseung shouted cheerful goodbyes as Young-hee scrambled to catch up to the old stone woman—a quick task, given Grandma Dol's pace. If she really was a stone there was no telling how old she might be, and in Young-hee's experience, the older someone was the more carefully you should treat them.

"Uh, Grandma Dol, your bag looks very heavy. Maybe I could carry some things for you."

Grandma Dol walked a while and then answered, "Thank you, Ms. Young-hee, but no. These are my wares, and mine alone to carry."

"Okay. But if I can help in any way, please tell me."

Another pause.

"You are not familiar with dokkaebi markets, I gather?"

"Not really. I mean, they have ... uh, where I'm from. But they're just kind of busy and dirty. Old people selling vegetables and things."

"… Oh."

"I mean, not *old* people. Not that there's anything wrong with old. I just meant, uh … just people."

"You like to talk before you know what you want to say," Grandma Dol said. Young-hee regretted her careless mouth, but, for once, Grandma Dol volunteered a comment. "That can get you in trouble in a goblin market."

"Are goblins really dangerous? Like those big, toothy dragonflies?"

"…Like what? Dokkaebi can be … treacherous in their way. They are not violent or fierce, like wild animals, but they are full of trickery. And you would make quite a prize, should you end up in a goblin's debt."

Young-hee didn't like how that sounded. "A prize? Like kidnapped?"

"No, dokkaebi have no power over free creatures. But debts can take away our freedoms, and can be incurred in a variety of ways. … Stay close. And do not take anything, not even a gift, unless I hand it to you."

Young-hee was not sure what Grandma Dol meant, but she thought it best to obey. After the quiet of the forest, Young-hee was startled by the goblin market, roiling with people and creatures, jammed into row after row of wooden stalls, each filled from the ground to high in the air. Everywhere were foods, powders, potions, trinkets, and caged animals being bought and sold. Roots, herbs, and plants hung from hooks, or filled huge sacks carried by squat creatures that lacked their own stall. Large pots full of *banchan* side dishes gave off aromas Young-hee had never smelled before. Most people wore hanbok clothing—from bright and fancy to off-white and stained. The air crackled with sounds—voices haggling, boxes clattering, birds squawking, dogs barking, and animals hubbubing in unfamiliar ways. One stall featured wires hung with cured animal parts in shapes Young-hee had never seen. The stall next to it featured parchments, papers, and scrolls, most of which seemed incredibly old. Hanging in the air in front of the stall, one scroll contained

Chinese *hanja* scratchings completely different than those she studied at school. A couple of stalls later, someone was selling a puzzling collection of metal instruments that looked vaguely scientific or astronomical.

As the market's name suggested, most stalls were run by goblins. Dokkaebi. Young-hee had heard of the troublesome little monsters—as common in Korean stories as trolls, leprechauns, and genies in Western tales—but she never expected to see one for real. They were short and wrinkled, with green-gray skin, heavy as a rhinoceros's, and as just as ill-fitting. Many had short, thick horns. Some had clumps of wiry hair on tops of their heads or in beards, but never a full head of hair. Their hands were stubby, with short, ungainly fingers; their mouths filled with large teeth. With their large eyes and half-grimacing expressions, most didn't look terribly threatening. They did, however, smell—*like soot*, she noted.

Grandma Dol trudged through the chaos, paying it no mind, until she came to an empty old wooden stall. Evidently hers. She slid her bag onto a table. "Are you hungry?"

Young-hee was about to say "no," when a deep, rumbling noise came loudly from her belly. "Sorry," she said guiltily. "I guess I am."

"Of course," said Grandma Dol. "I brought plenty for us both," and produced a large cloth bag from her sack, set it on a smaller table, and pulled out food wrapped in lotus leaves. And what food! She had pickled white kimchi made of acorns and chestnuts; thick slices of plant roots marinated in honey and rice wine until they were as soft as jelly; strips of seaweed—*gim*—that tasted unexpectedly of chestnut and flowers. There were colorful flakes that looked suspiciously like butterfly wings, spiced and rendered edible; garlicky chestnut cakes Grandma Dol called *meyrtawng;* and the whitest, softest rice balls ever, which Grandma Dol called *kaybal.*

"Please, enjoy," said the old stone woman.

"This is the most fantastic food," Young-hee gushed. "I recognize only half the things, but even those I know taste so much better here."

When they finished, Young-hee tried to help Grandma Dol clean the dishes and leftovers, but she didn't want help, and so, Young-hee just got out of her way. Grandma Dol opened her bag and laid out her wares: lanterns, boxes, carvings, and knickknacks.

"These wooden wares are the finest in the market, the finest this side of Lake Mey. All the fairies buy my lamps, and you know *they* appreciate quality," she explained. The rest of the market churned with such energy that Young-hee worried Grandma Dol would be ignored.

"Where are you, now?" the old stone mumbled as she rummaged through the box, and then lifted out a wooden shape. It was round-ish, painted on one side, with three holes in the middle, and two black ropes hanging from either side: a mask. Grandma Dol pressed the wooden mask to her face—and it seemed to come alive. The edges stretched and pulled at Grandma Dol's pale skin, latching on to the sides, her chin, and forehead. Mask and face both contorted horribly as they melded, and Young-hee feared the old woman was being hurt. Then, with a slight pop, there was just one face: a beaming young woman, with white skin, apple-red cheeks, bright lips, and black hair in two pigtails.

"Good day to you!" exclaimed Grandma Dol, no longer sounding like a grandmother. Or a stone. "Welcome to the finest woodware shop in the market. We promise lanterns that shine twice as bright for twice as long, mavelous boxes with hidden compartments guaranteed to protect your most valuable secrets, and *najeon* lacquerware that can repel even the foulest curse!"

"Uh, Grandma Dol?"

"No, not anymore. Well, sort of. I'm Boonae, Grandma Dol's business partner."

"You're what?"

"Not what—who. I'm Boonae! Grandma Dol knows how to find the best artisans, but she is not much of a saleswoman."

Young-hee had to admit this Boonae stood out, even in the mad goblin market. "Well, it's good to meet you, Boonae," said Young-hee. "I've seen masks like you on TV before, but nothing so … uh, real."

"*Teebee*?" Boonae repeated, puzzled. "Is Teebee a friend of yours?"

"No, I just meant …"

"No matter, the day's a-wasting, and I need to sell." The Boonae-masked Grandma Dol turned to the bustling hordes walking through the market and shouted a quick, engaging patter:

Deals, deals, the finest goods,

The finest crafts, all made of wood …

As the crowds gathered, Young-hee hung back and watched. Boonae worked them masterfully, teasing and entertaining them into a shopping frenzy. It was most impressive.

Just then, an enormous dokkaebi came down the crowded aisle, carrying a huge stack of poorly balanced, overflowing boxes. Shamelessly, he bounced and pushed into people. Young-hee pressed her back against one particularly smelly stall, full of cages containing small animals and insects. She felt a tug on her back pocket.

"Excuse me," came a soft voice. Young-hee looked around but didn't see anything. "No, down here, miss."

There, between the metal bars of a small cage, a hairy paw stretched to grab her lightly. Young-hee crouched down. It was a rabbit. "Hello?" she said.

"Greetings, miss," said the rabbit. He was brown, with a dark nose and mysterious, green eyes. "If you don't mind, do you see an old, short man with a wrinkled face and black, frizzy hair behind the counter?"

Young-hee craned her neck. "Is he wearing a brown cloak?" she whispered. "A bit stained and tattered?"

"He could be, yes," the rabbit whispered, sounding scared.

"I think I see him a couple of stores away, arguing with a gray lumpy thing." A man matching the rabbit description was talking to a woman selling textiles.

"A woman who looks like an old, boiled cabbage?"

Young-hee giggled at the description. "Yes, that's her."

"Mrs. Baek, then," said the rabbit. "My keeper likes to gossip with her when business is slow."

"You can talk," she observed. She found herself growing less surprised by this sort of thing.

"Yes, yes, it makes communicating much easier. At least most of the time. But I won't have long until he comes back." He looked left and right, checking if anyone could hear. "I don't suppose you can see a ring full of keys behind that stall? Perhaps hanging on a hook by the magician's stool."

"He's a magician?"

"If you'd just check, please. Hurry, he'll be back soon. But, yes, he is a shaman, of sorts."

This stall seem dedicated to powders and dried things (bugs maybe) piled into dirty glass containers, along with disorganized heaps of small, dusty boxes. "I don't see anything. I think I see a hook, but there's nothing on it."

"Thank you for checking," answered the rabbit sadly. "But I fear I am soon to become a stew."

"Oh, that's terrible."

"Maybe not, at least not for everyone. I'm told Kwon, my keeper, makes quite good stews. But for me, as I would prefer to continue living, it is distinctly problematic." The rabbit let go of the cage's bars and sat despondently.

"I'm so sorry," she said. "Could I just force the lock open? The cage doesn't look very strong."

"Regardless of how it looks, the magicks binding me here cannot be broken easily."

Young-hee turned and saw Grandma Dol a few feet away, negotiating with a couple of goblins. Or was it Boonae? She wasn't sure how masks worked. "Boonae, could you help us?"

The cheery young mask looked at Young-hee and the disorganized stall, excused herself and walked over. "Us?" she said. "Who is 'us?' "

"Me and my rabbit friend. I'm sorry, but I didn't ask your name."

"Quite all right," said the rabbit. "Call me Kkiman."

"Kkiman says that the magician that owns him will eat him tonight. Can we do something?"

Boonae looked down at the cage, unimpressed. "What kind of rabbit allows himself to be captured by a common magic man? Most magicians I know couldn't trick a tiger, let alone a rabbit."

"That is true," said Kkiman, looking a bit ashamed. "My father always said I was the least tricky rabbit he ever knew, and would end in a pie. 'Shameful,' he would say. It's a miracle Mrs. Kkiman agreed to marry such useless rabbit. But even Kwon never would have gotten me if I hadn't needed medicine for Soon-ja, my littlest kit. I let fears override good sense. I got the medicine, but missed nuances to my deal with the shaman."

"Obligations cannot easily be undone," Boonae confirmed. "If what he says is true, it would take more than a key to free him."

Young-hee was pondering Kkiman's plight, when a gruff shout caused her to jump. "What's this?" said the short, frizzy-haired man rushing toward her. "Have the ladies seen something they like?" Kwon asked, donning a fake smile that utterly failed to ingratiate.

Young-hee remembered how her mother bargained with the old women at the real-world market, and how important she said it was to hide how much you want something and treat it like something you don't care about. "Well, I was looking for some simple magic powders," Young-hee said. "My friend and I are going on a long trip and we'll need something, uh, for energy." Young-hee saw Kwon frown and worried, *Maybe that's not what magic powders do.*

"Surely I can help you out," Kwon said, rummaging through his wares. "As you see, old Kwon has all sorts of powders and potions. Ground ogre horn mixed with lotus seeds would allow you to travel at your best speed without sleeping for days."

"That might work," said Young-hee, trying to look cool. "Although I prefer my magic to be living. It's more potent than some old powders, don't you think?"

"Perhaps," said Kwon, trying to suss out his odd customer, "you have something in mind?"

"Well, I noticed that old rabbit. He might do."

"Oh, that foolish rabbit," he scowled. "I've been trying to sell him for weeks. But no one wants him, so I've decided he's best served in a stew. In a few hours, I should have plenty to share."

Kkiman shook in fear, but Young-hee pretended not to notice. "Hrm, I don't much like the taste of rabbit," Young-hee said. "Especially a frightened one like yours. But my friend here has a good recipe for powdered rabbit bones."

"I've not heard of any such thing."

"That doesn't mean it isn't really good," said Young-hee fishing through her pockets. "Now, how much would you like for him?"

"Well … he was going to be my dinner. But I supposed I could let him go for … ten jungbo."

Young-hee suddenly realized she had no idea how money worked in that place. *So annoying*, she thought. She looked at the money from her pocket—two 5,000-won bills and some coins. "Uh, I have a little over 10,000 won?"

"*Won*? What's a *won*?" said the magician. "Don't waste my time, girl."

"Boonae? Would you have any… uh, jungbo?"

"I'm so sorry, Young-hee, but I just gave all my money for a big shipment of new lanterns."

Young-hee dug into her other pocket, but found only a puffy hair scrunchy from a silly craft project using leftover fabrics—and it was not one of her better designs.

"What's this?" said Kwon, taking the hair band. He held it up to the light, tugging the elastic.

"It's just … " she started to say, but stopped herself. If the magician liked it, who was she to discourage him? "It's an old family heirloom, very rare." Kwon found one of Young-hee's hairs stuck in the hair band, which only excited him more.

"I'll trade you the rabbit for this, straight and even," he said eagerly.

Young-hee shrugged. She didn't understand this place at all. "Deal." The old magician took a ring of keys from an inside pocket and opened Kkiman's cage. The rabbit stuck his nose out tentatively, sniffed the air, then made a big jump to freedom.

"Oh, thank you, Miss Young-hee, ever so much!" he exclaimed as he danced about. He looked so happy, Young-hee laughed.

"Yes, quite impressive, for someone's first visit to a goblin market," said Boonae. "How did you know Kwon would trade on sentimental value?"

"I had no idea. None," said Young-hee. It felt so genuinely satisfying to help someone, especially someone so nice. "Can we help get your medicine, too?"

"Medicine?" Kkiman asked, looking confused, until memory clicked in and made his eyes sparkle. "Oh, yes, for my little one. I'm sure my lovely wife Soon-ja has found something by now. I'll just hurry home and check. I do love them so."

Young-hee glared at Kkiman. "You said Soon-ja was your baby's name."

"No-no-no, you misunder …, I mean, I misspoke. Of course I know my wife's … " his voice trailed off.

"You don't have a wife and baby," said Young-hee.

"Well, not exactly. I do have a couple of litters, but their mothers and I are not terribly close."

Young-hee thought him the least guilty-looking liar she had ever seen. She thought of several creative ways of telling him off and forcing an apology. But all she said was "Feh. Oh, just go."

"Very good, I think I shall," he said. But just as he took a step, Kkiman stopped. "I hope you will not be too angry. The magic man was going to eat me. And I do appreciate being freed. Here, please take this." The rabbit reached into his fur and pulled out, as if from a pocket, a bracelet, a tangle of flowers knitted into a pattern, as intricate as it was beautiful. "Please, take it. I owe you for your generosity."

Young-hee stood, hands firmly at her sides.

"It is a gift in exchange for a debt," said Boonae. "It is safe to take."

Young-hee didn't want the rabbit out of her debt. But she could feel Boonae and Kkiman waiting, growing more uncomfortable. "Fine, I'll take it," she said, holding out her hand. "Thank you," she added with reflexive, but instantly regretted courtesy, since she was definitely not thankful.

Kkiman hopped off. "And thank you, Miss Young-hee. It is a beautiful day not to be a stew." And just like that, he was lost in the market throngs. Kwon made a scoffing sound, but otherwise ignored them.

Young-hee looked at the bracelet some more. It looked delicate and felt like real flowers, but seemed incredibly strong with the solidity of silver.

"It is a special gift," noted Boonae. "I rarely see floral-silver of this quality."

That was something, she thought, admiring it in the light, and then put it on her wrist. It did look pretty. "What a jerk," she said.

"You mustn't get too upset, Miss Young-hee," said Boonae. "He is a rabbit. That's what rabbits do. They tell tales, they get caught, then, they tell more tales to get free. *His words have bones*, is what folks say about his kind. You're lucky he did not convince you to eat hot coals—rabbits have been known to do that. They are very tricky."

"*Feh*," Young-hee repeated. "*Jigyeowo*."

Boonae had an errand, so Young-hee walked through more stalls filled with more strange and amazing goods. At the end of one row, Young-hee spotted something much more interesting than any roots or drawings—a rickety, wooden stall full of fragrant cookies and cakes. *Now this is quality*, she thought. The merchant was a particularly homely dokkaebi, more squat than most, wearing old, sagging linens that said he didn't care about clothes at all. Which was fine with Young-hee, who didn't care about his clothes either. Just the food. "Wow," she said, "what is all this?"

"Just some simple pies and cakes, m'lady," said the dokkaebi, preparing to launch into a great sales pitch, when he did a double take. "Oh my, you're a bear child. A human female, if I'm not mistaken."

"Yeah, that's right. People seem fascinated by that."

He looked at her hard for a moment, calculating, and then all at once seemed to lose interest. "It's not my business. I just don't see many of your kind, is all. Is the old stone your master?"

"My master? You mean Grandma Dol? She's my friend, I guess. The jangseung in the forest just introduced us."

"Jangseung, *pah*," spat the dokkaebi. "Uptight, self-important prigs, thinking they control who comes and goes. Never trust 'em. You can be sure they are only nice for their own reasons. Besides, there are other gates the jangseung don't protect." The goblin rooted in some boxes stacked under a cracked wood shelf, before finding a package wrapped in simple, gray cotton. A pull on the cloth corner revealed a stack of *yakgwa* honey biscuits. "Here, take one. They're quite good. And just one cookie will keep you full for a year."

Full for a year, she thought, *pretty amazing.* Would it work in her world, too? "Wow, that's pretty neat," she said. "But will I just feel full, or actually be full?"

"I can guarantee that for the whole year, you would be satiated and healthy," said the dokkaebi, waving the biscuits before Young-hee. They smelled rich and flavorful.

Intrigued, she reached for them. *Surely, one taste wouldn't hurt?*

But just before she touched the cookie, a stony, chalky hand reached from behind and gently grasped her wrist. "What he means," said Grandma Dol—and despite the Boonae mask, it was clearly her—"is that if you take just one, you will belong to him for a year. You would be taken care of and well-nourished, but bound to him."

"If I ate just one?"

"If you ate just one bite. If you even took it. All exchanges contain obligations, even gifts. You cannot take something without giving something else."

The dokkaebi shot Grandma Dol an angry look, its fleshy, gray lips quivering slightly. "She would have been safe, interfering rock," he said. "Is that any worse than what you have planned?"

On hearing the accusation, a suddenly straighter, taller Grandma Dol glared at the goblin. "That is quite enough of your nonsense, goblin. Our business is done."

The dokkaebi's lip curled in anger as he grumbled foully. But he retreated into his stall.

"I'm sorry for that, Young-hee. Not all creatures here are as honorable as we would like."

As Grandma Dol led Young-hee away, the narrowness of her escape grew clearer by the minute. She could have been stuck in this world for a year. Or longer. Who knows if the dokkaebi would have ever let her go? And then she thought the dokkaebi, too, had a point—she didn't really know her new companions—except what they had told her. How could she know if they were honest? What if they had something terrible planned for her, like the goblin?

"This place is so scary," Young-hee said, as worry tapped across her brow. "Please keep a closer eye on me. This is your world, and I don't know its dangers." Young-hee was unsure where all this bitterness was coming from, but once out, she couldn't stop it. "It's kind of irresponsible," she charged.

The face and posture of Boonae or Grandma Dol were neither upset nor angry. They remained polite as ever. And yet … Young-hee felt them growing colder and more distant.

"I am sorry you feel that way," said Grandma Dol, or Boonae—or both. "If you do not think we have behaved appropriately, we do apologize. Perhaps it is best if we left now."

Young-hee knew she had offended them. She had been scared, but it was too late. "I should probably go home," she said, half-heartedly. "I've been here quite a while. My mom is probably worried. I should go back. If I can."

"That is your choice. But maybe it is for the best."

So Grandma Dol led Young-hee back to grove of jureum trees, where the jangseung stood guard. As they walked in silence, Young-hee felt a soft, persistent ache of regret in her chest. After wishing for escape from all the boredom and sameness, she had finally gotten the excitement she craved. But she ruined it, in just a few hours. She wished she could explain to the old stone woman how she felt: *Sometimes people just react badly, especially when scared or hurt. And getting angry doesn't mean someone's a bad person.* She wondered if the old stone woman was offended by her outburst, or hadn't liked Young-hee all along. It was too depressing to think about, so Young-hee did her best not to think at all.

Soon they came to the jangseung, standing guard at the edge of the forest. Behind them was the dark wooden door embedded in the massive tree root. She thought if she could just say the right thing, like she had to the jangseung, everything would be all right again. But she didn't know what to say or how to say it, so trying not to sound sarcastic, she said, "Thank you very much for showing me around and spending the day with me. Oh, and thanks for the food. That was really good. And for keeping me safe."

"You were my guest," said Boonae cheerfully. "A guest always deserves proper hospitality."

"And it was good to know there are still bear children in our realm," said the lady guardian. "It has been a long time."

The silence was awkward. *Tell them you're sorry*, she shouted at herself. *Tell them how much you like it here. Tell them!* "Okay, well, thanks again. I hope we can meet again." She gave a half-wave, but saw they were not going to wave back, so simply turned and walked to the stairwell door. It opened easily. One last chance to ask to stay. But after a brief pause, she walked through the door into the garage— a normal parking garage. There was her ball. As she picked it up, she saw that the bracelet from the rabbit, was just a knotted ring of dead flowers. She gently took it off, but even that soft touch caused half the leaves to fall to the ground like dust. When she turned around to mark the door, so she could find her way back, there just a normal blue steel door. It was locked. She looked at her phone—three bars (and still no messages), and the time said that less than an hour had passed since she first entered the basement garage. Spotting the wall marked 804 in white numbers, she walked toward her building and home.

The Pullocho and the Sanshin

There once was a man named Kang Manseop who lived in the Dharma Flower Hills of the ancient Gaya Kingdom, close to what is Mount Jiri today. Among the many powerful mushrooms, roots, and herbs in this incredibly fertile region, was insam, *wild ginseng roots much prized for* their medicinal and magical powers. Kang came from a family of sim-mani, *people who wander the hills and valleys, looking for damp, secret places where insam grows. Like all simmani, Kang never drank alcohol or ate meat or fish before heading into the mountains, and was careful never to offend the mountain gods. A single large root of the best insam could bring enough money to live on for a year, so over time more and more people tried their hand at insam digging—people who drank and ate before they dug and did not care about the mountain gods. Gradually the insam grew smaller and smaller, and ever harder to find.*

So Kang Manseop decided to stop hunting insam. He had a more special prize in mind—the pullocho, a magical root said to be so powerful, even the heavenly spirits feared it. While many people hunted insam, nobody dug for pullocho—for the good reason that it was nearly impossible to find. In fact, Kang had only seen one once in his entire life, and even then it was a small piece, the prized possession of a great lord in a nearby county. But he had seen pictures of pullochos and he read much about them and knew that while a good insam root could feed a family for a year, a single pullocho would make him wealthy for life.

Kang began searching all over the Dharma Flower Hills, but of course had no luck finding the magical ginseng. Determined to change his life, he walked every inch of those hills—from the rocky peaks to the deepest valleys—and waded every stream, in case pullochos liked the wet of the flowing rivers. But he never discovered even as much as a stem or a leaf of one. Weeks, months, years passed without any success, and eventually Kang had exhausted nearly all of his family's money.

But rather than grow discouraged, Kang grew angry. He was from a family of great simmani, and he worked harder than anyone else. This failure couldn't be his fault, but must lie with the mountain spirit. Perhaps it was angry at all the impious people who had dug up the insam. So Kang went to the governor of the Dharma Flower Hills and he complained about the lack of pullochos. "Your excellency! The mountain spirit who rules Dharma Flower Hills is too cruel! I have been hunting for years to find a pullocho, but he refuses to grant my small request."

The governor looked at Kang with surprise and annoyance. "What should I do about it? I am the governor of the physical world, not of the heavens and spirits. If you have a problem with the mountain spirit of Dharma Flower Hills, ask a monk for help."

"Your Excellency, I believe you are mistaken. As governor, your responsibility is true and profound. In a well-ordered kingdom, the heavenly realm and the physical are as one. You are responsible for everything that occurs in the Dharma Flower Hills. Even the spirits must obey."

"What you say is true," nodded the governor. "Come and we'll see what we can do." So the governor took Kang to the biggest temple on Dharma Flower Hills, and the shrine dedicated to Sanshin, the mountain spirit. There, the governor carved a petition to Sanshin on the sacred tree in front of the shrine:

To the Sanshin of Dharma Flower Hills:

As governor of Dharma Flower Hills, I command you to answer Kang Manseop's sincere prayers and allow him to find a pullocho. If you do not comply, I will send you into exile.

—Governor of Dharma Flower Hills

That night Kang dreamt of an old, bearded man, in simple clothes and with a serene expression. The old man apologized to Kang for making his life so difficult, and promised that if Kang followed the Three-Fingered Brook up the mountain to its source, where the Empty Forest meets Turtle Rock, he would find a pullocho growing in the wet shadow of an old, broken pine tree.

The next morning, Kang awoke early. He hiked all day until he found Turtle Rock and the broken pine. Just as the old man promised, in the damp roots of the tree, was a precious pullocho root. In fact, it was one of the largest pullocho he had ever heard of, and Kang cried with happiness.

When Kang returned to the governor's residence, he thanked him for his help and showed him the amazing pullocho. He told the governor how the dream led him to the root. The governor nodded solemnly. "I, too, had a dream last night, Kang. But in my dream, the Sanshin said he would follow my order immediately, but asked me to remove my petition. He said that he had been living in Dharma Flower Hills since before the first men emerged from the cave on Mount Taebaek, since before Tiger and Bear fought for the right to become the first man, before the great spirits divided the heavenly realm from the physical world. He couldn't bear to leave his mountain and the petition was a terrible burden. So I returned to the shrine this morning, removed the petition from the sacred tree, asked Sanshin to forgive me, and promised never again to order such a noble son of heaven."

5

The blaring television grated on Young-hee's nerves. Her school-books and homework lay scattered across her desk, poked at like a picky five-year-old eats peas. Bum raced through the apartment with some plastic robot toy, making sputtering noises somewhere between a jet plane and a machine gun, but Young-hee couldn't even summon the strength to yell *quiet*. She was beyond annoyed.

It was all because of the other place—the strange land of the jangseung. At first, memories of that realm, its market and creatures, filled her with a dizzying marvel. She could hardly believe there was something so much bigger and better than her dull little life. Her dull little world. Sure, that world was strange and scary, but also more vibrant, more alive. *No wonder they called this place a "mud world."*

Gradually, though, the flat, beige dullness of everyday life ate away at those memories. Bum's whining and pestering were worse than ever. Schoolwork felt more pointless. All her online apps and networks seemed so inane, she rarely bothered to log on. Everything felt like a dull shadow of that other world. Soon, everything annoyed her, and then became worse than annoying. The rains of *jangmacheol* were giving way to the heat of summer, turning those downpours into sticky, gooey humidity. The days burned and the nights stayed thick with moist heat. Everyone was miserable from the suffocating temperatures and the lack of sleep—sometimes, Young-hee wondered if her own bad mood was somehow making everyone else more surly.

Her mom asked what was wrong and tried to cheer her up but, stymied, went back to work. Bum just hoped Young-hee would please get over whatever was bothering her. Young-hee knew she was beyond getting over anything.

As the scare of the goblin market faded, she wanted more of the "strange land." She spent weeks searching every inch of the garage—at different times of day and days of the week, on rainy days and sunny—but she couldn't find the magical brown-green door; the lighting never changed, the colors didn't fade. When Young-hee was honest with herself, she was not surprised or even much annoyed.

She searched for clues, wandering through the five-day market where old people sold vegetables and side dishes that were tasty, but nothing compared to flower-scented *gim* or butterfly wings or acorn kimchi. She went to the supermarket, Internet cafes, the hillside park beside her apartment, but, there were no gateways to magical worlds.

Other times, she searched online or at the library for books about tradition and traditional stories—tales of silly tigers, powerful monkeys, mischievous goblins, and more. She read all the folktales she could find, famous and obscure alike. She combed the parts of Seoul where clueless tourists go to buy cheap masks and prints of old paintings. But everything seemed like a fake, a dim reflection in a tarnished mirror.

The boring, ugly sameness of daily life surrounded her without end, a desert of dullness. After a while, she began to doubt whether there even was a Strange Land, or just an afternoon dream born of boredom. She would occasionally look at the dead flower petals that used to be her bracelet, which she had hidden in a handkerchief in her T-shirt drawer. But after a time, they only seemed to be teasing her, so she stopped looking. She looked less and less often for a way back to Strange Land, and returned to her schoolwork and her life. She wanted to cry. She wanted to scream. She wanted to break things. She wanted everyone to just go away. She wished she could just go away too.

One day, after another fruitless search of the garage, Young-hee plunked down on a short, stone wall at the edge of the apartment complex near the plastic jangseung totem poles. One looked more bent than before. The sun was so high and harsh that it bleached out the colors, and she hoped that the glare would burn away her foul feelings. The hum of distant people going about their regular lives, complaining, playing, walking, living, sounded so very far away. "Feh," she said in quiet distain.

Just then, a shadow passed in front of the sun. "Is everything okay?"

asked a warm, old voice. Young-hee tilted her head up and squinted.

"Hello, Mr. Gyeongbi," she said, trying to be polite. "I'm all right, I guess."

"You guess? Because I've seen you walking around endlessly the past few weeks, like you had something on your mind."

"No, it's not that. … I just lost something," she said.

"Oh? What was it?" He sounded genuinely interested. Young-hee liked Gyeongbi Shin for always seeming to listen and care. He may have been older than anyone Young-hee had ever known, but he was full of life. Too many people fade as they age, she thought, but Gyeongbi Shin was as vivid as a teenager, only without all the spazzy nervousness.

"It's hard to explain. But I lost it and can't find it anywhere."

Mr. Shin thought for a bit. "Well, have you tried looking in the last place you saw it?"

"That's the problem," Young-hee said, "I can't remember where I lost it. I was lost when I lost it."

"I see," he said, although Young-hee thought he didn't see at all. "Well, if you lost something while you were lost, maybe you need to be lost again to find it."

It seemed like a silly thing to say, but Gyeongbi Shin's warm laugh made Young-hee feel a bit better. She smiled, which seemed to make him happy, too.

Just then, the orange kitten walked by. He was bigger than last time, but he still surprisingly friendly for a stray. The kitten crept out of some bushes and walked bravely to the guard. Gyeongbi Shin bent over to scratch it behind its ear. "All cats are really tigers," he said, laughing some more. "Even cute little kittens, so you need to be careful."

Young-hee reached into her pocket and pulled out a hairband and dangled it. The kitten instantly went crazy over the elastic toy, batting at it furiously. Young-hee remembered their first meeting, when the guard was telling Bum that silly story. "Mr. Shin, do you know a lot about fairytales? Tigers and goblins and magic things like that?"

"Sure, a bit, at least," he said. "My grandmother always told all sorts of old stories—'The Tiger and the Rabbit,' 'The Nine-Headed Ogre,' 'The Crying Green Frogs,' 'The Dragon King Under the Sea.' Before comic books and animation ruined the imagination, we had to imagine what everything looked like. But my grandmother could really tell a good story—about ghosts and dragons and dokkaebi goblins, and all sorts of creatures."

"Yeah, but aren't they scary, too?"

"Scary? Yeah, magic creatures can be cruel and capricious," he said. "If I got scared, she'd say that there are three rules to remember in those old fairytales: Don't accept any presents or eat food—except from friends, of course; never leave a path you are following; and, no matter whom you meet, be reverent and polite, because you never know who they really are."

Young-hee nodded solemnly. "And those rules keep you safe?"

"I guess so. Maybe. Sometimes," said Gyeongbi Shin, looking at Young-hee more deeply. "But in old stories, you're never really safe. I mean the real stories, not the boring cleaned up versions they teach in school—all mixed up with Western nursery tales and stories from other countries and other religions and things. The real old stories are always wild, but that's what makes them so exciting. If you want safe, you could just tell the story of Hanbit Mansions and the Incredible Shopping Discounts."

Suddenly, Young-hee had an idea. A great idea. She jumped up, but stopped herself and turned around. "Thank you *so much* for your help, Gyeongbi Shin," she said, giving him a serious bow before taking off for home. She had figured out how to get back.

Too excited to wait for the elevator, she bounced up nine flights of stairs. At the top, her face glistened with sweat, but she didn't care. Despite the summer heat, she put on a light windbreaker, stuffed a dark gray scarf into one pocket and a big handful scrunchies and hair bands into another. And without knowing why, she reached into her T-shirt drawer for the handkerchief with the dead flowers from Kkiman's bracelet and carefully pocketed it, too. Then she swept into the kitchen and crammed her jacket pockets with granola bars. Finally, Young-hee found Bum lying on the floor in his favorite yellow shirt, playing with his animal toys, and took him by the hand. She picked up Gangjee and found pocket space for the toy puppy. "*Let's go, Bum!*" she said to her confused brother. "Mom, how about I take Bum for a walk? Give you some quiet."

Young-hee's mom looked at her skeptically. "You're volunteering to spend time with your brother?"

"Sure, he's my brother. We'll have fun together, right?" Bum's confusion was quickly overwhelmed by his big sister's enthusiasm.

"Well, okay," said her mom. "As long as you keep an eye on him and make sure he stays out of trouble."

"Promise," said Young-hee. Getting into the elevator, she gave her mother an exaggerated happy wave goodbye, then pressed the ground-floor button.

But inside the elevator, Young-hee pressed the button for the parking garage. Bum looked confused. "We're going to play a game in the garage," she explained, and when the doors opened, led him into the garage. She took the scarf out and tied it over her eyes like a blindfold. *If you lost something while you were lost, maybe you need to be lost again to find it*, she recalled. "Okay, Bum, listen to me. I want you to play," she said, handing him Gangjee.

"Wha?" said Bum.

"Play. Just like normal. Here's Gangjee. You can make him fly. Or fire superlasers. Or anything. Just hold my hand and don't let go, no matter what." Bum looked from Gangjee to his strange sister, deeply confused. He sneezed for good measure. Young-hee lifted the blindfold from one eye, trying to figure out how to make this work. "What's wrong? You love playing with Gangjee."

"I don't know."

"*Aish*, so annoying," Young-hee muttered. "Look, Gangjee is the coolest dog in the world, right?"

"Mmm." That sounded like a yes.

"So this is like a giant cave. And you know what's inside of big caves, right? Treasure. Dragons. Lots of amazing stuff." Bum looked around, thinking. "And I heard Gangjee has a really cool friend somewhere down here. A dragon? ... a monkey?"

"Monkey-dragon?"

"Yes, a monkey-dragon. How cool is that?"

"Very cool."

"So? Let's go find monkey-dragon."

"Yeah!" Bum took off.

"Bum, wait!" Young-hee shouted, trying to sound playful, not annoyed. "With me, please. Remember—don't let go of my hand." Bum doubled back and took Young-hee's hand. She dropped the blindfold back over both eyes and let Bum lead the way. He bounced her off of only one car and a curb—thankfully, no concrete pillars—before getting the hang of guiding her. She kept her ears open for cars, and hearing one after just a couple of minutes, peeked under the blindfold and pulled Bum out of the way. A heavily made-up face stared dourly at them as the car slowly passed, and Young-hee saw that they were halfway between her apartment building and the next. *If I know where we were, we'll never get lost*—she thought, scowling and pulling down the blindfold.

Fortunately, few people were in the garage. She felt Bum lead them down a car ramp, which she hoped meant fewer cars. Ten minutes into the quest for the monkey-dragon, Bum found a new game, making "whoosh" noises and swinging his body in big arcs. It was all Young-hee could do not to peak. But she knew it was still just in the garage.

As they walked, accompanied now by Bum's rendition of motorboat sounds, Young-hee did her best to stop paying attention to where they were going. She concentrated on listening for cars as they went up a ramp, down another, got bored, and listened to her own breathing. They walked and walked.

"I'm tired," Bum announced.

"What? Already? Come on, you can play a while longer."

"*Aish*. I'm bored."

"But monkey-dragon?"

"I don't know," said Bum petulantly.

Uh-oh, thought Young-hee. *Once he's like that, he's not going to last long without a snack and a nap.* "How about ten more minutes?"

"I'm bored," he repeated. Young-hee's heart dropped. Another plan failed. But then Bum added: "I don't know where we are."

Cautiously, Young-hee slipped off the blindfold. The garage was gloomier than ever, the lights faded, the colors were strange. There were no cars anywhere and no people. It was impossibly silent and still. And right in front of them was the strange wooden door. She was back.

"Come on," she said. "Let's try the door."

The Story of the Mischievous Green Frogs

Once there lived three very mischievous green frogs. They never listened to their mother, always doing the opposite of what they were told. If their mother said move quickly, they went slowly. If she said "go slow," they would go fast. If she said "be quiet," they would shout louder.

After several years, their mother felt herself close to death. She knew she needed to be buried high on a hill, so her body would be safe from the summer rains that always caused the river to flood. But she was worried that if she told her naughty sons to bury her high on a hill, they would put her right at the riverbank. Worried about her afterlife, she decided to trick her sons.

On her deathbed, she called her sons over. "My sons," she said. "I am old and sick and will not be here much longer. Please, as a last favor to your poor mother, when I die, please bury my body beside the river."

Soon after that the frog mother died and her sons were sadder than they had ever been. "We've been such terrible sons!" they cried. "All our lives we have disobeyed our mother and made her life difficult. But now she is gone from us forever. At long last, let's listen to what she said and be good sons."

So the three sons buried their mother close to the river, as she asked. They were pleased with themselves for being so obedient. But a few days later, the summer rainy season started. It poured and poured, and soon the churning river overflowed its banks and washed away their mother's body.

Which is why today, when it rains, you can hear the frogs crying, "Gaegool, gaegool!" They are crying for their mother.

6

Young-hee carefully led Bum up the dark stairwell into the warm light and brilliant color of the Strange Land. "*Wa*," he said, blinking hard at the giant jureum trees, silky grasses, backward-flowing fountain, and all the other fantastic things. He was frozen in place, like when a sneeze tickles your nose but refuses to explode. And then— "*Ya!*" he exclaimed, bolting in a run of pure joy. *He's adjusting faster than I did*, Young-hee noted with approval, replacing her standard annoyance with pleasure in his joy—while keeping a cautious eye out for carnivorous dragonflies.

It was peaceful in the clearing amid the giant trees and the softly rustling leaves and burbling fountain. Young-hee knew she should introduce her brother to Jiha and Cheonha and make sure they were welcome. But with Bum shouting "*Ya*" and running in circles, Young-hee decided to let him tire himself out first. Young-hee wondered what Bum was thinking, but whatever it was inspired pure, simple joy, the kind that Young-hee knew she must have had once, when younger. Bum careened from fascinating to even more fascinating things. He rolled in the silken grass, enjoying its dance along his skin. He picked one green blade and divided into myriad thin strips. "Brush," he said, handing it like an offering to his big sister. "It's for you. A present." She accepted it with a droll "thanks."

Bum ran over to one jureum tree, and Young-hee didn't like the look in his eyes—a suspicion quickly confirmed when he scrambled up the immense trunk, effortlessly using the thick, cracked bark as hand- and footholds. "Bum, no!" she barked. She knew when her little brother was going to obey and when he was only pausing before the next onslaught of energy, so she turned up the authority in her voice (always far more effective than turning up the volume, she knew). "*Bum! Get down right now. Now!*" His eyes held hers in a test of wills, but reluctantly, he climbed down. But as he hit the ground, he dashed into the grass by the big hedge. Young-hee spotted Gangjee lying lonely on the ground, forgotten by Bum, so she slid him into her jacket pocket.

"*Ya!*" said Bum again, this time followed by a loud *thwack*. He had found a stick, about a meter long and fairly straight, that apparently made a good sword. He cracked it against the ground, the hedge, the tree, and anything else he could strike, while whirling in an elaborate, sword-fighting dance. Young-hee worried that someone, especially the jangseung, might take offense, even though Bum was not inflicting much damage.

"Careful, Bum," she said. When suffering through the dreariness of school and real life, she had imagined returning to Strange Land and making a new life—maybe never going back. She was resourceful and confident she could get by. Okay, maybe not *forever*, but at least for a while. But with Bum along, that wasn't really an option, at least not this trip. She had the granola bars, in case of trouble finding food, and a pocket full of the hair bands that passed as currency last time.

As her mind wandered through the possibilities, Young-hee walked over to the burbling, upward-flowing fountain. The waters laughed and cried, just as she remembered, and the water felt silky cool against her fingers. "Bum, come here a second," she said. But he didn't come. She turned around, looking for her ridiculous brother, but he was nowhere to be seen. The clearing was empty. *Oh, jeez,* she thought. *Did he run off already?* He couldn't have gotten far, but Young-hee felt that familiar pressure building in her chest.

Just then, a disheveled head appeared under the dense hedge. "*Hiya!*" shouted Bum, giggling as he wiggled from underneath the thicket of branches. "I fooled you." Bum bounded over, stick-sword in hand, completing a spinning-parrying combination on the way. Bum leaned over the fountain wall so far, his feet left the ground. "Wow, what's this?" he said at a flash of color. "Fish!" he shouted, trying to poke one of the poor creatures with his stick.

"No, Bum," said Young-hee, relieved that he wasn't lost, but tired of being a scold. "No hitting. Be nice to the fish." Bum put the stick down and slid his hand into the water, trying to entice the fish with a friendly gesture. *Boys,* thought Young-hee, *they're all the same. First thing they want to do is hit and smash.* Fortunately, Bum had quickly reverted to his usual sweet self. Young-hee watched carefully, just to make sure the cute, colorful fish didn't have large, colorful teeth.

"They're *pretty*," said Bum. One fish gave a funny shimmy, gathered speed and followed an upward stream to a higher part of the fountain. "Wow," said Bum. "That's so cool." He splashed the flow with his stick, sending water spraying upward before gravity re-asserted its hold on the little drops, pulling them to the ground. "Our apartment's fountain isn't like that."

"Hmm," Young-hee agreed.

And then it happened. "*Frog!*" shouted Bum, and quicker than she thought possible, he leaped into the fountain. She lunged, but clutched only air. With a deep *plunkt* sound, he was in the water, just like back home.

"Annoying!" she said, as his cannonball splashed all over her and Bum sank below the surface. The water was clean and clear, but the bubbling and churning from the force of the flow made it hard to see clearly. She could make out Bum in a dark corner of the fountain, distorted in the shimmering ripples, but he was not surfacing. "*Bum!*" she shouted. *What was going on?* He didn't look stuck on anything or hurt, but he just sat beneath the surface.

Young-hee had kicked off her shoes to jump after Bum, when suddenly a gush of water burst from the fountain. In it, a large, dark shape sprang rose high into the air, spraying water everywhere. It hopped in a big arc, landing at the foot of a tree, about twenty meters away, by the big hedge. It was a giant green frog. And, Young-hee realized in shock, Bum was on its back. Riding it like a horse. *That could not be good*, she thought. Before she could call out Bum's name, the frog jumped again, much higher and farther, flying between two jureum trees. *Oh, no*, she thought and took chase.

With each jump, the frog covered a lot of ground, as he zigged and zagged through the woods. Growing tired, it was all Young-hee could do to keep them in sight, but she pushed herself harder, determined to keep Bum safe. And then she heard it—Bum *laughing*. In fact, she was pretty sure she heard a "*Whee!*" coming from him, and resolved to kill him after she saved him.

Finally, as the end of the jureum tree forest neared and Young-hee thought she might be gaining on them, she saw an immense hole, like an old quarry, half-filled with water. "*Bum, don't go in there!*" she shouted. But even as the words left her lips, the giant frog stopped at the lip of the cliff, just long enough for Bum to slide off, and leapt into the water below. *Thank goodness for that*, she thought.

"What do you think you were doing?" she wheezed between gulps of air.

"The froggy was fun," said Bum, clearly delighted.

"Bum, that was very dangerous."

"No, froggy said we should go jumping," he answered.

"Froggy said?"

"Uh-huh. First he said I shouldn't be in his fountain, but then he asked if I wanted to play."

"That giant frog talked? Underwater?" she asked, surprised but not as surprised as she would have been the first time she traveled to the Strange Land. At least it didn't try to eat Bum. Or her. Yet.

"*Hi, froggy!*" said Bum waving at the water. Young-hee saw a large pair of eyes at the surface of the water, staring at them.

"Uh, hello, Mr. Frog," said Young-hee politely. "Thanks for not hurting my brother."

"Hurt him? *Phooey.* I wouldn't dream of it," answered the frog in a rumbling voice. "Frogs know how to treat guests."

Phooey? Young-hee recognized the sound of someone insulted, even if it was a frog. *Always be reverent and polite,* she recalled. Best to do damage control. "Oh, yes, of course," she said. "Frog hospitality is famous where I'm from. I'm just, as his big sister, it's my job care for him. I'm sure you understand what family is like."

The frog stepped from the water, droplets shimmering on its green skin. "Of course," he said, magnanimously. "I have many siblings and I love them all."

Young-hee remembered reading that frogs have thousands of tadpoles at a time and shuddered at the thought of thousands Bums running around. "I'm Young-hee, and this is my brother Bum. We're kind of new here. Are you from around here?"

"Indeed," said the frog, approaching. "This lake has been my family's home for generations."

"It looks very … big," said Young-hee, not sure what to say to a frog. "Say, would you know an old woman named Grandma Dol who lives in that jureum forest?"

"Granny Dol?" he said, now right in front of them. Young-hee marveled at how the amphibian's ugly gait carried its great bulk, and could probably carry her as well. A great hopper, but walking was not the frog's strongest point. "Of course. A fine old stone. My family has basked on her cool surface on many a summer's day."

"I see. The last time I was here, she was quite nice to me. I was hoping to see her again."

"Well, that might be difficult. Many creatures have been leaving those woods. Many bad rumors afoot these days. Changes."

"Oh, nothing too terrible, I hope."

"I'm a frog. By night I eat dew. By day I eat sunlight. How can I know?"

"To be honest, I don't know a lot of frogs. Where I'm from, they're a lot smaller … and don't really talk."

"I'm not surprised. Many of my people are not big talkers. Although we do enjoy a good cry, especially when it is raining."

"Ah, I know that," she blurted out excitedly. It was a story everyone knows. "I mean, I'm very sorry for your loss, but you cry because of your mother and the river, right?"

"Thank you for your sympathies, but to be honest it was long ago. And, personally, I think many of my brethren are too full of self-pity. But I am impressed you know of our sad story." He took a couple of steps closer, looking over Young-hee and Bum. "If you don't mind me asking, but would you happen to be human children? From the mud world?"

"Yes, we're bear-children," said Young-hee, trying to use what she had learned last trip. But her comment annoyed the frog.

"'Bear children'—phooey," he said with a rolling ribbit of disgust. "But I'm not surprised. That's all anyone talks about anymore. But keep in mind, Ms. Young-hee, there are different stories out there. Older stories. And in one of the oldest, it was actually frogs who helped the Son of Heaven create the first man. Frogs have ended kingdoms. Frogs have more power than most people realize." He half-hopped toward the water.

"I'm sorry, Mr. Frog," said Young-hee quickly. "I didn't mean to offend. I bet you are a very noble race."

The frog turned back. "I did not mean to sound so grouchy," he said. "There was a time when only our story was known, but that was a very long time ago, and I should not be surprised to hear of bear-sons and bear daughters. I guess I am just tired—I am a prince, too, of sorts, and I have been cursed."

"A frog prince? Are you waiting for a kiss?"

"A kiss? No. What does that have to do with anything?"

"Sorry. It's a famous story where I'm from."

"Well, please keep your story to your world. As for me, I cannot return home until I drink this lake dry and eat all the fish, among other things. It has been many years and it will be many more until I'm done. Sometimes it makes me short-tempered."

"Oh, I wish I could help," said Young-hee. "But I don't think I could drink much of that lake. It's very big."

The frog looked at her funnily. "It was nice of you to offer. One day, perhaps you can help me. But not today. I thank you and your brother for your company." And with that, the frog gave a big hop and dove into the water.

"Froggy's gone," said Bum, disappointed.

Young-hee wasn't sure of what to make of that conversation, but reminded herself of the need to be respectful to all of Strange Land's creatures. For all she knew, the next mouse she met could be a princess. Or a pile of wood could be a wizard.

She looked at the sky and wondered what time it was. Or if Strange Land had time. Her last visit had lasted seven or eight hours, but it always looked like early evening. *No telling how long days last here*, she thought. *We'd better get moving.* "Come on, Bum. Take my hand. I want to show you something."

Bum complied, and she led him back into the forest. The large jureum trees were disorienting, but she kept Haechi Hill on her left and tried to retrace her steps, aiming for Jiha and Cheonha. But when they emerged from the forest, the goblin market lay ahead. Young-hee thought about going back to talk to the jangseung, but decided it was easier to go straight into the market. She had a plan—buy some food and things, then go exploring. She could meet Jiha and Cheonha after, maybe ask for advice about places to go.

"Let's go," Young-hee said. A few other people were walking to the market, too—a long, elegant creature that looked like an elf; a bent, witch-looking woman; three beautiful, child-like women dressed in forest greens and browns, giggling and gossiping. They all ignored her, thankfully. At least four times Bum almost ran off in one direction or another, suddenly captivated—by a strange flower, a big rock that needed climbing, something high in the trees. She was determined that nothing would bite or hop off with—or, heaven forbid, eat—her brother, so she held tight to his hand.

"Did you see that big froggy?" he asked.

"Yes, Bum, I was there."

"Wasn't he awesome?"

"Yeah, he was pretty cool. Everything here is pretty cool."

"Did you see that big orange flower, the one that was *walking*?"

"Uh, no. Are you sure it was walking?"

"Uh-huh. I told you to look, but you weren't listening."

"Sorry, Bum." She did feel a bit guilty about that, actually. There was so much to see, but she wanted to make sure Bum was safe and under control. The market hubbub grew with each step closer.

"And did you see the doggy?"

"Huh? Do you mean Gangjee? He's right here in my pocket."

"No, the little brown doggy, playing in the long grass near froggy's pond."

Young-hee didn't like the sound of that. She hadn't noticed any dog. Did fairytales have dogs? But there are plenty of wolves, like in

Red Riding Hood or *The Three Little Pigs*. Or maybe wolves were just in Western fairytales?

"We're almost at the market, Bum. See?" She pointed at the stalls. "Now, Bum, this is *important*," she said, holding him lightly by the shoulders and looking seriously into his eyes. "You need to stay with me, okay? We're going to the market, just like home. And we're going to meet strange-looking people. Or creatures. Or something." Bum looked at her dumbly. "Anyhow, some are nice, but some can be a little scary. Don't get frightened or weirded out. Stay with me and we'll be okay, I promise. Right?"

"Okay," he intoned, only half-looking at her. So far, nothing seemed to have fazed Bum at all. He just took it all in, matter-of-fact, like it was as normal as a refrigerator or a roll of *gimbap*.

Young-hee feared he wasn't paying attention, so she pushed the point. "Do you *promise*?"

"Yes, I promise."

It would have to do. "Good. Then let's go."

The market enveloped them with noise and activity. Young-hee wasn't as overwhelmed as the first time and managed to take it all in better. What now struck her were the hanbok most of the creatures were wearing—many were white and baggy, like in TV dramas and traditional paintings, but others were brilliantly colored or made in exotic fabrics and fashions.

Most of the merchants in the goblin market were, unsurprisingly, goblins—squat, gray-skinned dokkaebi, with their gnarled, googly eyes—smelling of ashes. They were creatures of the fireplace, she had read on one trip to the library, and she even saw one handling hot coals with its bare hands. A large, jowly creature with three horns, shaggy hair, and hands the size of melons sat in his stall, polishing a huge array of copper, silver, and other metal pots. Past him—*it?*—four small, frail-looking women, like the one Young-hee had seen walking to the market, ran a stall for maps, beautifully drawn on heavy paper. Ignoring potential customers, they puffed on long pipes, gossiped, and pushed small stones on a game board. An old, skinny man with drooping skin and the longest pipe Young-hee had ever seen stood to one side. "*Unlearning!*" he called in a sing-song vibrato. "Give me the knowledge and thoughts you no longer need! Top coin for top ideas!" In another stall, was the most beautiful ogre ever—or the ugliest fairy—with long black hair in a bun, over a lumpy but graceful face. She wore a huge, brilliant hanbok, with a long, crimson *jeogori* jacket tied with a ribbon of beautifully stylized *otgoreum*. She sat around a huge stone wheel, grinding beans in colors both familiar and bizarre.

Young-hee checked to make sure that Bum wasn't scared, but the little brat, seemingly oblivious to the oddness all around him, just swiveled his head this way and that, enjoying the spectacle. "No, Bum, don't touch," she said gently, as a grubby hand reached for a cluster of fancy carved sticks. A glaring, grumpy-looking dokkaebi with extra-stubby fingers and large knuckles seemed almost disappointed when Young-hee and Bum passed safely without touching his merchandise.

Just as Young-hee was thinking they would need food and drink, a voice called from one shop. "*You again!* What evil is Ms. Young-hee bringing to our market now?" roared a large man with huge, burning white eyes and white dots covering his fierce, red face. Young-hee was sure she had never met him before. Leaning forward, he knocked over a couple of his stall's wooden carvings. "It's been so long. Who is your friend? Not a golem, I see." Neither dokkaebi nor ogre, the exceptionally strange man squinted at Bum. "*Hmm*, another human. Safe, then."

"I'm sorry, but I don't think…" Then, she noticed the man's giant, chalky hands and roly-poly body, as well as the stall full of wooden lamps and carvings. "Grandma Dol, is that you?"

"Of course," said the man. He reached behind his head and with an uncomfortable stretching and yanking, pulled off his red, big-eyed face. Underneath, there was the friendly, lumpy face of Grandma Dol, holding a bright red piece of wood painted with white dots and carved into a fierce face.

"Uh, what happened to Boonae?" asked Young-hee.

"Boonae is my main partner, but not my only mask. Mokjung, here is good for driving away evil spirits. But he's a bit angry. My apologies if he frightened you."

"Have you had a lot of evil spirits around here?"

"Many disquieting, odd things are afoot," said the old stone. "I don't like it." She looked down at Bum. "But listen to me, worrying, as always. That's what happens when I wear Mokjung too much. So what brings you back to our goblin market?"

"Just getting some supplies. I'm here with my little brother. Bum, say 'hi' to Grandma Dol."

"Hi there," said Bum. "I like your mask. Can I try it?"

"Greetings, young brother. I'm glad you like Mokjung, but save masks for the grown-ups. Keep your true face for as long as you can."

"Okay," said Bum, dutifully.

"Granny, we'd really like some basic supplies—rice cakes and such. Are there shops you'd recommend? I don't know the rules and don't want to get into trouble."

"Smart girl," said Grandma Dol. "Most of the dokkaebi are more trouble than they are worth. But straight down this aisle at the second right, is Lee Chul, who makes excellent foods—cheap and long lasting—and never adds magicks unless you ask. Tell him I sent you, and he'll give you a fair deal."

"Oh, thank you. Is Mr. Lee a stone like you?"

"Heavens no," laughed Grandma Dol. "But he was once a very impressive tree stump. Don't tell him I told you, though."

"I won't," laughed Young-hee. "Thanks so much."

"I'm pleased to help. By the way … could I interest you in a nice wooden lamp? Excellent workmanship with the delicate plum-fiber paper walls. Any candle placed in here will burn twice as bright and never go out, even in a hurricane. For you, just ten jungbo."

"It is lovely, but I need to save my money for the food. If some is left, I'll come back," she said. She was trying to be nice, but since goods from the Strange Land couldn't survive in the real world, she didn't want to waste her money. Or hair bands.

"Hey, *where* are you going, boy?" Grandma Dol yelled. Bum had wandered into the stall and was making a grab for a small metal globe. "*Don't touch* things that don't belong to you," she said, reaching to gently stop him.

"Thanks. He's fast like that," Young-hee said. They said their goodbyes and Young-hee, Bum firmly in hand again, headed for Lee Chul's stall. With so many food stalls run by untrustworthy dokkaebi, she was glad of the old stone's advice. She'd just buy some food and start exploring Strange Land. Hopefully, somewhere calmer. The market seemed busier and busier the deeper she went, with hordes of people and creatures surging chaotically like water down rapids. But with a bit of bumping and jostling, she found Lee's shop.

Lee was a sinewy man, lean from a lifetime of work—totally unlike a tree stump, thought Young-hee—and pleasant, if totally fixated on business. He sold them kaypal rice cakes he promised would stay fresh even on a long journey. Despite Bum's grabbing, Lee was not the sort to dole out free samples. He was startled but not shocked or angry when Young-hee admitted she didn't have jungbo—or *tongbo* or *jeongpye* or other local currency. The hair bands she offered were more often the currency of witches and magicians, he said, but since he dealt with magic folk in his travels, he'd make a deal for half her hair bands. He even threw in a few copper tongbo coins and a cloth pouch for the rice cakes in exchange for her brightest scrunchies. The food would last the day, so Young-hee was pleased with the trade.

As soon as they started walking, Bum started whining about food. Fumbling with the drawstrings on the rice cake-filled pouch, Young-hee got bumped hard by people and creatures surging the other way, all carrying boxes and bags.

Stepping back to avoid the throng, Young-hee almost lost her balance and stumbled into a stall. She automatically said "sorry" and gave a little bow. The merchant, smoking a large hookah pipe that filled the air with fruit-scented smoke, leaned across the counter. He was tall and thin, elegant and olive-skinned, with a neat goatee and mustache, and dark, soft hair that fell lazily into his eyes. A man, but definitely not Korean. "Might I interest you in something, young lady?" he asked. "I have a wide selection of beautiful cloths and garments from far off realms, quite unlike anything else at this market."

Indeed, his shop was full of luxurious linens and cottons, as fine as silk. Large bolts of cloth continually shifted color, like a spray of water in sunlight. Scarves and robes looked softer than a whisper, and cloaks and coats looked as light as air. "Sorry, I didn't mean to bump your stall," she said.

"Think nothing of it. But perhaps your accident is my good fortune. I have a thousand and one different items—certainly something you could use."

She looked closely. "You're a real person. Not a stone or a tree stump or anything like that."

"Of course."

"But you're not Korean," Young-hee said, more bluntly than she intended.

"Indeed, I'm not," he said, with the lazy calm of someone who has this discussion often. He swept his hand toward the market, "Like many here."

Young-hee couldn't tell if he was annoyed. "Right. I mean, no. You're different from them."

"And how am I different? I am a merchant like so many others, and I have been trading across this realm for a long time." He sucked on his hookah lazily and blew sweet, apple-scented smoke, but kept his eyes firmly on her.

"But you aren't from this realm?"

"That is true."

"And you aren't Korean."

"Also true."

"So … are you from the real world? From Earth, I mean."

"There are no real worlds, young one. All our worlds, *zamin* and *dastan* alike, are but shadows of the truth. But yes, I was born in the world of humans and science. Son of the bear, as they say."

"My name is Young-hee. I'm from Korea. But I'm not sure where I am or how I got here."

"Hello, Young-hee. That sounds like the wisest of paths. Far too many people stick to roads they know, but never go anywhere. I am Bassam Attar, of Neishapour, a fellow traveler and a trader."

"Hello, Mr. Attar," said Young-hee, bowing politely. She was getting used to not understanding all that was said in Strange Land, but was happy to find fellow outsider. "I'm sorry if my questions were rude. I was told that there were no other humans here."

"We are few, but we are here."

"So, Mr. Attar, if you're a traveler and trader, does that mean you know how to come and go between this place and the real world?"

"Call me Bassam, please. I have lived too long to cling to ceremony; plus, it is good to be friendly. Sadly, the answer is, no. I came long ago, and have never been able to leave. Back then, Korea went by a different name, but was famous among traders throughout Khorasan and the Abbasid Caliphate for its gold and treasures."

"Really?" said Young-hee skeptically. "The Korea I know is all ugly concrete and smog."

"I do not know about those things, but I think you mean cities, right?"

"Yeah, Seoul is a huge city."

"Cities are all like that, at least now. But in memory, they can become beautiful places, full of magic. When I was a young, I traveled through Khorasan seeking knowledge and enlightenment. However, I never found the peace I hoped for, so I searched further and further abroad. Eventually I took to trading along the way—at first just to finance my studies, but it turned out I was a much better trader than mystic. I grew wealthy and created a great name for my family. Across the many lands, I heard of Korea and its riches, and eventually came to see for myself and found a wonderful land."

"I've traveled a lot, too. My parents are always moving. It never makes me feel peaceful, just annoyed and worried by everything."

"I suspect it is different for a child. I was a young man, looking for understanding and mystery."

"I'm not a child."

"Yes, of course. I forget that few are as grown up as the young. My deepest apologies."

"Thanks," said Young-hee, not sure if Bassam was making fun of her. She thought it best to return the kind words. "At least you found out you are a really good trader. I have no idea what I'm good at."

"Thank you, but this store is but a speck, just one small stall in a small market in a vast land."

"So how did you come here?"

"Much like you, I do not know. As I was about to return home from my second trip to Korea, with a vast retinue and a caravan full of more treasures than I had ever dreamed of, I heard a most intriguing story: In a mysterious castle high in the northern reaches of the Gaema Highlands lived an incredibly wise and reclusive lord who had gathered more gold than the rest of Korea combined. Enough to rival the Middle Kingdom itself, maybe even ancient Babylon. I would like to say the tale stimulated my desire for knowledge, but the simple truth is, it fired my greed. So I commanded my caravan into the mountains to seek the strange castle. The trip was long and difficult, and one day, a great storm arose. It separated me from my caravan, my friends and soldiers, and my gold. After many days, when that storm calmed, I was in this world with no gold, no followers. I was just Bassam. Ever since, I have lived here, trading and living as best I can."

"Don't you miss your home and your family?"

Bassam took another long huff of his hookah, and his eyes grew sad. "I suppose I should say I do, but, no, not truly. It has been so very long, and the memories of people always fade. Instead, I live the most rare and extraordinary life, for days beyond counting, among creatures I thought were only from stories."

"That sounds really amazing and really sad at the same time," said Young-hee, wondering if she had begun to forget her father. "But if you're from Korasa... uh, from far away, does that mean creatures from your stories are here, too? Or from other places?"

"If they are, I have never seen them. I did look, but this realm is vast and, after a lifetime of traveling, I am content with much simpler life here."

"This world is simple to you? Wow, I think this is the most incredible place I could imagine. My other life is so boring and stupid. I want to meet more of the people here, the stones and guardians and whatever else they all are."

"If I may be so bold as to give you some advice, Young-hee—even though you are an adult and clearly do not need it. Go home with your brother as soon as you can. This world is very old and not designed for mortals. There are many powerful spirits and forces in the hills, and many of them don't get along. The ancient resent the old, the old fear the ancient, and few love humanity."

"But you're doing okay."

"Yes, in a fashion. I am known and have protectors. You don't." Another hookah puff as Bassam's eyes fixed on her. "You never asked for my advice. It was given freely and intended well. Make of it what you will."

"Well, thank you, Bassam. It was very nice meeting you, but I want explore before it gets dark. Maybe we'll talk again."

"Perhaps. It was a pleasure to meet another creature of the book. Go in peace."

Young-hee walked away slowly, thinking about what Bassam said. There *were* dangerous creatures here, but the jangseung and Grandma Dol had been kind and helpful. In fact, most of the creatures were reasonably nice. Maybe Bassam worried too much, or didn't like other humans on his turf.

First thing after the market, she should take Bum to meet the jangseung and ask about Bassam. Surely, they would know such a longtime resident. But then, they said they hadn't seen another person in a long time. Strange.

Across the aisle, a very old, witch-looking woman was polishing metal disks and spheres etched with stars and planets. In the next stall, a dokkaebi sat sleeping behind a wall of cheap clothing.

Young-hee looked for Bum to make sure he hadn't got into trouble, but didn't see him. All at once a familiar panic overtook her. *No, no, no, no*, she thought. *He was just here!* "Bum!" she half-yelled, startling Bassam and several people around her. Then, her voice rising: "Bum, come back *right now!*"

"Is there a problem, Young-hee?" asked Bassam.

"My little brother. He was just here, but I don't see him now."

"I'm sure he is close. I just noticed him a few moments ago myself."

"He always does this," she said to Bassam, her eyes darting over the market. She shouted again, louder. "*Bum!* Get back *right now.*" Young-hee looked down a row of stalls, then, moving faster, walked to the other side of Bassam's stall to check another aisle. She could feel her pulse quicken and that familiar stabbing in her chest. *No, no, no, this is bad.*

People looked at her with a mix of concern and annoyance. *There are too many big creatures*, she thought, *they make it too hard to see any distance.* She stuck her head behind stall after stall, panic quickening her pace. She kept telling herself that he had to be nearby, like always, just a little out of sight. Her head ached, but she couldn't tell if it was because she was breathing too heavily or not enough. "*Bum!*" she shouted. "Where are you! *Bum!*" She remembered how fragile her mother looked that day they moved to their new apartment, how fear that Bum was lost made her weak and helpless; Young-hee was certain she looked the same now.

Young-hee doubled back and down another aisle. She passed Grandma Dol, now wearing Boonae, and the four little women in green playing their stone game. Her chest hurt and her eyes stung. She looked behind vats of *anju* side dishes, spilling some, causing the shop owner to yell at her, but Young-hee barely noticed. Bum would turn up, like always. If only Gyeongbi Shin were there, he would have found Bum and had him laughing with one of his stories. But there were no guards here to care for him, and Young-hee felt very alone.

And, just like that, there he was. A couple of tall, thin creatures in billowing robes moved to one side, opening a clear path down the aisle. About five stalls away at an intersection, Bum stood, oblivious. "*Bum!*" she shouted and ran to him. He was smiling, holding a big *yakgwa* honey cake in one hand and crumbs all around his mouth, but Young-hee didn't care about his perpetual messiness and swooped to hug him. "Bum, I told you not to run off," she said. "Let's get out of here."

"Okay," he said.

Young-hee took him by his small, dirty hand and turned to go— but he didn't move. She was relieved, but in no mood for his obstinacy. "Bum, I said let's go," she said, but he stayed at the stall threshold, eating his biscuit. Young-hee pulled his hand, gently, then harder, but it was like tugging on a thousand-pound rock.

"I can't," he said in a plaintive voice. Catching a faint glimmer from Bum's ankle, she bent and made out a silver thread, wispy as spider's silk. It snaked around Bum's ankle and into the shop.

Confused, Young-hee looked around. The food shop, piled high with fragrant cakes and breads, was made of faded old wood in desperate need of repair. Young-hee realized she had seen the shop before, as well as the biscuit Bum was eating, on her last trip to the goblin market.

"Can I help you?" said a voice, full of malevolence. Young-hee looked up to find a dokkaebi grinning evilly at her. She glimpsed the tiniest flicker of light, a gossamer thread of ghostly silver, in the goblin's hand.

7

Which is how Young-hee lost her brother. After striking the deal with the dokkaebi—a pullocho in exchange for Bum—she went charging through the market, looking for a familiar, chalky white face. "Grandma Dol, I need your help," she said, voice breaking with sadness and rage.

"What's wrong, child?" the old woman soothed. She wasn't wearing any mask now, her real face was covered only by concern. Young-hee's words tumbled out, a mess of grief and anger, but Grandma Dol quickly understood. The old stone grew angry and threatened to put on Mokjung, or maybe even Yeongno—Young-hee didn't know that mask, but it sounded scary. Young-hee had hoped that her friend had the power or the connections to tear Bum from the goblin's clutches. But when Grandma Dol learned that Woo had followed the rules of the goblin market, she confirmed that the only way to save him was for Young-hee to fulfill the agreement.

At some point, Bassam joined them. He brought tea and talked to her while Grandma Dol went to Woo's shop to confront the goblin, only to return, shaking her head. Bassam and Grandma Dol promised to keep an eye on Bum as best they could from their part of the market, and see what they could learn about Woo. Bassam asked her to recount all that had happened several times, in all the detail she could recall. "This is a goblin market, and I have known many of those creatures in my many years in this land. They are a mischievous race, untrustworthy, to be sure. But I have not known them to be this evil before. Nor to eat human children."

"Well, this one is that bad," said Grandma Dol. She took charge of getting Young-hee properly equipped for a long trip, rounding up roots and rice cakes that would last as long as possible. She traded Young-hee's remaining hairbands for all the jungbo she could afford. "It's not a lot, but it should be enough," she said. She also gave Young-hee a small, wooden lamp with a candle inside. "It is a special type of soybean wax that burns very slowly," she said, "and the lamp is bright and light, so it won't weigh you down. It is one of my best."

Bassam, too, gave her items from his shop, a sturdy canvas bag, a sleeping roll, and a heavy linen cloak. She thanked them, but when she asked them to come with her, they shook their heads and said that it was not possible.

"I have my place in this market, and obligations of my own," said Bassam.

"Besides, Young-hee, this is your promise, your journey," said Grandma Dol. "I do not know why the great spirits of heaven allowed something so terrible to happen to you, but there are often reasons we do not understand, at least at first."

"But I need you," pleaded Young-hee.

"I am needed here, by those more in need than even you and your brother. Should I forget my other obligations just for you?"

Young-hee wanted to scream "yes," but gave a slight, reluctant nod instead.

"If it is your destiny to travel across our world and find a pullocho, you must embrace that, even if it is very difficult," said Grandma Dol.

Neither Bassam nor Grandma Dol knew much about pullochos or the Sacred City, but they said the jangseung could at least get her started in the right direction. Bassam thought Lake Mey was a couple of days' walk, then the Cheongyong mountains, and past them the Great Forest.

"But I believe the Sacred City was the great kingdom I sought, hundreds of years ago, when I first lost my way and ended up here," said Bassam. "If I may offer some advice—once the jangseung show you your path, stay on it as long as you can. Paths are ephemeral and strange, at once obvious and frustrating. This world is wild and dangerous, but the path is usually a safer place to be."

"And," added Grandma Dol, "as you have learned from your brother and Woo, refuse all gifts unless from someone who, like us, first grants you hospitality and calls you 'friend.' And whoever or whatever you meet, always be respectful. You have a fiery heart, and that is good, but it can get you into trouble."

"Thanks," Young-hee said. "I heard something similar not too long ago. I wish I had listened."

"One more thing," said Granny. "There are many dangers and dishonest creatures. But it is still good to make friends. Betrayal is a risk, but a good friend can help and comfort you on a long journey."

It had been a long day, so Granny Dol suggested that Young-hee sleep with them in the market. But knowing Woo would not let her stay with Bum, and that she couldn't bear to be so close, she decided to start right away, the sooner to return. So, with that, there was nothing to do but say good-bye.

As full and busy as the market was, it dropped away quickly. The sun was still the same rich, evening orange, as during the other visit to Strange Land. The beauty of the light and the rolling hills clashed painfully with her sadness and almost made her angry.

At the clearing, she saw the jangseung. "Who approaches the guardians of the Jureum Forest and the surrounding villages?" asked Cheonha gruffly.

"It's me, Young-hee," she replied in a flat voice. "Hi, Cheonha, Jiha."

"Oh, the human girl," said Jiha, always the friendlier jangseung.

"What's wrong, bear daughter?" asked Cheonha. When Young-hee repeated her story, both guardians showed great concern. "Such an evil goblin," said Cheonha, shaking his head—but they, too, could do little.

"There have been many rumors of bad things gathering, even war, unlike anything since the last divide," said Jiha. "You've chosen a dangerous time to travel our land."

"Great," said Young-hee, unable to hold in her sarcasm. "Do you know anything about the dokkaebi's instructions: The Sacred City and the sandalwood tree? Or the Cheongyong Mountains and Lake Mey? The animal spirits? Anything?"

"Well, the sandalwood tree is one of the most sacred sites in all our land. So sacred, in fact, that few can find it." Cheonha gazed into the distance. "Just a moment, I'll see what I can see." His eyes clouded over as he murmured odd noises, and then seemed to shine and pulse.

"Cheonha is just 'looking' for you," explained Jiha. "Guardians like us live in doorways and in-between places. We can see a great many things, very far away."

A minute later Cheonha's eyes returned to normal. "No signs of pullochos, sorry to say. But that is not surprising—strong magicks like pullochos can wreak havoc on far-seeing, discovery spells, and the like. However, I can say that your instructions, meager as they are, seem correct. If you keep walking past Haechi Horn, through the forest, you should come to Lake Mey in a day or two. On the far side lie the Cheongyong Mountains. And past them, somewhere, the Sacred City."

"*Aish*," said Young-hee. "And the—what were they called?—the 'animal women spirits?' "

"Yes, Bear, Snake, and Fox," said Jiha. "Three of the most ancient animals."

"But aren't foxes evil?"

"All three sisters are very powerful and dangerous, in their way. They live past the mountains, or so I've heard tell. If anyone knows about pullochos, they might."

"Somewhere past the mountains," repeated Young-hee. "I'm not some great explorer. I have no idea how I'll find my way through the forest to the lake, let alone around the lake or over the mountains."

"Well, at least for now you just need to follow your path."

"*My* path?"

"Yes, you're on it already."

Young-hee looked down and was startled to see she was standing on a dark stone path—almost two meters wide wide, that extended from underneath her feet toward Haechi Horn. "Wait, I never saw this path before."

"Yes, but you were never on a journey before," said Jiha.

Young-hee's thoughts swirled. This was weird. "So this stone path just … appeared? Just for me?"

"Indeed."

"And it just … knows where I'm supposed to go?"

"Yes and no, I would think," said Cheonha. "It won't take you to the pullocho, but it can take you Lake Mey."

"And over the mountains, too?"

"Perhaps," said Cheonha. "The thing is … "

"Oh, hush now," interrupted Jiha. "You'll scare the girl with your running on."

"What? Tell me. What is it?"

"Well," continued Jiha, "you have so much to worry about already. But if you really wish to know: The Cheongyong Mountains are large and treacherous, the biggest in our realm, and home to many great and terrible ogres … and worse."

"Ogres?"

"Some of the first ogres," said Cheonha. "Huge as these trees, some of them, with many cruel heads."

"And worse," Jiha repeated. Jiha's eyes rolled back as she used her far-sight. "At Lake Mey, on the far shore, is the cave of Darang. It is a short cut under the mountains."

"And no ogres?"

"Something protects the cave from ogres. However, you will have to cross Lake Mey by boat to reach the cave. And Mey is famous for its water dragon, I'm afraid. Very large and fierce."

"A dragon?"

"Yes, but the Lake Mey dragon is … ," began Cheonha, but Jiha cut him off again.

"Dragons are nothing to be trifled with," said Jiha curtly. "Especially for a bear daughter."

"Oh drat," said Young-hee, not needing more discouragement.

"Well, you can always go around the lake, I suppose, and take a road around the mountains," said Jiha. "But that would make your journey much longer. Weeks more, maybe; it is quite a large lake."

"I need to find that pullocho and get back as soon as possible, for Bum."

"Well, then, I do not envy you your choices, child. Do you have a light for the cave?"

"Grandma Dol gave me this," said Young-hee, taking the lamp from her bag.

"Ah, Glory Cedar, I do believe, very nice."

"And, Young-hee, be careful," warned Cheonha. "You are a bear daughter, and there are many creatures that would like to capture you, just like your brother. Everything in the goblin market becomes known throughout the land soon enough."

"*Aish*, it just keeps getting better," Young-hee said. "I don't suppose your world has any buses, does it? Maybe a taxi?"

"*Boosses*?" asked Cheonha. "A *taek-shi*?"

"I didn't think so. Never mind, I'll be okay," said Young-hee, muttering one last "annoying." She looked at the road before her. Flanked by dense trees, it curved up the steep hill that was Haechi Horn. She had no idea how far the journey might be. Or if she could find the ruins of the Sacred City or the pullocho that supposedly grew there. *I don't know anything*, she thought. *Why did I bring Bum to this place? I should have known it was too dangerous.* In that moment, though, she decided she didn't have the luxury of regret or self-pity. All that mattered was rescuing Bum.

She checked her cell phone for messages and emails she knew would not be there. But its clock told her it was after eleven at night in Korea. Back home her mother would be so upset, wondering what had happened to them. Young-hee wanted to feel bad about that, but doubted it was possible to feel any worse.

"What is that, child?" asked Jiha.

Young-hee closed and re-pocketed the phone. "Doesn't matter," she sighed. "Where does your, uh, guardianship end?"

"Just slightly up the hill," said Cheonha. "It varies."

"Yeah," said Young-hee. "And past that? Aside from dragons and ancient spirits and killer dragonflies and ogres, what else am I going to find?" She thought about the books she read in the weeks before returning to Strange Land. What else had there been?

"Ghosts," offered Cheonha.

"Oh, right, ghosts. How could I forget."

"Don't let them worry you, dear," said Jiha.

"You think I'll be okay?"

"Well, honestly, I don't know. It's a dangerous world, but you have spirit. And smarts. You'll need both. But you should have as good a chance as any."

"*Great.* Very encouraging," Young-hee said. "Well, I guess I should be going." And with that, Young-hee thanked the jangseung one last time, waved, and began her journey.

As she walked out of the jureum forest, along the path toward Haechi Hill, she thought about the doorway to the basement and back home. *Maybe this is just a crazy dream, and once I get home again, Bum will be there, and everything will be normal again.* She couldn't believe she actually wanted normal again. She wondered if she was doing the right thing, and had a chance of making it back in one piece. But then she looked at her feet and the road, stretching up over the Horn. Nothing to do but get started.

* * *

As she walked out of sight, Cheonha scowled at his partner. "Why did you interrupt me?" he asked. "She's a good girl, polite and respectful. I was going to tell her more about the lake's dragon, and the cave demon, and how to avoid the animal spirit sisters."

Jiha shrugged. "Some things she can learn on her own," she said coldly. "Other things, it would be better if she doesn't learn. At least not until the right time." Jiha looked at Cheonha with great purpose and seriousness. "We are guardians of this place, not of her. There are bad days coming, as you said, maybe even war, and I intend to be on the winning side."

Act II

The Children of Bear
Long ago, Hwanin ruled the endless expanses of the Heavens and was much beloved by all the great spirits of his realm. Hwanin and his favorite concubine had a son named Hwanung, and one day Hwanung decided that he wanted to rule over the lower world, much as his fa-

ther ruled the upper world. So Hwanin gave his son the Three Heav-
enly Treasures, the three great Masters of Wind, Rain, and Cloud, and
three-thousand spirits, and sent Hwanung to the world below. There,
by the Sacred Sandalwood tree on Myohyang-san—Mysterious Fra-
grant Mountain—Hwanung founded the Sacred City.

Down in the mortal realm, Tiger and Bear decided they wanted to
live as men, so they traveled to the Sacred City to meet Hwanung and
petitioned him to turn them into humans. Hwanung warned that the
magicks were powerful and the cost great, but both were undeterred.
Hwanung finally relented. He gave Tiger and Bear a large bag filled
with mugwort, twenty pieces of garlic, and a pullocho; and told them
to enter a deep cave high on Mysterious Fragrant Mountain. Hwanung
promised that if they stayed for one hundred days, never seeing day-
light and eating only the mugwort, garlic, and pullocho, when they
emerged they would be human.

Eagerly, Tiger and Bear went into the cave. But time crept slowly in
the darkness. Day by day the Mugwort grew drier and more foul, the
garlic more harsh, and the pullocho more bitter. Tiger said he hated
those plants, and Bear complained she was so very hungry, but they
had no choice but to endure.

After just a few day days Tiger gave up, leaving the cave with a
bitter growl. But Bear continued to suffer and wait. Finally, after one
hundred days, she emerged. Hwanung was very impressed with her
patience and turned her into a beautiful woman. But Bear had no one
to marry and was very lonely, so she made an altar under the Sacred
Sandalwood Tree and prayed. Hwanung heard Bear's prayers and took
pity; he married her and they had a son named Dangun.

Dangun would build the great city of Pyongyang, which grew into
the Gojoseon Dynasty, as well as the people of Shilla and Goryeo in the
south, and Okcho in the north, plus the Puyeo, the Ye, and the Maek.
Dangun governed them all for 1,038 years, until finally he left his king-
dom for Mount Asadal, where he became the Spirit of the mountain.

8

Young-hee felt as if she had been walking through the silent forest forever. At first she had passed the occasional house and, sometimes, other travelers, but now she was on her own. The path, such as it was, kept changing, seemingly without reason: sometimes it was wide and built of large, smooth stones, other times just a dark dirt path. When a hill crested, Young-hee would look to the mountains for a sense of her progress. But with no idea how far she had to go or even where she was going, the journey seemed timeless and endless.

Eventually the sun did go down, so Young-hee laid her sleeping roll in long grass, covered herself with the cloak from Bassam, and balled up her windbreaker for a pillow. She lay close to the road, re-membering instructions from Gyeongbi Shin and others about not leaving the path. Luckily, Strange Land's silky grass seemed clean and bug-free and the ground was reasonably soft. As Young-hee settled down, she noticed a big, round rock with a noble air and wondered if it might also be a person, like Grandma Dol. It was not talking now, but that didn't mean it couldn't. "Goodnight, rock," she said, just in case. Thinking about Bum, she looked up at the bright moon and strange stars, convinced she would never sleep but, after the hard day, she quickly drifted off.

When she woke up, the sun was warming the ground, evaporat-ing the dew around her. She had no idea how long she had slept, but felt surprisingly good after the deepest, most dreamless, purest sleep she had ever known. *I guess it's not surprising you don't dream in a world that is already a dream*, she concluded. Eating a granola bar and some rice cakes, Young-hee spied a pine cone by the rock, added it to her rather full bag, and set out again.

She walked and walked. Every so often, she thought she saw a movement in the woods or heard a rustling in the grass, but no matter how hard she stared, saw nothing. A dark speck moved high across the sky—*a bird?* The harder she looked, the less sure she was. But a shiver of discomfort that something was spying down on her was real enough. She could do nothing about birds or woodland animals. All she could do was keep walking the lonely path.

Finally, Young-hee just stopped. *This is crazy*, she thought. *I haven't seen another person for hours. Or a goblin or giant frog or talking totem pole guardian. Nothing.* Discouraged, Youngee kicked a small, gray stone at the edge of the road. She needed more advice, she decided. Maybe she could hire a guide. Anything would be better than this interminable walking.

So she decided to head back for help. Turning around, she immediately felt better. Her feet hurt less; her bag was lighter. She had started on this path too quickly, she thought, without proper preparation. Maybe she could even try negotiating with the dokkaebi again.

But she hadn't backtracked for more than five minutes when, ahead of her, the road split in two directions, and both paths looked the same. *Very, very odd*, she thought. *I definitely don't remember any intersections.*

Determined to get back to the market and the jangseung, she forked left. All the trees and hills had begun to look the same, and the road turned so much she lost track of which way she was going. But after a few more minutes, she came to another fork—this one with three roads diverging. "*Jigyeowo!*" she growled to no one in particular. "I *hate* this place. So annoying."

Once again, all the choices looked the same, and she was absolutely certain there had been no three-way intersection before. She must have taken the wrong path at the last crossroads, she decided, and turned back to take the other choice.

So she walked back. And walked. And walked some more. But even after what felt like forever, there was no intersection at all. *Where did it go?* she wondered. Just to be sure, she walked ahead a few more minutes, but nothing. And then, in the middle of the road, was a small, gray stone, exactly like the one she had kicked before turning around. Had she passed the intersection without seeing it again? "Bah!" she said, exasperated, and turned around one more time.

Once again, after a little while, she came to a forked path. Not in the same place as last time, but that hardly mattered to Young-hee. This time, she forked right, marching ahead full steam.

Again the road diverged … into four paths stretching into the forest. "*Argh!*" she shouted. *This place is mad!* Young-hee kicked at the grass. How could a road change depending on which way she walked? She plunked down on the grass at the side of the road and fumed.

Much fuming later, she resumed walking. Toward Lake Mey. She figured she had little choice but to advance, since return led to chaos. By this time, she was footsore and bored, but she forced herself on, for Bum, and because there was nothing else to do. Taking brief break to massage her feet and adjust her bag, she peered into the dense woods on either side, but heard only the sound of wind brushing the leaves and bushes. She was on her own.

At another break, as she removed her pack, a sudden sound startled her. She looked left and right, suddenly alert. *Was it anything?* "Hello?" she called and strained her ears through the silence. But nothing.

As soon as she started walking, she heard it again. It was muffled and unrecognizable, but it was something. A mouse watching from the woods? Another frog? "Who's there?" she asked.

The third time she heard it, she recognized it: *a sneeze. That's odd*, she thought. "Hello?" she asked, and as if in response, one more sneeze. Then she noticed a soft rustling coming from under a tree, right by the path. *That's it*, she decided, *I'm going to see who it is. Or what.*

The sounds were coming from the ground, very close. Young-hee stooped over, parted branches and leaves, and dug in the lightly packed earth. Her fingers fumbled and pulled—and, suddenly, Young-hee found herself holding a skull. A human skull.

"Gross!" she said. It must have been there a very long time. It was covered in dirt, with twigs and roots growing inside and through the nose hole. Most of the debris dislodged when she pulled the skull out of the ground, and Young-hee quickly brushed off the rest, revealing a smiling head of bone.

"Oh, thank you!" said the skull, most unexpectedly. "Those roots have been tickling me for years, making me sneeze and sneeze."

Young-hee had been in Strange Land long enough to get used to surprising things. "No problem," she said casually. "I hate it when I have allergies and can't stop sneezing." She gave the skull another brush and examined its empty eye sockets. They almost seemed soulful. Impulsively, she scratched the bone where a nose once sat.

"Ah, that is nice."

"It must be tough, being in the dirt so long, without any fingers. Or ones you can use." She wondered what other bones were buried there.

"I have been wanting to scratch that itch for more years than you know, girl. That's wonderful."

"I'm happy to help," she said, scratching again. "Would you like something to eat?"

"I'm afraid Bae's time for eating has long passed," laughed the skull. "But please, go right ahead. I would be honored to break bread with you."

Young-hee placed her sleeping roll on the ground like a blanket, and put the skull down beside her. Then she took out a few *kaypal* balls. "I don't have a lot, sorry."

"No, please. After being buried for ages, it is great to see the sunlight again, breathe easily, and have someone to talk to. Especially a bear daughter."

"Oh," said Young-hee, "you know I'm human."

"Well, I do now," said the skull cheerfully. "I was guessing."

"*Aish*," said Young-hee, telling herself to be more careful. She had a few bites and tried to act naturally. She wasn't sure of the protocol for skulls. "Um, if you don't mind me asking, are you a ghost?"

The skull laughed. "A ghost? Not like you mean, no. A ghost here must belong to the Ghost Queen, and I promise I am not on her side. No, I'm just a man who lived and died but, for some reason, endures."

"I see," said Young-hee, not really seeing. "Is the Ghost Queen not nice?"

"No, not nice at all. Ghosts are a nasty lot—all long black hair and pasty skin and fixated on bloody revenge. There are a few ghosts in these woods, but I never paid them any mind, and none were interested in helping old Bae. They're always upset about something and full of resentment. They never let anything go. And their Queen is the worst of a bad lot."

"Some girls said my school has a ghost—a student who died in a terrible accident years ago. I never believed them, though," said Young-hee. At least being stuck in Strange Land meant she wasn't stuck in class. "Say, don't people become ghosts because of injustice or suffering or something like that?"

"Bah, life is full of injustice. Look at me, I'm dead, and you don't hear me complaining."

"I suppose not." She scratched the skull a bit more, trying to think of something to say. "This really is an odd place." *Not a terribly creative comment* she thought.

"This forest?" the skull asked.

"No, this whole world. Talking stones and goblins and giant frogs. I think I saw a mountain wander off."

"And now you're talking to a bony skull."

"Exactly," she laughed briefly. "But it's stranger than that. I'm supposed to be on this big journey, traveling to Lake Mey and some cave called Darang through the Cheongyong Mountains, and on to the Sacred City. But I have no idea if I'm on the right path. I tried going back for more advice, but the path kept splitting. No one warned me that would happen."

"Hmm," said the skull. "Splitting paths are pretty common on big journeys and quests, I do believe. You can't just stop a quest, you have to keep going. That's what Bae's parents always said. But, then, it has been a long time since I walked anywhere."

"Great," she said without enthusiasm, unhappy to have another complication to worry about. She put away her food and things as she got ready to walk again.

"Before you go, do you think you could do me a favor?"

"Sure, why not?" she said.

"It's just that, I've been in that hole in the dirt for ever so long, and I'd really prefer not to go back there, not yet. Could you put me up in a tree with a good view of the valley and mountains below?"

That sounded very reasonable, so Young-hee found a thick, gray tree, like a maple, with a nook between two branches about two meters above the ground. "How's this?"

"Oh, excellent. Much better than the dirty, cold ground. Thank you again."

"It was nothing. I wouldn't want to be stuck in the ground either." She was happy to have helped, but she wanted to get moving. "By the way, you wouldn't happen to know if I'm on the right path?"

"To the Sacred City? I don't know. But to Lake Mey, definitely. Keep straight and you'll get to there soon enough. And past the lake lie the mountains."

"I was warned that the lake and mountains have a lot of big monsters."

"Ah, those. I don't suppose you can call on a heavenly warrior or someone to protect you?"

"No, I'm just me."

"I see," said the skull, thinking. "I'll tell you what—before you go, dig in the ground where you found me."

Young-hee nearly argued that she was in a hurry, but complied. "What am I looking for?" she asked as her fingers poked through the earth. But as she asked, she felt something cold and hard and metal. She pulled a golden ring from the dirt. It was filthy now, but was finely crafted with a large jade stone.

"In life, that was my ring. Everyone knows about Bae and his elegant jewelry. I'd like you to have it."

"Oh, thank you so much."

"At the lake, show it to my friend Mansoo. He'll recognize it and take you across the lake to the great cave."

"That's really nice. But how will I find your friend?"

"Mansoo? Trust me, you can't miss him. He's lived there a long time and knows all about the tricks and dangers. Tell him Bae sent you."

Young-hee held the jade stone to the orange sunlight. Beneath all the dirt, it was probably quite beautiful. "Thank you, Mr. Bae," she said waving goodbye. "I promise I'll keep the ring close." She put the ring in a pocket and was sure she heard the skull whistling happily behind her.

For the next couple of hours the path continued uneventfully, without confusing splits or talking skulls. When it crossed a small stream, Young-hee rinsed the ring in the cool water. The intricately shaped gold formed tiny ivy leaves and branches around the jade stone. She slipped it on her finger, and, although it was a bit big, it looked so nice she decided to wear it.

At last, the fat orange sun grew redder and fatter. On her first night in Strange Land, Young-hee had been surprised at how light the sky was, as if the stars shone brighter here than in the real world. Or maybe it was the sky itself, with its bluish shimmer, like Earth's during full moon. Even as darkness fell, Young-hee didn't feel tired and decided to walk a bit further before settling down.

The twisting path descended a slope. The hill loomed behind, casting a large shadow in the gathering gloom. And then, on one turn, the trees pulled back slightly from the path, revealing a good view of the hill above. Young-hee stopped cold—there was someone on the hill, looking down on her.

All she could make out was a distant shadow, a darker sliver against the evening sky. When she had almost convinced herself that it was only a stump or an oddly shaped rock, the shadow disappeared. She double-checked and checked again, but the silhouetted figure was gone. With a shiver running down her spine, Young-hee picked up her pace. She didn't like the thought of something following her. Not at all.

There were often noises in the forest. Until then, she had managed to convince herself they were little rabbits (cute, even if cunning liars) or frogs (funny, even if huge and grumpy) or other innocuous creatures (harmless, even if talking skulls). But, now, she was scared in a way she had not felt since coming to Strange Land. Losing Bum had been terrible, like a knife in her chest, but that was the pain of losing a person close to you. It was tears, anger, guilt, heartache. This was just fear.

Young-hee hurried down the hill, trying to put distance between her and the shadow. Finally, at the bottom, the road straightened into a nearly straight line. She didn't like how exposed it looked, so she hugged the trees on the left side of the path, hoping they would conceal her. She sped along, wishing for a curve that would make her harder to spot if anyone was following from a distance. She felt watched.

Finally, she sighed in relief to see the path curve up where the trees seemed higher and thicker. She welcomed the added shelter and began to feel embarrassed for getting so afraid. She was fine.

But just before the road made turned the corner, Young-hee gave one last quick look over her shoulder. And there it was—at the far end of the long, straight road, standing perfectly still: the shadow. Dark and distance shielded it, but whatever or whoever it was seemed to be wearing a light-colored robe.

Young-hee slipped around the bend and, once out of sight, broke into a full run. Behind her, a horrible rattling filled the air. Like a deathly howl. She didn't like this at all. The road snaked between two big hills. She liked being hidden, but also realized that a winding road also hid what was behind her.

The hill wasn't too steep, but after two long days of hiking, Young-hee tired quickly and her muscles burned. The road snaked again to emerge on a rocky outcrop. Maybe she could look down at the road, like the thing following her had done. Cautiously, Young-hee crouched and edged her way to the cliff face. She used the highest rock to shield herself as she looked over the edge.

It was hard to see the weaving path through the trees, but her eyes had adjusted and the stars cast light on the forest. No one was walking on the straight stretch, but the trees and darkness hindered a view of the curved sections. Not wanting to waste precious time letting that thing catch up to her, she would pause for just a brief moment, then be on her way again.

She was about to give up and resume running when she saw

something in a clearing, barely a hundred meters away. And it was not one, but two shadowy figures. Despite the darkness, she could make out the long, straight black hair, and white clothes—ghosts. And they were both looking right at her.

The Rabbit and the Water Dragon King

One day, Rabbit was taking a pleasant walk by a lake near his home, when Turtle appeared from the depths and crawled up on shore.

"Gracious Rabbit," intoned Turtle, "my master, the Water Dragon King, asks that you join him in his underwater castle. He has serious need of your unique talents. If you come with me, he promises you great rewards."

Rabbit was surprised to receive an invitation from such a noble creature, but still he thought about the request carefully. Being a small, weak creature, he always had to be wary of danger, but the potential for great wealth was most tempting. "All right," he said, full of rabbit chipper, "let's go."

Rabbit climbed on to Turtle's large, green shell and Turtle carried him into the lake's dark depths. Down and down they dove, to the deep bottom, until at last they came to the Dragon King's home. Turtle swam right up to the throne room, where he presented Rabbit.

"Ah, so you've accepted my invitation," exclaimed the Dragon King. "That is wonderful news."

"I'm pleased to be invited by a creature as regal and powerful as yourself, my lord Dragon. Please, tell me how I may be of service?"

"The truth is, Rabbit, that I have grown sickly recently. Very sick. And my greatest doctors tell me that the only thing that might save me is the liver of a rabbit. Which is why I've asked for you to come. My guards will remove your liver, which I will consume and return to health."

Now, it was immediately clear to Rabbit, even though he was not a doctor himself, that having his liver removed would be at least as bad for his health as it would be good for the Dragon King's. But the King and his guards were all mighty and Rabbit was no fighter. But Rabbit was a rabbit, so he knew how to think quickly.

"Why thank you, your majesty," he said with as much bravado as he could muster. "I can think of nothing more noble for a lowly rabbit like myself than to give such a precious gift to the mighty King."

"Is that a fact?" asked the King skeptically. He had been expecting more of a struggle.

"That is a fact. And it is also a fact that I would love to give you my liver right here and now."

"You would?"

"Yes, I would. But, alas, I cannot. Because when your emissary, Turtle, came to get me, he never told me that you needed my liver. And, as luck would have it, I did not have my liver with me then."

"You didn't?"

"No, I was, in fact, drying it on the rocks at the edge of the lake. However, if Turtle takes me back, I can pick up my liver and bring it right back to you."

The King grew angry. "What are you saying?" he roared. Rabbit grew afraid, but then the King turned to Turtle. "How could you bring Rabbit here without first checking for his liver? Go, now, with Rabbit, so he can bring back his liver to me."

Frightened and obedient, Turtle put Rabbit on his back again and swam to the surface of the lake. Once at the edge, Rabbit hopped off and ran up the rocks at the embankment.

"Okay, Rabbit, get your liver and let's go back to my lord's castle," said Turtle.

"Oh, I don't think I'll be doing that," said Rabbit as he hopped away as fast as he could. "Mrs. Rabbit probably thinks I've been gone too long as it is."

"Well, at least tell me where you left your liver, so I can bring it to the Water Dragon King myself," shouted Turtle toward Rabbit.

But Rabbit only laughed. "Foolish Turtle. What kind of creature can live without its liver? Tell your Dragon King that he is even dumber than you are. My liver is in my body, as with all creatures, and in my body I intend on keeping it."

9

Young-hee fled full speed as the rattling calls—this time two of them—filled the air. By cutting straight through the woods and avoiding the road's twists, her pursuers were gaining ground. She was in trouble.

Her lungs burned, but at least the pain distracted her from full-out panic. Ghost stories, comics, TV shows, and movies told about ghosts, but what did she really know? But even in the dark, from afar, in gloomy woods, she knew what they were from the long black hair, white skin and clothes, the deathly glare.

Bae-the-skull said they lived in these woods, that they were resentful and wanted vengeance. But why were they after her? She pumped her arms a bit harder and raised her knees a bit higher and struggled to think.

As she powered over a ridge, another rattle descended from high on the hill ahead. *Another ghost?* They were like a pack of undead wolves. *No, no, no!* a frightened voice inside her head screamed, but she willed herself to ignore it.

Young-hee kept running as the road dipped across a small stream before heading up again. She got an idea—a gamble, but if she couldn't outpace them she had to try something. She ran ahead, stopped, turned, and ran back toward the ghosts. They were close and would be on her at any moment. She was almost out of time.

Just as she neared the dip by the river again, she ran into a four-way intersection, like the mysterious path splits from the day before. Young-hee jumped off the path, dove into a dense bed of brambles, and covered herself with the linen cloak, leaving a small crack to peer through.

After what felt like hours, but was really a brief moment, the two ghosts came over the ridge toward the stream. They moved like cold wind on a wet November evening, freezing and miserable, and stopped short at the intersection. Fighting her racing heart, burning muscles and wheezing lungs, Young-hee was perfectly silent and still. She could just make out their dark, dead eyes and blue, cold lips. *They look hungry, but not for food.*

Soon, a third ghost joined them from another path, and as if they had an undead language, they issued their empty, rattling calls. This last horrifying ghost had no face at all—just a featureless surface, like an egg. With the path branching out in four different directions, they did not know where to go.

As Young-hee watched, she heard… *clopping.* The sound grew louder until she saw a huge, black horse, with a woman riding. Her rasping orders sounded more like talking than the others' sickly rattles. Young-hee shifted for a better look, but the blank-faced ghost turned in her direction. She froze—mid-shift—so that her weight rested on one side. Her leg began to hurt and cramp, but she dared not move.

The horse whinnied and twirled as the rider spoke. Young-hee bit her lip as her leg throbbed more and more. *How much longer can I last?* And, then, the ghosts were gone. The horse and rider, too. All just vanished. *Was it a trap?* she wondered. *Where did they go?*

She waited, but the dark forest was silent except for the soft rustle of leaves and the distant rush of the stream. Carefully, quietly, Young-hee unfolded her aching leg, massaging the cramps. It was darker in the woods than on the path, and spookier, but she waited, not sure how long.

And then she woke with a start. How long did she sleep? It was still dark, so it couldn't have been long, she hoped, and cautiously stood. The path was just ahead to the left. In the distance she heard the now familiar burble of the stream. The first gray streaks of morning comforted her. Dawn was coming. Careful to be quiet and not twist an ankle, she stepped tentative step-by-step, closer to the road. Any moment now she would rejoin the path and her journey to Lake Mey.

But the thing was, the path never returned, even after she had walked a good way. *It must have gone back to being a simple, straight path, without the strange intersection*, she thought, *and I'm probably just walking parallel to it*. It was easy to get turned around in the woods—she remembered hearing that once. She found a tree for reference—a bent, old thing with only a few desperate leaves hanging on. She turned ninety degrees, but after a few minutes, still nothing. She reversed, found the bent tree, and tried the other direction. Again nothing. *That must be why people say don't leave the path. Once you do, does it just disappear?* It was a terrible thought, but having run into so many terrible things lately, she almost felt comfortable being uncomfortable. After vengeful ghosts and scheming goblins, she could handle being lost.

She relaxed, listening for the sound of the stream. The cool gray of dawn showed flecks of orange. Cresting a ridge, she found the stream, and felt that finally something was going right. But a walk upstream revealed no path. She wondered what happened to people on a path when it disappeared or branched, but shrugged and thought, *First things first, get out of the forest. Maybe follow the stream to the hill top and look around.* But with mountains overshadowing the hill, a far view was unlikely. Then she realized that the stream had to go somewhere—to a larger river, perhaps even to Lake Mey. She could make the stream her path. Pleased, Young-hee set out again.

Downstream, the valley grew steeper, and the water sped up. Young-hee lunged from tree to tree, grabbing branches trying not to make noise or fall into the water. It was slow going, but at least she was going somewhere. And as the rising sun shone its warm, dull rays down on Strange Land, the light restored her spirits and blunted the awful memory of the ghosts. Feeder creeks joined the steam, which, after a few hours, was more like a river. It surged and churned, growing white with rapids and power.

She followed the river around a tight bend, and there she could see it—Lake Mey, or so she hoped, in the distance below. She still had a ways to go, but was happy to find a clear target and be one step closer to her goal.

Just as Youngee let herself feel a hopeful, a familiar, sickly rattling filled the air above and behind her. *Oh no, the ghosts have found me again*. As she spotted a ghost on a hill overlooking the river valley, a second rattling, louder, reverberated around the valley. Young-hee took off running.

The white, frothy river surged through the steep valley toward the distant lake. The ground sloped steeply, too, making running fast but treacherous. Then another rattle, this time in the woods on *her side* of the river, boosted her fear and her pace.

As the forest thinned, she could run faster, but was also more exposed. With nothing else to do, she ran even harder.

Then another noise rose over her fatigue and the river's roar—galloping hoof beats. The ghost on horseback, too, had found her. Young-hee looked back quickly, careful not to hit any trees, and there, on a ridge, descending toward her, was the mounted ghost. Young-hee felt her confidence flag. *How can I outrun a horse?* As a rattle rose up over the water, a ghost on the other side of the river—the faceless one—drew even with her. They were all closing in. There was nowhere to go. Except one place. Young-hee gathered her energy and launched herself as hard as she could into the river.

The first thing she felt was cold. Deep, sharp cold. The strong current grabbed her, but a couple of strong strokes pulled her to the surface. She was trying to right herself, when she realized that the canvas bag from Bassam was acting like a life vest, helping keep her head above the violent water. She floated feet-first downstream, ready to use her shoes to protect against rocks. Fortunately, the river seemed deep and fairly safe. As she rushed downstream, she silently thanked her mom for forcing her to take swimming lessons back in Canada. The ghosts, deterred by the water, followed, two on the right riverbank and two on the left, including the rider. As the speeding river left the others behind, only the ghost on horseback kept up.

With her head bobbing in the rough river, she managed to make out that the flow would slow and broaden as the river approached the lake. But first there was one last, big set of rapids—more like a series of mini-waterfalls. Four times she felt the freezing embrace of the water lift her into weightlessness and release her with a violent thump into the grasp of bubbly, churning waters. But once she passed the rapids, the river turned flat and peaceful. Under the stare of the ghostly rider perched on the left bank, Young-hee swam until she pulled herself onto the right shore. She knew little about ghosts, but this one seemed bitterly angry at the water separating them.

This was Young-hee's first chance to take a good look at the horse-riding ghost. The black horse was sturdy, more like a workhorse than a racehorse, but with steady, angry fire in its eyes. As for the rider, she wore a long, black veil that covered her face and hung nearly to the ground. Through it, Young-hee could just see pale, ghostly skin and dead eyes—but there was something different about her—she had curly hair, and instead of the white robes the other ghosts wore, was garbed in dark leather. Thin and severe, the rider seemed designed to command. She looked almost dignified. And definitely cruel.

She rode back and forth along the bank, as if trying to make up her mind. Then she made a noise and tugged the reins. Tentatively, the horse took one step into the water, then another. She was going to try to swim across. Young-hee's heart sank. The other ghosts couldn't be that far behind, either. She had to put some distance between them.

The lake was not far now. But it was huge. Mountains loomed ominously on the far side, just as the jangseung said. It would take forever to walk around, and then another forever to traverse the mountains. She had to find the cave, but how? She looked for a house or castle where the skull's friend Mansoo might live. But this land looked as uninhabited as everywhere else she'd been in the past couple of days.

Another round of rattling sounded behind her. The ghosts were still after her. She looked for somewhere to hide, but the shore was too exposed, the lake too big to swim across. Young-hee was running out of options. She ran along the shore of the lake until she was ready to burst, but the ghosts bore down. When she looked right at them they scarcely seemed to move, just hovered and stared with empty, terrible eyes. The black horse and its rider, her dark, curly hair and long veil flying behind, had emerging onto the shore.

Finally, at the edge of the immense lake, Young-hee stopped running and faced her pursuers. "What do you want!?" she shouted in a hoarse scream. "What did I do?"

But the ghosts kept coming. The rider pulled up, perhaps a dozen meters away, straight-backed, her face empty save for distain. "We want to be free," she croaked flatly. "We've been promised peace in exchange for you, bear-child." The horse snorted heavily through its immense nostrils, as if it, too, was proclaiming victory. Young-hee backed toward the water and, out of room, tripped over a rock and fell, one hand splashing as she instinctively tried to break her fall.

"Leave me alone!" she shouted in one last protest.

Young-hee heard rushing water and felt a cold spray on her head. *Someone's dripping water on me*, she thought as a huge gush of water surrounded her. She realized that something very, very large was surging out of the lake. An immense, scaly shape. There was a roar, not from churning water, but from a huge animal that suddenly loomed over her, all teeth and claws and scales—a dragon. A blue dragon, its eyes sparkling cold like black ice, its mouth bigger than Young-hee, and its great, serpentine body coiling out of the lake, right behind her. It opened its huge mouth, brandishing its great teeth, and roared once more.

10

Young-hee lay in the wet rocks and sand, feeling very, very small. The blue dragon, rumbling ferociously, was the biggest and scariest thing she had ever seen. It was so overwhelming that it took Young-hee several seconds to realize that the ghosts had all fled. Smart ghosts, she thought. Alone against a dragon, she knew there were no strategies or tricks to try.

The serpentine beast coiled and twisted, bringing his huge mouth right up the Young-hee. Two long, whisker-like tendrils hung menacingly from either side of its gaping, snorting snout. With a mouth full of razor-like teeth including fangs the size of her forearm, the monster could have easily swallowed her whole. It opened its mouth full and roared.

But as she felt its breath sweep her body, the dragon's eyes snapped to her hand, and shutting its mouth made a rumbling that sounded a lot like a deep "*Huh?*"

Then it spoke. "That ring, it summoned me, and I came. But where did a small bear daughter find a ring like that?"

"Er, a friend of mine gave it to me."

The dragon snorted, not liking her answer. "The bear daughter is a liar. I know that ring, and its owner is a good friend. You and I, however, have never met."

The monster's breath smelled like the spiced cider her mom gave to warm her up during winter in Canada. "Mansoo?"

The dragon looked surprised. "That is my true name, but it has been an age since I heard anyone use it. How did you know?"

"Bae gave me the ring and said I should look for you."

The dragon's fierce expression quickly turned soft and almost comical, the two tendrils along his nose bouncing lightly. "You know Bae? He has been a great friend for a long time."

"Yes, well, we met yesterday in the woods," said Young-hee, tactfully avoiding the part about Bae being a skeleton and dead. "I helped him, and in exchange he gave me this ring and said I should ask your help."

"Why, of course," said the gigantic serpent, its long neck and body coiling about her effortlessly, despite its bulk. One clawed foot slipped from the water, slicing the shore. "I owe him much. I would be happy to help a friend of his." His head bowed respectfully, so Young-hee bowed back, feeling somewhat ridiculous.

"I'm Young-hee. Would you happen to know of a cave around here called Darang?"

"Hello, Young-hee. Of course I do, on Mey's far side, between those mountains," he said, raising a giant claw from the water and casually pointing.

Young-hee scanned the faraway coasts. "And you wouldn't happen to know how far it is?" Shivering in her wet clothes, Young-hee blasted two sharp sneezes.

The dragon eyed her small, human legs and wet frame. "For you, quite far, I suspect," he said. "A thousand *li* if it's a *po*. But I could take you."

"Truly?" asked Young-hee, feeling torn. On one hand she really could use help, not to mention someone to talk to. On the other hand she also remembered the famous story of the Water Dragon King who tried to eat Rabbit's liver. He sounded so proud and dangerous in that tale—and he might even be the same dragon. But on the third hand (if she had more hands), the ghosts might re-appear if she tried walking around the immense lake. She'd take a chance. "A ride would be wonderful. Thank you, sir."

"Hop on," he said, pointing to the back of his head as he bent his long neck to the ground. "And 'Mansoo' is fine, please. Any friend of Bae is my friend too."

"Then, thank you, Mansoo," she said with a slight giggle. Climbing on as best she could, she happily discovered that the giant scales made excellent hand- and footholds. His neck was about the size of a large horse, and with a bit of stretching Young-hee straddled it. "Okay, I think I'm on," she said.

"Then let's go," Mansoo said cheerfully.

The blue dragon's five-clawed feet dragged its bulk into the lake, but as the water grew deeper, Young-hee felt him grow lighter and more graceful, until he was sliding through the dark blue-green water. The dragon's neck was comfortable and secure, and Young-hee settled in. For a scaly creature that Young-hee just assumed was some kind of reptile or dinosaur, the dragon was surprisingly warm. His heat radiated through her cold skin, helping dry her clothes. As the shore drifted away, Young-hee relaxed and barely needed to hold on.

After a moment's silence, Mansoo cleared his huge, dragon throat. "*Ahem,*" he rumbled. "So, how is Bae these days?"

Uh-oh, Young-hee thought. She had tried to finesse Bae's skeletal condition, but sensed that lying would not be a good idea. "Uh, dead," she said, more bluntly than she intended.

"Yes, of course. I mean besides that."

"Besides being dead, he seemed pretty well." Young-hee was relieved. He wasn't like the angry folktale king at all. The trees and hills whizzed by. "Very chatty and upbeat, especially for a spirit stuck in the ground. I put him up in the nook of a tree, with a good view of the valley."

"I bet he liked that," said Mansoo.

Beneath her body, she could feel the powerful surge of the dragon's muscles, cutting effortlessly through the lake, and a gentle pulse of speed with each flick of its mighty tail just below the surface. She felt safe for the first time in she couldn't remember when. It was a warm but distant memory she couldn't quite place, then, *"Oh,"* she recalled, *"when I was little girl, and my dad carried me on his strong shoulders.*

"You're crying," said the dragon.

Young-hee wasn't sure how he could see her face. "I'm okay," she said. "Just the wind in my eyes."

"I can slow down."

"No, I'm all right," she said, trying surreptitiously to squeeze her eyes dry with the back of a hand. Nonetheless, Mansoo slowed slightly.

After a few minutes, Mansoo spoke again. "So, why would three ghosts and the Ghost Queen be chasing a bear daughter along Lake Mey?"

"Ghost Queen? You mean the curly-haired woman on the horse? With the long veil? She was a queen?"

"Yes, with the *mongsu* veil, that was Mara, the queen of the ghosts—quite an enemy to have."

Fear and stress swamped Young-hee's short-lived calm. "*Aish*, no
…"

"It's okay," said the dragon, trying to calm his rattled passenger.
"Even the Queen of Mara is not likely to confront a blue dragon."

"But soon I'll be continuing on my journey, and you won't be
around. And I'll have someone else chasing after me and not know
why. It's so … *jigyeowo*."

"You have other things chasing you?"

"Maybe. I'm not sure. But ever since I came to Strange Land, it's
been really tough and scary." And so Young-hee told the dragon
about the dokkaebi, her brother's kidnapping, and the rest of her adventures. Mansoo listened more patiently and deeply than anyone
had in a long time, she thought. And when she finished, she watched
him carefully weigh the details and import.

"You are right to be confused," he said at last. "As others have told
you, the dokkaebi you met was most unusually cruel. But these are
unusual and cruel times. Divisions among the creatures of this land
are long-standing and growing worse. The younger spirits are tired of
the arrogance their elders, and the elders are angry at the impudence
of the young."

"Young spirits? Everything seemed so old here to me."

"You bear children do not live long enough to understand. But
even for long-lived creatures, there are ages and eras. Stories change.
Gods and spirits have come at different times. And many of the first
spirits resent the younger ones."

Young-hee thought about the old stories. "You mean since the
bear became human and gave birth to Dangun?"

"That's only one story, Young-hee. There are many others. Some
believe the world was born from an egg, sent from another world;
others that the great spirit Mireuk separated Heaven from Earth and
created the copper pillars that support your world."

"Wait, I've heard of Mireuk. My aunt said it's is another name for
the Buddha."

"Only in some stories is Mireuk the Maitreya. Older than the spirits of Buddha are those of the Tao. Older still are the first spirits, of the earth and hills and waters, stranger and angrier than the new gods. Before becoming the Maitreya, Mireuk was one of the oldest gods, and in one old version created two suns and two moons, then broke one moon into the fourteen great stars. After he created the world, he went to the grasshopper, mouse, and frog, and asked them all the meaning of justice, fire, and water. Then he decided to create humanity, holding a golden tray in one hand and a silver tray in the other. He prayed, and insects fell from the sky onto the trays, and became man and woman."

"That's deeply weird. Strange Land is so confusing."

"Strange land?" he asked.

"Yes, that's what I'm calling this world because it's so different than mine."

"Not an incorrect name" said Mansoo. "From 'stranger,' like foreigner."

"Huh? You mean in English or in Korean?"

"Yes."

"Yes which?"

"You don't know?"

"I don't even know what language I'm speaking," said Young-hee with puzzlement.

"No?"

"I mean, I assumed it was Korean, since this is all Korean magic and stories. But sometimes I'm more comfortable in English. Or … well, they're different, anyhow."

"I see."

"So what are you speaking?"

"Why my own tongue, of course," said the dragon laughing, sending a deep rumble through his long neck.

Just then, a big splash jolted Young-hee. And another, and then another. Keeping up with Mansoo's swift pace, one- and two-meter-long shapes shimmered, all fleshy pinkish-gold. "There are fish swimming with us," she said worriedly as the splashing grew. "Big fish."

"Hrm, yes. Lake Mey's many carp like swimming with the dragon."

"Isn't it good to dream of carp?" she said, remembering reading about *ingeo*—carp.

"I wouldn't know the dreams of bear children," said Mansoo. "But if dreaming of them is good, surely seeing them for real must be better."

"I read that dragons and carp are friends."

"Not enemies, but not 'friends' either. Now, turtles, they're a different matter. I've always gotten along with turtles."

"My little brother had a turtle once," said Young-hee, but thought better of telling the story. If Mansoo was a friend of turtles, he'd probably dislike how it ended … best to change topics. "So, you're a young spirit?"

The dragon laughed warily. "I have been lord of this lake for a very long time. Some might call me an old spirit. But, the truth is, I'm not much interested in the endless squabbles of the other spirits. I'm content to live peacefully in my waters."

"I just want to get my brother back and go home."

"Then perhaps that is your side."

Mansoo made steady progress. They talked some more, but at some point Young-hee fell into a deep, comfortable sleep. When she woke, the carp were gone and the Cheongyong Mountains loomed large. Even if they weren't full of evil ogres their high, unforgiving coils of snow-capped granite presented an intimidating prospect. She hoped the cave wouldn't be worse, but suspected that Strange Land's shortcuts always came with a catch.

She nibbled on a couple of kaypal cakes from her bag as Mansoo swam on. He politely rejected her offer to share, saying a young human's food was not much sustenance for a dragon. *I want to get my brother back and go home from this scary land*, but at that moment, eating magic rice cakes while gliding across a great lake on a blue dragon, Young-hee was so amazed, she almost didn't want to return to Bum. Trying to imagine his fear and her mother's worry, she felt guilty—or maybe just guilty that she didn't feel more guilty.

A cool wind whipped Young-hee's straight, dark hair. The shore raced toward them now, and mountains towered ahead. Great sheets of rock slammed straight into the water, with barely any shore separating mountain from lake. Trees clung desperately to the stony cliffs, branches and, in a straight line several feet above the lake, green needles gave way to bare bark. Young-hee thought that must be the high water mark, from when rains or melting snows swelled Lake Mey. Directly ahead among the rocks, she saw a dark spot that seemed to swallow light. Maybe it was Darang Cave.

In the setting sun Young-hee's shadow astride the dragon stretched toward the mountains. *How long had they been swimming?*

The quiet, rippling swishes of the dragon echoed off the rocks as they drew near to a lonely cove, nestled between the feet of two big mountains. Trees dotted the higher sides, gave way to patchy grass, and then yielded to stone.

Mansoo glided toward the cove's meager beach, backed by the cave's ugly maw. Its ominous darkness overwhelmed the torpid scenery. Young-hee felt a lurch as the dragon touched the lake bottom and walked forward, strength replacing grace.

Mansoo leaned over gently and she slid off, landing with a plunk, right in the middle of a line of dark, flat stones. Her path was back. It led from the water into the cave. *Why am I not surprised?* she thought.

Checking her things, she found everything in place. "Thank you so much for the ride, Mansoo," she said with unconvincing cheer.

"I owe Bae much, so I was happy to repay him a little, if only indirectly," said Mansoo, dipping his head in a slight bow.

"I don't suppose you'd be interested in coming with me?" she ventured. A dragon would be so much faster and safer.

"My home is this lake. I can leave the water, but only as a turtle, and that would help little. Please be careful in Darang Cave. It has no ogres, but legends warn of other dangers. Stay on the path and move quickly."

"Thanks, again" she said, unsurprised that more trouble awaited. The dragon took a couple of heavy steps into the lake, when Young-hee shouted after him. "Mansoo!"

He looked back at her. "Yes, Young-hee?"

"Did you really try to kill Rabbit?"

"Rabbit?"

"In a famous dragon story, you sent for Rabbit when you were sick because you needed to eat his liver to live."

"Ah, yes. And your people tell that story to each other?"

"Yeah. It's kind of famous actually—a *pansori* song and everything."

"*Hrumph*," Mansoo hrumphed. "I suspect that's Rabbit version. If you really wish to know mine … Once, when I was traveling the land in the form of a turtle, I was captured by an evil monk. Every day, after magically summoning my wife and one of our daughters, he cut open that daughter and ate her liver. Once, when the monk napped, I came on Rabbit and begged his help. Refusing, he fled in fear. And so the monk kept me prisoner, and more of my daughters died. Finally, with only one daughter left, I met an archer. Unlike Rabbit, he agreed to help. I showed him where to hide and watch. Shortly, the monk began to chant, and just when my wife and last daughter appeared, the archer fired an arrow and struck the monk in *his* liver. Wounded on the ground, the monk's magic faded revealing him to be Lady Fox, the animal spirit. I should have destroyed her then and there, but weak from long captivity, I let Fox go. The archer helped my family to the lake, and I have never left, since."

Young-hee groped for words, but all she came up with was: "I'm so sorry."

"It was long ago, and that is what Fox does," said the dragon, sounding so very old and tired. "But I appreciate your kindness, Young-hee."

Mansoo was just about to swim away, when Young-hee shouted once more. "Mansoo! The archer—was that Bae?"

"Yes," he said slipping beneath the surface with barely a ripple.

Unsure how to proceed, Young-hee sat on a square-ish, black stone and rubbed her ankles as she looked about. The only trace of Mansoo was the rhythmic slosh of tiny ripples. Across the great expanse of water she could still make out the rolling hills she had left. Beyond them was the goblin market and Bum, the jureum trees, and the way home. Each step toward the pullocho took her further from where she wanted to be.

Turning, she saw the great, jagged mouth of Darang Cave arched over a floor of broken stones. Twilight's glow lit the entrance, but as the cave quickly narrowed it dropped into black—like looking down someone's throat. *Or a dragon's gullet*, Young-hee thought, recalling her first meeting with Mansoo.

Rechecking her inventory, she removed Grandma Dol's Glory Cedar lamp. She was about to try her phone, but stopped herself. *What's the point?* At the cave, Young-hee felt dank, dead air swirl from the bowels of the mountains. She tried to ignore her dread as she lit the lamp. Ahead was only darkness. Young-hee raised her lamp and walked inside.

The Girl Who Couldn't Stop Farting

There once was a rich farmer who was sad because, try as he might, he could not find a husband for his youngest daughter. She was very beautiful, but had one big problem: She farted all the time. Really big, noisy ones.

Finally, the farmer found the son of a government official from the next province, who had not heard of the daughter's wind problem. He told his daughter, "This is your last chance. If you fart in front of your new husband or his family, they will send you back and no one will ever marry you."

The daughter and the official's son, Yi Chambong, were married and the daughter went to live with Yi's family, as was the custom. She was a good daughter-in-law and Yi's parents both liked her very much.

But after a year, the daughter grew very sick. She was pale and weak, and every movement brought her pain. Yi and his parents asked what was wrong, but she wouldn't answer. "Please tell us," they unsuccessfully implored, "so we can get a doctor and medicine to help you." But she only grew sicker each day.

Finally, the daughter relented, saying her sickness was caused by holding in her farts for over a year. "Dear girl," said the father, "break-

ing wind is embarrassing, but you should not ruin your health over something like that. If you need to pass wind, then do so."

So the daughter told everyone in the house, father-in-law, mother-in-law, husband, and servants all, to hold onto something strong and sturdy—a door, a windowsill, a big, wooden beam. Bewildered, they complied. And only once they were all secure did the girl fart.

And what a fart it was. A year's wind in one mighty break, wave after typhoon-like wave exploded as they held on tight, to keep from blowing out of the house.

When it finally finished, everyone was shocked into silence. They organized a procession to return the clearly unsuitable girl.

The journey took several days. On the way, they passed under three giant pear trees, where local villagers rested in the shade. The girl heard them say the pears were magical and could cure any illness. The villagers wanted pears for the dying king, but the only remaining fruit was on the highest branches that no one could reach, even with ladders or long poles. The villagers lamented that soon these pears would rot, their powers would be lost, and the king would die.

The daughter had an idea. "I will get those pears and save the king," she announced. The villagers laughed at her. "How could a young woman climb so high, where we men have failed?" But the daughter had no intention of climbing anything. Instead, she walked to a tree and bent over, lifting her skirt with her butt high in the air. And then the daughter farted once more, blasting mighty gusts into the air. The wind rattled the trees and knocked the pears to the ground. Her father-in-law laughed when he saw it: "Some farts are farts of blessing," he said. The villagers took the pears to the king, who ate them and lived for many more years. And they gave one pear to the daughter, who ate it and was cured of her wind problem, and the family lived long and happily.

11

Entering the huge underground cavern was easy enough. It began with a large grotto that gave way to a tunnel. She had to duck at one narrow point, but with the path under foot and her lantern in her hand, Young-hee felt confident. After several turns, the tunnel opened into a large chamber.

And it was really big—so big that the light from her lantern was swallowed by the darkness after just a few meters. While the path was mostly flat, its borders were dotted with boulders large and small. Some stalactites hung from the roof and stalagmites rose from the floor, occasionally even meeting in a solid column. After a little while the cave grew smaller, and Young-hee was able to see one side, then both, and then the roof, too. But before it grew too small, it opened up again, expanding into infinite blackness.

And so the path continued, through vast halls and narrow corridors—fortunately without signs of bats or spiders or anything living. The path wound steadily downward, utterly silent, save for the *tuk-tuk, tuk-tuk* of Young-hee's footsteps. It was a totally different from the quiet of the forest with its rustling of leaves and distant sounds of birds or tiny animals scurrying through the underbrush. In the enveloping, almost physical silence and darkness, without life's distractions, Young-hee really was alone with her thoughts, which steadily grew wilder and more random: *Will I ever get Bum back? What's mom up to now? Am I missing a lot of homework? Will anyone notice my Facebook page hasn't been updated? How long have I been gone in mud-world time?*

Sometimes she didn't notice the *tuk-tuk* of her steps, but other times their regular thumping rang in her ears like a lumberjack chopping down a great tree; sometimes, she was unaware of her breathing, then it seemed as loud as a summer storm. And once in a while, she'd stop, cover the lamp with her jacket and feel the most complete darkness and silence she had ever known. *Is this what it will feel like when I'm dead? What if this darkness is all there is forever?*

Maybe I'm on the verge of waking up, and this adventure will disappear, like a dream.

She lost all sense of time and direction. She had gotten a little hungry only once, and nibbled on a rice ball. Her feet hurt the way they had at the end of her first day in the forest. She took a break, sitting against a large stone at the path's edge, intending to rub her feet and then get going again. But she woke some time later—still in the cave, in the dark, unaware of actually falling asleep. Fortunately, the lantern candle was going strong. She didn't want to waste it, but wouldn't have wanted to wake to total blackness either. She checked it and found that less than half was used, and silently thanked Grandma Dol. With three more candles in her bag, Young-hee figured she could walk quite a while before worrying about losing the light.

And then, so far away she could barely hear it, was the slightest, softest of noises. She stood in place, straining to tell if it was just her imagination. As she walked on, the noise gradually built into the rippling, dancing sound of water. Not a lot, and still far off, but clearly water. She guessed it was another thirty minutes before she found the underground stream. It emerged from a crack in the rock as a small waterfall, then followed the path as it wound through the tunnel. The water was perfectly clear and cool. She held the light up but couldn't see fish or insects or anything in it.

After perhaps an hour, the stream disappeared, speeding up as it slid under a rocky wall. There was a dull, distant rumbling, like a plummeting waterfall nearby. After so much silence, she appreciated the sound and felt sad that it would soon drop away again. She filled her water bottle and kept going. Soon, there was only the little wooden lamp and the echo of her footsteps. *Tuk-tuk, tuk-tuk.*

The unending gloom had induced a kind of trance when, suddenly, she stopped short. She could swear she heard the sound. Perhaps a scuff? Maybe even a cough. She held her lamp higher and saw nothing but rocks that quickly faded to gray and then black.

She thought about following the sound, but there was no way she'd risk leaving the path and having it vanish, not down here. She was lucky in the forest to find the stream after losing the path. In this cave, she could be stuck forever—well, not forever, just until a rather icky end.

Scritch, came the sound again, and she thought she could tell its source. *Maybe it was just a bat or some rodent kind of creature?* But that didn't make her feel any better, and she quickly wished she could unthink it. "*Hello?*" she called out tentatively. "Is anyone there?"

She squinted and peered, and then, there it was—a shadow stepped from behind a large, rocky column. Something human, or at least human-shaped. It stood motionless, just beyond the light of her lantern. "Uh, hello?" Young-hee repeated.

"Greetings, stranger," rang out a young man's voice, high-toned and quivering slightly, as if he trying hard to sound cheery. "Welcome to my somewhat unfortunate and dim abode." With a step forward, he entered the outer limit of her lamp's glow—a tall, thin young man, wrapped in a ragged, faded hanbok. "I must say, you are the first person I have seen in a very long time."

"Hi there, I'm Young-hee," and unsure of what else to say, added, "Is this your home?"

"Home? No. Well, it's where I live, at least for the moment, that's true, but not altogether voluntarily."

"Not altogether voluntarily?" she echoed.

"No. Alas, I was captured by the demon who rules this cave, Yeonggam. Terribly clumsy of me, actually." The shadowy man raised a foot and gave it a jerk, jangling the chain tethering him to a rock.

"That's horrible. Have you been here long?"

"Longer than I would have preferred. I quite dislike being a prisoner."

"Of course," said Young-hee, thinking of her brother. "No one likes being a captive."

"I'm so glad you think so," said the young man eagerly. He slid forward a few more inches, and Young-hee's flickering lantern set his sharp features in distinct relief and illuminated an explosion of thick black hair, streaked with color. His eyes gleamed with the cool grace of a tiger. "Allow me to introduce myself. I'm the Samjogo."

"*The* Samjogo?"

"Yes, the one and only. The truest of the true bone."

"But is that your name? Or what you are?

"Why, a Samjogo is me. And I am a Samjogo."

"Yes, but, what I meant was …"

"Oh, I know well what you meant," he said, his words dancing lightly. "I am Samjogo, the three-legged crow of legend, true of bone and never born."

Surveying the decidedly two-legged man, Young-hee's eyebrows arched with more skepticism than she knew possible. "You don't look like a three-legged crow."

"Pish, posh," he said with a dismissive wave. "You should know by now not to be deceived by appearances. '*All that's gold doesn't glitter.*'"

"I think that's backwards."

"And I assure you, the Samjogo is legendary. More powerful than a dragon. Shining brighter than the phoenix."

"And yet you're chained to a rock. In the dark."

"Yes, that," he said, momentarily glum, and tugged on his chain.

Young-hee could feel he was going to be irritating. "Well, it's been nice meeting you. But I really should be going."

"Please, don't go," he called. "Not yet. The thing is, I could use some help."

"What could I do," she said, looking warily at the edge of the path.

"Well, would you have something I could use to free myself? Perhaps a releasing spell on you?" the Samjogo asked. "A small vial of dragon tears? A star key? Perhaps a shaman's lock curse?"

"Uh, no. Sorry."

"No, no, no, I understand," he said, disappointed, before taking one more stab: "Floral silver?"

"Floral silver? No. I mean, yes. I mean, not anymore."

"You lost your floral silver?"

"No, a rabbit gave me some, but it isn't floral silver anymore. The thing is, when I went through this door, see, the silver turned to dead flowers."

The Samjogo looked at her steadily, weighing her words. "But do you have those dead flowers?"

"Yes, actually. But I don't see how they could help."

"Please," he said, holding out his hand.

Young-hee puffed out her cheeks as she debated with herself. She wanted to get going, and was reluctant to trust a stranger, especially in a deep, dark cave. Finally, though, she found the handkerchief in a pocket and unfolded it. Despite her forest tumbles and river swim, it had survived, but looked less like a bracelet than ever. "How can I get it to you?" she asked. "It's too light to throw that far."

"It's okay, just walk over and give it to me."

Young-hee looked at the line where the path met the regular cave floor and the darkness extending around it. "I can't leave the path."

"Pardon me?"

"The path, I can't leave it."

"Oh, there's a path. That wasn't there before."

"I left it once, and it just disappeared. I was lucky to find it again, but if I lose it here, in this cave, I'll never find my way out again."

"Ah, yes, a questing path. They can be frightfully unstable."

"You know them?"

"Of course. Many people have them."

"You don't?"

"On the rare occasions I acquire one, the first thing I always do is step off and get rid of it. Paths are terrible things, always getting in the way of living."

"Very free-spirited of you. But, in my case, I need my path. I'm on a quest."

"Oh, really? You seem young to have your own path already."

"Yeah, lucky me." She stood, thinking. "So these paths work the same for everyone?"

"What do you mean?"

"They disappear if you step off of them? And they split into all sorts of side-paths when you try to go back?"

"Yes, that is the nature of a journey."

"*Aish.* Not where I'm from. In my world, a path's a path. It doesn't change." She thought about it a bit. "In my life, the paths are the opposite. When I look ahead, all I see are choices, but looking back, it's like there's only ever been one path."

"Fascinating," said Samjogo, not sounding at all fascinated. "But do you think you could get me those no-longer-floral-silver leaves? Before the demon returns? Perhaps you could weight it with a stone and throw it to me."

Young-hee tied the handkerchief to a rock as best she could then tossed it toward the Samjogo. It arched through the air and landed right at his feet. Unfortunately, the handkerchief had opened and the dead flowers fluttered to the ground halfway between them.

"Well, that didn't go as well as I had hoped," he said, still straining to sound optimistic.

"Sorry about that," said Young-hee, embarrassed. "But I think I've done all I can. I really do need to be going."

"No, please. Just stay a moment," said Samjogo, all flustered. "Just one moment." He looked at the dead flowers fell, thinking. "You know, I know these caves very well. Even if the path were to disappear—and it might not—I could lead you to Lake Mey?" he said, pointing ahead of her.

"No, I came from there," she said, raising a thumb in the opposite direction. "Lake Mey's that way. I was trying to get under the mountains."

"Oh," said the Samjogo, trying not to look crestfallen. "And why there, if you don't mind my asking?"

"I need to get to the Sacred City. Do you know it?"

"It is indeed most famous. But, alas, I have never been there."

"Yeah, well, you're not the only one. I was told it was this way. Somewhere near the Great Forest, wherever that is. Perhaps close to the animal ladies, wherever they are. So this path is the only clue I have."

"The animal ladies?"

"You know them?"

"Yes, they are well known across this realm. And much feared. I have not heard of anyone seeking their company by choice."

"Well, it's not really my choice. They are one of my few clues, and I need the path if I hope to find them."

"I see...," said Samjogo, thinking. "You said you lost the path before?"

"Yeah, when I stepped off."

"But you're on it now."

"When I got down from the dragon, the path was there again."

"Off a drag ...," said Samjogo with amazement before cutting himself off. "Anyhow, the important thing is, the path came back. So, it stands to reason, even if the path disappears again, it will reappear further on."

"I'm not sure I like that thinking at all."

"Yes, I promise you—I can lead you to the other side of the Cheongyong Mountains. And, if you lose your path, help you find it again."

"I'm sorry, but that's just too risky."

"Please, I've been a prisoner for so long. And, Yeonggam, the demon who chained me is quite terrible, even by demon standards."

"Why did he lock you up, anyway?"

"Demons do terrible things. I suspect he's aging me a bit before eating me—like a pot of pickled kimchi."

The thought made Young-hee sad—the being eaten part, not the kimchi. It was what the dokkaebi threatened to do to Bum. *I can't leave someone here in the darkness to get eaten by a demon.* Sometimes, you just have to do what you think is right, even if it's really stupid. She took a step forward and left the path.

It was hard to find the scattered, little pieces of dead flowers on the dusty cave floor, especially by candlelight, but she managed to gather a pile about the same size as what she had thrown.

Young-hee looked behind her. "Oh, *crud*," she said. "I knew it, the path's gone. *Jigyeowo!*" She scrunched her face in a ball of annoyance. Then she forced herself to breathe. "I really hope you're not lying to me."

"The Samjogo is a noble bird and he would never break his word," he said defiantly, taking the dusty petals into his hand. He held them close and examined them carefully, picking out specks of dirt. With his mouth open, he breathed a warm breath on the flowers, and lowered his hand to the chain. For a second, nothing—but then a warm, blue glow, and the chain fell off his ankle. The flowers faded into nothing. "It worked!" he laughed. "I'm free! For the first time in ages, and I have you to thank, Ms. Young-hee."

"I thought they were just dead flowers."

"They were. But floral silver is strong magic, and enough magic remained to break my lock." The Samjogo stepped boldly, kicking out with his freed foot. "I enjoy my freedom and have long made it a point to know all the unbinding magicks and techniques, should the need arise."

"*Aish*, I bet I could have used that to free my brother," she muttered sadly.

"Your brother?" he said, curious.

"I don't want to talk about it, not again. Can you please just help me out of this cave?"

"Of course. As easy as eating cold *chook*, as they say. I made a promise, and intend to keep it." He marched ahead confidently. "Come, the Samjogo is powerful, but I still need your lamp light."

"That's the wrong way."

"Yes, I was just scouting," he said, making a smooth about-face. "'Wherever a bird roosts, its feathers fall.' 'A rolling stone gathers no moss.'"

Shooting pains of annoyance jabbed just behind Young-hee's eyes. "Fine, let's get going."

Without the path, the cave was much tougher to navigate. The floor was rockier and more uneven. When a chamber opened wide, it was tough to find where the main route continued. And sometimes there were several options. In the lamplight, Young-hee examined her strange companion, trying to get a sense of him. He wore a casual, not-terribly-clean hanbok, with a gray *jeogori* jacket, yellow vest, and white-ish leggings. His clothing revealed the odd tension of someone who cares deeply about his appearance, but completely lacks the ability to keep tidy. After so long underground, he could see fairly well in dim light, and scouted the way while keeping up a cheery flow of banter. It was annoying—and probably not a good way to hide their presence from any unfriendly creatures—but after her long solitude, Young-hee appreciated the company and resolved to be positive. At least until they got out.

Young-hee tried to keep quiet about who she was and why she was making this long journey, but in the course of polite conversation she let out more than she intended—including that a problem with a dokkaebi had sparked her quest. "A dokkaebi?" he exclaimed, eagerly. "Silly creatures. Easy to outwit. One time, after a long day's hike in the hills, night fell as black as any night ever, as dark as this cave. Unable to go on, I rested on a grassy gravesite, and as, I snacked on half a melon, a dokkaebi came by. 'Is that you, skeleton?' he asked. It was too dark for him to see me, but I could tell he was a dokkaebi from his ashen smell, like an old fireplace.

"So I told him, 'Yes, it's me,' but I must have sounded different, because he angrily demanded who I was. I dropped my voice, trying to sound all dead and scary. 'No, my friend, it's really me. Here, touch my head,' I said, holding out the melon skin. 'Yes,' he said, 'it seems like your hairless head.' He still didn't sound convinced, so I held out my walking stick. 'And here, touch my arm.'

"'Ah, you have a skinny, bony arm, like you starved to death. You must be my friend skeleton.'

" 'What brings you out tonight?' I asked, and he told me his plan to steal the soul of the daughter of a rich landlord. I went along and watched him steal her soul, and put it in a little canvas bag. I told him I would keep it safe until the next night. He gave it to me and vanished. A few hours later, I went to the landlord's home, where everyone was mourning the daughter, who had died mysteriously in the night. I asked to see her privately, and once the door closed, opened the bag and returned her soul. She woke as if nothing had ever been wrong."

"That was really nice of you," said Young-hee, wondering what it would take to stop him from talking. She looked about as they walked into another large cavern. "What did the landlord do?"

"Oh, he was overjoyed, of course. He offered me the girl's hand in marriage and half his fortune. But the Samjogo is not tied down so easily. I took a modest reward and went on my way. It's a vast world, with much so see."

Young-hee tried gauging the vast emptiness of this latest cavern. Black was black, pretty much impossible to estimate, but Young-hee noticed the echo of Samjogo's voice getting deeper and delaying more, until the echo, too, was swallowed by darkness. This was the largest cave chamber yet, she thought. *What was this place?* "Didn't the dokkaebi come back to get you? I bet he was mad."

"I bet he was angry too. But the Samjogo has more tricks up his sleeve. One time, when walking through the mountains with noth-ing but a drum, I …" At long last, he went quiet, but the way he just stopped mid-sentence didn't fill Young-hee with confidence. Then she caught up and saw what silenced him.

Ahead, in the inky-gray distance of her lamp's light, was a tree. Huge and full of leaves, despite growing in the black of the cave. As they approached, more shapes emerged—something like a barn, a stone house, unkempt hedges, and perhaps a well. A big stone wall surrounded the property, crumbling in places, including where the path cut through.

"What is this?" Young-hee asked.

"This is the home of probably the worst ogre in a hundred realms, Agwi Kwisin, the nine-headed ogre. His is a very exciting story, with a noble warrior and a princess, betrayals, a magical life-giving pullo-cho, and Agwi the ogre."

"A pullocho?!" exclaimed Young-hee. "There was one here? In this cave?"

"Well, it's a famous part of the ogre's story, that much is for cer-tain. If I recall the tale correctly, it was…" But before Samjogo could finish, a loud, sulfurous *blam* exploded a few feet from them. Stand-ing in the center of the stinky cloud, was a hideous creature, seven feet tall, completely misshapen from head to toe, wearing dark armor, holding a jagged spear, and covered in a glow of blue flames.

"What is *that?*" cried Young-hee, shielding her eyes from the flames.

"Oh, him," deadpanned the Samjogo. "That would be Yeonggam, the demon of this cave. I would imagine he's pretty upset that I've been freed. And even more angry at the one who freed me."

Agwi Kwisin the Nine-Headed Ogre and the Warrior

Long ago, when the Tiger used to smoke, there lived a terrible ogre named Agwi Kwisin in the mountains of a beautiful kingdom. The huge, nine-headed rock monster would descend from his secret mountain cave and, armed with a great sword, ravage the land, stealing food, destroying villages, and sometimes taking young women.

One day, he stole the king's three beautiful daughters. The distraught king promised a great reward and the youngest daughter's hand in marriage for the return his daughters. But none would risk facing the monster, even for the reward.

Then a mysterious warrior came to the palace and said he would return the daughters. The courtiers laughed, finding the young warrior neither frightening nor famous. But the king, happy to have someone willing to try, offered three servants to help on the quest.

The warrior searched the kingdom's mountains and forests for weeks and months, but found no ogre. The three servants complained endlessly, and begged for permission to abandon the fruitless quest and return to the nice palace. But the warrior refused and persisted.

One day, they came across an old man sitting calmly under a tree, cooking soup on a fire. The servants ordered the man to give them the fire and food—because they were with the king. But the warrior told them to treat their elders with respect and apologized to the old man. Thanking the warrior for his kindness, the man revealed that he was in fact the great Mountain Spirit, Sanshin. He offered to share his soup and, as they ate, the warrior explained his quest. Taking pity, Sanshin advised, "Go past this mountain, then the next, and finally on the third, halfway up, you will find a big cave. Deep down in the cave you will find the ogre."

Then Sanshin thrust a bag into the coals, and it came out full of ashes. He held them out, saying the warrior might find them useful, especially if outnumbered.

The warrior thanked Sanshin and started walking with renewed purpose. And as promised, halfway up the third mountain was the cave and, far back within it, a great hole so dark and deep he couldn't see the bottom.

So the warrior tied all their ropes together, and anchored it to a big rock. "Servant, I will tie you to this rope, lower you into the cave. Tell us what you find." But the servant was too scared. "Just yank on the rope twice if you are in any danger," the warrior reassured, "and we will pull you right up."

The servant agreed, but he was not down long when the warrior, felt a tug, and pulled up the servant. The warrior turned to the second servant, but he was even more scared and yanked the rope after only a short way. The third servant did not make it much farther. "Okay," said the warrior, "I shall go myself. Stay here until I return."

The servants lowered the warrior deeper and deeper into the cave. It was vast and very dark, but gradually his eyes adjusted, and he saw a whole farm in the hole, with trees, giant buildings and more.

The warrior untied himself and went carefully forward. By one tree, not far from the huge, stone farmhouse, he found a well. Hearing someone approach, hid behind some bushes and spied one of the king's daughters, drawing water. Seeing her alone, the warrior emerged and introduced himself, saying the king had sent him to free his daughters.

She thanked him, looking him over, decided there was no way the warrior could beat the ogre. "Do you see that large rock near where you hid? Can you lift it?" The warrior tried and tried, but barely moved it. "If you cannot lift that rock, you can't defeat the ogre. His skin is like stone, and he can carry an ox in one arm. His sword weighs more than you." But then the princess had an idea. "Wait here," she said, as she turned and quickly walked away.

She returned with a strange piece of ginseng. "This is no ordinary ginseng," she revealed. "It is pullocho, a magical ginseng. Eat it." Every day the warrior ate the pullocho the princess brought, and every day felt stronger. Finally, after two weeks, the warrior could lift the rock.

"Good, you're ready," she said. "The ogre attacks our land for one-third of the year, does nothing but eat for another third, and only sleeps for the other third. He'll wake soon, so you must try to kill him tonight."

The princess took the warrior to the ogre's bedroom. The huge monster filled a huge bed, his nine heads (all snoring loudly) spread across nine pillows. His rocky hide rumbled as he tossed and turned. The princess gave the warrior the ogre's huge sword and, thanks to the pullocho's power, with one huge swing he cut off all nine heads.

Unfortunately, that only served to awaken the now-headless and extra-angry ogre. He swung at the warrior with his immense, stony hands even as he tried to recapture his heads full of huge, thick, snapping teeth. Dodging the jaws and arms, the warrior managed to cut off one of the ogre's hands, but the dismembered hand kept fighting too.

Nearing exhaustion, the warrior suddenly remembered Sanshin's advice. He grabbed the spirit's bag, opened it, and threw ashes at the hand. When they touched the severed hand, it turned to simple stone and stopped moving. Dodging the ogre's body, the warrior peppered the necks with more ashes, and the body stopped moving, too. With only the heads left, the warrior covered them with ashes, and they also stopped moving.

The princess was so happy to be free, but there still was work to do. They opened all the ogre's barns. In one were all the animals the ogre had stolen from the kingdom; in another, the princess's sisters, nearly dead from hunger. A third barn held all the ogre's stolen gold and jewels. So they loaded a cart with the jewels, freed the animals, and made their way to the rope. First, the warrior sent up the three princesses, then the jewels and gold. But when it was the warrior's turn, the rope did not move. He yanked on it, but no one pulled him up.

The evil servants had ticked him and stolen the princesses and treasure! The warrior climbed the rope to the top, but the servants had covered the hole with a stone so huge that even his pullocho strength could not budge it.

The warrior returned to the bottom of the empty cave to think. He heard a donkey approaching from the darkness and as it got closer, saw someone riding on its back—Sanshin.

The Mountain Spirit gave the donkey to the warrior and told him to ride into the cave, toward the tallest tree. There, at the back of the cave, the warrior discovered a small path. Riding the uncomplaining donkey, he followed it for days, through the endless darkness, and last came into the light.

The warrior rode the long journey back to the palace. There the king was feasting with the servants, celebrating his daughters' return. The king was surprised when warrior rode up on a donkey, because the servants had said he died fighting the ogre. When the warrior explained, the king had the wicked servants beheaded. He gave the warrior his prettiest daughter to marry, a great estate, and many treasures, and the kingdom enjoyed peace for many years.

12

The demon's lumpy, flaming armor clanked heavily as it menaced Young-hee and Samjogo with his spear. Large, misshapen fangs jutted from its mouth at odd angles, and three bumpy horns covered its forehead. Long hairs, thick as broom bristles, shot from its eyebrows and sideburns. A cool, blue flame licked its skin and hair without burning, sometimes dripping like water. The monster emanated a foulness and evil Young-hee felt deep inside. *I guess there's no chance this guy turns out friendly like Mansoo*, Young-hee thought, eyeing the jagged blade.

"Little bird," cackled the demon to Samjogo in his hoarse, bitter voice, "who opened your cage?" He gestured, and from his hand, a strand of blue flame dripped and transformed into two thin chains. "I think this creature wants to join you as my guest."

"Yeonggam, old friend, it's good to see you again," laughed Samjogo, shielded Youghee with one arm, and remarked, "I highly recommend against his hospitality—it's far too permanent."

"Samjogo," sneered the monster, "struggling will only make your meat more gamey, and I'll have to age you all the longer." As it jostled the magical chains, pools of flame gathered at its feet. "Don't be rude now. These dark caves are mine, and I have certain obligations as host. Introduce me to your friend. I like to have a friendly relationship with my meals."

With his shoulder, Samjogo edged Young-hee away. "I don't suppose you have any sort of blade on you?" asked Samjogo, never taking his eyes off of Yeonggam.

"Not even a sharp stick."

"In that case, I have what I think is an excellent suggestion," said Samjogo. "Run! Fast!" Before Young-hee could react, the Samjogo disappeared into the darkness, leaving her with her lantern and the demon. Not good. Then Young-hee ran, too.

"Where do my dainties think they are going?" the demon called out, amused. "There's nowhere to run. This cave is all mine." Young-hee sprinted past the tree and ducked behind the stone wall. Coming closer, the demon's steps crunched on the rocky cave floor. "I can see you," it sing-songed.

Only then did Young-hee remember her lamp. *Stupid!* she cursed herself. Covering it, she was enveloped by darkness—except for Yeonggam's blue glow—coming steadily nearer.

"I'm not a creature of sun," it chuckled. "I don't need lanterns to see in the dark. Please, feel free to run and hide. I like a little dinner entertainment."

She gathered herself, thinking if she couldn't hide, she could at least run, and took off full speed toward the barn. Shadows from her lantern bounced ahead of her. She hoped Samjogo was lurking nearby, ready to pounce, but he seemed completely missing. *More powerful than a dragon. Right*, she thought. Maybe a nine-headed ogre would show up to fight the demon for her. Of course, with her luck, the two would be friends, and would only fight over her best meat.

She searched the structures for an escape, but each moment looking was a moment not distancing herself from the demon. *Crunch, crunch, crunch* came its steady footsteps. Desperately reaching, she found something like a handle—she pushed then pulled, shoved then yanked, but the door stuck fast.

The blue glow shone brighter as the *crunch-crunch* got louder. The demon was right there. She turned to tug on the door one more time, but in her fear and haste Young-hee dropped her lantern. It hit the ground with a heavy *clunk*, and the light blinked out. The silent darkness that blanketed her in emptiness was pricked only by the steady *crunch, crunch, crunch* and the flick of dull blue flame. In a moment, he would be upon her.

Young-hee fled straight into the darkness, hands in front to avoid colliding with a cave or building wall. Instead, her foot slammed into something immobile, and she heard the demon laugh as she fell heavily, scraping her hands and bashing her toe. "Okay, dinner, that's enough," the demon called. "Stop running before I get upset." But Young-hee rose and ran through the pain, as hard as before. "*Hrumph*," the demon said disdainfully, "I told you to *stop!*" A crackling, whooshing filled the air, and a jet of blue flame shot past Young-hee's face. She recoiled and fell again, frightened by the heat and noise. A sickly smell hung in the air, and she realized it was her singed hair. *This is bad. Bad-bad-bad.*

As the burning monster approached, Young-hee saw that a flaming blast had hit the ground near the great tree, lighting the center of the cavern. She ran toward it, muscles pumping, lungs bursting, oblivious to Yeonggam's vile insults. She ran to the tree and then, not knowing how she did it, powered straight up the trunk, like a terrified cat. Reaching branches, she grabbed on and climbed. Up and up she went, until the branches became thinner and swayed threateningly. She struggled to breathe and clear her mind.

Far below, the blue, fiery demon paced. "You know," he said, "if I was trying to escape a creature who controlled fire, I wouldn't hide in a tree." With a great *thwack* of his spear, flames danced across the bark. "But that's just me. No judgments."

"For an ancient creature of myth and tradition," she shouted defiantly, "you're quite a big jerk."

"That may be the case," he said frowning, "but I'm the one holding the giant, flaming spear." He stabbed the tree again, harder, deeper, and this time, it started to burn.

Young-hee looked for the cave roof, or somewhere to flee. But no such luck. The flames rose up the trunk, larger and hungrier. "I don't suppose there's anything I could trade, in exchange for letting me go?"

"Sorry. I'm a simple demon. I don't collect trinkets. I just want some barbecued girl."

"I'm not a girl," Young-hee sniffed. If she was going to die, she it would be on her terms—defiant. "And you'll never get what you need to be happy."

Below, Yeonggam's fiery hand merged with the burning tree. "*Happy?*" he repeated quizzically. "I'm a demon. I'm supposed to be miserable. But, in my own way I will enjoy tearing the burnt meat from your bones, little bear daughter."

The demon started licking his lips, but suddenly his expression changed. His lips curled and parted. He coughed and clutched his throat. With horrid, bloody suddenness, a huge sword, wide as Young-hee's leg, burst from the demon's neck. A moment later, his head came clean off, rolling from his shoulders and disappearing in the darkness. Behind the demon stood Samjogo, holding a ludicrously large sword.

" 'If you can't climb the tree, you shouldn't look up at it,' as they say. Honestly, though, that saying never really made a lot of sense before. Now, I like it."

Young-hee looked down in shock. "Is he dead?"

"Just a moment," said the Samjogo, wiping demon effluvia from his eyes. Then, with a great heave, he swung the sword in a big arc and split the demon's body in half. "Yeah, I think that about does it." The lanky young man slumped to the ground, exhausted.

Young-hee was disgusted by the gore, but also unbelievably happy to be have survived—until she realized the tree was still burning. "I don't mean to sound ungrateful, but I'm still in some trouble here."

"Yes, of course," Samjogo said, standing with great effort. "You can't jump?"

"I'd break a leg, at least. That ground is all rock." A wave of thick smoke made Young-hee cough uncontrollably and stung her eyes. Through acrid tears, she looked for something to cushion her fall, but saw only stone—and the fire racing to the branches where she clung.

Then the Samjogo had an idea. "Young-hee, do you see the well?"

She peered through billowing smoke and there, a few meters from the tree, a circle of stones surrounded a deep, dark hole. "Yeah, I see it."

"If you can jump that far, there's water in it. Then I'll fish you out."

"Are you serious?"

"I don't know. Are you fireproof?"

A rather compelling argument, Young-hee thought. She threw

her cloak and bag and things beyond the reach of the fire, which was now perilously close. Soon her supporting branches would break.

With no time and no other options, Young-hee lined up the angle and distance and jumped. As she fell through the flames, everything grew very hot. Then inside the stone hole, darkness, a rush of wind, and a terrifying lack of control. She bounced off the side, but before she noticed the pain she plunged into freezing water, and for a moment she had no idea which way was up or where she was. But she followed the bubbles of air that rushed inexorably to the surface and felt cool air.

"Hello?" she called, coughing as she treaded water. High above, blue flames lit the air. "Samjogo? I'm here! I'm okay," she said. "Please help."

Something landed with a splat. A rope, and it led to the silhouette of a young man with crazy hair leaning over the mouth of the well. "Sorry, it took a moment to find a rope. Hold tight, and I'll pull you out."

Young-hee wrapped the rope around her hands. She held on as it tightened, pinching off the blood to her fingers. But she rose out of the water to the sound of Samjogo's grunts. At the well's edge, awkwardly, she pulled herself out and onto the ground, unwrapped her sore hands, and lay exhausted. Behind her, the tree cracked and burned, warming the air and lighting up the cavern like holiday fireworks.

"Thanks," she said, coughing.

"It was the least I could do. I owed you for freeing me," said Samjogo, slouching on the ground, splattered with demon gore. "This is the home of Agwi Kwisin the Nine-headed Ogre, so I went hunting for a weapon. As luck would have it I found the old monster's giant dagger. Not exactly a graceful weapon, and almost too big to lift, but, apparently, enough."

"I didn't need to be saved gracefully. But I hope that Agwi ogre guy doesn't show up."

"Huh?" said Samjogo, confused. "Oh, he's dead."

"What?"

"Had all his heads chopped off by some overambitious hero type. Ages ago."

"He's dead?" shouted Young-hee, exasperated. "You could have started with that."

"Well, I was going to mention it. But I got a distracted, what with the flaming blue demon and all."

"*Jigyeowo*," she grumbled. Then she remembered the story Samjogo had stared to tell before the fire demon showed up. "Wait, you said this troll …"

"Ogre."

"Ogre, fine, had a pullocho? The 'magic, life-giving ginseng of the Heavens?' "

"Oh, yes," Samjogo nodded merrily. "Certainly. Well, almost certainly. At least, that's the story."

"So it could still be here?"

Samjogo stood and started brushing himself off. "I don't see why not."

Young-hee sprang up, forgetting her wet clothes, sore hands and singed hair. "If it's here, I've got to find it."

As she scurried, randomly looking for the root, a great crack split the air, the tree fell and a ball of magical blue flame billowed hot sparks in chaotic swirls across the cavern. Young-hee kept exploring. *If a tree could grow here, surely a pullocho could, too.*

"Where's your lantern, Young-hee?" asked the Samjogo. "When that tree is consumed, it'll be pretty dark again." Young-hee, annoyed by the interruption, flicked her hand toward the barn, where Samjogo found it. "Any more candles? This one is about finished," he said, lighting the remaining candle stump with a burning branch.

Young-hee hunted furiously through the thin dirt covering the rocky cave floor. "Where would I find a pullocho? The dokkaebi said something about the shadow of some tree. This isn't the Sacred City, but it is a big tree. …or *was*," she corrected herself. "But does a tree in darkness even have a shadow?"

Samjogo half-heartedly looked at the ground. "It's been ages since Agwi Kwisin lived here. Or anyone else. I doubt you will find anything as valuable as a pullocho."

"You found a sword, strong enough to kill a demon," she said.

"A *dagger*. I could never have lifted Agwi Kwisin's sword."

"Whatever. The point is, I don't think anyone ever really checked out this cave." Young-hee grabbed a flaming branch to help her search.

"Maybe there's something inside the house," Samjogo shrugged and walked off. "Besides, I need to clean off these demon guts."

Young-hee kept searching, but found only bushes and smaller versions of the tree now rapidly becoming coals and ash. Her chest grew tight, as if someone were playing cat's cradle with her heart.

She moved on to the large barns. She fumbled with one huge wooden door, and this time it opened. Inside was rotting timber, a bit of messy straw, and the vague smell of ancient animal dung. *It must have housed livestock,* she thought, remembering the farms she visited with her friends outside Toronto. *Wait, don't mushrooms grow in poop?* Just to be safe, she combed through the barn, even poking at the petrified poop with a stick. But whatever the building once was, it had been empty for a long time. And the next building was even emptier than the first.

"Now, this is more like it," said Samjogo, even more jauntily than usual. Young-hee jumped, surprised by his voice as he sauntered into the barn, swinging a long wooden stick tipped with a nasty blade. "This is a really fine *hyeopdo*, which happens to be my weapon of choice. And the right size for a Samjogo."

"No pullocho?"

"I'm afraid not," he said cheerily, "just a cracking hyeopdo." In between mock cuts, he looked around. "Agwi must have kept one barn for treasure, one for animals, and one for kidnapped maidens. The knight who killed the ogre looted pretty thoroughly. Except for this hyeopdo."

"Knight? So you think the old story was true?"

"As true as any story ever is. The main house certainly looks like an ogre's—but with nothing left but huge bones and hide, thicker than any elephant's. And a stack of big, ugly heads."

"Ew," she said. It sounded gross … and cool. "Show me!" If she couldn't find a pullocho, at least she could check out dead ogre remains.

Proud as a cat with a half-eaten mouse, Samjogo took her to the main house. *I don't know what he's so pleased about. He didn't kill the ogre.* Scattered around a huge, hard bed, the ogre parts lay flaking and crumbling into dirt and dust. Each head, nearly as big as Young-hee, was frozen into expressions of fury and pain. She wondered if the ogre died once for each head or just once for the body, and almost felt sorry for the immense creature.

"Ogre beds are nearly as hard as stone, but a bit better than the cave floor," said Samjogo. "How about you get some sleep? Fighting demons is tiring work."

"I'm not tired," said Young-hee crabbily. The fire's pale blue light still shimmered with a creepy glow.

"Well, I need some rest," said Samjogo. "The ogre's chair is big enough for me to lie in. You take the bed."

"Great," said Young-hee, not sure she could climb up on it—or sleep in the same room as the ogre remains.

"I should be able to get you to the mouth of the cave, past the Cheongyong Mountains, after one day's good, long hike. It will be good to see the sun again."

"But I'll still be just as lost, without a path," she said climbing a crumbled piece of ogre to the bed.

"Nonsense. Get some sleep, and we'll figure details in the morning."

Young-hee was ready to argue some more. Was now day or night? Would they find the path? Could she fall asleep on the creepy, dusty bed? What if the ogre parts came back to life? Would Samjogo abandon her? But before she could to start arguing, she was already asleep.

13

Young-hee gasped as she woke in blackness so all-encompassing that she feared she had gone blind. She groped for the edge of the bed, before remembering how high it was.

"*Samjogo!*" she called into the terrible quiet. "As you there?" Had he left her by herself? As she sat in the void, she realized how sore her body was. Her whole right side ached from bouncing off the well wall, and her right wrist was too sensitive to take any weight or pressure. Her eyes still stung from the smoke. The battle with the fire demon had taken a lot out of her.

And where she left her bag? She had brought it to bed, she thought. Carefully she felt about until—success. She ran her hand inside, feeling the carefully wrapped foods, coins, and then a candle. *Yes!* But her victory was brief. She couldn't find matches. Perhaps she had given them to Samjogo?

Just then, she heard very faint scuffing noises and hoped it was not an ogre, demon or ghosts. "Samjogo?" she called again, louder. A glimpse of light reached in the window—not much, but definitely a wobbling glow. It had the warm yellow of her lantern.

The scuffing now sounded like footsteps. "Young-hee?" came a distant voice. "I'm coming." The footsteps fell faster and louder. It was Samjogo.

The light bobbed past the window to the door, where Samjogo entered, looking upset. "Very sorry, Young-hee. I woke earlier and thought I'd look for that pullocho you so need. I lost track of time."

"I was worried you had left me."

"I would not do that. I promised to help you," he said, looking hurt. Then his eyes lit. "Oh, I found this!" he said excitedly, pointing at a bow and a quiver with a single arrow.

"Great. One arrow."

"It's not for hunting."

Young-hee was confused. "Did you find anything else?"

"No, sadly. No pullocho. There's very little left, just plates and knickknacks. For an ogre, Agwi Kissin was quite cultured. But the bow will let us find the path."

Young-hee was too tired to ask what he meant. "Great, let's get going then."

They had a brief breakfast of some unusual *gimbap*—kaypal rice filling with marinated *dureop*, all wrapped in pickled sesame leaves— while sitting on a large rock just outside the ogre's house. The fire had totally burned out, but smoke still hung heavily. Just past the lantern light lay a lumpy shape that Young-hee realized as Yeonggam's body. "I wonder what will happen," said Young-hee between bites. "Can the trees and bushes keep growing in the dark without magic to sustain them?" Samjogo shrugged.

Done eating, they set out again. The going was hard, and at first Samjogo started back the wrong way again, but Young-hee recognized the tunnel and turned him around. The ground was rocky and uneven, but eventually they found what seemed to be the main route. "Ah, yes, I know this," Samjogo would say every so often, or "Of course, not long now," inevitably followed by confused muttering as he slowed or halted. After some looking about and mumbling, Samjogo would spring to life, recognizing some stalactite or arch, and pick up his pace.

The whole time, he prattled on for the sheer joy of talking with another person. Young-hee tried to be understanding. *He must have been terribly bored, stuck in those chains for so long.* But it did get annoying, and she decided if he was going to talk and talk, at least the topic could be interesting or useful for her. So she asked about Strange Land, the creatures she had met, and his history.

"Were you born a Samjogo with three legs and feathers?" she asked. "Or was it a title you, uh, earned?"

Vaguely perturbed by her questions, Samjogo, nonetheless remained genial. "As a matter of fact, I was an orphan, adopted by fairies when I was very young. Not your normal fairies—unusually savage ones."

"Savage fairies?"

"Indeed and indubitably. They loved hunting deer and boar in the wood, and wrestling with mighty fishes in their lakes. They rode wild, one-horned *girin* like horses, and warred with mountain ogres."

"Wow. I didn't know fairies were like that."

"Most aren't, not anymore. But mine taught me to track prey through forests and fields, read the winds and stars, and fight bravely."

At one point another river gushed out of the walls and followed their trail, but this one blasted like a fire hose. The tunnel narrowed and the rocky outcropping they walked on shrank to a skinny ledge above the torrent of white water. Samjogo used his hyeopdo to steady them across the slippery, wet rocks. Young-hee was happy for Samjogo's lighthearted chattering then, as she surely would have been too scared to walk undistracted, but also happy that the rush of water partially covered the prattle.

Once past the water, Samjogo grew more confident. "Not much longer," he assured. "The deepest parts of Darang Cave can be confusing, but now I'm certain of the way." In fact, the tunnel had narrowed to just a few feet wide. There were no options anymore, no side passages or vast caverns. There was only forward.

The cave floor angled upward, little at first, then so steeply that their walk was more of a climb. Up and up and up they went. Young-hee hoped for the path again, but no such luck. Still, she followed Samjogo.

"Yes, it's a bit of a climb," he said. "It was even tougher going down, way back when I first entered the cave."

And then Young-hee saw light—natural sunlight, high above. She redoubled her pace, straining forward. As the light grew brighter and closer, Young-hee grew anxious.

Then, finally, the cave mouth opened onto the top of a green, grassy hill. Young-hee blinked hard, unaccustomed to the sun. *It must really hurt Samjogo. He's been underground for so long.* Behind them, the Cheongyong Mountains loomed, all rock and ice. In front was just green—grass and trees and all things natural, but too bright and, well, too *big*—hills and forests and mountains stretching forever.

"So," she said, "where to now? There's still no path."

"No worries. That's why I brought this," said Samjogo happily, unslinging the bow from his shoulder and handing it to Young-hee.

"What do I do with this?"

"Shoot an arrow."

"Uh, where?"

"Anywhere. It doesn't matter."

"I don't understand."

"That doesn't matter either." He wrapped her left hand around the water buffalo horn that was the bow grip and took the single arrow from the quiver. "Take the arrow and fire it into the air."

"Anywhere?"

"It's completely up to you. Just really give it a good shot."

Examining the bamboo arrow, with its pheasant-feather fletching, bush clover nock, and sharp metal arrowhead, she felt a little ridiculous. She had no idea how to fire an arrow and seeing it in a movie didn't compare.

Reluctantly she nocked the arrow, but there was nothing resembling a target, only green and rocky hills. She tried pulling back the string, but it was harder than she'd anticipated, and the bow snapped from her hand. The string released with a heavy *thwang* and the arrow wobbled free, careening by Samjogo's head. He jerked away, although the slow and ungainly misfire presented no danger. The arrow flopped to the ground. "Sorry," Young-hee said, embarrassed and shaking out her fingers, which had been stung by the string.

"Maybe we should try again," said Samjogo. "Don't think. Just relax, take a deep breath, exhale, and let go."

This time she was ready for the pull of the string and strain of the bow. As she drew the arrow back, pointing it into the sky, instead of fighting the pressure, she just exhaled and imaged herself expanding. *You're not even aiming.* The string dug into her fingers, and her shoulder burned, but she ignored the pain. When the string was drawn as far back as she could manage, she let go. With a sharp *ping*, the arrow shot out true, into the sky, so impossibly high. And it kept going. "Wow," said Samjogo, squinting, "that was good."

Finally the arrow—now just a small speck—slowed, hung in the air, and arched into its fall. Faster and faster, it plummeted, until it slammed into the field, halfway to the forest by a lonely, brown rock. "Okay, then," said Samjogo. "That's the way we go."

With no better options, Young-hee followed Samjogo down the grassy hill toward the barely visible arrow.

"Aha," he said, reaching the rock and picking up the arrow. "There it is."

"Yes, the arrow. So?"

"No, not the arrow. There. The path."

Young-hee gasped. Maybe two meters across was a path of shiny, black, stone blocks extending toward the forest, where it cut between the trees. "Wait, there wasn't any path here a moment ago," she said, confused and trying to understand.

"That's true, there *wasn't*," said Samjogo. "But there is now."

"But … your arrow formed the path?"

"No, of course not. It's just an arrow."

Young-hee scowled. "So what happened?"

"When the mountain spirits of Mount Chungak asked the venerable monk Simgong to build them a temple, he shot an arrow from the mountain top, and the built the temple where it landed. When the three first men emerged from a cave on Mount Halla to divide up the world, they fired three arrows, one each, to determine their lands."

"Oh, nice trick," said Young-hee. "I don't suppose we could just fire an arrow to find out where a pullocho is?"

"No, I'm afraid it doesn't work like that."

"Of course not," said Young-hee. "It never does." She sat on the brown rock and looked around. "Wait, wait, wait. 'First men?' I thought Bear was the first human."

"True. Ungnyeo the Bear became human in a cave atop of Mount Baekdu and then married the King Under Heaven and gave birth to Dangun. And three divine men shot three arrows to divide their kingdom. And Mireuk created man and woman from insects he caught on a golden plate, with the help of Frog, Mouse, and Rabbit."

Samjogo, full of patience and contentment, smiled at Young-hee. She couldn't stand that. "So which story is right?"

"'Right'?"

"They can't all be true."

"I don't know which is 'true.' But they are all true stories. The same way the path splits into an endless maze of options whenever you try walking back along it."

"So. Only forward then?"

"Forward. Or off the path altogether."

"No, I need the path," she said. "*Aish.* So annoying. But thank you for helping me find it again."

"You only lost the path because you saved me. It was the least I could do."

Very true, she thought, struggling not to snark out loud. "Well, I should probably get going."

"You know, you did more than just free me from almost certain death from Yeonggam. You distracted him long enough for me to defeat him. And you shared your food. I feel that I owe you more."

"Don't worry about it."

"I do not worry. But I pay my obligations. Perhaps you would allow me to continue on and help find your pullocho?"

Young-hee was not sure how she felt about that. Samjogo seemed flaky and strange. Plus his constant chatter made quiet travel impossible. But he knew much more about Strange Land than she, and about fighting and weapons. Plus, it would be good to have company—no telling how long before she found a pullocho. "Let's get going, then," she decided. "Thanks."

The trail wandered down the high hills, through a rolling valley. In the distance, she spied small clusters that looked like villages, and the countryside here was a little less lonely. With leafier and more fern-like trees, the landscape was more arid than the jureum forest.

"Are we traveling south?" she asked. "The climate seems more tropical. But the sun is on our left."

"What does the sun have to do with south?"

"You know … the sun rises in the east, sets in the west. During the day it is in the south."

"Does your sun only have one route?"

"Well, yeah. I mean, it changes a bit with the seasons—its angle mostly. And really it's the Earth that moves, not the sun at all. But every day, it rises in the east and sets in the west."

"Sounds horribly boring. The sun here has far more options."

"But, wait. … If the sun shifts, what about seasons? How can you tell directions? I mean … " Young-hee snapped silent. Atop the next hill, looking down on them, she could see it—a ghost. Long, straight black hair, smooth skin, and faceless, just smooth skin like an egg. One of the ghosts from Lake Mey had found her again.

14

"Do you see it?" asked Young-hee fearfully, tugging on Samjogo's sleeve. "On top of the hill—a ghost."

"An Egg Ghost," he looked worried. "That is not good."

"There could be others," she warned, searching frantically.

"Yes, you said even the Ghost Queen herself pursued you. I had better make sure the Egg Ghost does not contact her sisters." Samjogo drew his hyeopdo and jammed the arrow into the path between two stones. "That should hold the path. Stay out of sight. I'll return soon."

As he sprinted across the field, the Egg Ghost retreated into the woods. Young-hee looked for a hiding place, but the hills were mostly open, rocky grasslands, with clumps of trees here and there. Some small villages seemed not too far, but the way there was far too exposed—assuming, of course, that whoever or whatever lived there was friendly. So she headed away from the Egg Ghost, toward a solitary and ancient-looking zelkova tree. In its majestic canopy, a flock of birds looked down on Young-hee with expressions between bemused and inscrutable. Well, not a flock exactly—all the birds all seemed to be from different species. She could lay low in the tall, thick reeds around the tree and keep an eye out for ghosts, and Samjogo.

And so she sat, as inconspicuous as possible. As the stalks and blades rustled against her, rough and pointy, she remembered the marvelously silky grasses she had run through so happily on her first Strange Land journey. Maybe they only existed around jureum trees, or maybe it was she who had changed.

Shifting her weight, she felt a lump in one coat pocket. Her cell phone. Without thinking, she took it out, and flipped it open. *(Flipped? Who still has flip phones? Only her, it seemed)*. Unthinking, she pressed the "on" key and, after a pause, the phone hummed and lit up. The logo danced across the screen as the phone dragged itself back to life.

The power bar had just one small, red bar. Not much at all. The big clock-calendar was a confused jumble of almost times and nearly dates. *Poor thing can't figure out where or when it is*. No messages either. *Same useless hunk of plastic as ever*. But just as she was about to power down, there it was—just for a moment and just one tiny bar—a brief flicker of reception. A glitch? An electronic spazz-out? Not daring to get her hopes up, she pressed the "4" key. Speed dial. For home.

Ten blips sang as the phone counted out her phone number. Then silence. *This is stupid*. She looked out across the hills with the phone cupped to her ear, but heard nothing. *Maybe I should have dialed it like an international call*, she joked to herself. But just as she was ready to give up, there came a click. Followed by a buzz, a whirring, and then a ring. *A ring!* Young-hee couldn't believe it. But just as quickly, she thought, *What can I possibly I say?*

"*Hello?*" The answering voice was distant, distorted and staticky. But it was clearly mom. "*Young-hee? Is that you?*" Young-hee froze, suddenly too happy and too heartbroken to speak. "*Hello? Hello?*" the voice repeated, each word more urgent.

"M-Mom?" said Young-hee at last.

"*Young-hee?*" the voice repeated, a wash of relief audible even over the bad connection. "*Young-hee, where are you? Where on ea… … you been?*"

"Mom? Yes, it's me. I'm here."

"*Young-hee? … can't … … clearly.*"

"Mom? Can you hear me? It's Young-hee."

"*I can't … ….*"

"I'm okay. I'm here."

"*… sta… … Where's Young-beom?*"

"Mom, I'm trying to get Young-beom back. I promise."

"*Where's Young-beom?*" Even through the static, her mom sounded panicked.

"He's with me, kind of. I mean, he was. It's a little hard to explain, but I promise I'll bring him back soon."

"… *don't … … -ation … … a … ever!*"

"I said, I promise I'll bring him back do you. Mom?"

"*What do you mea… …?!*"

"Mom? Can you hear me? Mom?" Cut off, Young-hee immediately hit redial. The numbers beeped, but then only silence. She hit end, then redial. And again. But before the digits finished counting, the sounds stopped and the screen faded to black. Out of power. "*No!*" she cried at her phone. "No, no, no. Mom, I'm so sorry." Feelings flooded across her like waves in a storm—misery, longing, guilt, anger, ache, despair, helplessness. She couldn't distinguish one from another, but they all hurt too deeply to contain. She was crying. "Mom …," she said.

She wasn't sure how long she lay in the grass—only that she was nearly cried out—when she thought she heard a strange noise. *Another ghost? But no, someone else was weeping, calling for help.* "Hello?" came the sad voice, deep and rumbling. "Terrible, how terrible… Is anybody up there?"

"Uh, just me," said Young-hee, seeing no one. A light breeze swished the grass and tickled the zelkova leaves, but otherwise all was still. "I don't see you, whoever you are." Up in the tree, the mismatched birds gazed silently down.

"I'm over here," said the voice unhelpfully.

"Here?"

"I'm under the ground, in a trap. Between the thick grass and the big tree."

"That sounds dreadful. I'm coming," she said, adding, "I hope I don't fall in, too."

She crept through the grass, testing each step, in case of more traps. Under the hulking, arching zelkova, there it was—a big hole, partially obscured by reeds. Young-hee peered carefully over the edge. It wasn't what she expected. "Hey, you're a tiger!"

"Indeed, I am Tiger," said the big cat, obviously embarrassed. He was a large tiger, at least in Young-hee's opinion, and the hole was barely larger than his bulk, but deep enough that he couldn't get out.

His ears lay back against his head, and his tail slinked limply behind. "If you would be so nice, please help me out before the villagers who dug this trap find and kill me."

"There's a long coil of rope here."

"Probably the villagers left it to string me up."

Young-hee tied one end around the tree, but before she threw the other end down the pit, she stopped and frowned. She had been tricked before. "What a minute. You aren't going to eat me as soon as I help you out of that pit, are you?"

"Oh, no. That would not be nice of me at all. I would owe you my life."

"You promise not to eat me?"

"Of course."

Her forehead wrinkled with stress as she decided, then tossed one end of rope down the tiger trap. Young-hee knew real world tigers cannot climb ropes, but neither could they (or frogs or rabbits or bony skulls) talk. Indeed, this Strange Land tiger spilled out of the hole with a lumbering, undignified scamper, falling heavy onto his back. He growled with joy and wriggled in the grass, scratching his back. "Oh, thank you, thank you," he said. "I was certain that the villagers would find me, mount my head above a door, and use my fur as a blanket. Terrible." Tiger rolled over onto his feet. "I must say, I was stuck quite a long time," he said, his voice rumbling deep. He walked slowly and deliberately toward Young-hee. "Several days, alone in the dark, not knowing when my life would end. With nothing at all to eat."

"Er, I'm sure my friend, when he gets back, will help you get something to eat," said Young-hee with a nervous laugh as she backed away from Tiger just as deliberately. "He's the Samjogo. Do you know him? Three-legged bird of power. He's very protective of me."

"I'm sure he is," said Tiger, who suddenly sprang forward and wrapped himself around Young-hee like a kitten cozying the feet of its owner. A very, very large kitten. A very, very hungry kitten. "But I am so very hungry. And you do look quite delicious."

"But you promised." She felt growing panic, and scanned the hills for Samjogo.

"Well, perhaps. But I am a tiger, after all. I can only act according to my nature."

"You said you owed me your life."

"And now I am starving. So perhaps you can help me a second time. One last time."

"That's so … rude," sputtered Young-hee, who suddenly found herself more angry than scared. "Besides, you could *never* hurt me. I'm far too powerful for you."

"Don't be silly," said Tiger, looking Young-hee all over. "Your teeth are small and flat, your claws are weak, your body is tiny."

"You cannot judge so easily—you know that, Tiger. I have a, uh, a mandate from the … King of Heaven." She struggled to remember things she had heard in Strange Land, anything intimidating. "My arms may look skinny, but they were, um, gifts from the, uh, Monkey King."

"Your arms came from Seonokong?"

"Yes, Seonokong the great Monkey," said Young-hee, trying to sound confident, remembering an old comic book, but feeling mostly silly. But silly was better than eaten, so she dove in. "And my bag contains great fire, a gift from the Ten Kings of Hell. Very hot." *Ten Kings of Hell? Where did I come up with that?*

"Ooh, I do not like fire," said Tiger, backing down slightly, but still staring with menace.

Just then, in the distance, Young-hee saw people walking up the hill toward them. Farmers perhaps, dressed in off-white, simple hanbok and carrying farm tools. Whoever they were, they were probably her best chance. "Come on," she semi-commanded. "Follow me as I attack those villagers—the ones who imprisoned you, no doubt—and you will see my powers."

Young-hee moved with a confident stride just ahead of Tiger. She wasn't sure how Rabbit pulled off this part in the folk stories, but she concentrated on keeping herself between Tiger and the approaching people. The tall reeds partially concealed Young-hee and her furry companion but the villagers finally spotted them, stopped walking, pointed and grew ever more animated. Young-hee just kept walking, closer and closer with Tiger right behind. When a hundred meters separated them, the farmers' frantic cries filled the air. Young-hee kept walking, and the villagers broke into an all-out run, scattering every which way.

As they stampeded, they shouted: "*Tiger!*" and Young-hee glanced nervously at her companion. His furry ears pricked up, and his yellow eyes narrowed as he listened to the panic wailing. Tiger was not the most brilliant creature in Strange Land, but his hearing was sharp. *Rabbit never faced this problem.* But out of her racing mind jumped an idea "See? There's your proof," she said, trying to look composed and serious. "They're yelling 'Die, girl!' They're terrified of me."

He stared right into Young-hee's eyes, weighing her words—until suddenly his gaze broke. "Yes, I can see how frightened they are of you! I had no idea. Please forgive me and do not punish my impudence." He stretched out his front paws and lowered his head to the ground, bowing.

"You've had a terrible time, with the trap and all. I accept your apology this one time," said Youngee, hiding her shaking hands. She couldn't believe the old story worked.

"That was impressive." Young-hee spun around and saw Samjogo leaning against a nearby rock, hyeopdo in hand, grinning.

"You saw that?"

"Yes, I was on my way back, when I saw you and Tiger 'talking.' I was ready to intervene, but you had the matter well in hand."

"I was so …" She let her thought trail as she directed a glance at Tiger.

"Rabbit couldn't have done better," Samjogo reassured. If he noticed her red eyes and runny nose, he said nothing, instead turning to Tiger. "Greetings, Tiger. I see that you've already met the mighty Young-hee and gotten a taste of her power."

"*Ya-oong*," said Tiger sheepishly, covering his eyes with a huge paw. "Yes, she was kind enough to help me, and although I rewarded her generosity with betrayal, she forgave me."

"And don't you forget it," scolded Samjogo.

"I only did it because I was so very hungry I couldn't think straight."

Young-hee felt bad for the silly cat. "I'm sorry, Tiger. I would share my food with you, but I don't think Tigers eat rice and vegetables."

"We don't, *ya-oong*, but thank you."

"Young-hee, I think we should be going," urged Samjogo. "Now that he's out of the trap, I'm sure Tiger will find food soon enough."

"But what if that 'something' is a villager? Or Rabbit?"

"Tiger has been trying to catch Rabbit since the dawn of time. I don't think there's much danger of that. He's not exactly the freshest kimchi in the *ong-gi* pot." He turned to Tiger. "No offense."

Young-hee's face lit up. "You know, when those farmers ran away, they some dropped their bags. I bet they had food in them."

They hurried over, and sure enough, there were two bags, along with many sticks, hats, and a nice long pipe. They first bag had wrapped rice balls and pickled vegetables. But the second held thick pieces of thick-cut *samgyeopsal* meat. "They must have been going on some kind of picnic," noted Young-hee.

There was plenty of meat for a team of farmers, but not so much for a hungry tiger. While Tiger ate gratefully, and Young-hee and Samjogo enjoyed some kaypal *gimbap*, Samjogo told about the Egg Ghost. "She escaped, I'm sad to say. And once she tells the Ghost Queen, we're going to have trouble. So I think we need to get going."

"The Ghost Queen?" said Tiger, shaking his head. "If she is after you, then all the ghosts must be coming. I wouldn't like that at all."

"Yeah, it's not fun," said Young-hee.

"Well, thank you, Tiger, for your company," said Samjogo, as he packed the remaining food. "We must be going if we are to stay ahead of the ghosts. Please, in the future, try to stay out of traps."

"Yes, and thank you again for your kindness." Tiger took a couple of tentative steps, but didn't look in a hurry to get anywhere.

"Wait, don't go," said Young-hee.

"What?" said Samjogo.

"Maybe he'd like to come with us."

"I don't think that's a good idea. He already tried to eat you once."

"Yes, I know. But I was thinking about all the Tiger stories I know, and, the thing is, they are all pretty short. He gets tricked, he runs away. Or he eats a traveling monk or something. But none say what happens next. There are no stories about Tiger living his life, making friends, hanging out. If he sticks around, he wouldn't be bound by those stories. He would be free to do anything, be anything."

Both Tiger and Samjogo looked at Young-hee as if she were crazy.

"It was just a thought," she said, deflated. "I thought we could use the muscle. And another friend."

"Why, may I ask, are all the ghosts chasing you?" asked Tiger.

"I don't even know," said Young-hee, as they found the path. "I think it has something to do with my quest to find a pullocho for a goblin, to get my brother back. But no one knows where pullochos are. So for now I'm trying to find the three animal spirit women. I'm told they can help."

"And that is why we must get going," said Samjogo, pulling the arrow from the path and putting it in the quiver on his shoulder. "We have get as far away as possible before the ghosts come back. Plus there's no telling how long before we find the animal spirits."

Tiger looked at Young-hee and Samjogo as they started down the path. "But I know where the animal ladies live," said Tiger. "I could take you there."

How Tiger Got His Stripes

One day Rabbit was hopping home, when suddenly hungry Tiger sprang from the grass and said he would eat Rabbit.

"Why would you want to eat me?" asked Rabbit. "I'm far too small for a big animal like yourself."

"You may be small," said Tiger, "but I am ever so hungry. So I must eat you."

"But I have a better idea. All around us in the tall grasses, there are dozens of swallows. Hundreds. If you open your mouth and just wait here, I will run through the grass making a huge racket and scare them all right into your mouth. Dozens of swallows would make a much better meal than just one little Rabbit, don't you think?"

Tiger thought about it and had to agree that the birds sounded a lot bigger and better. He nodded.

"Okay," said Rabbit, "just stay here, close your eyes, and open your mouth as wide as possible. When you hear the big rustling noise all around you, you will know the birds are on their way."

So silly Tiger did just what he was told and closed his eyes and opened his mouth. Rabbit went hopping through the grass, but instead of scaring the birds, he lit the grass on fire all around Tiger and then ran away. The flames leapt higher and higher, with a great crackling noise. "Oh boy," thought Tiger, as he heard the crackling getting louder, "that sounds like the flapping wings of a lot of birds. This will be a great meal."

But as the flames closed in on Tiger, he began to notice how hot it was getting. He opened his eyes and realized he had been tricked, and was barely able to escape the blaze. To this day, Tiger's fur remains singed black from Rabbit's trick.

15

Young-hee and Samjogo stopped at Tiger's words and turned around. "You know the animal spirits?" asked Young-hee, surprised to get some good-ish news for once.

"Fox, Bear, and Snake, yes, I know them," said Tiger. "They live a couple of hills away. If we walk quickly, we could get there by dusk."

"That's wonderful. See, another good reason for Tiger to join us."

"I just wish we could trust him," said Samjogo. "For instance, how does he know where the animal sisters live?"

"A good question," said Young-hee, and was about to ask Tiger when she remembered they were being chased. "But shouldn't we hurry before the ghosts return? We can question Tiger as we walk and go our separate ways if we don't like his answers." Tiger cocked his head and purred.

"Tiger, we thank you for your generous offer," said Samjogo, "and hope you will not hold our wariness against us. But we need to leave."

"Of course," said Tiger, his face lighting up as he bounded ahead, his tail swishing fancifully. "Come with me then." And they did. Young-hee shrugged and adjusted her bag; Samjogo scanned the hills and horizon for ghosts.

After walking alone through the woods and cave, Young-hee found traveling with others easier and more pleasant, despite the threat from the Ghost Queen and her minions. It was an easy walk, over rolling hills, through occasional clusters of palms and elms, more baroque than any in Korea. They moved quickly and made good time.

"The ghosts or whoever can't follow us?" Young-hee asked again.

"No, this is your path," said Samjogo. "No one can see it when they cannot see you." But Young-hee noticed that Samjogo kept looking about nervously.

Soothed by the gentle landscape and great varieties of birds, Young-hee, nonetheless, thought about the animal sisters. Could they locate a pullocho? What made them so special and worrisome?

At least Tiger was in good spirits, walking briskly, but not going too far ahead. Although not as talkative as Samjogo, he made pleasant conversation. "That village over there is famous for its spiced *makgeolli*," he would say. Or "That valley past the rocky cliff was where the dokkaebi rebellion once hid, until the Thunder General and his army drove them back to their ashen home." *It is hard to believe he tried to eat me*, thought Young-hee. But then Tiger added, "I'm not always so silly. I'm sure you could find tales of my prowess— eating a minor immortal or a wicked priest." *Okay, so maybe not that hard to believe.* Young-hee grew comfortable with Tiger. Perhaps he was like most cats, which can ingratiate themselves once they decide to be friendly.

"I hope the animal sisters can help us," Young-hee said.

"I'm not so sure," Samjogo warned. "They are not the most popular spirits in the realms under Heaven."

"What's wrong with them?" asked Young-hee, ready for the more usual bad news.

"They are … difficult," said Samjogo. "Very old. Very powerful, in their own way."

"So, are they on the side of the elder gods?"

"No, the sisters are forbidden from taking sides. That is one of the few things all creatures here have agreed on," said Samjogo. "Ungnyeo, the Bear, was the first woman, the source of all humans, and so she is the mother of all loss. Sanyeo, the Snake, served the Ten Lords of the Underworld, corrupting the King of Heaven's most pious servants. And Fox … "

"That's Gumiho, right? The nine-tailed fox?"

"Yes, Gumiho. She is a special kind of evil. She only wants two things: to become human and to destroy everything in creation."

"Wow," said Young-hee, "that's really psycho."

"Indeed."

"Everyone knows about the becoming human thing. But I thought Fox was more like Rabbit—playing tricks and being sneaky."

"No, Gumiho is the most dangerous of the sisters, but none can be trusted. Which is why I am skeptical of your plans."

"But I don't know any other options."

"You could forget about the pullocho. Our world is a vast and splendid place. You could step off the path and make your own way, as I have done."

The memory of the phone call still stinging, Samjogo's suggestion just upset Young-hee. "The pullocho is not for me, it's to get my brother back. He's just a little boy. And it's my fault he got in trouble. I have to save him."

"Maybe he doesn't need saving. Besides, didn't you say you found him more annoying than anything? Perhaps he's getting what he deserved."

"You should *shut up*," snapped Young-hee. Guilt stung deep as she recalled things she had said and thought about Bum. Just then, she felt something warm and furry. Tiger was rubbing his cheek lightly against her, like a kitten trying to get attention.

"So, Tiger, tell us," said Samjogo, changing the subject, "how do you know the sisters?"

"I've had … business with all three," he said, grimacing.

"Business?"

"Ungnyeo, the Bear, and I competed to be the first humans."

"That was you?" exclaimed Young-hee.

"That was Tiger, so yes, me. You probably have not heard of Sanyeo, the Snake, though. After she seduced the holy servant of the Heavens, causing him to lose grace and protections, it fell on me to eat him. He was tasty but, I assure you, you don't want to upset Heavenly servants," he looking a little guilty.

"And Gumiho?" asked Young-hee

"It was wicked and cruel Fox who gave me my stripes," he grimaced at the very thought.

"Wait, I know that story," said Young-hee. "A fire singed black lines onto your body. But didn't Rabbit start it?"

"Only kind of. Rabbit is not cruel, though he is smarter than I am and always escapes me. This one time, he promised to scare swallows into my mouth, so he could run away while my eyes were shut. But as he ran, he met Fox, who convinced him to set the fire and kill me."

"Wow, that's terrible."

"She's done it before. Once I caught Fox—not my usual meal, but you eat anything when hungry enough. She held up these stones and told me they were bread rolls. Even I am not that dumb, but she promised that cooking would make them soft and delicious. Foolish me, I believed her. So evil Fox was heating the stones in a fire, when she said, 'Oh, I have to go get some kimchi to go with the buns. Now, don't you eat any of my ten rolls.' Well, there were eleven, so I thought at last I'd outsmart Fox. I could eat one, and there would be ten left. So I swallowed a stone—and, of course, it burned my mouth and belly so badly I stayed in bed and couldn't eat anything for a month. Fox just laughed and told all the other animals, who laughed too."

Tiger's stories were grisly and horrible, but also so foolish, Samjogo tried to hide his amusement. Young-hee scowled. "How can you laugh?"

"I think you misunderstand Tiger and our land. He acted according to his nature. It would be an affront not to laugh at his silliness."

"Still, it's pretty crappy to laugh at suffering, no matter whose."

Eventually the sun grew heavy and more orange. Sundown was approaching. The path took them through a birch grove, so white that the trees glimmered. Young-hee noticed the birds again, perched in the birches.

"Are those birds watching us? I think they're the ones from that zelkovia tree, where we met Tiger."

"Why would you think that?"

"Because they're all different kinds, with no two matching. I've never seen a flock like that."

His interest peaked, Samjogo looked up. "Hmm. No pigeons—terrible animals—so that is good. But you are right, they all seem different. I see a finch, a nightingale, a *hootooti*."

"A hootoo-what?"

"A hootooti. An *odisae*. That bright yellow bird with the big crown of feathers." Samjogo seemed distracted, his lips moving; Young-hee realized he was counting. "Huh, thirty birds. That is … odd."

"Don't you mean thirty-one?" she countered. "Including you."

"Me?"

"You are the three-legged bird of great power, as I recall."

"Not the same thing. But, still, very odd."

But before Young-hee could ask what Samjogo meant, Tiger interrupted. "That's it," he said, motioning ahead. Past the birch grove, on the grassy hill, stood a wall made of stone and wood, surrounding a run-down *hanok* house. "That's where the animal sisters live."

The Tale of Frog, Rabbit, and Deer

One day, Frog, Rabbit, and Deer decided to have a party. Each would set a table with food and drink according to his customs. But they needed to decide the tables' order. All agreed it should go by age, with the eldest in the most prominent position; however, they didn't know their ages.

Deer spoke first: "Before there were any men in the land, I climbed the Sacred Sandalwood Tree and hammered all the stars onto the sky. Clearly, I am the most ancient of creatures."

Rabbit was unimpressed. "Ah, that was you?" he said. "For I was the one who planted the Sandalwood Tree. So clearly, I am older than you, younger brother."

The Frog started to cry. "Oh, I'm sorry to weep in front of you like this. But your stories reminded me of my three sons. When young, each planted a tree. I used the wood from one tree to make the hammer Deer used to nail the stars in place; from second son's tree, I made the great plow that furrowed the tracks in the heavens for the Milky Way; and from my third son's tree, I made the carts that carry the sun and the moon across the sky. But all three sons have passed away, and I miss them very much."

And as Frog finished his story, Deer and Rabbit agreed he was the eldest of the animals.

16

In the evening dusk, the animal sister's hanok was eerily silent. No smoke emerged from any chimney. Young-hee wondered what to do if no one was there.

Ramshackle and decrepit, the hanok's curved, tiled roof sagged and lacked many shingles, the white walls were faded and mildewed, and the stone fence surrounding the property was cracked and uneven. A sad, half-dead persimmon tree rose over one wall, before drooping—as if gathering sunlight wasn't worth the bother. The whole estate had definitely seen better days.

"This wreck is home to the mighty animal spirits?" asked Samjogo in disbelief.

"It's nicer on the inside, I am told," said Tiger. "But impressive appearances are not the ladies' priority."

"Come on. Even if it's rundown, it's better than being out in the open," Young-hee urged, unable to shake the bad feeling from the ghost that spotted her that morning. Samjogo may have driven it away, but there were always more.

The surrounding stone walls were too high to look over and, even in decay, they looked daunting. Around a corner, they found a heavy wooden gate. It looked new and strong, with a fresh coat of varnish, and well-polished *moongeori*. These brass knockers, centered on each of the double doors, were shaped like the heads of growling, fierce animals. As Samjogo reached for a knocker, Young-hee thought she saw the animals bare their sharp teeth. She had been in Strange Land long enough to yell: "Samjogo, stop!" He looked at her quizzically. "The door knocker. I don't think it's safe to touch."

Just an inch beyond his fingers, Samjogo saw an open mouth, poised to take a bite. He drew back his fingers, leaving the ornament snapping at air. "Well now," he said. "That's just not nice."

"Shove off!" "Get lost!" barked the knocker.

"And rude," noted Young-hee.

"You're not wanted here," snarled the other knocker. "Not invited.

No trespassing."

Tiger examined the surly ornaments. "Lions—*pah*," he said. "Powerful guardians, but no manners."

"But how do you know we are not wanted if the ladies of the house don't know we're here?" asked Samjogo.

"We are the guardians of the doorway," sniffed the right-hand brass lion. "It is our duty to protect this home and bar outsiders."

"I'm sure you are excellent guardians," Young-hee flattered, "and we would never ask you to shirk your duties. But we have important business and promise we would never make trouble."

"Oh, you promise?" said the right-hand lion mocked. "Well, that changes everything. Go right in."

"Really?" ventured Young-hee.

"Of course not," said the other brass lion. "Beat it."

"Take a hike," echoed the first lion. "Get lost."

I am lost, thought Young-hee. But each insult changed her insecurity to anger. "So, what do you think?" she asked Samjogo. "Maybe we can just open the door." Seeing no handles or latches, she gave a good shove, careful to avoid the metallic mouths. But the door would not budge.

"Hanok doors lock from the inside," said Samjogo. "Usually a heavy wooden *bitjang* crossbar between two *doontae* supports."

"Nice try, loser," sneered one ornament.

"Should we just go over the wall?"

"Hah!" laughed the lions.

"No, doubtless this home is protected by magicks," said Samjogo. "Climbing the walls will only bring trouble. I'm guessing the hanok will just appear deserted."

"Oh, look who's so smart," said the left lion.

"You be quiet or I'll hang a big hat on you," snapped Young-hee.

Suddenly, a great crashing noise rung out as the stone walls and great wooden gate rattled and shook. Tiger had thrown himself full-force into the doors. But the gate held, leaving Tiger with nothing but bruises for his efforts.

"Careful, silly Tiger," said Young-hee, petting her furry companion behind his head. He looked goofy as he nursed his bruised body and pride, but Young-hee appreciated his willingness to help.

Just then Samjogo's face lit with a pleased-with-himself smile. "Guardians!" he exclaimed. "Perhaps we were not clear. We are not asking you to let us in. We are telling you. We are on a mission … from Moonjeon."

"Moonjeon?" said the right lion warily.

"The god of doorways?" said his partner.

"None other," crowed Samjogo. "Moonjeon sent us with orders that you let us pass."

"And why should we believe you?" asked the right ornament.

"What evidence do you have?" asked the left.

"Why, we are the evidence, noble *moongeori*. My friend here is Tiger. And I am Samjogo, the three-legged bird as well as a man, which makes me a type of rooster. And everyone knows that the god of doorways exists between a Tiger and a Rooster."

Samjogo's words clearly impressed the two lions. "Between tiger and rooster, that is true," offered the left guardian. "And if they are emissaries from Moonjeon, we would not want His Greatness angry at us."

"But if we let them pass, and Moonjeon had not sent them, the god of doorways would rip us off this gate and melt us for chopsticks."

As the guardians bickered, it grew ever darker. As Young-hee was thinking how little she liked standing exposed on the lonely hilltop, she heard it—the slow, sickly rattle of ghosts, rising over the hills like the dry howls of a wolf.

"Oh no," said Young-hee, as a deathly chill passed over her.

Samjogo gripped his hyeopdo.

Tiger forgot his bruises and stood guard in front of Young-hee and Samjogo. "I can smell them," he said, "Ghosts are in the air, all around us—along with their horse-backed Queen."

"You are being chased by the Ghost Queen?" said the right lion.

"Yes," said Young-hee, as the shadows shifted, maybe closer, in the evening gloom "They've been after me ever since I started my journey."

"The Ghost Queen is no friend of our ladies," said the left lion, suddenly commanding, "Pyeonbok, *open up!*"

"*Pyeon*-what…?" More shadows, moving closer.

"I wasn't talking to you, but to the *doontae*—the latch guardians—behind this gate."

With a heavy, sliding rumble, both gates swung open, revealing a small lobby and another set of doors. Young-hee, Samjogo, and Tiger stepped inside, but not before Young-hee saw several ghosts gliding eerily toward them at frightening speed, black hair covering their pale faces, white robes fluttering.

And then just as the doors slammed shut, something smashed against them, hard. "The ghosts?" she asked.

"Don't you worry about those ghouls," said a good natured voice on the door. Not a brass lion this time, but a wooden bat, one of two that supported the thick wood latch. "Once this door is closed, nothing passes without our say-so."

The door thumped again, followed by the sickening sound of fingernails against the wood. Young-hee shuddered.

"Oh, thank you so much," said Young-hee, bowing slightly, "uh, Pyeonbok." The two bats twittered appreciation.

The undecorated vestibule was cramped for three people (well, two and a large tiger). *What now,* Young-hee wondered as an inner door clicked and groaned opened, filling the vestibule with lantern light. Holding the lamp was a thin, young woman with black hair and an expressionless face.

"Welcome, travelers," she said. "Few guests make it past our overly zealous guardians—but you are welcome in our home, and protected by the rules of hospitality. Tiger, it is good to see you after so long. All of you, please, enter peacefully." Leaving the door open behind her, the lithe woman slid inside, taking the light with her.

Young-hee looked for guidance. Visibly worried, Tiger stepped into the hanok, followed by Samjogo, looking typically bemused.

Young-hee shuddered at what was scratching and banging on the outside doors, then followed her friends into the old building.

Samjogo slowed and leaned in close to her ear. "Remember, none of these spirits are to be trusted," he whispered. "Gumiho least of all." Then he straightened up and walked on with seeming cheer.

Past the second doors, Young-hee was surprised to find a brightly lit and luxurious hanok. As Tiger said, it was much nicer on the inside—larger, too. Bright paper lanterns hung from the eaves, bathing the *madang* courtyard in a warm, golden glow. The house formed a horseshoe in front of them, then sprawled back into a conglomeration of rooms. The house frame was warm-hued wood, the walls white plaster, and the wooden sliding doors backed with immaculate white paper. Around the interior was a wooden path, about three feet above the ground, with a series of gentle steps leading up to it. The largest, lushest persimmon tree Young-hee had ever seen sat in the center of the madang. She had seen traditional Korean hanok before, from lavishly restored museum pieces in the heart of Seoul, to ramshackle dives that survived high-rise development projects in unfashionable neighborhoods. But never one of this size and opulence.

Setting her lantern on the wooden path, their escort clasped her hands together modestly. She had a strangely serene look, with her black, straight hair slicked back and held by a long silver pin. She wore a traditional hanbok, covered by a long, pale red *durumagi* jacket with elaborate gold trim. "I hope your journey was not too arduous," she said. "It is no small thing to be chased by the Ghost Queen and her terrible servants. But I think you will find our home safe." She glanced briefly at Young-hee and Samjogo before turning to Tiger. "Tiger you know all the parties here. Won't you make the introductions?"

A soft but slightly menacing rumble accompanied Tiger's "Of course." Through gritted teeth (as much long fangs can grit), he said "Ms. Young-hee, Samjogo, I would like you to meet Sanyeo, one of the three ladies of this great house. Sanyeo, like all the others, is one of our realm's oldest spirits. And Sanyeo, this is Young-hee and the Samjogo, my travel companions. I met them only recently, but they have already have shown me much kindness and generosity." Everyone bowed, polite and a little uncomfortable.

"Thank you for letting us in," said Young-hee. "I've never seen such an amazing hanok." Young-hee wondered why the quiet woman was so creepy, then realized—Sanyeo never blinked. *I guess she does look a bit like a snake.*

"Thank you for your kind words. It is good to meet you all." Sanyeo's words slid smooth and seductively, and smiling her empty smile, she called "Sisters, come greet our guests."

A door slid open, and two more women emerged from the labyrinthine building. The first was huge, with broad shoulders, a thick neck, and big hands. She wore a heavy, casual hanbok, in brown and green tones, finely crafted, but designed more for comfort than to impress. Her face hung heavy, as if all she had ever known were sorrows. Behind her came a sharp-faced woman with a red-tinged her hair and a smile as cold as the rivers of Darang Cave. Young-hee thought her hanbok the most fantastic she had ever seen—the finest silk, jet-black with blood-red accents and matte black embroidery.

"Ah, the travelers we've heard so much about," she said.

"It seems the star signs were true," said the large woman. "I apologize, sisters, for doubting."

"Greetings, Tiger," said the woman in black, projecting like an actor in a large theater. Behind her, shadows flickered furiously, as if a great many tails waved before the lanterns. "It is always a treat when we get together. So glad you got your tail out of the ice."

Tiger winced a little at what Young-hee assumed was yet another past humiliation. "Hello, Gumiho. We thank you for granting us your hospitality." Young-hee wondered if he was thanking her for the protection or reminding her of it.

It was an odd threesome, alike yet totally different. Their interactions were both casual and uncomfortable. *Family*, Young-hee thought.

"Hello again, Tiger," said the large woman. "It has truly been ages—not since the cave. Why have you ignored me for so long?" She knelt and put her face near his and ran her massive hands through the lush fur around his cheeks and neck. "Truly a 'tiger out of the mountains,' aren't you?"

"Ungnyeo, Hwanung's precious gift has been a great boon, I see," said Tiger, struggling to keep his manners as the large woman pawed at him. "You make a fine human. Although I can't help but notice a whiff of garlic."

Embarrassed, Ungnyeo stopped rubbing Tiger's fur and turned to the other guests. "Greetings, bear daughter," she said to Young-hee. "It has been so long since I've talked with any of my children. Especially my true children from the mud world."

"You can tell?"

"Of course, a mother always knows her children," she said with a sigh. Then gazed at Samjogo. "And greetings to you, too, bear-son."

Young-hee gasped. Samjogo looked human, but she never thought he was. Samjogo, however, just laughed. "I'm afraid the wise old Bear is mistaken. I am Samjogo, the three-legged bird of power. Famed across the heavens for my skills and might."

"No, bear-son. I can recognize my offspring, but call yourself what you wish."

"Well, now that the pleasantries are out of the way, we'll let our guests rest and freshen up," said Sanyeo, ringing a small bell.

"Uh, please, Ms. Sanyeo, sisters," interjected Young-hee. "We've come hoping you can help us. I'm looking for …"

But Sanyeo interrupted her with a gesture. "Plenty of time later. For now, please enjoy our hospitality. Our servants will show you to your rooms, where you will find warm water and anything you need after your long, tiring journey. We dine in eight *gak*, when you can tell us news from across the land, and why the stars are so interested in such diverse travelers."

"What's a *gak*?" whispered Young-hee to Samjogo.

"About fifteen of your minutes, so eight gak is a couple of hours."

As Sanyeo spoke, a troop of servants appeared, all small, but otherwise almost comically varied: rusty green, or brown and earthen, or bronze. Some shone like polished glass, others looked dirty and tarnished. Some seemed quite human, others beastly or monstrous; still others seemed an odd combination of both. They ushered Young-hee and her friends ever deeper into the labyrinthine structure. With each slap of a sliding door Young-hee worried they were entering a trap.

The servants made a few noises and only responded with a token "yes, yes" or "there you go." *Like drones*, Young-hee thought, and realized why they were so mismatched and odd—they were living sculptures, made variously of clay, bronze, brass, celadon, stone, and possibly of gold. All moved stiffly, like puppets.

"Golems," said Samjogo, noting her stares.

The servants showed them to three rooms surrounding a small, common courtyard, brightly lit by lanterns. Young-hee was relieved they were together.

"Water," said one clay servant, pointing. "Blankets."

"You, there," said a sad-looking celadon servant, showing Samjogo to his room. But Young-hee grabbed his wrist.

"You're human," she said. "A real-world human, just like me."

He held her gaze, annoyed. "I wouldn't listen to old Bear. All those spirits are liars with their own agendas. I am Samjogo, the three-legged crow, raised by the fairies of Three Rivers, and truest of the true bone. I am true to my word." He gently lifted her hand and retired.

Young-hee was looking forward to a good rest and warm food. Maybe even something delicious. A wooden servant opened the door, and Young-hee tumbled in, sprawling over a stack of blankets and pillows. The room was exquisite, with thick pillars of fine pine, intricately carved window frames, and floors of the thickest oiled paper Young-hee had ever seen. "Ah, pillows," she sighed and immediately fell into sleep that was ended only when the same wooden servant repeatedly poked her. "I'm not sleeping," she immediately protested.

"Dinner. You'll be late." It continued poking.

"*Jigyeowo*," she snapped. "I'm coming."

"New clothes," it said, pointing at a pile. "Hot water. Bath," pointing at a large tub. *How had the servants brought the full tub without waking her?* After the long journey, it was inviting. "Hurry," the servant urged.

"Okay, but you've got to leave," said Young-hee, feeling modest. The wooden creature protested, but Young-hee brushed him out with a busy rush of hands. The hot water felt as glorious as it was painful, and as she scrubbed until a lifetime of dirt and grime slid off her skin and hair. She wanted to soak forever, but the servants' rapping on the door broke through her relaxation.

Toweling off, she eyed the laid out clothes. The hanbok, all deep blues and reds, was soft, like the finest linen, better than silk. Young-hee didn't think she could have endured a long meal in a suffocating, formal hanbok, with its poufy skirt and tight, wrapping layers, but this one was remarkably informal, with a relaxed skirt, a shirt, and a loose-fitting *jogeori* jacket. It fit perfectly, and felt like a dream. Looking in the silver mirror, she thought, *Not bad.* "Okay, I'm ready."

The servant made a noise resembling exasperation, but said only, "Your clothes, clean, tomorrow," and led her through a maze of corridors to a large dining room. Everyone was there already, waiting.

"Uh, sorry I'm late," she said sheepishly. Everyone stared, making her feel self-conscious, except for Tiger, who was busy eating, chewing and slurping with enthusiasm. "Thank you for the clothes. They are really lovely."

"Oooh, fancy," said Samjogo, teasing her like a big brother. "I had no idea I had promised to save a princess." He was trying to keep the mood light, but Young-hee could see his attention was really on the three sisters.

"If I recall, I saved you."

"Indeed, scarcely the same girl," noted Sanyeo, now changed into a green and pink hanbok with light blue trim. "We've been making small talk as we waited—well, as most of us waited. Please, come sit by your friends and we shall dine and talk."

It was a great, long wooden table, low to the ground like Koreans tables are. The walls were decorated with nine images from nature: a deer drinking at a stream, a pine tree forest, bamboo, a cloud, a crane, a turtle, a rock, water, and the sun. One panel was strangely empty.

Everyone, save Tiger, sat on maroon cushions around a table filled with a vast number of small bowls and pots, each holding different foods. Young-hee's eyes opened wide as she sat between Samjogo and Tiger, whose greedy breach of etiquette clearly annoyed his hosts. But he was as oblivious to their scorn as he was to Young-hee's outfit.

Young-hee settled close enough to Tiger to use his large furry side as a pillow, but far enough to avoid his dangerously indiscriminate mouth. "Wow, I've never seen such a selection," she said.

"Thank you," said Sanyeo, blank-faced and empty-voiced as ever. "We do try to be good hosts for our *special* guests. But I wonder if Tiger did not want our hospitality."

"I suppose we should be flattered," said Gumiho. "What is it they say about delicious food? 'When two are eating, one wouldn't know if the other person *died*.'"

It was a famous saying, but Young-hee did not like Fox's emphasis. "What are you doing?" she whispered to Tiger.

"What?" he asked between mouthfuls.

"You're eating before your hosts invite you to start. Everyone is staring." She smiled at the ladies, trying to look relaxed.

"I've been in a hole for days, starving," said Tiger defensively. And you shared barely enough to quell my pangs. This is a real feast. And 'an eating person is never guilty,' as they say."

"Is that what they say?" said Young-hee, annoyed at so many old maxims being flung around.

"Maybe there's a beggar in his stomach," offered Samjogo.

"I've heard that before," said Young-hee. She casually but firmly set her left hand on top of Tiger's right paw, before he could grab another bite. He reluctantly stopped. She gave the ladies another strained grin, which they returned with disapproval. "As I said, it looks lovely. So many delicious dishes. We *all* appreciate the hospitality."

"Sister, please," said Gumiho to Snake. "I'm sure Tiger means no offense. Sanyeo is proud and cares about protocol and manners. We've prepared foods good for humans, Tigers, and spirits alike."

"One hundred and eight dishes, I can't help but notice," said Samjogo, disapprovingly.

"It was one hundred and eight," said Gumiho, glaring at Tiger. "Now it is one hundred and six."

"Please, eat well and enjoy," said Ungnyeo. "We can talk of more serious things later." She reached a big hand across the table and, with her chopsticks, pushed choice dishes toward Young-hee. Her grandmother had passed away before the family left for Argentina, but Young-hee was warmed by the memory of the ancient tiny woman pushing bowls of food at her and Bum.

Surveying the impressive bounty—pickled vegetables, meats marinated in unusual sauces, dumplings steamed and fried, rice cakes of all different colors, shaped into half-moons, stars, and all sorts of shapes—Young-hee couldn't help thinking of Bum and the goblin's cookie. The apartment guard had warned against food and presents—*except* those given in hospitality, which the animal sisters had clearly extended. Certainly Tiger seemed okay, and the ladies were eating everything, too, so the food was not poisoned. Assuming the animal women could be poisoned. None of her worries *seemed* right. Samjogo started eating, too, if perhaps a little warily, so Young-hee dug in, too.

When the long meal was finally done, the servants whisked away dishes, cloths and decorations, broke up the table like a jigsaw puzzle, and removed it. They spread pillows and cushions across the floor so the room resembled a sultan's tent, with only a small table in the center holding a few light desserts and a couple of large candles. At last it was time to talk.

"This is a really beautiful hanok," Young-hee repeated. "Have you been living here long?"

"Very long," said Sanyeo. "Even by how time works in our world— so different than in yours—we have been here a long time."

"And not, it should be noted, entirely by choice," added Ungnyeo.

"After some … disagreements with the other creatures, both above and below the heavens, it was agreed that it was best if we stayed here."

"Are you prisoners, then?" asked Young-hee with sympathy.

"In a manner of speaking," said Sanyeo. "We can leave these walls; but our safety outside is not ... guaranteed."

"That's terrible. But at least your home is amazing."

"The most beautiful cage is still a cage, Ms. Young-hee," chided Ungnyeo.

"Of course. I'm sorry," said Young-hee. Samjogo was strangely quiet, and Tiger looked like he was in a food-induced coma.

"I cannot remember the last time I left," said Ungnyeo. "And my man never visits."

"Oh, here we go again," said Sanyeo, eyes rolling.

"Uh, you have a man?" asked Young-hee. "Like a husband? Do you mean Hwanung?"

"Not Hwanung. A man. A brave hunter who pursued me for many days through the wilderness, over hills, across rivers. He captured me by trapping my shadow. But he loved me so. We had two beautiful children, who ... drowned."

"That's horrible," said Young-hee, shocked.

"He was a fisherman. Hard-working and resourceful. He loved me, but a storm swept him out to sea ... "

"I thought he was a hunter."

"There's more," added Sanyeo, obviously annoyed.

"He was the most pious and kindly man," said Ungnyeo, "so remarkable that he was adopted by a lord of heaven. But his father disapproved of our union ... "

"So, which one was your true love?" asked Young-hee.

"All of them."

"That is Bear's story," explained Sanyeo, "to always love a man and lose him."

"That's horrible."

"They always die," said Ungnyeo, sadly.

"But that is Bear," said Sanyeo. "That is what always happens, and what she always says."

"I'm sorry she's so sad so often," said Young-hee.

"That's very kind of you, daughter," said Bear. Young-hee disliked being called "daughter," but manners silenced any objection.

"I should change my clothes," said Sanyeo.

"And that is what my other sister always does," said Gumiho, her fiery hair spread behind her on a pillow. Sanyeo shot her a look as she left the room.

Although Gumiho had made no threats, Young-hee felt an inexplicable chill. All she knew about Fox, from movies and comics in the real world, and from Samjogo and others here, portrayed her as pretty and deadly, like a newly polished blade. She decided to take a chance. "Gumiho, why does everyone fear you so much?"

Tiger and Samjogo looked aghast. Even Ungnyeo slinked back slightly. Gumiho, however, smirked ever so slightly. "A brave question. But, tell me, what does *everyone* say?"

"Um, you know," said Young-hee carefully, "stories about Fox eating humans hearts, hurting Tiger, wanting to destroy the world. And how all you want is to become human, no matter how many people you hurt."

Gumiho, if anything, seemed bored by the accusation. "Human? *Pah.* Yes, there was a time I wanted that, very badly. But times have changed. I've changed. Humanity has changed. Humans ruin everything. When their mud world replaced our realm as the prime, true world, that threw the heavens out of balance. That's what caused the rupture between the old spirits and the younger, between ghosts and fairies, gods and animals. And then humans ruined their own world with pollution and war, with statistics and concrete, and all the rest. Who would ever want to be human anymore?"

Young-hee had expected Gumiho to deny her past, not to confess everything. Plus, much of the time, Young-hee shared Fox's assessment.

Sanyeo returned, wearing a sprawling yellow hanbok. It had trees and mountains, like a painting, embroidered across the large, hanging sleeves. Without comment, she sat on a stack of pillows, close to her sisters.

"So, tell us Bear daughter," said a languid Gumiho, "what brings you to the home of the dangerous and untrustworthy animal spirits?

"Well, the thing is," Young-hee began, "I need to find a pullocho. And I was told that you and your sisters might help." At the word "pullocho," all the sisters had snapped to attention.

"A pullocho?" said Gumiho savoring the word. "Now there's a magic I have not heard mentioned in a long time, or seen in even longer. Why a pullocho? You are too young to be looking for more life. And I doubt the gold and currencies it would bring are much good back in your world."

"Oh, it's not for me," she said. "It's for my little brother."

"Is he sick?" asked Ungnyeo, concerned. "It is so terrible to lose anyone close."

"Not sick. He's been captured by a dokkaebi who refuses to give him back, except in trade for a pullocho. So I need to find one if I want to get my brother back."

"Such a dutiful sister," said Ungnyeo.

"Do you even know what a pullocho is?" asked Sanyeo coldly.

"Uh, it's like ginseng. The dokkaebi showed me pictures."

"A pullocho is more than ginseng, girl," said Sanyeo. "It is the root of life. It is what turned sister Bear into a person. It is the dream that consumed the first emperor of the Middle Kingdom. It is a magic so powerful, its effects could be felt in your world. It is the most precious thing in our world."

"I had a husband once, a *simmani*," said Ungnyeo. "He would leave for weeks to dig the mountains for pullocho. And that's how he died."

"What my sisters are saying," said Gumiho, ignoring her sister, "is that you may have underestimated the seriousness of your quest. All known pullocho were dug up and used ages ago. If there were any left, the spirits would be lining up to acquire one, certain it would tip the balance of this realm. Why if I had one…"

"You can be sure no spirit would let you have one, sister," said Sanyeo, pointedly. Gumiho scowled, but held her tongue.

"I had no idea," said Young-hee, her spirits sinking. "I was told that I might find one beneath the ruins of the Sacred City, in the shadow of the first sandalwood tree. The dokkaebi said you might help me find that."

"That is an … interesting description," said Gumiho.

"Does it mean something?" asked Young-hee.

"It doesn't matter," cut in Sanyeo. "The pullocho is too dangerous to be found again. Give up this quest. Nothing good can come of it." Her voice cut through each syllable, leaving no room for debate. Bear and Fox looked at her. "That is my decision," Sanyeo said.

"Sanyeo, dear sister, please don't be so quick to strike," Ungnyeo soothed. "I know what it is to lose family. A brother's loss is just as terrible as that of a son or husband. We should be merciful to my daughter," Ungnyeo implored. Sanyeo, however, looked most unconvinced.

All eyes turned to Gumiho, who relished the attention. Something cruel rested just behind her face. *This is where I'll see Fox's true nature*, she feared. *Surely Fox will side with Snake, and Bum will be lost.* Young-hee thought she might be sick. But then something like gentleness filled Gumiho's eyes. "Sisters, I must agree with Bear," she said. "This bear daughter has traveled far in a clearly noble cause. Even the heavens foretold of her visit. We should help if we can."

Sanyeo's eyes narrowed, displeased. "You are siding with a human," she said skeptically. "A true human?"

"It is out of character, I admit. But I feel for her. And Ungnyeo was most convincing."

Sanyeo stared dumbstruck at her sister. Gumiho tried a kind smile. "Fine," said Sanyeo, "if both my sisters want to help, I bow to your wills."

"Oh, thank you! Thank you, thank you!" exclaimed Young-hee, taking Ungnyeo's huge hand and kissing it. Ungnyeo blushed, unaccustomed to such emotion.

Samjogo, however, was less enthusiastic. "I thought you said you didn't know where any pullocho were," said Samjogo. "Or wasn't that true?"

"None of my sisters would dream of lying," said Gumiho indignantly.

"It's true, 'Even the spirits do not know,' as the old saying goes," said Ungnyeo. "However, someone might help."

"What? Someone else?" asked Young-hee, seasick from rocking between hope and disappointment.

"There is one possibility," said Sanyeo, reaching for a *yakgwa* covered in a delicate floral design. Young-hee wondered if Snake was drawing out the subject just to annoy her. "If anyone knows where to find the ruins of the Sacred City and the sandalwood tree, it is Namgoong Mirinae, the astronomer and geomancer. She has the greatest collection of maps and star charts in the land."

"She is the one who told us you would come," said Gumiho. "We sisters are not *jeomjaengi* who can foretell the future."

"I was married to a jeomjaengi once … ," said Ungnyeo.

"And you do *not* want to know what happened to him, trust me," said Sanyeo, trying to keep the conversation on track. "More knowledgeable about the strange contours of our land than any creature under heaven, Mirinae is also wise. Her huge stone home and workshop has the most fantastical inventions, books, and devices."

"Is it far?" asked Young-hee, worried how long the journey would take.

"Not too far," said Gumiho. "She lives atop the Lion Head Cliffs, a long day's hard walk."

"Does it look like a lion's head?" asked Tiger, finally finding something interesting in their conversation.

"Not now," said Gumiho. "The whole cliff face fell off in a storm, many years ago, but the name stayed."

"Oh, that's too bad," Tiger muttered.

"Anyhow, that is fantastic news," said Young-hee. "Thank you so much—for the advice, the shelter from the ghosts, the food and everything. You have all been very kind."

"Perhaps we could go to bed now," yawned Samjogo. "It has been a long day and we want to start at first light, to reach that astronomer's before dark."

"Very well," said Sanyeo, ringing a bell to summon their short, mismatched servants. "We will have supplies ready in the morning."

"Well, this has been a delightful evening," said Gumiho, holding out a sweet. "Would you like a yakgwa?" she asked Young-hee.

"No, thanks. I'll just go to bed, too."

"Suit yourself. Few can resist such a delicious treat."

Is she teasing me about Bum? Did I tell her how he was captured?
Young-hee decided to ignore the comment, whatever Gumiho meant.

The little golems led Young-hee, Samjogo, and Tiger to their
rooms. As soon as they left their hosts, Samjogo regained his tongue.
"The animal spirits sure have become so … domesticated. I was certain they would try something underhanded. Or, worse, that Bear
would enlist me as her latest husband and victim. But it appears a
few centuries of house arrest has changed the ladies."

"You were pretty quiet during dinner," said Young-hee.

"It was your conversation, your path," said Samjogo. "It felt it
more strategic to listen. And watch. Besides, everyone knows the
Samjogo is not much of a talker."

Young-hee snorted. She thought him the chattiest person she had
ever met.

Back in her room, Young-hee happily found her clothes, washed,
dried, and folded neatly. A few servants rushed about—three brass-
faced golem changing candles, a stone one carrying a huge armful
of cleaning supplies, a wooden one poking about aimlessly in the
shadows. Youngee, Samjogo, and Tiger gathered around the *madang*
courtyard.

"The stars here are all so different here," said Young-hee as they
gazed up.

"I am curious what maps and star charts this astronomer has in a
land where unmappability is a defining trait, and locations are more
ideas than geographic coordinates," said Samjogo. "The stars are none
too reliable, either. I once went traveling with a star for a few months.
He was a silly thing, barely a flickering flame, not your regular astral
body. He had lost his father's three treasures and he promised me
a great reward if I helped recover them. So we traveled to the sun's
lands …"

"I'm sure it's exciting, but can you tell us tomorrow?" interrupted

Young-hee, suspecting the tale could last until sunrise. "I need sleep, and we need to start early." Tiger agreed with a sleepy rumble, and they all retired to their rooms.

Young-hee spread blankets on the floor and donned her own clothes—washed so quickly and emitting an indescribable flower scent. Her sleep was quick and deep, but her dreams were full of dark shadows and looming threats—the sort of nightmares that vanish instantly on waking, leaving only a lingering dread.

Finally, just before dawn, Young-hee awoke to silence. Flickering in from the hallway, lamp light danced faintly across the top of the walls and ceiling. She was just about to light a candle when she realized she was not alone. A wooden servant stood motionless in a shadowy corner by the dresser. Her heart raced as the servant stepped into the soft orange light from the hall—revealing its wooden cheeks, painted red; its small, cheery, cherry-red mouth; and two pigtails hanging below its hat. "Boonae?" said Young-hee in surprise. "Is that you?"

"Quiet, Ms. Young-hee," said the masked servant. "We haven't much time, and you and your friends are in much danger."

17

Overjoyed to see the girlish mask of Grandma Dol, Young-hee re-flexively picked up the small servant and squeezed. "Boonae, how did you ever find me? Is Grandma Dol okay? Have you seen my brother?"

"Careful, Ms. Young-hee," said the familiar voice, emerging from the very different body. "We are friends, but this body belongs to a servant of the animal women and is not to be trusted."

Young-hee took a step back, instantly serious. The mask Granny Dol had worn at the goblin market was indeed seamlessly fused with the golem; it looked real, except that none of the hanok's servants had blush-red cheeks. "Are we safe?" asked Young-hee.

"I think so. These servants are simple magicks without much fight in them. But, still ..."

"How did you find me?"

"No time for that now. Much has happened since you started your journey. All manner of creatures are marshaling and the mountain fairies are on the march. Suffice it to say, Grandma Dol and Bassam have been finding out what they can and how to help you. A great crane spotted you here yesterday, but it took me a day to arrive and find a way in. The important thing is—I have two warnings for you. First, watch the skies. There's a Storm after you."

"A storm? But the weather has been nice since I came to Strange Land."

"Not a *weather* storm. A Storm Lord, Nwaegongdo, is looking for you, like the ghosts. And when a Storm Lord comes, the skies will howl."

"Together?"

"I don't think the Storm Lord gets along with ghosts. But word of your quest and hunger for a pullocho are stirring old rivalries and ambitions. Your path is growing more dangerous."

"Oh, geez."

"Sorry I don't have better news, dearie. But I have a second warning: Do not enter the Great Forest. I do not understand why, but Granny was firm that I tell you."

"Thanks. I guess," said Young-hee. "I don't really control where the path takes me, though. And there are trees all over this world."

"Just remember the message. Grandma Dol had a reason. And now, we have to do something about me. If I linger, the sisters will find me soon enough."

"Is that so bad? They are a lot kinder than I expected."

"No, they aren't." Boonae examined the room as she talked.

"But they helped me."

"Maybe it seems that way, but I doubt it." Boonae said, giving the dresser a shake. "Okay, I need you to push the dresser over so the top crashes onto me as hard as possible."

"No, that could smash you."

"That's the point."

"I'm not going to do that."

"Quick. The rest of the servants will arrive in a moment."

"Can't I peel you off and then break the servant?"

"No. Unfortunately, the moment I separate from his face, he would control his body and doubtlessly inform the animal spirits that I was here. You must break the body with me still on it."

"Won't that be dangerous for you?"

"Yes, I fear it will be."

"Well, I won't break you, just to help me out."

"There really isn't any choice."

"There's always a choice," said Young-hee, defiant.

Noises came from down a hallway. Servants were on the move. "Listen, Young-hee. You must do this and make sure the servant is well and truly broken. Judging by the dresser's size, I'll get cracked up pretty good, too. Collect the pieces of me and hide them in your bag. The animal ladies cannot know I was here. Hurry."

Young-hee walked reluctantly to the dresser and got a feel for its weight. "How is Bum, I mean, my brother?" she asked.

"Not so great, to be honest," said Boonae. "Now, don't go looking like that. No crying. Your brother hates being that dokkaebi's captive and is making the goblin's life quite a trial. If your agreement had a loophole, the dokkaebi would have dumped Young-beom a while ago. He's safe for now, but sooner or later that goblin will find a way to get what he wants. His kind always does."

Young-hee felt rotten. "I'm so sorry."

"I know, dear. But it's not that awful. Really."

She heard heavy footsteps on the courtyard's wood floor. As the servants drew closer, Young-hee closed her eyes and heaved at the dresser. It was heavier than she expected and she worried she hadn't used enough force. But then, all at once, it toppled, slamming onto the wooden servant. And Young-hee's friend. The servant smashed into chunks, splinters, and sawdust, instantly and completely lifeless. Boonae, too, now looked like a regular Korean mask, but busted into three jagged, lifeless pieces. The door slid open, and four very concerned and confused bronze servants entered. "What, what," they said, over and over.

Young-hee swept the three pieces of Boonae under a sleeve. "I'm so sorry. I lost my balance and knocked the dresser right onto your poor friend."

The bronze creatures looked the broken servant, then at the dresser, and then, suspiciously, at Young-hee. As she pushed the pieces further up her sleeve, one golem noticed, leaned forward, and reached to grasp at Young-hee. Just then, the other bronze servants demanded help righting the dresser and cleaning up the mess. Outnumbered, the suspicious golem returned to the pack and apparently forgot all about Young-hee's secret.

Young-hee slipped quietly out. Tiger and Samjogo were waiting in the courtyard. Discreetly slipping the broken pieces of Boonae into her bag, she joined them.

"Good morning, Tiger," said Young-hee, affecting good spirits.

"Good morning to you, too, friend," said Tiger cheerfully. If he noticed her reddened eyes, he thankfully said nothing.

"What's wrong with you?" asked Samjogo, less diplomatically.

"I'll explain later," said Young-hee. She threw her bag over her shoulder and trudged off, with the servants leading them to the front gate again. Sanyeo's hanbok today was light green with orange trim. As for Ungnyeo, it was immediately obvious to Young-hee that something was off, but only as she got closer did she notice Mother-Bear was sporting a black eye, with a couple of deep scratches along her neck.

"Good morning bear daughter, bear-son, Tiger. I trust you slept well," said Sanyeo, as inscrutable as ever.

"Excellent, thank you, ladies," said Tiger, his spirits still buoyed by having gorged himself so spectacularly the night before. "Just as the Diamond Mountains are best appreciated after eating, I, too, am most refreshed by your fine food and hospitality."

"The servants have prepared food for your journey," said Ungnyeo, distractedly.

"Excellent," said Tiger, as Samjogo took the bag.

"And now, we must say goodbye and wish you well on your quest," said Sanyeo. She waved her hand and a stone servant opened the big doors to the inner lobby.

"Not so fast, sister," said Gumiho. "I fear the Ghost Queen and her servants lie in wait."

"Ghosts in the daylight?" said Sanyeo. "Show me," she ordered the door guardians. As she looked through them, the eyes of the wooden bat on the back of the door glowed. "You are correct sister. Disturbing." With a flick of her hand, she signaled the stone servant to close the inner gate.

"That sounds bad," said Young-hee.

"Indeed," said Gumiho. "Our servants will escort you to a secret exit, well away from the outside wall while my sisters and I talk with the Ghost Queen about protocol. Our hospitality does not end at our walls. You should be well on your way before the ghosts realize you are gone."

"Oh, thank you so much," gushed Young-hee. "I've heard so many things about the animal sisters, especially about you, Fox. But you've all been so nice and helpful. You can be sure I'll tell everyone how wrong those stories are." Before Young-hee knew what she was doing, she sprang forward and actually hugged Gumiho. Fox was too surprised to move for several seconds, eventually raising a hand to half-return the enthusiastic gesture.

"Yes, well," said Gumiho uncomfortably. "That is kind. But you must be going. Please give Namgoong Mirinae kindest regards from all of the animal spirits."

"Goodbye sisters," said Tiger. "I am happy to know our relations are much improved. Thank you."

Samjogo turned as if to speak, but decided against it and hurried after his friends. The stone servants escorted them quickly down a deep maze of corridors. Doors slid open and shut, *madang* courtyards appeared and were left behind. They rushed through an amazing but cold and cavernous hall.

Eventually there were no courtyards or paper-covered windows let in translucent daylight. Up some stairs and down many more, the servants broke the darkness with metal-framed lanterns. Finally, at the end of a long corridor, was a heavy wooden door with a thick iron bitjang crossbar that took three servants and many heavy grunts to slide open. Then another set of wooden doors with fish-shaped doontae.

The stone servant stopped at the top of a staircase pointing into the black. "You, go," and repeated, "Here, go."

"Uh, hello?" Young-hee said. "Are you the guardians of this door?"

"Hello dearie," said the right fish, springing to life. "The bats at the front door told us to expect you, and that you needed a quiet getaway."

"Yes, something like that. You talk with the bats?"

"Sure, guardians of in-between places often keep in touch. We're never really in any one place, so in a way we're everywhere. Or every nowhere. Or something like that. I was never terribly clear."

"That's all very nice," said Young-hee, trying to be patient. "But can you tell if it's safe on the other side?"

"Just a moment," said the other fish. Its eyes glowed like the bat's had. "All clear. No one around at all."

"Good. Then could you open up?"

"But of course … " And with a moan, the bitjang slid away and the heavy door swung open. The flood of bright sunlight made Young-hee blink hard as her eyes adjusted and she saw a flowing stream and green rolling fields unfurl in all directions. The beauty contrasted with Boonae's warning: *There's a Storm Lord coming after you.*

Young-hee thanked the fish for being such good guardians. They seemed to enjoy the flattery, or maybe they were just lonely, since a secret entrance might not get much use. As she ducked under the exposed roots of a huge willow tree that hid the door, there in the distance, Young-hee saw the profile a steep cliff topped with a building.

"Doontae?" she asked.

"Yes, dearie?"

"Do you know the home of the astronomer Namgoong Mirinae?"

"Of course. That's it on the cliff. A fantastic place for a fantastic woman, I'm told. She is one of the most learned people in our land, with all sorts of amazing gadgets and devices."

"Thanks so much," Young-hee said happily. She felt closer than ever to the pullocho—and to getting Bum back. Then she noticed the path was back again, leading her ever forward. "That cliff is our destination. Let's go before anyone finds us again."

She stepped onto the path, as Samjogo and Tiger followed. It was a beautiful day.

* * *

In a lookout atop the hanok walls, the three sisters surveyed the valley below. Gumiho watched Young-hee, Samjogo and Tiger; Sanyeo watched Gumiho. Gumiho looked pleased, which displeased Sanyeo.

"What are you scheming, sister?" asked Sanyeo.

"Whatever do you mean, sister?" answered Gumiho.

"In our hundreds of years together, I have seen you eat humans' hearts, drink their blood, but never once did you help them. And now you have helped this human girl three times in one day—you sheltered her in our home, advised her, and ran off the Ghost Queen. I hope you are not planning to use this girl in the coming war. We are pledged to help no side."

"Do not worry sister," said Gumiho, suppressing a grin, "I am on no one's side."

18

Act III

Young-hee wheezed as she pushed up the steep slope as fast as she could, but cold rain and wind froze her to the bone. Thunder boomed and echoed like colossal drums. Looking equal parts misery and exhaustion, Samjogo and Tiger sped on, so Young-hee refused to slow either. They had escaped the ghosts outside of the animal spirits' hanok; but, now, something new was chasing them, something at least as terrible as the undead ghouls: the Lord of Storms himself.

"I don't think he has found us yet," said Samjogo, "or he would be here already."

"Why isn't that very comforting?" asked Young-hee, shivering.

"For now he's just trying to slow us, maybe blow us into the open."

At first, Tiger's thick warm fur protected him from the rains, but eventually the constant downpour soaked him through, too, and his tail and ears fell with his spirits.

"So, what is Nwaegongdo the Storm Lord like?" Young-hee asked.

"Terrible," said Tiger. "Very scary. *Ya-oong*." A flash of lightning in the sky, much closer than before, and then a loud crackle, accented Tiger's point.

"Yes, terrible," said Samjogo. "Nwaegongdo is a younger demon, who became Storm Lord after defeating the previous spirit of the sky. He's fierce, with a demon's face, bat wings, a serrated blade, and hammers that he carries with his feet."

"His feet? Does he have monkey toes or something?"

"No, ... well, I don't know. That's not the point. The point is..."

"He's terrible," said Young-hee glumly.

"Yeah."

Another cold wind froze their bones and deadened their fingers. "Ow!" shouted Young-hee, rubbing her forehead in pain as a hard, white ball bounced to the ground. "Hail? Really, hail? *Jigyeowo!*"

Soon thousands of acorn-sized balls of ice pummeled down. The trees lessened the barrage, but hiding under them only slowed them more. Her bag held protectively over her head, Young-hee wasn't sure which was worse, hill or hail. Samjogo shielded his head with his hyeopdo, but it didn't help much. Another flash, with a huge, frizzy crack, followed almost instantly. "It's closer," Young-hee said.

"He's trying hard to find us," said Samjogo, scanning the clouds.

"*After many flashes, the thunderbolt will fall*," said Tiger.

"Indeed," agreed Samjogo. "We should keep going." So they set out again on the steep path as it wove through folds of rock, their eyes on the distant cliff-top building.

After what seemed forever, they crested the rocky slope. Their destination was still far, but Young-hee was relieved that the way looked fairly flat. Soon, the burning in her legs cooled and she moved quickly again, determined not to get stuck in the countryside at night.

But then—*boom*! A fat palm tree beside the path exploded in a bright yellow flash and a deafening roar. The explosion knocked them to the muddy ground.

"Lightning," explained Samjogo, his voice a muddled smear in Young-hee's ringing ears. "Are you okay?"

Young-hee nodded and struggled to stand. She saw Tiger furiously licking his fur, which was covered in tiny pieces of burnt wood and splinters. She realized she was, too.

"We need to keep moving," urged Samjogo.

They moved almost at a jog, listening to the hypnotic rain. No one talked. Young-hee felt the ringing in her ears slowly fade. Every so often she extracted another splinter from her skin without breaking her stride. Samjogo kept his eyes on the sky.

Young-hee noticed it become colder, then darker. She was fearfully contemplating a night spent in the drenched; freezing woods, when suddenly they stumbled on a large stone wall. The astronomer's home.

Up close it was a lot larger than it had seemed from the animal sisters' home below. With huge walls of precisely fitting stones the size of small cars, it looked more like a European castle than anything she had seen before in Strange Land. Its huge wooden gate had no moongeori, and as Young-hee was wondering to get in, a slot slid opened, and a pair of eyes peered out.

"Is that the bear daughter and her friends?" It was the voice of an older woman, but sharp and potent. A light suddenly cut through the evening murk, illuminating the three of them.

"I'm the bear daughter, the human. My name is Young-hee. May we come in?"

"Fascinating," said the woman, sliding the slot shut.

The rain redoubled, and wind howled, or Young-hee hoped it was wind, not a ghost or some other foul creature.

With a series of clangs and thumps, a person-sized door in the huge gate opened. Inside looked warm and dry. "Come in, come in, before you catch your deaths," said the woman. None of them needed to be asked twice.

The hallway beyond the gate was huge—as wide as a Seoul road. Two lanterns lit the entrance surprisingly well, with a glow so steady it didn't resemble flame at all. The giant hallway stretched as far as Young-hee could see, slowly sloping up into darkness. *At least it's shelter from the freezing rain*, thought Young-hee shivering.

"So," said the woman, raising a small lantern, "a human, a tiger, and a … whatever you are, traveling some of this realm's more remote fringes. All the lands under Heaven going crazy, but the stars tell me to expect you. Fascinating."

Young-hee assumed this was Namgoong Mirinae, but assuming often went awry in Strange Land. She wore a long, flowing *dopo*—a scholar's robe—with a white collar and a fine yellow belt. Her hair was up in a complicated braid, with streaks of white as thick as scallions. Her face was lively with the kind of scowls gained by a lifetime of dealing with people who didn't understand.

"Thank you for letting us in," said Young-hee. "It's been pouring all day."

"Yes, hailing, too. Most unusual," she said, looking them over.

"I'm sure you'll tell me all about it. But, first, you should get dried off and warmed up."

Rather than take the wide hallway, the woman walked to a wooden platform and a complicated beamed structure nestled in an alcove in the stone. "Watch your step," she said, mounting the platform.

Once everyone followed, the woman grabbed a lever and gave it a tug. With a jerk, the platform rose like an elevator. Thick hemp ropes pulled it up the wall, although there was no sign of electricity or servants. "This was a war fortress, before I moved in," she said matter-of-factly. "I made a few modifications."

After the platform clanked to a stop to the top of the wall, the woman led them through a short corridor to an immense room, as big as a banquet hall, that served as living quarters and workshop. Dominating the space was a gigantic series of thick iron circles and gears that took up nearly half the hall, swooping and arcing high overhead. If it was some kind of machine, Young-hee had no idea what its function might be.

Only after coming to terms with the mysterious machine was Young-hee able to take in the rest of the hall. Clothes and all manner of personal things lay in a tight haphazard space by the entrance, while the rest of the hall was crammed with an endless array of odd gadgets and devices on wooden benches and work spaces. There were trinkets small enough to hold and large metal contraptions with complicated cogs and interlocking wheels. Stairs led into the gloomy rafters above the iron circles where stone walls gave way to the wooden roof, with its own platform full of large metal gadgets. *It looks like a telescope,* Young-hee thought. And everywhere were tables full of rulers, calipers, and glass beakers, along with scrolls and papers covered in mysterious writings and numbers.

"I couldn't prepare properly, what with all the rain and clouds," said the woman, rooting through a chest. "But the worst seems to be over. If it clears up and I can see some stars, I might be able to make a few predictions." Finding a stack of towels, she threw them to her guests. Samjogo and Young-hee began drying themselves. Tiger shook vigorously, then began licking his fur.

"So, are you Namgoong Mirinae, the astronomer?" asked Young-hee.

"Who else would I be?" she responded, a little annoyed.

"I'm Young-hee ... "

"Yes, the human child. I hope we won't have to re-state everything. Once is usually enough for me."

"Uh, yes, of course," said Young-hee, taken aback. She pulled the towel around her for warmth, then sneezed violently, twice.

"You're cold," said Mirinae. She tossed another towel, walked to the wall, and pulled a metal bar. A thump. Deep rattling. Then, a prolonged hiss. A moment later, Young-hee felt the stone floor heating up beneath her feet.

"*Ondol* heating," said Young-hee. "Nice. But how?"

"Water power," said Mirinae. "You need energy to get anything done, and my workshop has the best clepsydra in all the land. Come, see." She turned up the hall's lanterns with a handle connected to a rope and pulleys, and motioned Young-hee to a massive cage of hard white bones. It churned rhythmically up and down. "It's a water pump made from the backbone of a dragon," Mirinae said proudly. "Extremely hard to acquire, but they make the most powerful pumps. It powers not only my clepsydra, but also that armillary sphere, my astrolabe, orrery, and torquetum. And the lights and ondol floor heating. Very useful." She pushed a small lever and the interconnected brass rings inscribed on the table started rotating and spinning in arcs.

"Wow, what is it?"

"It's an astrolabe—for charting the movement of the stars and the heavens. I have mapped all eighteen trigrams and the one hundred celestial systems. She pointed up at the largest machine, at the huge rings overhead that filled the hall with thick, iron arcs and massive metals gears. "That is my armillary sphere for more precise measurements of more distant bodies."

"Wow," Young-hee repeated, before sneezing a third time.

"Enough of my boasting," said Mirinae. "Sit here on the floor's hottest spot. I'll make you some *naengmyeon*."

"Cold noodles?" said Young-hee, finding the spot blessedly warm. "Thank you, but if you had any hot food …"

"*Pah*, don't you know anything?" said Mirinae, shuffling off to the kitchen. "Only the ignorant eat naengmyeon to cool down. You must wait until you are truly cold, then sit on the hottest spot on the ondol floor and eat them. It's a scientific fact." She started cooking, paying little attention to her guests.

"What do you think?" Young-hee asked her friends.

"Tigers don't know much about machines and measurements," said Tiger, stretching his massive body to full length to soak in the maximum heat.

"Knowledge is a disease," scoffed Samjogo. "Wisdom, happiness, the important things in life don't exist in books or science."

"Well, I think it's pretty cool," said Young-hee, a little dejected by her friends' indifference."

Mirinae brought a big bowl of the cold, buckwheat noodle soup in an icy broth for Young-hee and Samjogo. "I don't suppose a Tiger would like a bowl of noodles and vegetables?" she asked.

"Oh, I could eat a little."

"Really? Fascinating," muttered Mirinae, as fetched him a bowl, and a small one for herself. She barely picked at it as she waited for the others to finish.

"So, why do you live high on this hill, all by yourself?" asked Young-hee drinking the last of the broth.

"Science," said Mirinae.

"Science?"

"Yes, this location has excellent *pung su*, with the ridge behind, the cliff in front, and a river below."

"Ah, that kind of science."

"*That kind of science*? Please, science is science—it doesn't have *kinds*. And, by the science of pung su, this location is ideal for learning, thinking and, most importantly, seeing. Being so high makes it easier to see both the heavens and the worlds under the heavens. I need to see them all to be accurate. And I need to be accurate to know … what I need to know." After clearing their empty bowls, Mirinae sat with a plunk facing Young-hee. "Okay, you've traveled far to my little observatory, eaten, dried off, and rested. Your visit was important enough to stir signs in the stars and winds, so, now, tell me why you've come?"

"Well, the thing is," Young-hee said, thinking about her words and then just blurting, "I need to find a pullocho."

"A pullocho?"

"Yes, it's a kind of root, like ginseng."

Mirinae rolled her eyes. "Yes, I know, but why would a simple girl like you want such a powerful magic?"

"It's for my brother," said Young-hee, and repeated the whole dreadful story. "I was told it is in the shadow of a sandalwood tree in the ruins of the Sacred City. No one knows where that is, so they said I was to ask animal spirits. They didn't know either, so they sent me to you."

"Fascinating."

"But can you help me get my brother back?"

"Hmm… this isn't as easy as eating *juk*. It's more like plucking stars from the heavens."

"Yes, but can you help?"

"Perhaps."

"You know where the pullocho is? Or the Sacred City?"

"No."

"No?" cried Young-hee, readying for crushing disappointment.

"The Sacred City is more a concept than an actual location, and it tends to move around."

"*Jigyeowo*. But … you said you can help me."

"I said 'perhaps.' I do have one idea." Mirinae stood and went to her workshop. She hunted through clocks and gears and strange devices before plucking out a small metal circle with a metal bar in the middle, attached to an angled plane. "It's a compass, of sorts, combined with a torquetum. But I have replaced the usual *chinam-*

chim—the 'south-facing needle'—with a device of my own making. A chi-*oon*-chim."

"What's that?"

"'*Oon*' … That's fate," said Samjogo.

"Ah, so he's the brains of your group. Yes, fate, or fortune, or luck, depending on who's asking. My compass points toward your fate."

"Or future?"

"Or luck. I've never been able to get it to work properly."

"Oh."

"You're not the only seeker of Namgoong Mirinae's help. And not even the first in search of a pullocho. Which is why I invented my chioonchim."

"To help people find their destinies?"

"To help me make money. Science doesn't come cheap, and as you can see, my work burns through a lot of capital. So I thought a machine that could help spirits, demons, and other creatures on their many and various quests could be very profitable. Sadly, though, the chioonchim has a bit of a flaw. Instead of pointing to one's fate, it only pointed to the past."

"That's not helpful," agreed Young-hee.

"But couldn't you just turn it around?" interjected Samjogo.

"What?"

"Well, the whole point of a regular compass is, if you know north, you can figure out its opposite, south, and all the other directions. So if your chioonchim points to the past, shouldn't it also tell someone's future and present?"

"It doesn't exactly work like that," said Mirinae. "There are more … planes involved. More dimensions. It's not a front-back, either-or problem. Spiritual space isn't the same as physical. It's not about where you are, but who you are. What you want and what you need."

"Choice," said Young-hee. "The problem is choice."

"Choice?" repeated Mirinae.

"Strange Land's creatures don't really make choices. Who they are, what they do or want, it's all been written down for them already. It's all a reflection of the real world, of our stories. Your world *is* stories, mine writes them."

"Fascinating theory," said Mirinae. "A bit condescending, but fascinating. And just a theory. I suppose the only way to know is to put theory into practice." Mirinae walked off, poking her chioonchim thoughtfully.

"Where you are going?"

"To the lookout platform to test your theory. Come on." They followed Mirinae up the steep wooden steps that curled around the great chamber's inner wall. It was steeper than it looked and, without a banister, quite scary.

Up top, the workshop below shrank to messy details, except for the massive armillary sphere. The platform was nearly as full of mysterious equipment as the lower level. One table was full of lenses of different sizes and colors; others with tubes and charts and levers of all kinds. Large slats in the wooden roof and walls could slide open and closed with ropes and winches.

"This is an observatory?" asked Young-hee.

"The best in the land, yes," said Mirinae, fiddling with the chioonchim. "I can see for many *li* in all directions. And with my *cheolligyeong*, I can see even further."

"Ah, it *is* a telescope," said Young-hee. The device was covered in star charts, although no Big Dipper or Orion or anything Young-hee recognized.

Samjogo picked up a large, red lens and held it to the light. "Careful, that's a fire pearl," said Mirinae. "You don't want to know what I went through to get it, or the cost if you broke it." Samjogo placed it back down quickly and very carefully.

Mirinae finished placing a spring inside the chioonchim and admired her handiwork. "Okay, I need something personal of yours," she said. "The lodestone is made from *essentite*, a very emotionally sensitive mineral. When wrapped with something uniquely yours, it is imbued with your spirit and sensitive to your field."

Standing with her hands in her pockets, Young-hee's fingers fell on something small and springy: one last hair band. She took it out and stretched it. "How about this?"

Mirinae examined the simple elastic like a jeweler with an uncut diamond. "Not bad. These are your hairs caught in there?"

"Yeah, I think so."

"Let's give it a try then." Mirinae slid the hair band over the thin lodestone and twisted it around twice to make it reasonably tight. "Okay, hold the chioonchim, and keep this plane level with the floor."

Young-hee took the device awkwardly. The lodestone was certainly moving, spinning this way and that. Young-hee relaxed her arms and tried to stay still, to help the needle settle. The spinning slowed, swung in ever smaller arcs, until it came to rest—pointing right at Samjogo.

"Oh, you've *got* to be *kidding!*" Young-hee shouted, monumentally frustrated. She had appreciated Samjogo's help, but he was at least as annoying as he was interesting. And whatever their relationship, it was more like family than anything. It certainly wasn't her fate or future.

Samjogo arched his eyebrows in surprise. "Well, now, that's … uh, well, that's something."

Mirinae looked from the device to Young-hee, then to Samjogo, and back to Young-hee. "I don't know what's wrong." Shrugging, she reclaimed the chioonchim and began fiddling again.

"Could I try?" said Samjogo suddenly.

"Eh? You?" said Mirinae.

"Yes, me. I've been traveling with Ms. Young-hee for several days now. She saved me when I was imprisoned, and since then I have fought for her more than once. The pullocho is her quest, but I feel it has, in a way, become mine too."

"I thought you said you were some kind of bird thing. How can the chioonchim work for you?"

"I think Samjogo-the-three-legged-bird is more of an honorary title," said Young-hee.

"Most definitely *not*," snorted Samjogo.

"Well, Ungnyeo the Bear called him a bear-son," said Young-hee. "Maybe he has some mud-world human blood."

"Fine. But we'll need something of yours for the lodestone. Do you have a hairband, too?"

"No, I'm afraid not," said Samjogo. "Oh, but how about …" He fished through the pockets of his *jeogori*, and pulled out—well, Young-hee wasn't sure what—the remains of a dead, mangy rat, or something just as dreadful.

"What is that?" she asked.

"It's a good-luck charm from a fairy. I've carried it as long as I can imagine. And if it has protected me this long, it must have powerful fairy magic. What do you think, Mirinae? Fascinating?"

"Definitely not," Mirinae scoffed. "It's not alive, is it?"

"No, just a faded memory."

"All right. By now, it should carry some of your essence, but I don't detect any fairy magic, whatever you were told. It's too big, though." Mirinae found a knife, and cut a small piece, then replaced Young-hee's hairband with Samjogo's charm. Satisfied, she handed the chioonchim to Samjogo. "Okay, keep that plane level."

But before she finished that sentence, the lodestone swung back and forth so violently that they all started. "I hope it's not …," began Samjogo.

"Quiet!" Mirinae barked. "Don't disturb the search."

The lodestone swung left and quivered, then right, then spun furiously—and then, just as suddenly, came to a full halt, pointing into the distance. Mirinae held her finger up to her lips, ordering silence. She opened the wooden slat in front of the needle, adjusted the chioonchim, angled the plane up and down, then carefully rotated a dial surrounding the lodestone needle. "Uh-huh," she said, followed by "Hmm" and "Fascinating." She spun around, fumbled through a table of scrolls, picked one, and read the indecipherable scratchings. "So that's that, then," she said.

"Wha- What is it?" said Young-hee.

"I think I know where your pullocho is, dear," said Mirinae. She pointed to a star low in the sky, in a break in the clouds. "That way."

"What way?"

"Come, I'll show you," said Mirinae, hurrying downstairs, with everyone anxiously following. She found what she sought in stacks of scrolls, brushed aside the clutter, and unrolled a map. "There," she said, jabbing it with her finger.

Young-hee found no meaning in the purple-green squiggles, almost-but-not-quite Chinese characters in circles and jagged blue lines. The ornate wind rose in the corner featured animals in each direction instead of the words north, south, east, west. It looked more like a map of ideas than actual locations.

"That is your pullocho," Mirinae said. "This line is the ridge we are on. This blue line is the Hungry River. And this is where the Sacred City should be."

"And the big green shape between the river and the city?"

"That's the Great Forest. You'll want to go around it. It's a long journey, but the Great Forest is, well … "

"Great?" offered Young-hee. "Very, very big?"

"Cheeky," said Mirinae, not amused. "The Great Forest is very large, but also very peculiar. No path or quest can penetrate it. And it is full of dangers."

"She speaks truly," said Tiger. "It is the home of the Forest Fairies and their unfathomable spirits. Even I know that no one enters the Great Forest. Or, more precisely, no one leaves."

"So we go around instead?" asked Young-hee.

"Yes, although that could take a very long time," said Mirinae. "Going over the forest might be easier. Can any of you fly? No? So, around it is. Crossing the Hungry River will be tough, too, especially as it is swollen from the rains. But once over it, you can circle the forest in, oh, ten days or so?"

"Ten days?!"

"Or so."

"And then all the time I'll need to get back. Assuming we even find a pullocho there."

"I'm with you, no matter how far the journey," said Tiger.

"Mirinae's machine and my heart say the pullocho is there," said Samjogo. "You can trust both."

But I don't trust either, thought Young-hee. Of course the chioon-chim directed her right into the Great Forest, undoubtedly the one that Grandma Dol and Boonae warned her about. And Samjogo—well, he was brave, well-meaning, and fought well, but far from trustworthy. But what other choice was there? "Okay, let's get some sleep, and start in the morning," said Youngee, without much conviction.

Mirinae took blankets from a chest, and they all bedded down on the floor. The warmth of the ondol floor soothed the constant rattle of worries in Young-hee's mind.

"Young-hee?" said Mirinae, "you need to sleep the other way. If your feet face that direction while you sleep, your soul might walk away." Lacking energy to argue, Young-hee turned round and Miri-nae seemed satisfied. "It's science."

* * *

Dawn came quickly, and when the bright sunlight awakened Young-hee, she felt barely rested. Her grogginess was made all the worse by Samjogo's excessive keenness as he bragged of lucky dreams.

Mirinae descended her great staircase. She had been using the clear skies to re-check last night's observations and, unwilling to give up the original map, had sketched a copy for Young-hee. She wished Young-hee well on her journey and pronounced the weather a good omen. "Science."

But all at once the sunlight was blotted out and Mirinae's house grew dark and—*boom!* With a huge explosion, fragments of wood and stone rained from above, followed by Mirinae's precious gadgets tumbling from the overhead platform. Only the great iron armillary sphere protected them being hurt by the downpouring shrapnel.

Shielding her eyes, Young-hee looked up to see dark storm clouds beyond a newly formed hole in the roof. In the hole stood a bizarre demon. Its head was like a mutant ox, bald save for two wild patches of hair around his ears and unkempt whiskers on his chin. Each foot held a great hammer, and his right hand gripped a long sword, ridged like a bread knife. Cymbals with long ribbons hung off his waist. His two great leathery wings beat against the sky. It was Nwae-gongdo, the Storm Lord.

"Give me the girl!" he roared. "Or I will take her!"

"Oh crap," said Young-hee.

19

"*My house!*" shouted Mirinae. "What have you done to *my house?!*"

Nwaegongdo's lightning strike had filled the air with smell of ozone and charred wood. A brass ring from an astrolabe fell to the floor beside Young-hee, along with a hail of gears, glass, and other bits of gadgets. The whole observation platform moaned, shuddered ominously, and threatened collapse.

Samjogo swung his hyeopdo to deflect debris hurtling at Young-hee's head. "Go, take cover," he said, pushing her under a row of benches as he brandished the weapon. Tiger danced about avoiding falling objects, his feline skittishness rapidly turning to big-cat anger. Mirinae, sheltered along a wall, continued wailing at the demon.

The Storm Lord's beating wings swirled wind and rain through the broken hall as he slowly descended onto a huge iron ring, just overhead. He wielded his serrated sword with menace and thumped the wall with hammers. Tiger growled as he prowled underneath. "Move, little kitty," the Storm Lord warned. "My mistress wants the bear daughter, not you. Don't make me clip your tail."

"Oh, hush, you ugly, empty breeze," laughed Samjogo, stepping forward. "I've farted angrier winds than you."

"And who in the heavens are you? Besides a soon-to-be stain on my hammer?"

"Your threats mean nothing, but not knowing who I am—now, that hurts. I am Samjogo, the three-legged crow, and one of the mightiest creatures under the heavens."

Nwaegongdo's forehead wrinkled. "A samjogo? Not like any I've seen."

"*The* Samjogo, thank you very much," Samjogo corrected.

"Well, *the* samjogo," scoffed the Storm Lord, "I'd like to introduce *the* hammer." With swift violence, Nwaegongdo swung his bludgeon, using his feet as dexterously as hands. Samjogo barely dodged the heavy weapon, which smashed through tables and instruments, sending debris in all directions, then shook the whole stone house as it landed on the floor.

The Storm Lord next swung his sword, chopping a table in half. Then his other foot swung the second club, destroying more of Mirinae's precious devices. Parrying, Samjogo swung his hyeopdo at the Storm Lord's neck, but the demon easily knocked it aside. He raised his blade and charged again, but this time Tiger dove to head off the attack, swerving in that impossible, coiling feline way—he twisted once, then doubled back in the same motion, clamping his jaws hard around the Storm Lord's thick wrist. With each bellow of the demon's pain, wind and rain whipped harder. Seizing the chance, Samjogo swung his hyeopdo at the Storm Lord's body.

But the moment didn't last. Nwaegongdo deflected Samjogo's blow with his cymbal. Then he hammered the ground so hard the stone floor split and cracked, breaking Tiger's grip. Flapping his wings, he rose out of reach, readying his next attack. In a flash of orange, Tiger bounded up the wobbly stairs, light as a housecat. Leaping off the stairs, he pounced onto the Storm Lord, teeth aimed at the demon's throat. Tumbling backwards, Nwaegongdo wrapped his immense wings around Tiger and, rolling with the attack, swung his hammer. The blow flung Tiger through two stairs, shattering them. But having twisted his body in the air, Tiger had righted himself before landing in a mess of scrolls, breaking a table, and rolling to the floor, stunned but alive. Wincing, Young-hee hoped he would be okay. Good fighters though they were, Tiger and Samjogo were no match for such a powerful demon.

"This is ridiculous," snapped Mirinae, bolting from her hiding place. She ran past her dragon-bone clypsedra and started rooting in a particularly messy corner.

With boastful and angry cries, Nwaegongdo reached behind his back and pulled out a great drum and one of his hammers. The air crackled as he readied to summon a lightning bolt—and, just then, Young-hee realized that nearly every machine of Mirinae's was made of metal, including the giant iron rings of the huge armillary sphere for mapping the heavens. Electricity plus metal sounded like a formula for a very bad outcome. "*Everyone, get down!*" she shouted.

The Storm Lord hammered his drum with a joyful solemnity, and a huge bolt of lightning shot out with a blinding flash and deafening clap. But in the enclosed hall, full of conductive materials, the electricity went wild. It bounced and ricocheted everywhere, filling the chamber with a vast web of errant forking zips of electricity. It would have been beautiful, had it not been so deadly. Young-hee screamed.

Luckily, the giant armillary sphere absorbed most of the strike, sending much of it back at Nwaegongdo. He crashed to the stone floor, stunned and smoking slightly. Samjogo recovered quickly, dashed at him, and swung his hyeopdo in a big arc. Nwaegongdo rolled away, but Samjogo's blade ripped into his large wing. The demon shouted something Young-hee was sure were demonic swear words.

The rush of battle gave way to a spontaneous lull. Then, with an unceremonious waddle, Mirinae pulled a square wooden cart from the messy corner. Behind its two big wheels were rows of tubes in a five-by-ten grid, each tube with four sharp points sticking out. Young-hee's eyes widened. It looked like an ancient weapon she had seen once while on a class trip to a museum—a *hwacha*, a "fire cart" that shot hundreds of explosives and flaming arrows at a time. And Mirinae was lighting it. "This is *my* house," she repeated, more pissed off than ever.

At first the sparks popped and crackled so lightly it was almost comical. But as the burning fuse jumped from tube to tube, the hwacha lit up like holiday fireworks. All at once, the sparks gave way to a roar of rockets, as hundreds of arrows caught fire and blasted out. The first salvo, right into the Storm Lord's chest, drove him back. The next volley blasted the demon with an explosive fury of flaming arrows.

It was a brutal barrage, but not only for Nwaegongdo. Burning slivers of wood and roasting wreckage bounced off the walls and rained down. Samjogo heaved and shoved Tiger to the side of the room, away from the worst of the shrapnel. Young-hee pulled her legs under the bench, becoming as small as possible. The hail of burning debris seemed interminable, and the noise so overwhelming that Young-hee couldn't think straight at first. Then, the hall fell largely quiet—save for the crackle of burning wood and irregular thump of falling rubble.

"That did it," said Mirinae, sounding satisfied.

"Yes, I think he's gone," said Samjogo, emerging from a wreckage-strewn corner.

Mirinae, uninterested in gloating, rummaged through her stacks. "Science," she said. "Don't get too happy, though. The Storm Lord is made of sterner stuff than that."

Tiger was smoldering slightly from hot ashes that had dropped on him. He had new stripes burned into his fur. Young-hee looked for water and blankets. "You think Nwaegongdo survived?" she asked.

"Probably," said Mirinae, still poking around. "But hopefully, not very well. Still, I recommend moving with some haste."

"Will you come with us?" asked Young-hee.

"With *you*?" said Mirinae, with an incredulous huff and a hollow laugh. "You're the reason my laboratory and home is so much scrap." Overhead, the observatory platform—empty of telescopes, desks and devices—moaned and sagged. Mirinae pulled out an interconnected jumble of bamboo sticks, large sheets of paper, gears, and ropes. She carried it through another hole in the wall that had been created by the fleeing Storm Lord to the field outside. The after-storm sun shone bright and piercing. "I'm going my own way, as far from you lot as I can. I would thank you never to come to me for help again."

"Not unreasonable," said Samjogo.

The bamboo and paper looked like a chaotic mess, but Mirinae began turning and snapping pieces into place, aligning the wood into rectangles, and filling the space between with the paper. After a couple of minutes, Mirinae's latest device was clear—a large kite, with a seat and controls. A glider.

She went back into her home, avoiding unstable objects, and returned with a couple of bags bulging with star charts and blueprints. "My machines, I can rebuild, but the science, that I need," she said. She put the large piece of red crystal into a bag and half-smiled. "Consider yourself lucky my fire pearl survived."

"What is it?" asked Young-hee, not sure why.

Mirinae huffed again. "It grants farsight. It holds sunlight. And much more." Then mounting her kite-glider, she waited. A moment later, a cool, gentle wind swept over the plateau, lifting Mirinae high into the air. She headed back toward the Cheongyong Mountains, and in just a couple of minutes, was out of sight.

"Fascinating," said Samjogo.

"She never said goodbye," said Young-hee.

"I don't think we were very good houseguests," noted Tiger.

With a huge boom, the house shook and trembled, and a cloud of dust billowed out. "That must have been the platform," said Samjogo. "Come on, let's see if we can salvage anything and get moving."

* * *

Young-hee's path continued from Mirinae's house down a staircase cut right into the cliff. From the top of the cliff, they had surveyed the land Mirinae described—at the precipice bottom it receded in a rocky slope for several miles, until cut through by the Hungry River, which stretched from horizon to horizon. Across the river lay vast, dense woods—the Great Forest that everyone warned about. And beyond that, a looming ridge of purple mountains, with one peak towering over the rest. Somewhere high on that hill were the Sacred City and the sandalwood tree—and the pullocho.

The stone stairs were narrow, and time had smoothed some and worn others cracked and fragile. For four-legged Tiger, still shaky from the battle, they were especially treacherous. But the three kept moving, motivated by the knowledge that the Storm Lord and Ghost Queen were out there somewhere, still after them.

After a little over an hour they reached the cliff bottom. Ahead, a rocky plain rolled from the highlands far in the distance. Samjogo wanted them across the river, for safety, so they headed as straight as they could. The black stone path was visible on the uneven ground, but barely. "When you know where you are going, paths tend to follow your will," explained Samjogo. Young-hee had heard enough about path science and just looked ahead to the mountain that held the Sacred City. Hope of actually finding the pullocho gave her renewed urgency and relief—along with increased anxiety from the Storm Lord's attack.

They were halfway to the distant river when a distant rattle wail swept the plain. Tiger guessed it was a ghost spotting them from the cliff top.

"At least Nwaegongdo won't be flying soon with his messed up wing," said Samjogo.

They talked little as they hurried to the river. Debilitated by the fight, no one relished another showdown. A good couple of miles away, the river roared with the ugly sound of flooded water moving hard, tearing up anything in its way. But Young-hee welcomed it as one landmark closer to getting her brother back.

Then it was Tiger's turn to slow and look around as he picked up a scent. "Up the hill, there," he said, nodding toward two large figures on horseback, still a ways off, but closing in.

"The Storm Lord appears to have gotten a horse," said Samjogo. "And he's pulling a cart."

"And his friend?" asked Young-hee.

"Another evil spirit, I assume."

As they broke into a run, Young-hee saw the sky darken and fill with clouds; the Storm Lord at work again, she thought. The rough and rocky ground made running tough for them—and their pursuers.

"I'll go head them off, buy you some time," said Tiger.

"No, we should stick together," said Young-hee, between breaths.

"She's right, stay with us," said Samjogo. Tiger obeyed, but moved between the riders and Young-hee.

Her lungs burning from the run, Young-hee reached the river—

but it was completely impassable. Swollen from the Storm Lord's rains, it churned brown and bellowed with fury, licking at its banks and, in places, spilling greedily over. She understood why it was called the Hungry River. "What now?" asked Young-hee breathlessly.

Samjogo scanned up and down the river, for a passable place, a ferry, anything. But there was only the great and terrible water, at least a hundred meters across. They were stuck.

Nwaegongdo and the other man on huge workhorses stopped about fifty meters away. The second man was gigantic, too—eight feet tall, with a face as red and rough as lychee rind. Dressed in dark green, with golden script embroidered on his sleeves, he carried a wide, heavy sword. The fierce, blood-red horse pulled a cart carrying a large wooden box full of baskets.

"This time, I brought help," Nwaegongdo laughed. "Meet the Lord of War."

The red-faced man dismounted silently, walked to the cart, picked up the box, and placed it on the ground. He touched the small flame that rose from his open hand to the box of baskets. Flames quickly flared into a massive bonfire. Young-hee shielded her eyes from the brilliance, wondering what was going on.

"That fire is how the Lord of War carries his army," said Samjogo. "We cannot fight his hordes. We need to get out of here." *Hordes?* Young-hee wondered.

"There's nowhere to go," taunted the Storm Lord. "And the Lord of War has a present for you. It is rude to just run off."

As fire consumed the box and baskets, they tumbled to the ground, releasing something bumpy and busy. Smoke and fire obscured whatever was pouring out, but it didn't move like a regular liquid. Dark and jumbled, like a dense swarm of black ants, it moved toward them.

And that's when Young-hee realized what was pouring out of the flaming baskets—swarms of tiny soldiers, just an inch or two tall. By the thousands. Tiny soldiers clanking tiny swords off tiny shields, pounding the earth with tiny boots, and charging with tiny battle cries joined in a sickening, high-pitched cacophony. Closing fast.

Tiger crouched, ready to fight. Samjogo readied his hyeopdo. Young-hee just gulped. *How do you fight against thousands of tiny soldiers*, she wondered.

Just then, she heard a noise over the roar of the river. Searching about, she heard it again, clearer. "Excuse me?" it said. Young-hee looked behind her at the river's edge. There was the head of a large turtle sticking out of the water. "Are you Miss Young-hee?"

"Uh, yes?"

"Please, the Water Dragon King sent us to help."

Mansoo? How did the Water Dragon King know they needed help? But how didn't matter, they just needed help. The thousands of tiny warriors screamed as they rushed forward. "Can you help us fight Nwaegongdo's warriors?"

"Fight? Oh, Turtles don't fight." Twenty feet and closing fast. "Please, climb on. We'll get you to the other side."

"We?" asked Young-hee. But even as she spoke, dozens of turtles rose out of the water, locking together to form a bridge with their shells.

"Hurry, please. The current is very strong, and it is hard to hold on."

Young-hee grabbed at Samjogo and Tiger. "Come on! Run!"

"Where?" said Tiger, too busy preparing to fight to notice their new allies. The tiny soldiers were almost on top of them when he looked and grasped what was happening.

"Come on, come on!" Young-hee shouted as she tugged on Samjogo. He saw the turtles, too, and in an instant they were all rushing over the turtle-back bridge, just inches above the gushing water.

As soon as the three crossed one turtle, it would sink back into the river and swim away, so that the bridge disappeared as quickly as they ran. The stampeding warriors, running too hard to stop, poured into the fierce river, which quickly swept them away. With only her feet wet, Young-hee stumbled to the far shore of the river, along with Tiger and Samjogo.

"There are entirely too many creatures trying to capture you," said Samjogo.

"I'm not exactly enjoying this either," she said, plunking down in the wet grass. She turned to the turtles in the water. "Thank you so much. And thanks to Mansoo. We never could have gotten away without you."

"We are always happy to serve the Water Dragon King and help his friends," said the lead turtle.

"The Dragon King sends servants to help you?" said Samjogo, dazzled.

"I told you before he was my friend," said Young-hee.

"Yes, but, I didn't … I mean … wow! A good friend to have."

"Oh, Miss Young-hee, one more thing," said the turtle. "A message from the Dragon King—our lord says you shouldn't be scared to give up what you most want."

"What? Why would he say that?" *Did he mean my brother?*

"I do not know. That was the message. But now, my siblings and I need to go, before the evil spirits return." And without so much as a *blup*, the turtles sank beneath the brown, churning waters.

Tiger kept an eye on the far side of the river, while Samjogo unhappily surveyed the forest a few dozen meters ahead, as dense as a wall.

Young-hee looked at the path, which split into two, following the edge of the forest upstream and downstream. "Which way are we supposed to go?" she asked.

"We might not have any options," interjected Tiger, meekly. "Oh, dear."

Young-hee and Samjogo looked across the river. Nwaegongdo's tiny warriors were still streaming from the burning baskets into the rushing river in such numbers that they were starting to create a barrier. At first it was a small outcropping, but as more and more ran into the water, they began to form a living dam. There was no end to the soldiers under Nwaegongdo's command. In just a few moments, the dam extended about ten meters into the water.

The Storm Lord first, followed by the Lord of War, rode to the barrier. Nwaegongdo's horse placed a tentative hoof onto the barrier and, convinced it would hold, strode forward, its rider laughing and sneering.

"Oh, jeez, you've got to be kidding," said Young-hee. "Are they actually going to cross like that?"

"I'm afraid so," said Samjogo.

The living dam was now a quarter of the way across the river.

"We cannot fight them," said Samjogo.

Young-hee had a terrible feeling she knew the alternative. No one even had to say it. They just turned and walked off the path, toward the Great Forest. Where they had been warned not to go. Where there was no path.

As they approached the forest, the evil spirits urged the tiny soldiers into the river even faster. The Storm Lord shouted something at Young-hee, but the pounding water snatched his words away.

Young-hee went first, pushing through the dense, fence-like wall of the Great Forest's edge. Just what she had been warned not to do.

20

The Great Forest was absolutely still and silent. Despite the on-slaught of evil that had been rushing toward them, the moment they crossed the threshold of the woods, the sounds of the spirits, their horses, the charging tiny warriors, and even the roaring river dropped away. Here, it was as cozy and comforting as a warm bath. Young-hee thought she had never before been enveloped by so much utter nothingness, even in the depths of Darang Cave.

The wall of trees guarding the perimeter had made entering the forest a tight squeeze. But once inside, white and lonely trees like young birches were spaced out, with little brush on the ground. So it was easy to walk wherever they wanted. There just was no path, or sign to guide them. Just sameness and stillness, a pleasant emptiness stretching as far as they could see.

They had entered in a panicked rush to escape the spirits chasing them, but after a few meters they slowed to a walk, their sense of the danger melting away. "Shouldn't we be running?" said Young-hee.

"Yes, yes, the Great Forest is not safe for us," said Samjogo, sound-ing more bored than hurried. "Let's catch our breath, and speed up in a few moments."

And so they walked. There were no sounds of animals, no birds, no wind rustling through the leaves. Just a beautiful, vacant forest. Peaceful, like the beginning of a good nap.

The sameness made it impossible to know the right direction. Samjogo and Young-hee tried climbing the trees, but the upper branches were too weak to let them get high enough to see over the forest canopy.

At one point the trees parted, giving way to a small, shallow pond. Young-hee felt as if she had read about the scene in a book. "Do you think I could get back home if I jumped into the pond?" she asked. "Or maybe into yet another world?"

"It's just a pond," said Tiger, with a yawn.

In fact, they were all yawning, more and more. The soft, grassy ground looked ever more comfortable, and Young-hee contemplated a nap—just a short one, of course.

"*Young-hee!*"

Samjogo's sharp call snapped her to attention. *Did I nod off while walking?* she wondered, happy to have avoided a tree. "Sorry, just a little sleepy," she said sheepishly.

"Yes, we all seem strangely tired," said Samjogo, blinking hard to force himself awake.

"I don't see the problem," said Tiger, yawning again. "The forest is perfectly safe and peaceful. We could sleep until we're feeling refreshed."

"No, Tiger, we need to keep going. We can sleep in a proper camp once it gets dark. Or did you forget who was following us?"

Tiger grunted a reluctant acknowledgement and kept walking. "I don't hear anyone following us," he said. But they were all slowing down, finding it harder to continue.

Finally, Tiger plopped to the ground and curled up, his eyes closed, his mouth smiling. "Tiger, *no!*" said Young-hee. "Don't sleep. This isn't natural."

"Just a short nap," he said, without opening his eyes. "Then we'll walk more."

"No, we need to keep going."

"You keep going and I'll catch up in a bit."

There was no moving him. Tiger was out cold. Young-hee envied him. "I wish I could sleep, too. Just for five minutes?"

"No, Young-hee," said Samjogo. "Something or someone is trying to stop us from moving forward. We have to keep going."

"But what about Tiger?"

Samjogo shouted into Tiger's ear, but got no reaction. He pushed hard on the big cat's hindquarters. He even tugged Tiger's whiskers, earning a reflexive paw-swat in the chest. Still Tiger would not wake.

"I fear we have to leave him behind," said Samjogo. "Whatever magic is operating here has him firmly in its grasp. We need to get away"—Samjogo yawned big, too—"We can come back for him once we are safe."

Young-hee agreed, so they set off without their friend. She steeled her senses, determined not to succumb to the magic. But the deeper they moved into the forest, the worse the sleepiness. Soon it began to rain—not Nwaegongdo's cold, nasty rain, but warm, relaxing drops that turned the air sultry and thick. She put on her jacket to stay dry, but the sound of raindrops on its hood was ever more hypnotic.

They kept walking, drifting in and out of strange sleep. One would catch the other nodding off and shout a warning. Each drift grew deeper and harder to wake from.

At one point, as dreams were sneaking up, Young-hee snapped awake. At first she couldn't see Samjogo—sleepwalking had separated them by a good twenty meters—as good as a mile in a forest. Young-hee considered herself lucky to spot her friend.

She and Samjogo kept going, forcing each step.

When she woke again, she was leaning against a tree and, judging by the trail of spittle running down the rain-soaked trunk, she had stopped walking for some time. Beginning to cross back into sleep and dreams, her thoughts floated to Bum, and that shot her awake.

She stood up, wiped her mouth, and shook her head to clear her thoughts. "Samjogo!" she shouted. "Where are you?" No answer. Just stillness and silence, punctuated by the pulse of rain.

Young-hee felt panic rising up again. *Where was he? He couldn't be far away.* She ran about, trying to retrace her steps, calling out. Still no sign. At least panic would help keep her awake, she noted wryly. "Samjogo?" she cried again. Nothing.

There was nothing to do but keep walking. Perhaps he was ahead and she'd run into him.

So Young-hee continued, fighting off overpowering drowsiness. *How large is the Great Forest, anyhow?* She realized she had no idea how long it would take to the other side—or what awaited her there. But without options, she kept walking.

After what seemed ages—although she had lost all sense of time—she saw something moving ahead. *There he is*, she thought. But relief quickly dissipated. *That's not Samjogo.* It was a man, walking slowly toward her. He clearly had seen her. It was too late to hide.

The stranger stepped through the trees, right up to her. Tall and elegant, broad-shouldered with a back ramrod-straight, his face was obscured by a large hat, his body by a flowing *durumagi* overcoat. *Who was he? What was he doing in the woods?*

"Greetings, stranger," said the man. "Not many outsiders try passing through our forest."

He looked oddly familiar, but it was hard to see him clearly. "Uh, hello. Yes, my friends and I seem to have gotten lost," she said.

"Your friends?"

"Yeah. First we got lost together. Now I've lost them, too."

"Few outsiders try passing through our forest, and even fewer succeed."

Well, that sounds ominous. "Oh. I hope I'm not … trespassing or anything like that. I didn't mean to be rude or break your rules." *Where have I seen him before?*, she kept wondering. "Uh, do you think you could help me out? Maybe point me in the right direction?"

"Why are you here?"

"We were trying to get to the Sacred City. Some … bad people chased us across the Hungry River, and we entered the Great Forest to hide. We were told that the Sacred City lies on the other side of this forest." Young-hee wasn't sure why she was so honest. "I was on a quest, to help my little brother. But there are no paths in your woods, and it is so hard to know where to go."

"Yes, it is easy to get lost here. But the Sacred City is in that direction." He pointed behind him, just to Young-hee's left.

"Thank you. Thank you so much." She got ready to resume walking.

"However, I would not advise it."

"Oh?" *There's always a hitch*, she grumbled silently.

"Trying to leave the forest seldom works well. I recommend going that way"—he pointed to her right—"deeper, into its heart."

"Deeper into the forest?"

"Yes," he said. "Sometimes you need to get more lost before you can find your way out."

Young-hee recalled similar advice before. If she had learned anything in Strange Land, it was that the direct, most logical route was rarely the best.

"Into the heart…"

The man nodded. "If you go straight that way, you will come to a stream. Follow it to a house. There you should find the help you need."

"Oh, thanks," said Young-hee, straining to see where the man had been pointing. It looked the same as any other part of the forest. "Could you tell me who you are? So I can tell the people in the house who sent me?"

But when she turned back, he was gone. The forest was deathly quiet again. She nearly called out "*Jigyeowo*," but caught herself. Strange Land had thrown her another odd obstacle. She could handle it.

She considered choosing the most direct way out, but took the stranger's advice, turned right and resumed walking.

After a while, Young-hee began to worry that she had not followed the man's directions properly. Or perhaps he had lied. But too sleepy to think, she pushed forward.

And, then, there it was—a small brook, winding lazily through the forest. It didn't look very deep, and despite the rain was perfectly clear and gentle. Plus there seemed something strange about the riverbed—it looked … smooth.

Young-hee walked right into the water. A few inches deep, it reached just above her shoes. The bottom was smooth, white, and hard, like marble, although luckily not as slippery. *This is very odd.* Walking in the middle of the brook, she followed its twists and turns downstream.

Right around then, the rain stopped. On the other side of the river were countless bamboo trees, their long, thin trunks reaching high into the air. The soft murmur of the water was the only sound. *Maybe having wet feet is waking me up a bit because I don't feel so sleepy any more*, she thought. In perhaps a mile, she saw the house— a simple hanok, good for a small family.

Stepping out of the stream, Young-hee walked to the front gate and knocked using the iron ring. It was just a ring, not a biting animal. After a few moments, there was a sound from inside, and an old, thin man opened the door. Long whiskers clung to his face like ivy on an aged stone wall. *He looks like an old, cracked piece of bamboo*, she noted.

"Uh, hello. Sorry to bother you. I'm trying to get out of this forest, and a man I met back there"—she pointed behind her—"said I should follow the river to a house and ask for help."

"Ah, yes. Very good," he said. "I've been waiting a long time for you."

"Oh, sorry? I came as soon as I could. I think it was just an hour or so."

"No, you don't understand. I've been waiting a long time for you, Miss Young-hee. Please, come with me." Without another word, the man took a jade, nine-segmented walking stick from his home, closed the door behind him, and led Young-hee into the woods, away from the stream. Young-hee wanted to ask about leaving the forest, but somehow the thought, light as a shadow, kept slipping away, so she just followed him.

They walked quietly for a mile or so until at last they came to a slight hill where the trees thinned into a large clearing. The entire hillside was filled by an immense palace. Even from the outside, with great walls surrounding it, the building was spectacular. The parapets were covered with colorful jewels, precious stones, and exotic crystals. The roofs of the buildings inside the walls were made of beautiful, ornate ceramic tiles, curling in long, baroque eaves that spread like fir trees. The main gate of the palace was open. The old man led Young-hee to the gate and stopped.

"I can go no further. But you are invited to enter," he said.

"But whose palace is it? Who's inviting me?"

The old man offered no answers. "In the great hall, you will find the lord of the palace. You must talk with him," he said.

Entering cautiously, she found wooden halls, pavilions and residences around a courtyard of white stone bricks. To one side was a great pool, surrounded by bamboo trees, where myriad birds swam and perched. *The same ones Samjogo and I saw a few days ago?* All the palace buildings were beautiful, with curling eaves and thick, wooden beams painted red; elaborate green, blue, and red designs covered the halls.

But only one building could be the great hall. Large as a soccer field, and three times higher the others, it loomed in the center of the palace grounds. Each floor was set off by flaring, curling eaves. The hall rested on a ten-meter high stone base topped with balustrades, each carved in the shape of a different animal. The Gyeongbokgung and Deoksugung palaces Young-hee had seen in Seoul looked like mud huts in comparison.

As she walked through the grounds, she realized it was full of forest fairies, all so slight and beautiful in their hanbok of earth-toned greens and browns. They looked at her, nodded respectfully, then resumed their work.

She climbed the stone steps to the great hall's entrance, marked by a large marble table holding a jade brazier of burning incense. Inside, hundreds of fairies in scholarly robes sat studying at low tables running across the cavernous hall. One of the tables pointed to the hall's deep heart. Young-hee passed row after row of studying fairies until the tables came to an end.

In the center of the room, reclining alone at a great table, sat a broad-shouldered fairy in green ceremonial robes. It was the man she had met earlier in the forest, the same person who had told her to travel this way. But this time she recognized him. He was clearly a fairy, but he also looked exactly like her father.

21

Young-hee stood before the fairy's table, too shocked to react. *How could this man look like my father? Could it be him?* She had not seen her father in more than a year, since the police came and her life in Canada had fallen apart.

The fairy looked at her kindly. "Please, sit. You've had a long, difficult journey. Have something to eat."

"B-but," she stammered. "I don't … I mean, but…" Face to face with her dad—well, what *looked* like her dad—Young-hee was suddenly speechless. She had not realized how much she missed him. Her heart ached so badly, like she had been stabbed in the middle of her chest.

He gave a signal, and servants quickly filled the table with all manner of foods. "Sit. Eat first. Then we'll talk."

Not knowing what else to do, Young-hee sat on a mat across from the fairy. There were noodles as light as gossamer. Amazing-colored fruit. Steaming soups that smelled of dawn after a night of rain. She picked up her chopsticks, but then stopped. "Who are you?" she asked.

"I am the king of the Forest Fairies," he said matter-of-factly.

"Is that all you are?"

"What else would I be?" His voice was so warm it sounded like a laugh. Young-hee couldn't recall ever hearing a voice so wonderful.

"You look like …"

"But *that* would be impossible," he interrupted. Even then, he sounded kind. "Eat."

So Young-hee ate. And as she ate, other fairies played music—complex rhythms, with wisps of melancholic melodies above the deep percussions. The music was sad, but somehow evoked a sort of joy. Or maybe the other way around. When she couldn't eat any more, the servants cleared the table.

"Did you like the food? The music?"

"Very much."

"It is said that when the forest fairy play their songs, even the clouds stop to listen."

"I believe it. It was very beautiful. And sad."

"Like a dream, perhaps."

"Am I dreaming?" asked Young-hee, suddenly afraid. "Am I lying in the woods, asleep, just dreaming all this? Or maybe this whole world has been a dream, and I'm still home, in my lousy apartment?"

The king smiled softly. "Have you ever had a dream like this?"

"No."

"It is no dream, I promise. And tomorrow is a lucky day. I'm happy you made it in time."

"In time for what?"

"My eldest son will marry a princess of the Cloud Fairies. It will be a beautiful ceremony, with all of our finest foods and music, dancing and joyfulness. A fairy wedding is a wonderful celebration, and a marriage of fairy royalty is beyond imagining."

"Yes, that does sound very nice. But…"

"But?"

It was so hard to think, to remember. "But I came here for help to get out of this forest so I can find a pullocho and save my brother."

"Yes, I know all about that. After the wedding, there will be time for serious talk. Come celebrate with us. I promise it will not delay your quest. It will be a very joyful occasion. And necessary."

Young-hee breathed heavily through her nose, trying to keep calm. She couldn't stand any more distractions from saving her brother—but a few hours' sleep wouldn't be so bad. "Okay, but then you must help me."

"Wonderful!" said the king. "So, tonight, enjoy our hospitality. Rest. Bathe. And tomorrow I will show you so many things."

He stood and told the servants to prepare the nicest residence, the finest clothes, and everything his guest could need.

Before dismissing her, the king took Young-hee's hands in his and kissed her fingers lightly, just like her dad had done when she was little and had been crying. Then he gave her a big hug. Many dads she knew could be so distant, but not hers. He was warm and kind, which is why it hurt so much when he went to prison.

It was dark when the servants escorted her to her very own residential hall, a long, wooden building covered with precious metals and jewels. Inside, beautiful paintings, long panoramas of animals and mountains and spirits covered walls and screens. Young-hee soaked in a hot bath for over an hour, trying to settle her busy, worried mind. Later, servants brought new clothes of impossibly soft cloth woven by fairy magic. A hanbok, dark blue with golden trim fit perfectly, its light silk as warm as a fleece. Incense burning in the hall smelled of lavender.

The next morning she woke to hot soup and kaypal rice on a table in her room. She ate voraciously and felt immensely satisfied—at least until she remembered her brother. *How could I have forgotten?* she chastised herself.

Sliding open the door to her hall, she discovered the fairy king waiting patiently. "Are you ready?" he asked.

"I guess so. I don't really know where we're going."

"First the wedding. Then further in."

A palanquin carried them to the Great Hall. Emptied of scholarly tables, the huge hall was decorated for the wedding with jewel-lined flowers, silk ribbons, and all the fairy fineries. Jade bells rang out, and delightful perfume filled in the air. The Cloud Fairies, beautiful but more wispy than their Forest cousins, wore light blues and whites. The princess, wearing a great string of pearls, stood at the front with the king's son, and Young-hee thought they were the most gorgeous couple she had ever seen. Music, dancing, and happiness filled the hall. Wedding hall ceremonies in Korea were always so deathly dull and tacky, but this was both dignified and fun at the same time. After the ceremony, despite her anxiety, Young-hee joined in the joyful feasting and celebration.

The day was nearly gone when she finally remembered her great hurry. Hunting through the crowds of fairies, she found the king, at last. "Your majesty, I'm sorry to interrupt, but … "

"Ah, there you are. Would you like to see how fairies see the world?"

What a peculiar question. "Yes, I guess. Maybe next time."

"Nonsense. This is the perfect time." So the king led Young-hee deeper into the palace. They passed resplendent streams and waterfalls winding through the grounds. The estate was even more huge than she had noticed yesterday, another world unto itself, full of green hills and a menagerie of animals, all living peacefully with the fairies.

The king led Young-hee to the estate's center, where its largest hill was crowned by a tall tower. They climbed stairs to the top where he showed her the full view of the palace. All around, waterfalls and hills and buildings and animals fit together in perfect harmony, with a golden halo hanging over it all. The sounds of the fairies' music—*gayageum* zithers, *haeguem* fiddles, *daegeum* flutes, and *buk* and *janggu* drums—floated from the wedding, echoed through the hills. The king regaled Young-hee with fabulous stories from fairy history. Before she knew it, the sun had set. The fairy wedding went long into the night. Young-hee sang and danced and made many friends, and forgot her worries. Before bed, the king recited a *shijo* poem:

You ask how many friends I have?
Water, rocks, pine, and bamboo.
And when the moon rises over east mountain,
I feel even greater pleasure.
Enough:
To these five why add more?

Young-hee thought it sounded marvelous, even if she didn't totally understand it. *Why add more?* she thought, drifting off to sleep.

She woke up late the next day, another great meal by her bed. For a brief moment she remembered her quest, her brother. *There's some sort of magic here, making me forget.* But by the time she finished eating, she had forgotten yet again.

That day, the fairies hosted games for their Cloud Fairy guests—running, archery, riding, and more. The following day, the king showed Young-hee the most precious and magical creatures in his zoo—the eight-legged *cheollima* horse, capable of traveling a thousand *li* in one gallop, and the great cranes, bigger than a house, like Young-hee had seen in the sky when she first entered Strange Land.

And so it went. Each day was special with exotic and entertaining happenings. There were people to meet, songs to sing, and fun to have. Time slipped away. Days, then weeks, then months, and before Young-hee knew it two years had passed. Time had turned into nothing, and she rarely thought about why she come or what lay beyond the Great Forest. And as soon as she half-remember her other life, a new delight arrived to distracted her.

One day Young-hee was seated beside the Forest Fairy King at one feast or another when the king's son and daughter-in-law entered. Young-hee, laughing at a joke, suddenly noticed that the Cloud Fairy carried a small child, her firstborn. All at once, Young-hee thought of her brother. "Young-beom!" she exclaimed. *How could I have forgotten him? How long have I been here?* "No, no, no! This is all wrong!"

Everyone fell silent and stared at her. "Is something wrong, Young-hee?" asked the fairy king.

"Something is *very* wrong! My brother—I came to find my brother. Instead I've been stuck for ages." Young-hee knew she was making people uncomfortable, but didn't care.

"I'm surprised you remember your brother, after all this time," said the king.

"I can't believe I forgot," said Young-hee, struggling to free her thoughts.

"It's okay, these things happen in the fairies' home. Tomorrow we will talk about him."

"*No!*" said Young-hee, louder than she intended. "No, *not* tomorrow. No more tomorrows! *No laters! No more mysteries!*" Once she started yelling she couldn't stop; one frustrated bellow swept into the next, until her heart raged like the Hungry River. All eyes were on her. "You said you could help. I need to leave and save my brother. I-I need … I'm sorry," she said, embarrassment battling rage, and started to cry. *Great … blubbering like a little girl.* The more she cried, the angrier it made her, and the angrier she got, the more embarrassed she grew, and the more embarrassed she was, the more she cried. "Stupid," she muttered and stood up, determined to leave immediately.

The king reached across the table and placed a large, strong hand on hers. "This world is very different from the world of mud and dust you came from. It can seem … difficult."

"I'm sorry," Young-hee repeated, happy to be all cried out. "It's just … I can't stay here any more. I have no idea how long I've been here or what's happened to Young-beom. If you won't help, I'll go by myself. Maybe I can't get through the forest, but I have to try."

The king looked into Young-hee's eyes, steady and thoughtful. "Yes, I believe you."

"You don't need to believe me. Just watch me go."

"No, that's not necessary," said the king, rising, "We can go together." As they left the hall, the celebrations started again.

"Is this a trick? To make me forget again?"

"No, no tricks. I just wanted to talk before you left."

Young-hee walked to her private pavilion, packed her belongings, and donned her own clothes. The king was waiting outside. "Which way do I go?" asked Young-hee, suddenly aware it had been years since she saw or thought of the main gate.

"I will walk you there."

Young-hee noticed that the palace seemed less and less magical with each step. The jewels faded, the great pond turned mossy and shrank, the buildings grew older and more run down. "Why did you make me stay?"

"We never made you. You've been in the realm of immortals, beyond the attachments of mud. Had you stayed, you could have forgotten everything from your mud world—anger, longing, sadness, hate, fear, ambition, selfishness."

"But I would have forgotten my family, too."

"Yes, everything. In time."

"That's terrible."

"Terrible? Weren't you happy here?"

Young-hee thought for a moment. "No," she said. "I mean, it was all wonderful, everyone was fun and delightful. But I feel … distracted, not happy."

"I see," said the king. "Before you go, may I show you one more thing? It will only take a moment, and it is about your family."

"A moment?"

The king nodded and led Young-hee to his private pavilion, now a rotted relic of the splendid mansion. They mounted a staircase to a tower where there lay a large, jade-colored crystal, uneven and unclear.

"This is my dragon glass. It grants far sight."

"Like a fire pearl?"

He laughed. "Yes, a little. As a grain of sand resembles a mountain. Look into the dragon glass."

So she looked. The blue crystal warped her vision, magnifying some things, shrinking others. "I can't see anything."

"Keep looking."

Gradually, blue crystal cleared and the views sorted into near and far. She saw the forest fairies in the palace, playing, studying, and living. She saw miles of bamboo beyond the walls. And, slowly, she began to see ever farther—to the Great Forest and across the vast expanses of Strange Land. She saw past Cheongyong Mountains, the Ogre's Fist, Lake Mey, and more. She saw the Wandering Mountains and the Jade Forest and the great Orange Sea. The more she looked, the faster she sped across wider and wider plains and realms, always with startling clarity. She saw Bassam walking across desert wastes with a treasure-caravan laden.

Then, all at once, she was looking into a Korean apartment—large and modern, but tasteful. It looked lived-in and happy. Young-hee had lived in an unhappy apartment for long enough to know the difference. Happy homes lacked that nervous edge, the dreadful anticipation of the next thing to go wrong.

A door opened, and a young girl ran through, in a pretty skirt and fashionable haircut, followed by her mother. *Her* mother. It took Young-hee a moment to realize she was looking at her mom. And herself. They were laughing, happy. She felt confused. A moment later a man entered. Her father.

"What is that?" she asked.

"It is you. Or it could be, if you wanted."

"Me?"

"You could be back home, in your world."

"Oh, really? You can do that?" After all she had been through in Strange Land, it seemed too good to be true. Young-hee blinked hard, trying to believe that the vivid scene before her in the blue glass was real. "But that's not my world," she said. "Or my apartment. I don't wear skirts"—that struck her as quite odd—"Or live with my dad."

"Yes, but you could. Just tell me that's what you want, and I have the power to return you to your world."

"My world. But in a nice home. With my father."

"Yes. Just like you always dreamed. Just tell me you want it, and I can send you there. No more quest, no paths, no more monsters chasing you, no scheming spirits."

Young-hee didn't want to let herself believe it. After all she had been through, the forest fairy king return her home? Not just home, but a better home. With her father back. It was … perfect. And then …

"Where's Bum?"

"Sorry?"

"Young-beom, my little brother. Where is he?"

"Ah, your brother. That, I'm afraid to say, is the one thing I cannot give you. He was captured by a goblin. That is an old magic, strong and true—one I cannot simply undo."

"But … you can do all this other stuff."

"Yes, I can give you everything you have wanted for so long. Everything except that one thing."

"But the whole reason I've traveled so far, is for Bum," she trailed off. In the crystal's images —her father back, her mother happy—everything seemed so right. But … "He needs me."

"Does he really? Can you really be so sure? He is stronger and more resourceful than you realize. And didn't you always resent him?" The king's words stung her. "Wouldn't the family be happier without him?"

"No. I have to get him. I promised." As she said the words, she knew they were true. Even though losing her dad again was just as terrible. "I have to go."

"That is your choice. But know this—even if you find your pullo-cho and complete your quest, you will lose your brother."

"You don't know that."

"I do."

"I have to try. Wherever he is now, I will find him."

"Of course you will try. I know that, too."

As they descended the steps and left the king's residence, rotten timbers creaked and collapsed behind them.

"My leaving is destroying your palace."

"Only for you. For us immortals, it will forever be glorious and beautiful. But before you go, we have a gift, to thank you and, perhaps, to help your journey."

A ragged servant approached, head bowed, carrying the finest lacquer box, with mother-of-pearl designs so vivid they seemed alive. The fairy king opened it. Inside were three small vials, one white, one red, one blue. "Blue is for water," he said, "red for fire, and white for nature. When you are desperate, open a vial and let a single drop fall to the ground—but no more—and it should help."

"Oh, thank you so much," said Young-hee. The box was too big, so she put the vials in her carrying bag. The bag had seen better days, but was still sturdy, and Young-hee felt quite attached to it.

Finally at front gate, she saw that the wall was collapsed rubble, jutting with broken timbers. "Head toward the sun," said the king. "You will reach the end of the forest by the end of the day, on the side of the Sacred City."

"Toward the sun, check."

"When you see your friend, Samjogo, please tell him that the Forest Fairy King remembers his service and wishes him well."

"Okay. But I have no idea where he is. It's been so long since I left him."

"Thank you for your time with us. The forest fairies wish you well."

Young-hee climbed over the rubble. When she turned to bid the king one last farewell, there were only ruins where the palace once was, with no signs of fairies or king.

"Of course," she said. Feeling vacant, Young-hee found the sun through the bamboo and started walking. She had grown so comfortable and content in the palace, Young-hee could scarcely believe she had left it. *Even if you find your pullocho, you will lose your brother.* The silent forest turned the memory into a shout. Was that why Boonae warned about the forest? After months free of care, Young-hee felt crushed by all her old worries and fears.

After a couple of hours bamboo gave way to cedars and birch, then after a couple more hours she saw the forest end and a clearing await her. She squeezed through a particularly thick grove of trees and stumbled into it.

A disheveled man saw her emerge and stood up suddenly. His goofy friend smiled broadly and wagged his tail. "Hey, there she is," said Samjogo to Tiger.

22

"You waited for me!" gushed Young-hee as she ran to hug her friends. They looked just as she remembered. "I can't believe it. How long has it been? Months? More? I lost track." She couldn't believe they had waited. She didn't think she could endure the quest alone.

Tiger responded with typical purrs. Samjogo seemed pleased, but concerned. "Young-hee, it has been only a day since we entered the Great Forest," said the three-legged crow.

"A day? But … I was …"

"Gone much longer? Yes, the forest can be like that, especially the palace of the immortal fairy king."

Young-hee was confused, but not surprised. Time was just one of many things that didn't work the same in Strange Land. She scratched behind the ear of the happy big cat. Then she scowled. "How did you know I went to the king's palace?"

Samjogo looked away, troubled. "Because I know the fairy king very well. He was the father who found and raised me as his son."

"Wait, the king of the Great Forest was *your* father?" Young-hee's mind raced, amazed, bewildered. "You know, that would have been useful information before we entered the forest."

"I tried to keep us out. We only entered because there was no choice."

"But once we entered, you could have said *something*."

"I couldn't tell you," he said. "That is the test of the Great Forest and why we tried to go around it. There are no paths through, and you must face its tests alone. I am bound by the same forest rules and tests as everyone else."

Young-hee let go of Tiger and stood. Her head throbbed as she tried wrapping her brain around what had happened. "I thought you said you were raised by savage fairies? Hunting, fighting, and all? The fairy king I met was very kind."

Samjogo scuffed the ground as he talked, troubled by memories. "True, today, the immortal fairy king is peaceful, beyond the concerns of this, or any realm. But he was not like that when he took me in. Only after great suffering and the Dragon Wars did the king renounce his old ways, devoting himself to sutras and enlightenment, to becoming forever joyful. When he moved into the forest, he took over the palace of the immortals and turned the woods into that fearful test."

A test? She thought about all she had given up to leave the palace—its simple happiness, the promise of regaining her father. It had taken more strength than she knew she had to reject those offers. "So, the test is the fairies' promise of happiness," she said, trying to understand. "Which, for some reason, you aren't allowed to talk about."

"Basically, yes."

"And I got sucked in for a while. But eventually, remembering my brother and love for my family helped me pass the test."

Samjogo pushed a clump of earth with the end of his hyeopdo and looked sad. "No," he said, "you failed." Pressing his lips together grimly, he started up the hill.

Young-hee stood stunned, until Tiger lightly nudged her forward. "We should be going."

Ahead loomed a rolling expanse of hills, and right in front was the largest of all, a huge, flat-topped mountain—home to the Sacred City. Most of the slope was treeless but green, yielding to rock and snow near the top. *So close now.* But conflicting thoughts made it hard to concentrate.

Young-hee and Tiger walked together, while Samjogo took the lead. As upset as Young-hee was, she also worried about Samjogo. He had lost his chatty optimism, and gained an almost sullen look. *The king is the Samjogo's father? And he looks like my father?* Something about those ideas cut too close and too deep. The Great Forest was yet another Strange Land mystery, she decided, free from the burdens of logic. Sorting it rationally would only give her a headache, so she decided to just keep going.

"If it helps, I didn't know the fairy king was Samjogo's father either," said Tiger. "After I fell asleep, I woke up at the edge of the forest, beside Samjogo. Only then did he tell me the nature of the forest and the fairy king's tests."

"So the fairies didn't tempt you?"

"I would never get the chance to take the fairies' test. It is not for all creatures. Just you ... and Samjogo, too."

"He looks ... upset."

"Because he failed the test, as well, or so I understand. And since then he has not been able to see his father or the other the forest fairies."

"None of this sounds very fair. What was the test? Was I supposed to stay forever? How would that be passing?"

Shrugging, Tiger walked on.

The slope they trudged up was not as lush as it appeared from a distance. Under sparse grass, the ground was all black rocks and coarse soil. Looking closely, she thought some of the stones resembled the magic path she followed since her quest's start. And that's when she realized that the whole mountain was now her path. As her journey neared its end, the path grew, converging on the Sacred City.

Up and up the long, difficult climb. The clouds grew closer, larger, and fiercer. Young-hee worried that the Storm Lord might have a hand in it, but saw no signs of him. Nor of the ghosts or any other pursuers. Had they tried following through the forest? Or gone around? Maybe they lay in wait at her destination. It couldn't be a secret that their goal was the Sacred City, not now.

As they traveled higher, the wind rose and the temperature cooled. She put on her cloak and all the clothes she had, but the wind bit through. Only the strain of climbing provided warmth. Even when the sun poked through a cloud, it beamed half-heartedly. Young-hee remembered the perfect, ethereal warmth and eternal twilight that was Strange Land when she first arrived. Everything had seemed so magical and wondrous. Now, it was gray and ominous, as if her fears, worries, and doubts had infected the entire realm.

Young-hee certainly had a lot of all three—she was afraid for Bum, worried about her family, and doubtful she would find the

pullocho. But increasingly she wrestled a concern she couldn't iden-
tify. Something about this whole excursion didn't add up. Why were
the Ghost Queen and her minions after her? Little of what the animal spirit sisters had told her made sense. And what was up with
Mirinae's chioonchim working for Samjogo but not her? More and
more, Young-hee thought that there must be something else she
wasn't aware of. Something bigger. But no matter how much she
mulled and imagined, she found no good answers.

At one point, shifting right to avoid a steep bit of cliff, they crossed
a ridgeline that awarded a view of a previously hidden mountain
side. Below was a great swathe of small, light blue shapes. Whatever
it was, it was too small for Young-hee to make out clearly. Samjogo
noticed her confused stare. "River fairies, most likely," he said simply.
"The blue would be their banners."

"That looks big enough to be an army," said Young-hee.

"That's because it is." With no more explanation, he led the way
forward.

Up ahead, the mountain leveled into a plateau. Even from this
distance Young-hee could see odd rocky formations and figured the
Sacred City must be there. Or had been, if any ruins remained.

Despite fatigue from the long day's trek, she walked faster,
spurred on by anticipation. *The pullocho just has to be there. I'll get
it, then I'll get Bum back.* Samjogo was climbing faster, too, and Tiger
casually leaped ahead of them both.

She smelled the city before she saw it—the rich, oily scent of sandalwood filled the air with perfume that reminded Young-hee of her
mother's favorite incense. The beautiful smell meant she was close to
her goal. *A noble-hearted* simmani *might be able to find a pullocho in
the ruins of the great Sacred City, in the shadow of the first sandalwood
tree.* That's what the dokkaebi had told her. Of course, why should he
be any more right than any other creature Young-hee had met? Most
advice since beginning this quest had been dubious at best, and some
was just wrong. Leaving the path didn't seem to matter because a new
one emerged. Gifts didn't always come with strings. Even the Great

Forest, difficult as it had been, was surmountable. Now Young-hee was ready for her quest to end. She wanted the pullocho. She scampered over a large rock and spilled onto the plateau. Before her lay the ruins of the Sacred City.

A large, lonely sandalwood tree sat in the middle of the plateau. Scattered all around were deeply decayed ruins, with only crumbled stones where walls or foundation once stood. In a couple of spots, splinters of rotten wood hinted at a large hall or palace. A few tufts of grass clung to life on top of the ruins. It was impossible to imagine what the Sacred City has once been. Behind the ruins, the mountain—just bare rock—continued up. The clouds closed in on them, darkening the scene. Around the ruins' edges were four large, stony mounds, with another behind the sandalwood tree.

But that one … moved. Brown and earth-like, it looked like a cross between a lion and a hippopotamus, but huge, twice the size of an elephant, with a thick, earthen hide, wings, and a single, stubby horn on the middle of its forehead. The creature walked lazily toward Young-hee making *hrumph* noises, its steps shaking the earth and shattering stones.

"Oh wow," said Young-hee, "that's a *haechi*."

"Indeed. And that's really bad news for us," said Samjogo, reaching for his hyeopdo.

"Is it another evil monster trying to kill us?"

"Worse. It's a guardian of goodness, honor, and justice."

"That sounds like a good thing."

"Not for us. You only summon a haechi to guard something very, very important that you firmly intend to keep from anyone else. Haechi are not the smartest guardians in the realm, but they are probably the most powerful."

"Oh. Great," Young-hee said. Tiger stood bravely in front of her, ready to defend her as always. The haechi came to a stop halfway between Young-hee and the sandalwood tree. Closer now, Young-hee saw swirling designs rippling his hide like the surface of a stormy lake. "Uh, hello, Mr. Haechi?!" she called and waved, suddenly felt foolish, halted, felt just as dumb giving a half-wave, so resumed. In the end, it was probably a three-quarter wave, and she still felt dumb.

The haechi blandly tilted his head. "Hello, young travelers, and Tiger. What brings you to such a distant, difficult part of our realm?"

Young-hee gulped and walked forward. She felt Samjogo trying to pull her back, but she brushed his hand from her shoulder. "Well, Mr. Haechi, I am here for a pullocho. I have traveled very far and encountered many trials, but I need it to save my little brother."

"I see," boomed the creature. "That does sound like a noble venture, suffering and sacrificing for family. But, alas, I cannot help you—there are no pullochos here."

"No pullochos?" cried Young-hee, equal parts disappointment, frustration, and anger. That couldn't be right, not after all she had been through. "No, everyone said it's '*In the shadow of the first sandalwood tree*.' Please, let me search, just for a while."

"That would be impossible," said the gigantic guardian. "Outsiders are not allowed. Now, please leave my home." Haechi turned and walked slowly toward the tree.

"But ... But, please, Mr. Haechi. I need the pullocho. Surely I could at least look."

"I understand your frustration. But my words were clear." The haechi didn't bother turning to look at them.

"*Noble haechi*?" shouted Samjogo, his voice full of mocking. "Truest of all the great guardians? What kind of noble creature lies like that? There is nothing noble about lying and turning your back on those who need your help." The haechi stopped and turned, definitely displeased. But Samjogo continued defiantly. "He won't let you look because he knows full well there is a pullocho here. Look at him, he knows what I say is true. The pullocho is here, but he just wants to stop you from getting it."

The haechi glowered at Samjogo. The clouds grew purple and began to churn. "I do what I must and I say what I must, not to insult, but to protect my charge. If you realized what you asked, and what it could do, you would not be so quick to cast aspersions. Now leave, unless you think three small travelers can stand against an angry haechi."

As lightning flashed across the sky and thunder boomed, the haechi looked as troubled as Young-hee and friends.

"Uh-oh," said Tiger, "I think this storm is not the haechi's doing."

A great wind whipped, rain fell, and lightning exploded in their midst, booming like an unholy drum, and knocking Young-hee, Samjogo, and Tiger off their feet. As the roar of the thunder and the rattling in her head faded, Young-hee realized that the lightning had struck the haechi. His skin steamed and smoldered, but otherwise he looked unhurt—just very, very angry.

"Look at this—kitty, bear daughter, and the sparrow have found the lost ruins where the last pullocho lies," came a cackling cry from over the ridge. "Why, I do believe that's a haechi. A crispy, barbecued haechi." Riding a huge black horse was a monstrous figure, carrying cymbals and hammers—Nwaegongdo. With him was the Lord of War carrying a cart full of even larger baskets.

"Storm Lord, War Lord, I will tell you what I told the others—this place is under my protection," said the haechi, his thick tail slapping the ground. "Leave at once."

Nwaegongdo smirked. "With that pullocho, we'll be strong enough to challenge the Lords of Heaven. And we'll happily go through you to get it." At a signal, the red-face Lord of War dismounted, walked to the cart of baskets and set them alight.

"Oh, jeez, not those again," said Young-hee.

Just then, beyond the wind's gusting, another sound whipped the plain—an empty, terrifying rattling. Across the field Young-hee saw a mass of figures with long, black hair and white hanbok, led by a thin, hollow-faced woman on horseback—the Ghost Queen leading her minions, more of them than ever.

"Enough!" shouted Haechi. He stomped the ground angrily, sending broken chips of rock flying, then stomped again and again. The third time, the ground shook and cracked as the whole hill rumbled. And then, with a great roaring, the four hills surrounding the ruins came to life. They shook off the dirt and grass that covered them, revealing more guardians, each as big as Haechi—a red bird that swirled with flame, a huge white tiger, a blue dragon, and a black thing between a turtle and a snake.

"Holy crap," deadpanned Young-hee, gaping at the great guardians of the four directions, sent by the King of Heaven. Ordinarily she would have been pleased at recognizing the mythical creatures, but at the moment she was far too frightened.

"Is he a relative?" Samjogo asked, pointing to the hulking white cat flexing its huge claws just a hundred yards away.

"Very distant," Tiger replied.

"This is really getting out of hand," said Young-hee, reeling at all the creatures rapidly filling the mountaintop. The bird flapped its wings, sending a plume of flame across the field. "I'm assuming that's the Phoenix," she said. "Dragon, Tiger … and some kind of snake-turtle creature."

"Hyeonmu," said Samjogo, "the Turtle-snake."

"This is far too dangerous for all of us, but especially a bear daughter," said Tiger. "We should get going. Stay close, and I will keep you safe." Together, Tiger and Samjogo protected Young-hee as they backed away from the battlefield. Luckily, the spirits were intent on each other.

As the Lord of War's burning baskets crashed to the ground, tiny soldiers streamed from the magic fire. The four guardians snapped and growled themselves into fighting frenzy.

Young-hee wasn't so sure if either of her friends should put himself in front of her. The creatures squaring off against them looked quite out of their league. "Are they after me or the pullocho?" she asked.

"Does it even matter at this point?" said Samjogo, his blade moving in a tight arc in front of them. "The four direction guardians wouldn't even notice if they squished us flat."

"Great … "

The wind howled as Nwaegongdo beat his drum and whipped

up the elements. Each bash of his cymbals caused lightning to fly. "Come, lords and ladies of the underworld!" he chanted in time with his deep drum. "Join us in the Sacred City as we, at long last, vanquish the servants of Heaven, the guardians of nothing! Fight with us, demons of the deep, hateful spirits of the first things, creatures of the ancient darkness! Come Chiwoo, come Mother of the West! Come demons of the home and hearth, come spirits of the trees and rocks, of the ash and kettle and grave!"

And they came. As the storm lashed the lonely plateau, beating all with rain and hail and wind, Nwaegongdo summoned demon after demon to join the battle. Some came from storm clouds, others from cracks in the ground. There was a heavily armed ochre warrior—half-man, half-bull. There was a woman wearing jade jewels—her broken teeth were outside of her mouth and she had a leopard's tail. And more and more strange, disgusting creatures appeared.

The haechi and the four guardians roared and stomped, displaying their ferocity and unwillingness to back down, even though faced with ever-growing opposition.

"They're not really going to fight, are they?" Young-hee asked.

"I'm afraid it looks that way," said Samjogo, warily eyeing the gathering hordes.

"And this is because of me? Because I led them here?"

"You were only trying to save your brother," said Tiger. "Their actions are their own."

But as Young-hee watched the forces growing she wasn't so sure. Demons may be demons and guardians, guardians, but she felt her presence had thrown Strange Land horribly out of balance.

Suddenly, on the far side of the ridge, the battle began for real, as the ghosts and their queen circled the Blue Dragon and attacked. The long, snaking dragon swirled and rippled like a ribbon on a stick—beautiful, if not for its violence. When the ghosts had been chasing Young-hee, they were all creep and menace—aggrieved spirits from beyond the grave, starving for vengeance. But here, on an open field, in daytime, squaring off against a dragon, they were almost cat-like, claws out and coiled, as they darted around the great, scaly guardian.

The battlefield quickly filled with the noise and cruelty of fighting. Surrounded by his tiny warriors from the flames, the Lord of War swung a giant sword and a heavy mace as he charged the haechi.

It is an awesome and frightening sight, Young-hee thought, *seeing immortals and magical creatures clash.* As more demons materialized, the five guardians of the Sacred City fought ever more ferociously, the phoenix breathing fire, the turtle-snake upturning huge mounds of earth and rock and flinging them. Young-hee, Tiger, and Samjogo fled to the edge of the plateau, their backs to a huge stone slope. This was all so much bigger than they were, there were no illusions of heroics or bravery—self-protection was the only real option.

As the Lord of War marshaled his forces and directed the attack, he turned to Young-hee and her friends with an evil laugh. She wished he would quit that sort of thing; it never ended well. He snarled orders at two human-ish and heavily armored demons—one with a goat's horns, the other, a bull's. They turned, looked at Young-hee, drew their spears, and charged.

"Great, livestock demons," said Samjogo. "Get ready, Tiger."

Tiger growled and extended his claws. As Young-hee scrambled in vain for a rock or something to use as weapon, she heard a hard rattle from her bag. Stones? Then she remembered—the vials from the Fairy King. Opening her bag, she extracted one vial at random—the white one, a rough, vaguely crystalline bottle, totally unassuming. *Nature,* the fairy king had said, whatever that means. She uncorked it.

"What are you doing?" said Samjogo. "Stay back. Those demons will be upon us in a moment." He tried to push her back behind him, hoping he could keep her safe.

But Young-hee slipped by him. "Both of you, stay close," she said, strangely confident. Holding out the vial, she tipped it and let a single clear drop fall to the ground.

The earth heaved, like the mountain itself was vomiting, it writhed and churned. Instantly, green stalks covered in heavy, sharp thorns sprang from the ground. Their vines and branches split and twirled and thickened, rising all round Young-hee, Tiger, and Samjogo. As the stalks grew, their thorns grew, too—except the barbs were not just growing around the charging livestock demons, they were growing through them. Broad and jagged, the spines surrounded the demons, who disappeared into the tangle so that all that was left were the sounds of dying and pain before they finally fell quiet.

"Oh my," said Samjogo with mixed shock and admiration. "Nice trick."

Across the thorn-filled field, the Lord of War bellowed furiously, surprised to find two of his soldiers suddenly so well aerated. He barked another order, and a stream of the miniature warriors broke from the main force. Like locusts swarming a field of crops, they streamed toward Young-hee,.

"They're too small for your thorns, I fear," said Tiger, the fur on the back of his neck rising. "They can run straight through."

Young-hee reached again into her bag and withdrew the red one.

"They're fire demons," said Samjogo. "If red is fire, it might have no effect on them."

"Right," she said grabbing the pretty azure vial, polished so smooth the ceramic glaze looked like glass. The tiny fire warriors rushed like a tsunami of smoke and shouts, weaving between the thorns without even slowing down. Young-hee pulled the stopper from the vial, carefully tipped it, and let a drop fall.

The moment it touched the ground, earth and stone turned into a lake of the clearest, cleanest water. Deep and cold, it swallowed the fiery creatures, so that all that was left was an undignified little *hiss*.

The Lord of War grew angrier than ever, but before he could shout a new round of orders, the Blue Dragon attacked. With his massive jaws he grabbing the Lord of War and threw him into the newly formed lake with a massive splash. The demon didn't re-emerge. The dragon, at home in the water, began fighting the evil spirits from there; soon Young-hee's crystal clear waters darkened with the wreckage of war.

Separated from the worst of the fighting by the lagoon, Samjogo led his friends up the rocky wall, further from the fray. The battle noise was deafening as lightning flashed, fire roared, and each side took turns attacking and defending, rallying, and succumbing. One evil spirit with green, decaying skin—a plague spirit, Samjogo told her—was locked in a brutal fight with the much larger and stronger white tiger guardian. But the more they fought, the more the spirit's diseased body infected the guardian. The tiger pinned the plague spirit with one great paw, and split it in half with huge jaws. But it was too late; the great guardian crashed to the ground, overcome by a wasting sickness. The shredded plague spirit continued to move, too resilient to die so easily. But then the phoenix flapped its wings, and in a cloud of fire, swept across the body of his fallen comrade, turning both bodies to ash. Young-hee's Tiger looked on sadly as his distant relation vanished. With just five guardians, the loss of even one, Young-hee feared, could changing the tide of battle.

Just then, a great chorus of horns rang out, echoing across the battlefield. Young-hee saw hordes of soldiers with blue armor and banners, charging up the hill. "River fairies are joining the fight," said Samjogo matter-of-factly, as the fairies stormed the hill, banners waving and steel menacing.

"Fairies! Now the guardians will win for sure," said Young-hee.

Samjogo looked unhappily at the swarm. "I don't know whose side they are on, if anyone's. They are a wild tribe, untamed and unenlightened. I suspect they only represent more danger."

Indeed, the fairies joined no side, attacking any and all with equal ferocity. What had been a fight between two sides devolved into a chaotic fight of all against all.

Next, the mountain itself rumbled, this time from above the cloud line. The source of the pounding, hidden in the mists, was coming closer, down the slope.

"Something big's coming," said Young-hee.

"Yes," said Samjogo, scanning the fog. "Ogres."

Indeed, from out of the clouds and mists, a giant ogre emerged, huge and dumb, swinging a massive club. With a few giant steps—

each rattling the whole hill—the ugly brute was out of the clouds and upon Young-hee and her friends. His tree-sized club smashed a great rock beside them, sending a wave of sharp, jagged debris flying everywhere. Young-hee yelped as the stony shrapnel struck her skin, raising red welts.

Before Young-hee could get the last fairy vial from her bag, the huge ogre raised his club a second time, ready to turn her and her friends into a sticky paste. He swung, but Tiger jumped onto the ogre's ankle, sinking teeth and claws into the giant's Achilles tendon. The monster roared as he buckled and fell. But the ogre was monstrously large, and even as he fell, he kicked Tiger with his other boulder of a heel, arching the great cat into the air. Tiger landed limply and bounced down the slope and into the water.

"No!" cried Young-hee. She dug into her bag for the red vial. The ogre was pulling himself up with his club. With a stupid, angry look, he faced Young-hee. Samjogo was saying something, trying to hold her back and calm her down, but Young-hee was possessed by a sweeping fury that left her deaf to soothing words. *That thing hurt my friend!* She pulled out the stopper and poured out the liquid—a lot of it.

The ground was ablaze. The hottest fire Young-hee had ever felt swept across the rocky slope. It swirled orange and yellow, rushing like a blow-torch, billowing thick, black smoke. A wind, created when the sudden flash of heat fought the cool air, whipped the fire into big, rolling waves. Rocks glowed red. From the heart of the flames came the saddest, most brutal cry, as the giant ogre shook and seared. Moments later, he dropped to the inflamed ground, dead.

They had no time to savor the victory, though. Too many arrows flew, too many enraged spirits battled to the death. More ogres, some with multiple heads, marched from the mountaintop. From below, the sound of pounding hooves signaled new combatants.

Understanding their plight, Samjogo reached into Young-hee's bag, took the white vial, and poured several drops in an arc around them.

"What are you doing? They king said only a drop."

But even as Young-hee spoke, the ground burst again with life, as the barbed vines towered over and around them, larger and denser than before. Within seconds, Young-hee and Samjogo were completely encircled in a safe nest while the battle raged.

With the realization that she had killed the ogre, Young-hee's anger was replaced by a sad emptiness. Samjogo sat silently, lightly holding her and stroking her hair, like she used to do to Bum when he was upset.

"How can you enjoy these adventures?" Young-hee asked, as the ground shook. "This isn't fun at all anymore."

"This isn't an adventure," he said quietly. "This is something else."

At first, the sounds from beyond the thorn bushes grew louder as the fighting intensified. The whole mountain shook and rattled, but Young-hee and Samjogo could do nothing but wait. Beyond their thorny oasis, the most powerful creatures in the realm tore at each other with the unmatched fury of the ancients. It seemed to last for hours.

After a time, the noise faded. The thunder grew less frequent, the warriors' cries less fierce. The roar and flash of fire gave way to the hiss and puff of smoke. And, gradually, quiet swallowed the battlefield.

* * *

Once they were convinced that the fighting was truly finished, Samjogo used his hyeopdo to hack at the hedge. "I think the thorn bush is dying," he said as he thwacked away. "It's getting a lot more brittle."

Finally he cut through enough to see a boulder so big that it nearly cleared the towering vines. Samjogo and Young-hee clambered atop it, surveying the plateau. Nothing moved. Endless bodies—huge, tiny, fairy, monster—lay everywhere. Some were burnt, some bleeding, others had turned to stone or changed by other magicks. From the largest guardians to the tiniest basket soldiers, everything was still.

"What happened?" asked Young-hee.

"I, I think they fought themselves out."

"Yeah, but ... It doesn't make any sense. There's no one left at all." It was the most terrible thing she had ever seen.

A great, coiling, octopus-looking monster lay half-in and half-out of the lake, covered in a thousand gaping wounds. A giant crane was draped across the battlefield, covered in a thousand arrows. After looking across the plain for a while, Young-hee finally saw the haechi, too, or the ruin that was left.

Samjogo hacked his way out of the thorn bushes, leading Young-hee to the smoking remains of the battlefield. She just couldn't believe there was nothing left. Together, they walked through the carnage, in shock at the spectacle all around them.

"Even the grass is dead, everything," said Young-hee, running her hand over the burned ground.

"Not everything," said Samjogo, pointing across the blackened plain. The sandalwood tree was somehow still standing, only a bit scalded about the edges. The clouds were breaking up, and a weak evening sun poked through, illuminating the sweet-smelling tree.

Just then, with a thump and a jostling, the body of large demon rolled not far from them. Samjogo raised his hyeopdo, ready for anything. But the demon wasn't moving, it was just being shoved aside from underneath. By Tiger, clearly in bad shape.

"Young-hee," came the wheezing voice, barely loud enough to be heard. Cut, bruised, and horribly hurt, Tiger limped slowly toward them.

"Tiger," gasped Young-hee.

Samjogo rushed forward to help, pouring cool water from a canteen onto a cloth to soothe him. "Here, friend, let me help," he said, full of sadness. Tiger was dying.

Tiger shook him off with what little strength he had left and turned. "Come, please," he said, leading them slowly toward the sandalwood tree.

"Tiger, please stop," said Young-hee, almost crying. "You need to rest."

"No time," said Tiger, coughing weakly.

"Young-hee's right, Tiger," said Samjogo, even though he knew she was wrong.

But Tiger would not stop walking. Together, they climbed over burnt wreckage and broken pieces of armor until they came to the tree. Lying in the tree's shadow was the body of the haechi. All about were dead fairies and demons. Whatever had happened, he must have been in a terrible fight, thought Young-hee, as she looked tight-lipped at the remains all across the plateau. Tiger leaned against the guardian's side and started pushing. The haechi was too big, and Tiger too weak. Samjogo quickly joined him, and finding a good leverage point under the guardian's front right limb, rolled it over. On the ground, crushed by the haechi's bulk, were the flattened remains of a small green plant, with a single, red flower.

"Take it," wheezed Tiger, growing weaker. "It's your pullocho. The haechi was protecting it until his last breath. He died on top of the pullocho to protect it."

Young-hee just looked unbelieving at the crumpled flower. Samjogo dropped to one knee, furiously moving dirt and stones with a knife. He quickly uncovered the thick, twisted root of the pullocho.

Just as Samjogo pulled out the magic root, Tiger fell to the ground on his side. Young-hee ran up and cupped the cat's head. The pullocho didn't seem so important now. "Poor Tiger," said Young-hee, rubbing her friend's head softly. "I should have listened to Samjogo and never let you come with us."

"You saved me from that tiger trap," he said weakly. "You were kind to me."

"But I never wanted my journey to hurt you. Why did you attack that ogre? Why didn't you stay close to us?"

"Because … You gave me a chance … to be brave. And good. In all my eons as Tiger, I've been ferocious and I've been … foolish. But you let me be a hero."

Young-hee felt her eyes growing wet as she stroked the ears and big neck of Tiger. She tasted salt. She wanted to tell Tiger not to go, to order him to stay, but no sound escaped.

"Take it," panted Tiger, each breath weaker than the last. "It's why you came so far. It's what we wanted. Take it. We've won." Tiger closed his eyes and breathed no more.

23

Young-hee looked at the twisting root Samjogo placed in her hand, underwhelmed. It looked like ginseng—just slightly yellower. Big deal. *Dragon head, snake tail*, as the saying goes.

"Now what?" she asked Samjogo.

"Now? We bury our friend and honor him with the rites he deserves. Then we go, quickly, before scavengers and other bad things come to pick through the dead. And we get you back to your dokkaebi."

The ground was hard and rocky, but Samjogo found a good place close to the sandalwood tree and got to work, digging earth and piling it high for a burial mound. He had changed into black linens, although Young-hee never saw him do it. Young-hee helped as best as she could, wanting to commemorate her friend, but Tiger was large and piling the stones was hard. As Samjogo stacked the stones, he sang the *bawijeol hosangnori*, or funeral song.

By the time they finished, the sun was setting. But rather than sleep in such a grim, terrible place, Young-hee and Samjogo walked down hill to a safer, quieter place. By a glowing fire, Samjogo regaled her with stories about Tiger, some familiar, others new to her. He told of a shrine spirit stopping Tiger from eating a tired traveler by fooling him into thinking they were brothers. Of nine generations of men Tiger had eaten before a *mudang* shaman broke the family curse. Of Frog beating Tiger in a game of riddles. Of why Tiger began to smoke, back when Strange Land was still young.

The next morning, they readied to return to the beginning. They searched the sky and land for threats, but all was quiet. Every so often Young-hee checked her bag for the pullocho root, still not really believing this was the all-important herb of life.

"If this pullocho is so powerful, can't we use it to bring Tiger back?" she asked. But Samjogo only shook his head.

As they broke camp they heard the clambering of hooves. A horse appeared over a nearby ridge, walking toward them. Not really a horse—but a horse-like animal with eight legs and small, feathery wings around each hoof.

"It's a cheollima," said Young-hee, recognizing it from her time with the fairy king.

"The king's great horses can travel a thousand *li* with a single gallop. Majestic animals."

"Yes, the fairy king used to take me to feed him, if it's the same cheollima." She scratched the animal behind its head.

"Ah, then I suspect my adopted father sent it to help you return to the goblin market."

"But why now?"

"You spent a long time with the forest fairies, enjoying the king's hospitality. That counts for a lot. Even if you were not ready to leave behind this life, the king can sympathize with your connection to your mud world."

"I don't know how to ride a horse. Or a cheollima. It looks dangerous." Unbridled and unsaddled, its back was six feet high.

"Nonsense. Any cheollima that would allow you onto its back would never let you fall," said Samjogo petting its thick neck. "I'll steer. You just hold on."

"You're coming back with me?" asked Young-hee, not-so-secretly relieved.

"I promised I would get you out of the cave, and I did. I said I would accompany you all the way to the pullocho, and I did. It is only right that I see you to end your journey."

"Well, it is much better traveling with someone than alone."

"Besides, I am very curious about this unusual dokkaebi of yours. I would like to meet him for myself."

Samjogo led the steed to a large rock. "Sorry, old man rock," he said as he used the stone to mount the cheollima. The animal shifted with the weight of its rider, but soon settled.

Young-hee followed, climbing the rock, then with Samjogo's help, mounted the cheollima. She was surprised at how comfortable and steady she felt.

"Keep your balance with your knees, and hold fast to me," said Samjogo.

"How will you steer without a bridle?"

"You don't really control a cheollima. You just tell him where you want to go, and he leads the way." Samjogo kept petting the animal's neck, soothing and bonding with it.

"Wow, he sounds smart. And he really goes that fast? And we can hold on?"

Samjogo tussled the cheollima's mane. "To be honest, I don't really know. I've never ridden one before," he said. Young-hee felt herself about to freak out, but Samjogo just leaned close to the cheollima's ear. "The goblin market by the Haechi Horn," he whispered, and before Young-hee could voice her concerns, they were gone.

* * *

In an instant, the cheollima was moving faster than a sports car. In a few seconds, more like a jet. And once it hit its stride—its impossibly long, eight-legged stride—faster still. They went around the Great Forest in minutes, skipped across the surging Hungry River as if it were a leaky faucet, and onward past green fields to the Cheongyong Mountains. The faster they traveled, the smoother the ride, almost like they were not moving at all. Even the air seemed to part for them, so it felt like a soft spring breeze. It was a cool, gentle exhilaration.

At one point, a great airplane-sized crane swooped and raced along, a few feet off the ground, matching the magical horse's pace in what seemed to be a game. Samjogo laughed with amazement. But after a few moments, the cheollima raced ahead.

"That was really incredible," said Young-hee, laughing, too.

"Much better than being chained in a dark cave," agreed Samjogo. "Awesome." But then he glanced back at Young-hee, and his smiled dropped.

"What is it?" she asked.

"It's just … When we do see that dokkaebi, remember, whatever happens, he cannot really hurt your brother."

She didn't like Samjogo's words. "What do you mean?"

"I'm just saying … There's no need to freak out or go crazy. It's going to work out."

"Uh, okay. Thanks."

Just as Young-hee was getting used to racing across Strange Land, they slowed and then stopped—at the clearing on the edge of the jureum forest. The journey that had taken Young-hee so long, the cheollima did in an hour.

"Is this where you started?" asked Samjogo.

"Yeah, except …" said Young-hee, seeing two broken stumps of woods. "Except the jangseung are gone." The cheollima knelt on its front four legs. Young-hee slid off the magic horse and hurried over to where Jiha and Cheonha had been, followed closely by Samjogo. "They definitely were here when I started my journey, and a path ran right past them."

"*Hmm*," said Samjogo, thinking. "That is a bad sign. Jangseung are strong guardians. It looks like they were snapped off at their base—and the break in the wood is most jagged."

Young-hee looked past the jureum forest to where the market once lay. It looked still and deserted. "This isn't good," said Young-hee. "What if the market was attacked by ogres or some other terrible monster? What if whatever attacked the jangseung also attacked … Oh, baby brother!"

She ran to the market with Samjogo just behind. It looked long abandoned, with overturned boxes and papers everywhere. No one shouting or selling. No merchants or customers. No rabbits or other magic animals chained up or caged. No dokkaebi or fairies, and no signs of Bassam or Grandma Dol. Young-hee walked through the silent chaos, bewildered and panicking, certain the worst had happened—she had lost her brother forever.

Then, as she turned a corner, there, once again, there was the same rickety stall, still full of biscuits, rice cakes, and cookies. And at the entrance, holding a thick wooden cane, stood the thin, brown, all-too-pleased-looking dokkaebi. "Oh my, oh my, so you actually came back," he said, sounding not at all startled. "I can scarcely believe it." He played it cool, but there was an eager, even voracious look in his eye.

"What happened here?" asked Young-hee.

"New management?" huffed the goblin. "A sharp change in market conditions? It makes no difference to Woo." Just then the dokkaebi noticed Samjogo. "What's this? Did you bring a warrior to fight Woo?" he said, pointing with his cane, obviously agitated. Stepping into his stall, the goblin put one hand behind a table, as if he was reaching for something. "You made a vow, sealed with a *yeouiju*. No tricks, no force."

"He's a friend, he's not here to fight," said Young-hee, pushing Samjogo back lightly with one hand. "I kept my promises."

"Is that so?" said Woo, eyeing Samjogo uneasily.

"I wouldn't waste my time, fighting an ashen worm like you," snapped Samjogo.

"*Samjogo!*" said Young-hee, appalled. She didn't need her friend making trouble, not when she was so close to getting her brother back. Assuming he was even here. "My friend isn't a problem. But how about you? Have you kept your word? Where's my brother?"

"Of course your bratling is here," he said, irritated. He turned to the depths of the messy stall. "Brat! Come here."

A moment later, Bum shuffled out, still clutching his doll, still as dirty and snotty as ever. But for once Young-hee didn't care. She was happier than she could remember being in a long, long time. She dropped to one knee and gave Bum a big hug. "Oh, baby brother, you're okay," she said, on the verge of crying, before pushing him back and examining him at arm's length. "Are you okay? Did you eat? Did that goblin hurt you?" She slid one hand to the thread that still bound him.

"Your filthy sibling is fine. I made a vow, too." The dokkaebi narrowed his eyes and wet his lips. "But this cheery moment won't last long without the pullocho."

"I have your pullocho."

"So you say. But because you have a straight mouth doesn't mean your words aren't bent."

"Here, see for yourself," she said. But before she could hunt through her bag, Samjogo put his hand on hers.

"Don't," he said. "You cannot trust a dokkaebi. Make him free Bum before you give him the pullocho."

That riled the goblin. "Trust? The filthy crow talks about trust? We don't need trust, we made a deal. Now. Give. Me. My. Pullocho!" He brandished the cane.

"Don't listen to him, Mr. Woo," said Young-hee, desperate to placate. "He's not part of our deal or family. He doesn't count. Let's just make the exchange and be done with it." Samjogo looked angry, angrier than she had ever seen him. *He can't ruin it for me now, not when I'm so close.*

"He's a nasty creature," said Samjogo. "You can see in his eyes, he'll never give the boy back. He knows the pullocho's power and will use it as soon as he gets it."

"You, three-legged *chicken*, should be more polite. And you, silly bear daughter, should pick your friends with more care," he growled. "You don't have Tiger to hide behind any more." He tapped the cane to the ground three times, shouted, *"Tukdak, tukdak!"* and Bum flew from Young-hee's grasp, pulled by an invisible thread back into the stall.

"Bum!" cried Young-hee.

The dokkaebi walked between Young-hee and her brother, his wooden stick hovering ominously. "Now, give me the pullocho, or leave."

"How do you know about Tiger?" asked Young-hee.

"Eh?"

"Tiger. How would you know I was traveling with him?"

"Oh, *uh*, spies, of course," he muttered convincingly. "I never trusted you, so had my trees and squirrels report your little adventures."

Samjogo drew his hyeopdo and took a fighting stance. "He's lying," Samjogo said. "He's lying about this like he lied about everything." He wriggled the blade toward the goblin.

The threatening gesture outraged the dokkaebi. With his free hand, he bent low, grabbed the gossamer thread, pulled Bum off of his feet, and dangled him upside down from his outstretched arm. Bum yelled with surprise then began to cry, then wailed with ear-shattering howls.

"Put him down!" Young-hee ordered, digging frantically through her bag. "I have your pullocho here." And pulled it out.

"So you have." he said with a massively evil grin. "Excellent. But I told you, no tricks, no threats." And with that, he tapped his stick twice and said *"Tukdak, tukdak!"* Poof—Bum was gone!

For a moment, the abandoned market turned unearthly quiet, as Young-hee's crying brother disappeared and everything just stopped. *No, this can't be happening. No, no, no!*

"Now, give me the pullocho," said the goblin, "or I'll do something really nasty to you next."

"*No!*" she howled. Samjogo spoke and tried to pull her away, but her emotions overpowered her, and Young-hee couldn't hear her friend or feel his hand on her shoulder.

The dokkaebi ignored her shout and grabbed greedily for the pullocho. But Young-hee held on, gripping the magic root with a ferocity the dokkaebi didn't anticipate. With her other hand she reached into her bag and pulled out the white vial. Recognizing the little bottle, the dokkaebi recoiled with fear. She popped it open with her thumb and poured it onto the ground.

There was a brief, painful pause, and then the thorny hedge exploded, wrapping the dokkaebi with thick vines and sharp barbs, enveloping him and tearing him away. The giant stalk tore through market stalls and discarded sundries, smashing wood, piercing furniture, and breaking apart pretty much everything around them. The devastation was total.

Young-hee knelt, clutching the pullocho. *This can't be happening.*

Bum is gone, and it is the dokkaebi's fault.

She was shaking, but it took a moment to realize that it wasn't from emotion—Samjogo was holding her shoulder, trying to get her attention.

Finally, his words penetrated. "I said, we have to move. Those thorns won't stop him."

"*You*," she said, dripping with scorn. "You did this. I told you not to make trouble. But you had to run your mouth and act all tough, like always. Now my little brother is gone because of you."

"That's not what happened," he said, hurt and concerned.

"The thorns stopped two demons by the sandalwood tree, and protected us from that war of the spirits. They should be enough for a little goblin."

"You really don't understand yet," he said. "I didn't..." But before he could finish, the sounds of wood breaking and vines snapping filled the air, like something gnawing its way through. "He's almost here."

Young-hee went digging through her bag again. She found the red and blue vials, so dropped the red one and got ready to use the blue.

"No, we'll need fire," he said.

"No good against a dokkaebi," said Young-hee. "They're creatures of the hot coals, practically half-fire."

"Trust me," he said. "That's no dokkaebi."

The thorn bush burst open in front of them, splinters and thorns flying everywhere. The dokkaebi emerged unhurt, eyes blood red with rage. "Silly fairy tricks won't help you," he spat. "I want my pullocho."

The goblin swung his cane, but Samjogo stepped forward and parried it with his hyeopdo. The two began to duel, each attacking with full force. Young-hee held the blue vial ready. Seeing Samjogo fighting feverishly for her, she put aside her anger and heartache and decided to listen to him; she switched vials. The dokkaebi tapped the ground with his cane, causing the soil to roll like a wave, knocking down Samjogo and half-burying him. Then the goblin turned to Young-hee and raised his cane, ready to strike.

At that moment, Young-hee tipped the red vial. Even as the fairy water fell, it roared with red and orange fire, pulsing with heat. Fear washed over dokkaebi's face. Then the liquid touched the ground, and waves of thick, oily fire rolled forward in a great curtain of destruction. Billowing black smoke covered the sky as the inferno consumed all it touched. Shops and thorns shimmered and flickered into ash.

As Samjogo lightly pulled Young-hee back, urging her to leave, a dark object strained its way through the flames, trying to escape. Covered in smoke and ash, barely recognizable, the dokkaebi tumbled out. "That *hurt!*" it yelled, its voice breaking with confusion and anger. "You ridiculous humans actually hurt me!" But its voice was higher, less ugly than the dokkaebi's, almost lady-like. The dokkaebi tugged at its burnt ear, pulling it right off. Then its nose came off, too. And its horn. The goblin's entire skin sloughed off in big chunks.

Underneath, a creature obscured by ash and gore, lay breathing heavily. As Young-hee watched, horrified and fascinated, she began to see short, reddish hairs all over the creature's body. A tail burst out, and then another, and another, until nine tails spilled from the dokkaebi's burnt remains. The creature stood in her fox form—red-brown fur and a sharp face full of teeth.

"Gumiho," said Young-hee, shocked.

"Hmm, yes," it answered, a mix of pain and boredom and perhaps a touch of respect. "I was tired of that disguise anyway. Now, bear daughter, I will take my pullocho, that you so thoughtfully brought me." She walked steely, steady, and without fear toward Young-hee,.

"But why?" asked Young-hee, as she and Samjogo backed away. "Why the elaborate scheme? Why not just take what you wanted? Or just ask me for help?"

"Silly bear daughter, that's not really your concern," she said.

Samjogo swung his hyeopdo, trying to keep Gumiho back. "Because the guardians and other creatures of this realm would never let her have a pullocho. The elixir of life is too precious to be trusted with any creature, especially one as evil as Fox."

"There's some truth to that," Gumiho said. "For regular creatures—a witch or dokkaebi—a pullocho grants long life and great powers. But for me? I could do anything. Rival the lords of Heaven. Became a *real person* and cross into your world." As she came closer, her eyes grew redder, her claws longer, she teeth sharper, and she grinned. "And, to be honest, this way was a lot more fun."

Young-hee felt a knot of fury choking her. "You … terrible … *rotten…*"

The Fox just arched her eyebrows. "Thanks to you two, there's no one left in this realm with the strength to stop me. Your great war by the sandalwood tree ensured that. Now I'll take my pullocho, and all I need to become human is to eat a human heart—*yours*."

As the words left her lips, Gumiho pounced, impossibly fast, all teeth and claws. Turning to flee, Young-hee tripped and fell. But before Fox could reach her, Samjogo swung his hyeopdo. "Stay behind me." Samjogo was without bravado now, focused solely on the evil creature.

Again and again, Fox snapped and slashed, a flurry of deadly attacks. But Samjogo parried and kept her at bay. Young-hee scrambled for her bag, but its contents had scattered when she fell. There were crushed rice cakes, her smashed lantern, and the broken pieces of Boonae's mask, but no blue vial.

Samjogo swung his hyeopdo, sweeping Gumiho's feet then doubling back and aiming for her belly with the sharp blade. But Gumiho twisted away with just a scratch, sinking two claws deep into Samjogo's shoulder. Then she brought up her back legs, clawing at Samjogo's stomach. He just avoided getting gutted by butting her snout with the wooden end of the hyeopdo. Gumiho flipped over backwards, head over heels, landing lightly.

"Why do you care?" hissed Fox, her nine tails quivering behind her. "Let me have her and the pullocho, and I can give you anything you want."

"You already gave me my freedom, Fox. What more could I want?" he said. "Except, perhaps to save my sister."

Samjogo swung his hyeopdo once more, but Gumiho dodged. Then, seeing Young-hee sprawled on the ground, Fox bounded over Samjogo, aiming for easier prey. Samjogo shouted a warning, but Young-hee didn't have time to rise or run. She realized she was clutching the three busted bits of wood that once were Boonae. Not knowing what else to do, she squeezed them together, restoring Boonae's face, then rolled over and pushed the back of the mask at the lunging Gumiho. Fox was too close and charging too fast to evade Boonae, and as they met, the mask came to life, sucking itself onto Gumiho's face.

Gumiho's face disappeared, and Boonae came to life once more. Her red cheeks flushed and her eye's bulged, her lips quivering. A voice screamed, but Young-hee didn't know if it was Gumiho or Boonae.

On the ground, Fox shook and shook.

"*Young-hee*, you're all right," Boonae said weakly.

"You, too, Boonae, you're still alive."

"Barely, I'm afraid," the masked wheezed. "Gumiho is far too powerful … even at the best of times and I'm not a fraction of my best self at the moment."

The Fox's body jerked back and forth, her front paws, trying to rip off the mask. "Off … me!" she hissed from between Boonae's cracks.

Bleeding, Samjogo aimed his hyeopdo at Fox's stomach.

"No," said Young-hee.

"Why not?"

"Because … I don't know, it doesn't seem right," she said.

"Young-hee, pour the fairy water on us," said Boonae. "Wash us away with a great river. I'll be okay, but Gumiho will be swept away." Young-hee found the blue vial, but hesitated as Fox kept clawing at the mask. "Hurry!"

"Thank you, Boonae. I'll make sure we find you, wherever you end up."

"No, no," said Gumiho. "Our pullocho. It's *ours*. We had it."

Young-hee poured the vial onto Gumiho, nearly the whole thing. As the water touched her body, it turned into a great rushing river, twice as big as the Hungry River. With a roar of churning water, Gu-miho was swept away and vanished into the great waterway to parts unknown.

"What happened?" asked Young-hee, near collapse.

"I'm not sure," said Samjogo, "but I think we won."

"Won?" echoed Young-hee incredulously. "Gumiho didn't kill us, but that's hardly a win. She killed Bum."

"No, she didn't kill him. She just sent him away."

"Okay, she sent him away—but I don't know where. Or when. Or how to even begin to look for him."

"You don't need to," said Samjogo. "You already found me. I'm your brother."

24

Young-hee flopped to the ground, utterly exhausted by her fight with Fox and the terrible things she had lived through that day. "*You're … ?*"

"Young-beom. Bum."

She looked at his wild hair and angular face. "That's not possible."

"And yet that's the truth," he said.

"I… I don't understand."

"I didn't either, at first. It happened so long ago, and I was so young, I barely remembered any of it."

"But you're so old."

"That's because I've been here for years. After the dokkaebi—well, Gumiho, I guess—made me disappear, she didn't just send me far away, she sent me back in time. I was found by the savage fairies, and the fairy king took me as his son. I grew up in this world and became Samjogo. You, mom, the mud world were like a dream, and the fairy king was my father, as far as I was concerned."

"When did you know?"

"I started suspecting soon after we met. You were like a long-forgotten dream that had come to life, but I did not know what it meant. And, I was angry, too; I thought you hated me and had abandoned me. When did I know for sure? When you were holding Namgoong Mirinae's chioonchim and it pointed at me. She said it would point at the thing you most wanted, and I guess it did."

As Samjogo—*no, Young-beom*, Young-hee reminded herself—talked, he rubbed at dirt on his face with the back of his hand. The gesture reminded Young-hee of her little brother, a simple action, yet filled with his essence. His eyes, nose, crazy hair—the more she looked, the more she saw Bum.

"I never hated you," she said sadly. "It was just hard, coming back to Korea, losing my friends, losing dad…"

"Yeah, I know now," he said.

"I was so alone and sad and angry that dad was gone. I didn't mean to…" What began as tears of relief and regret, broke open until she was weeping uncontrollably, her whole body shaking.

As she thought she'd lose the strength to stand, Young-beom put his arms around her—just as she used to hold him when he was little and crying.

"I missed you, Young-beom," she said.

"I missed you, too, big sister."

"So what's up with that streak of white in your hair?"

"I don't know. I just thought it was cool."

As they hugged, Young-hee felt a warm stickiness on her brother's shoulder. "You're bleeding."

"Yes, Gumiho cut me. It's not that bad."

Young-hee ripped strips from the cloak from Grandma Dol, soaked them in the river she created from the blue vial, and cleaned the wound, wrapped the shoulder with one longer strip and applied pressure.

She had one last, big worry she didn't voice: *Now what?* She had her brother and a pullocho, but how could they escape Strange Land? And even if they got home, how could she explain a grown-up Young-beom to their mom? Plus she worried about her new friends—Grandma Dol, Bassam, the jangseung. The raging river, now receding, had swept away most of the thorn bush and busted stalls, but a big mess remained.

As Young-hee and Young-beom celebrated their reunion, they noticed a man, bent with age, approaching.

"Hello, bear children." He had a flowing white beard and wore a long, white hanbok.

"Greetings, Sanshin," said Young-beom, bowing respectfully.

"Hello, sir," said Young-hee. Recognizing the mountain spirit she bowed, too, but wondered, *Where have I seen him?*

"My, what a fearful ruckus," Sanshin said. Despite his venerable age and imposing presence, he had a youthful spark. "I'm pleased you both survived intact. Physically, at least. Although I understand there are other costs."

"Yes sir," said Young-beom, his awe of the great spirit rendering him atypically quiet.

"Your shoulder, it's hurt," said Sanshin, touching Young-beom's shoulder lightly. The bleeding stopped.

"Hey, nearly as good as new," Young-beom said, unwrapping the bandages to reveal pink but healed skin.

"It's the least I could do," Sanshin said. "I owe you far more."

"You owe us?" said Young-hee, surprised.

"Indeed. As do all the creatures in Strange Land," he said, chuckling softly.

"Stra … That's what I call this place."

"Yes, a good name, and easier than the mouthful the first spirits use; simpler than the grandiosities the young spirits prefer. Or the spirits who remain, at any rate."

"Sanshin, I'm so sorry. So many died over this pullocho," she said, taking the sacred root from her bag. It seemed right to offer it to the old spirit. "I never meant for any of that to happen. I just wanted to save my brother."

"Do not be troubled, bear daughter. Gumiho has long schemed to become human and destroy both our lands. She used and manipulated you, but, in the end, with a bit of help from me, you saved us all. So I am guilty, too, of manipulations, and for that I am deeply sorry. That is why we owe you."

"But so many are dead."

"Yes, but they'll be back soon enough. Such is the way of Strange Land." He touched the pullocho without taking it from Young-hee's hand. "I don't need any pullocho. I am of the mountains. My power is much older than animals or stories or even storytellers. You earned this pullocho."

"But… What would I do with a pullocho?"

"Anything you want."

"What if I ate it?"

"Hmm, interesting. I don't think a bear daughter ever has. Emperor Jin Shi Hwang sent three thousand warriors to find one, but died without succeeding."

"I don't think I want to be the first. No, I give it to you freely, by the rules of hospitality."

Sanshin smiled kindly. "That is very generous. I promise to keep it safe and only use it when most needed." He took the pullocho from her hand and hid it in the folds of his hanbok. "If I could trouble you for a bit more help, do you have a pine cone?"

"I do, actually," she said, rummaging through her tattered bag. At the bottom, beaten up and stomped, was the pine cone she had taken from the forest after her first night in Strange Land. "Here."

"Thank you, bear daughter," he said and buried it in the ground. "We owe you thanks, but, sadly, have little to give you. It is time for you both to return home."

"Home?" said Young-beom, uncertainly.

"But how can we go home? My brother is older than me now.

"Yes, that would be embarrassing—or at least highly inconvenient. But I assure you, when you walk through the wooden door, in the stairwell in the jureum forest, he will be a four-year-old boy again. And you will be the same young woman as when you left your home."

"The same?"

"Physically, at least. After years the realm of fairies, magic, guardians, and spirits, I doubt you could be quite the same inside."

"And my friends—the jangseung, Grandma Dol and Bassam?"

"In time, I'll repair all Gumiho destroyed, including your friends. Except for Bassam, who is not of this world. I sense he has departed, but do not know where."

"Oh," she said, thinking. "And my magic potions from the fairies? And clothes and everything?"

"Will lose their magic and turn to rags and dust and plain things."

"Oh," said Young-hee again, somewhat disappointed.

"Cheer up. We can't have magic spilling into your mud world. For starters, it would wreak havoc with your science, at least as I understand it."

Young-hee giggled, suspecting he was teasing. "Can we ever come back to Strange Land?"

"I do not know. Perhaps in dreams."

As he talked, Young-hee became aware of a soft rumbling and gentle swish of fur. "Tiger!" she exclaimed. She hugged her old friend—as full of life as ever—around his shaggy neck. Tiger rumbled a happy purr and kissed across her whole her face with his big, rough tongue. "Ack, gross!" Young-hee laughed.

Tiger walked to Sanshin and lay down beside the venerable spirit, who rested a hand on the back of Tiger's neck. Young-hee didn't know how it happened, but suddenly Sanshin and Tiger were sitting under a huge pine tree—it looked like the oldest thing in the world. And that's when she saw it—Sanshin looked like gyeongbi Shin from her apartment, the day she found him playing with that tiger-orange kitten.

Saying goodbye, Young-hee and Young-beom headed to the jureum forest and the doorway home. At the top of the stairs, they cast one last look of the magic world.

"Do you think we'll ever come back?" Bum asked.

"I don't know. But I think I'm ready for the real world. At least for a little while."

She opened the door open, letting Bum walk down the steps first. She was about to follow, when she heard the mishmash of squawking. In a massive, wrinkly tree, the birds were back, looking at her again. Thirty birds. She waved goodbye to them, then followed her brother into the darkness.

* * *

And so they stumbled back to the real world, as if nothing had happened. One moment Young-beom was a young man, the next a four-year-old boy. Young-hee's canvas bag was a pile of old, dead leaves; her linen cloak looked and felt like dried spider web; the three vials from the fairy king were ugly, faintly-colored stone. Her shoes and clothes—and Bum's—were still horrible messes. *Mom is going to freak when she gets a load of us.*

And freak she did: "What *on earth* have you two been up to?!" mom said as soon as she saw them. Their whole adventure had taken scarcely two hours in mud world time, Young-hee noted, but time enough to worry mom—especially after Young-hee's choppy phone call. As they bathed, she ordered spicy chicken from Young-hee's favorite restaurant. Nothing was different, thought Young-hee, and yet somehow everything was better.

After they ate, her mom asked her to do the dishes. "I know, 'It's annoying,' but I have more work and would appreciate the help."

"It's okay," said Young-hee, surprised by her answer. "I don't mind." It was nice to have something so mundane to do again. But then:

"*Young-hee!*" her mom yelled. "What did you do to Young-beom's *hair*?" The white streak was still there.

* * *

The next day, after an impossibly long sleep, Young-hee bounded outside, eager to see Gyeongbi Shin. "Teacher!" she said as she knocked on the guards' office.

"Eh, what?" It was another guard.

"Oh, ... I was looking for gyeongbi Shin."

"Who?"

"Mr. Shin?" she repeated. "The really old guard, thin, wrinkles." *Did he even exist?*

"Ah, Shin. Why do you want to see him? Nevermind, I don't want to know. Anyhow, he's retired. Yesterday was his last day."

"Oh," she said, disappointed that he was a real person after all. "Any chance he will be back? I, uh, promised to bring him something."

"*Aish*, just a minute." After much shouting back and forth with another guard, he returned to the door. "Nope, you're out of luck. He apparently left to live with relatives in Gangwon Province."

"Well, thank you." Just because she was back in the real world, she didn't expect things to start making sense now.

She walked through the apartment complex, wondering what she would do next. It was going to be a hot, beautiful day.

"Hey, dork!" someone shouted, and there were the three mean girls from school. "I've been meaning to teach you another lesson."

Even though there were three of them, Young-hee wasn't frightened any more. "Hi there. Nice day, isn't it?"

"Who said you could talk to us?" said the sharp-faced ringleader. "Well, good. I'm in the mood for teaching a worm some respect."

Young-hee shot them a look—nothing angry, in fact she was smiling—that warned not to press their luck.

"Uh, maybe we should just be going," said the heavier friend.

"What for? We can't let losers just do whatev... *Ack!*" the sharp-faced girl cried suddenly. "*Ouch! Ouch!* My foot's stuck!" A long thistle plant had caught her sandals and stuck fast, wrapping around her foot and digging into her skin. "*Ow!* Get it off!" she yelled, panicking, it got worse. "What *is* this, anyway?"

Young-hee smiled and walked away. In her right pocket, her hand rubbed against a dull white stone she was carrying for no particular reason. "Yep, it's a great looking day," she said.